BLEEDING
TARTS

Published by Kensington Publishing Corporation

Also by Kirsten Weiss

The Quiche and the Dead

Published by Kensington Publishing Corporation

BLEEDING TARTS

Kirsten Weiss

KENSINGTON BOOKS
KENSINGTON PUBLISHING CORP.
http://www.kensingtonbooks.com

First Printing: May 2018
ISBN-13: 978-1-4967-0897-7
ISBN-10: 1-4967-0897-0——

eISBN-13: 978-1-4967-0900-4
eISBN-10: 1-4967-0900-4

10 9 8 7 6 5 4 3 2 1

Printed in the United States of America

ACKNOWLEDGMENTS

A special thank-you to Linea Van Horn, who not only contributed the recipes in this book, but also gave me better insight into life in a bakery!

Chapter One

I gripped the pie box as the Jeep bumped along the winding, dirt road.

Charlene, my octogenarian piecrust specialist, yanked the wheel sideways. Her white cat, asleep on the dashboard, slid toward me and the Jeep's open window.

One-handed, I steadied the cat, Frederick. Charlene believed Frederick was deaf and narcoleptic, so she carted him everywhere. I thought he was rude and lazy and didn't belong on important pie-selling business.

Oblivious to Frederick's near-sudden exit, Charlene hummed a western tune. The breeze tossed her white hair, its loose, glamour-girl curls shifting around the shoulders of her lightweight purple tunic.

Certain in the knowledge I wasn't getting that tune out of my head in the near future, I sighed and leaned closer to the windshield. My rollercoaster fear mingled with optimism in a heady brew of nervicitement. We were zipping toward a faux ghost town as super exclusive as only an event site on the bleeding edge of Silicon Valley could be. The Bar X was so private, I'd only learned about it three days ago, and I'd been living in San Nicholas nearly nine months.

Now, not only was I going to see the Old West town, but I was delivering pies that would be featured in its charity pie-eating contest. If all went well, the Bar X would become a regular Pie Town client. If all didn't go well, I didn't want to think about it.

Frowning, Charlene accelerated, and gravel zinged off the Jeep's undercarriage. "I don't know why Ewan had to make the roads so authentically awful. Now about our case—"

"Mrs. Banks is a lovely person." I gripped my seat belt. "She buys a strawberry-rhubarb pie every Friday. But she's a little distracted, and she's not a case."

"You mean you think she's gaga. Not every old person is nuts, you know." Her white curls quivered with indignation.

"I know."

"She says when she buys groceries and brings them home, they disappear from her backseat."

"Mrs. Banks is forgetful, and no," I said before Charlene could object, "I don't think all old people are forgetful. But she is. She might not have remembered to load the groceries into her car in the first place." And the Baker Street Bakers, our amateur sleuthing club, didn't have time for another tail-chasing case. I had my hands full with my real job.

Four months earlier, in a fit of sugar-fueled enthusiasm, I'd doubled Pie Town's staff. Now, the pie shop I'd put everything I'd owned into was barely scraping even. At the thought of the financial grave I'd dug for myself, nausea clutched my throat.

"I've researched Banks's problem." She veered around a curve, and my shoulder banged the passenger window. "I'm thinking fairies. They're known thieves. I wouldn't put a few bags of groceries past them."

"It's a well-known fact that there are no fairies on the California coast." Or anywhere else, since they're not real.

"You're wrong there. There've been reports of fairy activity in the dog park. Of course, most people think it's UFOs."

"Right. Dog park. Because where else would they be?"

The late summer morning was already warm. I smelled eucalyptus and sagebrush and a hint of salt from the nearby Pacific.

"Or the cause might be ectoplasmic," she said enthusiastically. "The groceries could be apporting."

I struggled not to ask, and failed. "Apport? What does that mean?"

"It's when ghosts suck objects into another plane." She made a whooshing sound. "Then the spirits make the objects reappear in different places in our dimension. I told her we'd stop by on Friday night and try out my new ghost-hunting equipment."

I rubbed my brow. Right now, *I* wouldn't mind apporting to another plane. Our armchair crime-solving club was all in good fun . . . until Charlene left the armchair. "I really don't think it's a case."

"We don't know that. And it's not as if you have other plans for Friday night."

My cheeks heated, and I braced an elbow on the window frame. Charlene knew very well what I'd scheduled for Friday night. "Sorry, but Gordon and I are going on a date on Friday. Remember?" My insides squirmed with pleasure. It had been a long time since I'd been on a date—not since my engagement to Mark Jeffreys had gone kablooey earlier this year. Detective Gordon Carmichael and I had been dancing around going out for months, and it was finally happening.

"Are you sure it's a date?" She quirked a white brow. "Not just two people getting together?"

"Of course, it's a date."

"Because you two have been having a lot of 'not-dates.'"

"We've been getting to know each other," I said, defensive.

"Usually that happens on dates."

"It's the twenty-first century, Charlene."

She grimaced. "Don't remind me. Have you bought new knickers?"

"What?" I yelped.

We rounded a bend. Charlene cut the curve close and scraped the yellow Jeep against the branches of a young eucalyptus tree.

"You heard me," she said. "You can't be too prepared."

I sputtered. "It's only a first date!" And knickers? Who even talked that way anymore? It's not like she was from Regency England.

"High quality unmentionables—"

"Unmentionables?" Had we time traveled to the Victorian era?

"Are a confidence builder."

And Charlene knew all about confidence. She'd been in the roller derby. Had scuba dived off the Great Barrier Reef. Had gone skydiving. And if it hadn't been for her, there never would have been any Baker Street Bakers.

I hadn't quite forgiven her for that.

"Besides, your date will be over by the time the ghost hunt starts. Things don't really get going until midnight or one AM."

"And you know I have to be at work by five. If I'm not in bed by ten, I'm done for." I yawned just thinking about it.

We trundled into an Old West ghost town. Its single dirt road was lined with ramshackle wooden buildings. Hills carpeted with low, green scrub cascaded from the east.

"I wonder where Gordon will take you," she mused.

"Your options are limited in a small town like San Nicholas. Maybe he'll take you to the . . . Marla!" She slammed on the brakes, and I careened forward.

The seat belt caught me in the ribs, but not quick enough to keep my head from banging into the windshield.

"The pies!" Ignoring the thudding pain in my skull, I whipped around and peered anxiously at the pink and white boxes stacked in the rear of the Jeep. I exhaled a shaky breath. The boxes hadn't fallen.

A growl vibrated beside me.

I turned, eyeing Frederick. The sleeping cat hadn't budged from the dashboard.

Charlene's knuckles whitened on the wheel. "Marla, here. Here!"

"What?" I looked around. The street was empty. "Who's Marla?"

Charlene floored the accelerator, whiplashing me against the seat. We rocketed down the dirt road and flew past a saloon, a chapel, and other random Old West buildings.

I yelped. "Pies. Pies!"

She braked hard. The Jeep screeched to a halt, engulfed in a cloud of dust.

Coughing, I rolled up the window. "What was that about?"

"Marla, is what," she snarled. Opening her door, she gently dislodged Frederick from the dashboard and arranged him over one shoulder. Charlene strode into the dust cloud and vanished.

I unbuckled myself and clambered over the seat. Holding my breath, I lifted the lid on one of the pies in the cargo area. The air whooshed from my lungs. The pie had survived. The others might be okay as well.

Pie-eating contests are traditionally messy, but it wouldn't do to prebreak the inventory. Not when I wanted to make a deal with the Bar X to be their regular pie supplier. Aside from guns, cowboys, and those old-timey photos where you dress like a prostitute, there's nothing that says "Old West" more than hand pies. And we made awesome hand pies.

Lurching from the yellow Jeep, I dusted off my pink-and-white Pie Town T-shirt. Beneath its giant smiley face was our motto: TURN YOUR FROWN UPSIDE DOWN AT PIE TOWN! I'd designed the shirts myself, one of the perks of owning my own business.

The downsides of entrepreneurship? Baker's hours and knuckle-biting payrolls. If I could add this wholesaling business, the latter worry would be a thing of the past.

The dust dissipated, leaving a brownish ground fog. We'd parked in front of a squat wooden building set amidst a stand of eucalyptus trees. A sign above the one-story wooden shack read: POTTERY.

At the far end of the dirt road, Charlene vanished into a carriage house, its ginormous, barnlike doors wide open.

A shot rang out, and I flinched.

Mr. Frith had warned me about the gunshots. It was only the sharpshooters, practicing for the event later today. But since a homicidal maniac had attempted to shoot me earlier this year, I was an eensy bit sensitive to gunfire.

"Charlene!" A woman shrieked inside the carriage house. "You look awful. What happened?"

Three more shots rang out in rapid succession, and my jaw clenched.

I trotted into the carriage house and slithered past a massive coach that looked like it had driven out of a Wells Fargo ad. Straw lay scattered about the wood plank floor, and the massive room smelled strongly of manure. Past the coach were rows of empty stalls, and a second set of open doors on the other end of the building.

An elegant, silver-haired woman in a salmon-colored silk top and wide-legged slacks was awkwardly embracing

Charlene. Diamonds flashed on the woman's fingers. An expensive camera hung from one slim shoulder.

An older gentleman in jeans and a crisp, white button-up shirt beamed at them both. "I'd no idea you two knew each other." He chuckled. "That's life in a small town. I should have guessed."

The woman released my piecrust maker. "What are *you* doing *here*?"

"Pies," Charlene said, gruff. "For the event today."

"You're the pie maker?" The woman's lip curled. "Charlene, I would have thought you'd have retired." She sighed. "That's California though. So impossibly expensive. Fortunately, I've got my real estate rentals. I had no idea I could make so much money renting houses. *So* much money."

Charlene stiffened. She owned rentals as well. And as one of her tenants, I didn't like that this conversation was headed toward higher rent.

The snowy cat looked up from Charlene's shoulder and yawned.

"I work because I want to," Charlene said. "I like to keep my hand in, stay busy."

"Of course, you do," the woman said. "Ewan, take a picture of the two of us. I can't wait to compare this to our old yearbook photos."

The man stepped forward, and she handed him her camera.

The woman—Marla?—pressed herself next to Charlene and struck a pose.

Charlene flushed, her fists clenching.

Uh-oh. For some reason, Charlene was seriously annoyed. I cleared my throat. "Mr. Frith?"

He returned the camera to Marla and swiveled, his teeth gleaming white against his rough and ruddy skin. "And you must be Val. I'm Ewan. Welcome to the Bar X, young lady!" He strode forward and took my hand, pumping it enthusiastically.

I was twenty-eight, but I'd take young lady, and I grinned.

"Charlene's told me so much about you," he continued. "Not that she needed to. Your pies speak for themselves."

I grinned. That sounded promising. "And this is the famous Bar X! I'm excited to finally see it."

The mystery woman—Marla, it had to be—sidled up to him and draped a diamond-spangled hand over his broad shoulder. "And who are you? Charlene's employee?"

"Ah . . ." I darted a glance at my piecrust maker. "We work together," I said, deliberately vague.

Charlene's shoulders dropped. She raised her chin. "Val owns Pie Town. I run the piecrust room. Val Harris, this is Marla." Her voice lowered on the last syllable, dripping with disdain.

Marla scanned me. "How adorable. And your skin! What I wouldn't give for the skin of a twentysomething, right Charlene?"

Adorable? I'd always figured myself for kind of average, and I warmed at the compliment. I was a normal California gal—blue eyes, five foot five, and a little curvy (the tasty tragedy of owning a pie shop). I touched my brown hair, done up in its usual knot.

Charlene harrumphed. In her mind, she still was a twentysomething. Or at least a fortysomething.

"When Ewan suggested a pie-eating contest for our little fundraiser," Marla said, "I'd no idea you two would be involved."

"Who is it supporting?" I asked.

"The local humane society," she said. "All those poor lost doggies and kittens. I'm on the board. You know how it is when you're retired. It does help to stay involved, even if my passion is helping others rather than baking pies."

Her nose wrinkled, and she linked her arm with Ewan's. "Now, did you say something about a private tour?"

"Of course," he said. "The carriage isn't hitched up, so we'll have to walk. Charlene? Val? Would you like to join us?"

Yes!

"Val can't," Charlene said. "She needs to get the pies out of the Jeep."

I shuffled my feet. The pie retrieval wasn't that urgent. "But—"

"Before they get soggy in the heat," she continued.

Grrr!

"But *I* could go for a walk," Charlene said.

Marla's face tightened. "Lovely. We really do need to catch up. Are you sure you can manage the exercise, Charlene? You look rather tired."

Charlene glowered. "I'm fit as a fiddle."

"Oh, Charlene." Marla laughed, a jewel-like tinkle. "You haven't changed a bit. At least, not on the inside." She snapped a photo of the carriage house, and the three ambled toward the open doors on the other side of the barn.

Another shot rang out, and I started. "Wait," I said. "Where should I put the pies?"

"The saloon," Ewan called over his shoulder. "My daughter Bridget will be there to help you."

"Okay," I said. But they'd already disappeared around the corner of the carriage house. My lips compressed with disappointment. I wouldn't have minded a tour, but I could take a hint, and Charlene's had been as obvious as an elephant on Main Street. She didn't want me around.

I stomped to the Jeep, opened the driver's side door, and paused, chagrined. Charlene had the key. I could get inside, but I couldn't drive the pies closer to the saloon, which was across the street and down a bit. I'd just have to make lots of trips.

Another shot cracked.

A murder of crows rose noisily from the nearby eucalyptus trees. Uneasily, I watched them flap toward the hills.

I stacked six pink pie boxes in my arms and clamped my chin on the top box to steady them. Nudging the door shut with my hip, I lurched across the road, automatically looking right, then left. I gave a slight shake of my head. It wasn't as if buggies were racing down the—

A shot cracked. The top box flew from beneath my chin. It exploded in a burst of pink cardboard and piecrust and cherry filling.

I shrieked, the boxes swaying.

I slapped my hand on the top box, and they steadied. Okay. Okay. I was alive. But what-the-hell? Another shot rang out, louder.

Heart banging against my ribs, I scrambled for cover behind a horse trough. My tennis shoes skidded in the loose dirt, and I half fell against the trough. I clutched the remaining boxes to my chest. Someone. Some stupid person . . .

My fingers dented the pink cardboard. Probably some kids, or hunters, or a random idiot. The trick shooters couldn't have been this careless.

I forced my breathing to calm. "Hello?" I shouted. "Hold your fire!"

No one answered.

Still clinging to my pies, I squirmed about and peered over the trough. Since I hadn't been hit, the bullet that had taken out my pie must have come from an angle, from my side rather than my front or rear.

The eucalyptus trees across the street shivered. They would have made a good hiding place for a shooter.

Hiding place? The shot had to have been an accident, but suddenly all I wanted was to get out of here.

I hunched over my remaining pie boxes and speed walked toward the saloon, the nearest shelter. It now seemed light years away. Its front doors were shuttered closed.

I scooted up its porch steps and set my pies by the door, rattled the heavy wood shutters.

Locked. I gave a small whimper.

Abandoning my pies, I ducked into the alley between the saloon and a bath house. Panting, I peeked into the main street.

I was probably safe here. I'd probably been safe behind the watering trough. This was twenty-first century California, not the Wild West. But cold sweat trickled down my neck. I backed deeper into the shade of the alley.

My heel bumped something. I staggered and braced my hands against the rough, wood-planked wall. Legs wobbly, I exhaled, turned.

A man lay sprawled on the dirt, his plaid shirt soaked with blood. Mouth open, he stared sightlessly at the cloudless sky.

Chapter Two

I gaped at the dead man. And, I'm sorry to say, I've seen enough dead bodies to be certain he was dead. There was too much blood pooling in the dirt, soaking his button-up, plaid shirt. His eyes were dull, unmoving. A breeze ruffled the man's brown hair, exposing his receding hairline.

"No," I moaned.

My brain turned to mush. I shook my head, shut my gaping pie hole. I needed to call the police. And my cell phone was in Charlene's Jeep.

I pressed my back against the wall and ducked my head out, glancing up and down the road. It was empty.

The sniper could be waiting for me to make a run for it so he could pick me off.

Or he could be circling around the building to shoot me.

I cursed softly, so the hypothetical mad gunman wouldn't hear.

Gritting my teeth, I raced across the exposed street to the Jeep and yanked open the driver's door. I grabbed my phone from the cup holder.

My chin jerked up. I'd left the body. You shouldn't leave the body. The police frowned on that sort of thing.

I raced back to the alley. No murderer bent over the

corpse, muddling the crime scene. No detective prowled
the narrow alley, searching for clues. Hands shaking, I
crouched in the shade and dialed nine-one-one.

A side door to the saloon flew open and banged against
the wall.

I jumped and swore.

A fortysomething woman in jeans and the ubiquitous
plaid shirt stepped into the shaded alley. A long braid of
blond hair flecked with gray cascaded over her shoulder.
"Devon? Where the . . . ?" Her mouth slackened. "Is that . . . ?"

The phone squawked. "Nine-one-one, what is your
emergency?"

"Uh—"

The woman gasped and spun toward me. "Oh, my God!
You killed him!" she screamed, her voice echoing through
the ghost town.

"I didn't! I'm calling nine-one-one."

"What is your emergency?" the dispatcher repeated.

"You're covered in his blood!" She clapped a hand to her
mouth and sagged against the saloon's rough wooden wall.
"Oh, my God. Oh, my God."

"What? I never touched him." Maybe I should have.
What if he wasn't dead?

Shaken, I glanced at the body.

No, he was definitely, definitively, indubitably dead.

"Hello? Can you hear me?" the dispatcher asked.

"Uh, yeah. This is Val Harris. I'm at the Bar X. Someone's
been shot. He's dead."

"Who's dead? Who's been shot?"

"I don't know who he is," I said. "Please send the
police."

The middle-aged blonde bolted through the saloon's side
door. The lock snicked shut.

Footsteps pounded in the dirt, and Ewan and Charlene
rounded the corner.

I lowered the phone to my side.

Charlene skidded to a halt, her purple tunic flapping in the breeze. "Val! Where were you hit?"

"I wasn't." I rubbed my temple.

"We heard a scream." Ewan glanced down and his ruddy face paled. "Devon?"

Charlene, who only had eyes for me, raised her palm. "Hold up. Is that cherry?"

"What are you talking about?" I motioned toward the body. "A man's been—"

Charlene swiped a gnarled finger across my cheek. "It *is* cherry. Did someone decide pie throwing would be more fun than pie eating?"

"Forget the pie." I swiped a hand across my chin, and it came away sticky. "Someone shot the pie, and I guess the same person shot . . . whoever that is." I turned to Ewan.

Looking flattened, the big man braced his hand against a wall.

"I'm sorry, Mr. Frith," I said. "Did he work here?"

Charlene tore her gaze from me, looked down the alley, and her eyes widened. She staggered sideways, one hand clutched to her chest. "What the . . . ?"

Ewan swallowed. "We have to call the police."

"I already have." And whoops, I hadn't ended the call. Tentative, I lifted the phone and whispered into the receiver. "Are you still there?"

"What's happening?" the dispatcher asked. "Are you in a safe place?"

"More people have arrived. And yes, I'm safe."

"If it's too late to administer first aid," she said, "keep everyone away from the body. I've dispatched units to the scene. They should arrive in a few minutes."

"Okay. Thank you." I hung up, swallowed. "The police are on their way. We're not supposed to go near the body."

Marla rounded the corner, her silk top and loose slacks
rustling. "Who screamed?" The older woman stopped
dead, her gaze bouncing from me to Charlene to the man's
body. She clapped her hands to her silver hair. "It's not
possible. He was just . . . He's dead! You killed him! You're
covered in his blood." She pressed a hand to her forehead.

"What *is* that on you?" Ewan asked. "Cherry tart?"

"No, it's pie," I said. "Cherry pie."

Marla moaned. "I feel faint."

Ewan hustled to her and cradled her in his arms. "Come
sit on the porch. It's all right."

"Blood. So much blood." She slumped against his broad
chest.

He half dragged her around the corner, presumably to
the saloon's porch. His voice drifted around the side of the
building. "Head between your knees."

Charlene whipped toward me. "Quick. Before the cops
show up. What happened?"

"I didn't kill him!"

She rolled her eyes. "Of course, you didn't kill him.
Now what did you see? Who shot the pie?"

"I don't know. The pie exploded in my hands, and then
there was a second shot."

"A second shooter. It's the grassy knoll all over again."

"I don't think someone could have hit that pie from the
hills," I said, scanning them through the gap between the
buildings.

"The grassy knoll. JFK. Lee Harvey Oswald. Keep up!"

Oh, *that* grassy knoll. I didn't respond, determined not
to be pulled into another of Charlene's conspiracy theories.
"At first, I thought the shooter was in the trees near your
Jeep, so I took shelter in the alley. And then I saw the body."

"Where was the pie shot?"

"In the street. You can still see the remains." I gestured vaguely toward the broken pie box.

"Okay, that should help us figure out the trajectory."

"Us?"

"It's a case!"

My chest caved. "No."

"Yes."

"Charlene, we can't." Our so-called cases tended toward missing surfboards and suspicious lurkers. The first and last time we'd been involved in a murder, we'd almost been killed. "This is too big for us. The police will be here any minute—"

"Too big? We busted open the biggest crime syndicate San Nicholas has seen since Prohibition."

"I wouldn't call it a syndicate—"

"And we're here, on the scene. Someone shot a man, and you could have been killed." She tapped my chest with a crooked finger and lowered her voice. "This, my girl, is personal."

A siren wailed in the distance.

I prayed for sanity. "Charlene. Someone didn't just shoot a pie. They shot an actual person. This is serious."

"The Bar X is going to need our help." She drew a leather-bound notebook from her pocket. "Think of what last spring's murder in Pie Town did to your business. It nearly wiped us out."

"The killer nearly wiped us out. He literally, nearly wiped us out."

"Do you want that to happen to the Bar X? For Ewan to lose his business because of a crime he had nothing to do with?"

"How do you know—?"

The siren stopped, and I fell silent.

Ewan shouted, "Over here!"

"The real question," she said, "is why did they shoot the pie? Was it a diversion?"

I counted to ten. "Forget the pie. It's not about the pie."

"Maybe you were the target. What if the killer meant to kill you and accidentally shot this Devon fellow instead?"

"Who would want to kill me?"

She shot me a dark look. "You *know* who."

Except I didn't. "Who—?"

Gordon walked into the alley, and the tension I didn't realize I'd been holding, released.

He halted, staring. "Val?" In spite of the heat, he wore a blue suit jacket, and I almost smiled. He'd worked hard to become a detective again after transferring to San Nicholas, and he was determined to dress the part. He looked like a TV detective, tall and square jawed, dark haired and handsome.

"Detective Carmichael," Charlene said. "The body's here. The killer shot a pie right out of Val's hands. Cherry." She shook her head. "Real mess." She departed the alley for parts unknown. Probably to keep an eye on Marla and Ewan.

He blinked, his eyes hardening to jade, and strode forward. "What happened?" He knelt beside the body and checked for a pulse.

"I was walking across the street, and someone shot a pie out of my hands. I thought the shooter was in the trees, by the pottery shed and Charlene's Jeep, and I ran into the alley. That's when I saw him."

"Who is he?" Rising, Gordon pulled a notebook from his breast pocket.

"Mr. Frith called him Devon," I said. "I've never seen him before. Oh, and there was a blond woman. She came out of the side door to the saloon, saw the dead man, and me covered in cherry filling, and panicked."

He ran me through a series of brusque questions. Why

was I at the Bar X? When had I arrived? When had I met
Ewan and Marla? When did I hear the shots?

EMTs arrived. More police. A firetruck.

Finally, the interrogation ended, and he closed his notebook. "There goes our date," he said under his breath.

So, it *was* a date. I wasn't feeling super romantic about
it with a corpse nearby, but ha! Take that Char . . . wait.
"What?"

He scrubbed a hand across his chiseled face. "We'll have
to cancel."

"Because you'll be busy investigating on Friday?"

"Because, by virtue of discovering the body, you're a
suspect. Again."

"What? No! I'm not. It's only cherry." I peeled the T-shirt
away from my skin. The filling had soaked through and
was starting to feel icky.

"And you look delicious." He rested his hand on my
shoulder. "I know you didn't kill the man, but I have to
follow procedure. And if a woman saw you standing over
the body covered in blood—"

"Cherry filling!"

"That she thought was blood. I'm going to have to in-
clude you in the field of suspects, even if it is only on a
technicality. And I can't date a suspect."

And San Nicholas only had one detective. And this
would be his first homicide case here. And he wouldn't
give this case up to an outside investigator from another
town. I smiled weakly. "It's fine. I get it." I did not get it.

"It's only a delay," he said. "Once this is cleared up—"

"Grumpy Cop!" A voice boomed from behind us, and
Gordon's fist clenched, crumpling the notebook. Our new
chief of police, hawk nosed, narrow faced, and skinny as a
scarecrow, strode down the alley. His steps slowed, and his
brown eyes widened. "Val Harris? You're the last person I
expected to see at a murder scene." His voice was hearty.

"Hello, Chief Shaw," I said, glum. I knew he loved it when people called him "chief." His position was new too. Shaw had moved up from detective to chief, and Grumpy . . . I mean, Gordon, had taken his spot as San Nicholas's lone detective. It was a good change for the town, but Shaw was, well . . . Shaw.

"We can't be certain it was a murder at this point," Gordon said. "Stray bullets were flying. One took out a pie Miss Harris was holding. It's possible the death was accidental, though we can't rule out—"

"Don't tell me a cherry pie was heinously murdered during the perpetration of this crime?" Shaw's gaze raked me.

"A few witnesses have mistaken it for blood," Gordon said.

"I suppose Miss Harris could have murdered the man, and then covered herself in pie to obscure any bloodstains," Shaw said. "Very Agatha Christie. Well played, Miss Harris."

"I didn't—"

"Right," Shaw said. "I'm afraid we'll need your clothes, Miss Harris."

"What?!"

"It's for the best, Miss Harris." Gordon clapped me on the shoulder, as if there was nothing at all between us. The big faker. "You'll get them back, and this way, there'll be no doubt of your innocence."

"Or guilt," Shaw chimed in.

"My clothes?" I stepped backward, bumping against the bath house's rough wooden wall. Of all the ways I'd fantasized about Gordon getting me out of my clothes, this wasn't one of them. "But I'm wearing my clothes."

Shaw rubbed his hands together. "Well, I'm here now. I may as well pitch in. Why don't I tackle Mr. Frith?" Without waiting for an answer, he sped down the alley.

"Thanks," Gordon said to his chief's departing back. I knew what he was thinking—his big case had become a joint effort. I also knew that in the end, Gordon would be the one to figure out whodunit. And Shaw would take the credit. At least Gordon would have the satisfaction of knowing he'd solved the crime.

"My clothes?" I squeaked.

"Sorry, Val, but it needs to be done."

A policewoman appeared and escorted me to the saloon's bathroom. She swabbed my hands for gunpowder residue. Beneath her watchful gaze, I stripped off my T-shirt and jeans.

I handed them over, realized the problem. "I don't have a change of clothes."

She nodded. "Wait here. We'll find something for you. Worst case scenario, I've got a blanket in my trunk." She left me alone. Though it was warm outside, the blue tiles seemed to pull in cool air, and I shivered as I washed my torso free of cherry goo. I turned on the hand dryer and huddled in front of it for warmth.

Fifteen minutes later, Charlene hollered through the door. "Are you decent?"

"No!" And the hand dryer had stopped working. I might have blown the fuse.

"We found you something that might fit. Open the door."

I cracked it open, and Charlene passed through a garment bag on a hanger. "Just to get you home. They want it back."

Edging the door shut with my foot, I unzipped the bag and a tumble of crinolines cascaded from the gray plastic. "What is this?" My voice echoed weirdly off the slick tiles.

"One of the costumes from the photo shop."

I eyed the striped satin skirt and corset. There didn't seem to be any outerwear involved in this costume. "Couldn't you have gotten me a miner's costume?" Something with pants?

"Couldn't find anything else in your size," Charlene said. "Time to lay off the pie, my girl!"

"I have not gained weight."

"That's what they all say." A door banged shut.

"Charlene? Wait!"

No answer.

Dang it all!

Annoyed, I rummaged through the bag. It contained some sort of chemise with short, puffed sleeves. I guessed it went under the red and black corset, which I would not be wearing. Steampunk might be hot, but this was a murder scene, and the dead deserved respect.

I slipped into the skirt. The satin was sheer and clingy, so I added the petticoats for modesty and buttoned up the chemise. The tiny mirror over the sink couldn't capture the entire effect, but I'm sure my tennis shoes were the touch of elegance needed to pull the look together.

I jammed the corset into the garment bag and zipped it up, opened the door.

A flash blinded me.

Charlene lowered her phone and squinted at the screen. "That's going on Twitter."

I rubbed my eyes, and the saloon came into focus. Wooden floors thick with sawdust. A long, polished bar and, behind it, a mirror speckled with age. Green felt tables for gaming and plain wooden ones for eating. A player piano. "Please don't post that on Twitter."

"Too late. No take backs. The Internet is forever."

Frederick raised his head from Charlene's shoulder and yawned in agreement.

"Now come outside and meet the other suspects." She wound through the tables.

Resigned, I followed and adjusted my thin top. The arms were a little pinchy. "*Other* suspects? I'm not a suspect."

"If they find any blood on that T-shirt, you are. So,

what about it? You didn't cut yourself slicing fruit today, did you?"

My skirts swished around my knees. "Charlene—"

"I know you didn't kill anyone, and more importantly, so does Detective Carmichael. I expect you to pump him for information on Friday. Or at least pump him—"

"Charlene!" My face heated.

Her eyes widened with innocence. "What?"

"Friday's off."

She stopped with one hand on the swinging, batwing doors. "Why?"

"Because he's in the middle of an investigation," I said, "and I found the body."

"Oh." She snapped her fingers. "All the more reason to help the police wrap this up quickly. Solve the crime, salvage your love life."

"I don't think Gordon wants us to interfere—"

"Asking questions isn't interference. What can it hurt?"

"You always say that, and things always go—"

"Besides," she said, "it's human nature to discuss tragedy. We'll just be there to listen. And if we hear anything useful, you can pass it on to your Detective Carmichael."

"I guess," I said, uncertain. Charlene wasn't wrong about human nature. Everyone would want to talk. My stomach churned. Everyone except the killer.

She pushed through the doors.

Feet dragging, I followed her into the sunny street.

She beelined toward a small cluster of people: two men and the woman who'd screamed at me, convinced I'd been covered in blood.

"Everyone all right?" Charlene stopped in front of the trio. They edged apart, making way. She tapped a pen on the cover of her little leather notebook. "Val, this is Bridget, Ewan's daughter."

Bridget winced, deepening the fine lines around her caramel-colored eyes. "Sorry, Val. Charlene explained about the pie. I guess I panicked. Are you all right? I hope the clothing fits okay."

I tugged on the sleeves. "It does, thanks. And I wasn't exactly at my best either. I didn't expect to find . . ." A corpse.

"And these are the Bar X trick shooters," Charlene said. "Moe and Curly."

The men bobbed their heads. They wore cowboy hats, khaki slacks, and denim shirts. Empty holsters were slung low about their broad hips.

"I'm Moe," said a fiftysomething with unnaturally dark hair, a down-turned mouth, and beaky nose. He stepped forward and shook my hand.

A man built like a fireplug and with a military haircut stepped forward. "I'm Curly." He tipped his hat.

I blinked. The men looked unnervingly like their Three Stooges namesakes. I'd always been more of an Abbott and Costello fan. "Is there a Larry?" I asked.

"Not anymore," they said in unison.

"And yes, those are our real names." Curly lifted his hat and rubbed his uber-short salt-and-pepper hair.

"Chief Shaw already took their statements," Charlene said.

I crossed my arms, uncrossed them. If Shaw really believed it was murder, those were quick interviews. As the Bar X trick shooters, Moe and Curly had been firing weapons around the time of death.

"Did you see anything?" Moe eyed me intently.

"I saw . . ." What had I seen? I wracked my brainpan. But I'd been fixated on the exploding pie and then the corpse, and not much had made it into my peripheral vision. "I'm not sure what I saw."

Moe's brow wrinkled, and he fingered his empty holster. "Chief Shaw confiscated our revolvers," he said, mournful. "Guess he figures if one of us did it, the ballistics will tell him."

"Who was Devon?" I asked.

"Devon Blackett, our bartender." Bridget's full lips quivered. "It must have been an accident. I don't know why anyone would want him dead."

"If by 'accident' you mean Curly or I did it," Moe said sharply, "we don't have accidents with our weapons."

"No, I didn't mean . . ." Bridget flushed. "I know you're careful. Maybe someone else was around the Bar X, hunting or goofing around. You know we've had to chase kids off before."

Curly wrinkled his sun-reddened face. "I did see a bunch of wild pigs earlier today. There could have been a hunter chasing after them, I reckon."

"A stray shot would explain why someone shot Val's pie," Charlene said. "Two stray bullets, and one was deadly."

"Maybe," I said, though I didn't quite believe it. The bartender had been in the alley, which wasn't over four feet wide. He would have been fairly well protected from random bullets.

"For all we know," Curly said, "it was the Phantom of Bar X." He slapped his cowboy hat against his thigh.

Bridget's shoulders hunched. "Not that again."

"What phantom?" I asked, and immediately regretted it. The only thing Charlene loved more than a good conspiracy was the paranormal. Knowing my luck, she'd try to drag me into a spot of ghost hunting.

"Something Ewan invented to drum up business," Moe said. "Tourists love a good ghost story."

"It's not a story," Bridget said, her words clipped. She spun on her heel and stalked into the saloon.

Curly winked and replaced his hat. "Right. It's *not* a story, and her father *didn't* dream it up to attract tourists."

"What have you heard about this phantom?" Charlene asked casually. "What does it do?"

"It wanders the Bar X at night, looking for vengeance on the man who killed him," Moe said. His broad face hardened. "It's a fairy tale."

"That can't be right," Charlene said, pocketing her notebook. "This whole setup isn't more than five years old. No one was killed here, were they?"

"This site is part of a ranch from the eighteen hundreds," Curly said. "Who knows what happened way back when? I'm sure lots of folks died around here, even if they weren't murdered."

"There's been a murder now," I said.

"Maybe," Moe said. "When the ballistic tests come back on our revolvers, that'll prove we didn't do it."

"Don't worry, Miss," his partner said. "This probably will turn out to be an accident. Maybe Devon shot himself. Murder is rare in San Nicholas."

If Devon had accidentally shot himself, the gun would still be nearby. I hadn't seen a gun by the corpse, and I had a sick sense the gunslinger was indulging in wishful thinking.

Chapter Three

We left Curly, Moe, and Bridget and walked down the dusty road. The sun walloped us, glinting off the storefront windows of the fake ghost town.

A trio of cops in blue turned to stare at my "fallen woman" getup.

Wishing I'd brought my Pie Town apron today, I tugged up the low collar of the revealing blouse. "The Jeep's back thataway."

"And Ewan lives thisaway." Charlene pointed at a Victorian perched on a hill. To the home's west, a piebald horse peered over a wooden fence and munched dried grass.

Unenthusiastic, I gazed at the two-story yellow Victorian, iced with white gingerbread trim. Charlene was right. We couldn't leave yet, even if my sleeves were pinching. Not with a Jeep full of pies.

"Just wait 'til you see the inside." She huffed, crunching up the gravel driveway. "Now let me do the talking."

"We need to find out what's going to happen to the pie-eating contest," I said, determined to be cold, businesslike, and efficient. My stomach twisted with selfish nerves. I'd pinned my hopes on regular pie sales to the Bar X. If this deal fell through, Pie Town was on the edge of real trouble.

I shouldn't have been thinking about pies. A man was dead. But Pie Town was still a new business, and aside from Charlene, it was pretty much all I had. My thoughts cravenly turned to its welfare.

"Don't worry," she said. "I've got it handled."

That was what had me worried.

She lumbered up the front steps and rapped smartly on the screened door. It swung open, and Marla beamed with patently false sympathy. "Charlene! They didn't arrest you after all. What a relief."

Charlene's nostrils flared. "Here to comfort the bereaved?"

"Hardly bereaved," Marla said. "Poor Ewan barely knew the dead man, though, of course, it is a terrible shock." Diamond rings twinkling, her wrinkled hand gripped the door handle. "Can I do something for you?"

"Who's there?" Ewan's voice called from inside.

"No one important," Marla said.

Charlene grabbed the screen door handle and pulled. Marla tugged in the other direction. They struggled for dominance, grunting. I had a brief, horrible image of Charlene keeling over from a heart attack.

"It's us," I shouted. "Val Harris and Charlene! May we come in?"

"Of course," he called. "Come inside!"

Marla let go, and Charlene tumbled backwards into my arms.

She turned and glared at me, brushing off her purple knit tunic.

"Please, do come in," Marla said, opening the door.

Ewan loomed behind her in the foyer. He raked a hand through his silvery hair. "What a day. How are you two holding up?" And then his gaze traveled from my skirt to my head, and his mouth quirked.

"They took my clothing for evidence," I said, and stepped inside. The entryway glowed, natural light from the tall windows reflecting off the wood floor. Pegs hung on one wall for coats, but aside from that, the room was barren. "Your daughter lent me these from the photo shop." I plucked at the skirt. "How are you managing? Did the police say anything about the fundraiser?"

"Ewan and I were just working that out," Marla said.

"We can't use the saloon and have to block off the alley," he said, "but the fundraiser will go on."

I looked heavenward and sent a prayer of thanks to St. Ivan Rilski, the patron saint of pies and pie makers.

"Why close the saloon?" Charlene asked. "Devon was killed in the alley."

"Fire code," he said. "The alley's a crime scene, and that means we can't use the saloon's side door. Without that exit, we're breaking fire code if we let people inside. We'll set up tents and move the bar and gaming outdoors." He turned to me. "I'm sorry this had to happen on your first visit, Val. I hope this won't turn you off the idea of letting us sell your pies at future events."

"No!" That hadn't sounded too eager, had it? I cleared my throat. "It wasn't your fault."

"Even so," Ewan said, "I don't like this hanging over our heads. Devon was a recent hire, but he seemed a decent fellow. And even though our trick shooters had nothing to do with this, it won't do anything good for their reputation, or ours."

He walked onto the porch, and we all trailed after him. Ewan crossed his arms and stared at his ghost town below. A faint blue rim of Pacific peeked above the eucalyptus trees.

Charlene leaned against the porch railing. "And I don't like that someone took a potshot at Val. If you don't mind, we'd like to look into this."

I cringed. And this is where it began. Fortunately, no

sensible person would ever agree to letting us play detective. "Charlene, I don't think—"

"The Baker Street Bakers." Ewan's eyes lighted. "I wouldn't mind seeing our local amateur detectives in action."

"Please." Charlene sniffed, brandishing her notebook. "Consulting detectives, not amateurs. Though technically, we can't even call ourselves detectives, since we don't have a license. Let's just stick with consultants."

"Detectives? You're a detective?" Marla snorted with laughter. "You must be kidding."

"Didn't you hear?" Ewan asked. "She and Val helped the police solve two murders—"

"Three," Charlene said modestly.

"Three murders earlier this year. These two ladies were nearly killed in the process."

"How unfortunate," Marla said.

My eyes narrowed. Unfortunate someone had tried to kill us, or that they'd failed?

Ewan turned to my piecrust maker. "Speaking of local news, is it true Mabel Merriweather saw fairies at the dog park?"

I gaped. Was Ewan a lover of the paranormal too?

"That's what she says, but it was dark." Charlene tapped the notebook against her chin. "So, it doesn't seem likely."

I waited for it.

"My guess is she saw an alien," Charlene said.

A shiver crawled across my skin. I knew there were no such things as aliens. But there *could* be. And I'd watched enough *X-Files* to know nothing good comes from an alien encounter.

"That dog park has always been haunted," Charlene continued. "Little wonder it's started attracting fairies."

"Ghosts attract fairies now?" I asked.

"If you read my Twitter feed, you'd know," she said tartly.

I sighed. At least the conversation had shifted away from

"Val and Charlene, Consulting Detectives." If Gordon found out I'd been soliciting the Bar X for detective work, we'd never have our first date.

"Back to Devon's murder," Charlene said. "If we take the case—"

"You mean you're serious?" Marla uncrossed her arms, her gaze ping-ponging between the three of us. "This isn't a joke?"

"Nope," Ewan said. "I've tried to join their crime-solving crew, but Charlene's told me I'll have to prove my baking skills first."

I stared, aghast.

"He wasn't serious," Charlene said to me.

Marla lowered her sunglasses to her eyes. "A detective. You. Charlene McCree. A detective."

"Yes, me, Charlene McCree. Did you forget to put in your hearing aid?"

On Charlene's shoulder, Frederick twitched his ear.

"Well, your last case mustn't have been a very challenging murder," Marla said.

Ewan rubbed his chin. "I dunno. I thought it was a real three-pipe problem."

"A what?" Marla's face was as blank as an empty plate. "What does smoking have to do with it?"

"Duh," Charlene said. "It's a Sherlock Holmes reference."

Marla bristled. "I do know who Sherlock Holmes is."

"Saw the movies, did you?"

I squeezed between the two. "Mr. Frith—"

"Ewan."

"Ewan, please let us know if there's anything we can do to help. I've still got most of the pies in the Jeep, and the—" I swayed, horrified. "The pies. I left a stack of them on the saloon porch. Did you take them?"

"On the porch?" Ewan said. "I saw a cop carrying some pink boxes away from there."

I swore. "Come on, Charlene. Those pies are *not* evidence." I dragged her to the porch steps. "Don't worry. If something's happened to them, we've still got time to return to Pie Town and get replacement pies before the contest. It's all under control!" I turned back to him. "Oh. Where do you want the other pies I've got in the Jeep?"

"Put them in the photo shop," he said. "It's unlocked."

"Righto."

I hustled Charlene down the hill and to the ghost town's main street, still bustling with police.

"How could you leave pies on the porch?" Charlene asked.

"Where was I supposed to put them? You were on the porch with Ewan and Marla, why didn't you rustle up the pies?"

"Rustle up? What is this? A western?"

"I can't help it," I said. "I was an English major. I'm easily influenced when it comes to words. On my trip to London senior year, I came back speaking Cockney. Everyone thought it was an affectation, but I couldn't get it out of my head."

"All right." She patted my arm. "It's only a pie-eating contest. They'll be shoving pie down so fast, they won't be able to taste it. Worst case scenario, we thaw some frozen pies. They'll never know the difference."

"What if they do? I can't leave a bad first taste in their mouths. Everyone at that fundraiser could be a future customer."

"That's crazy talk."

"That they might be future customers?"

"That they won't like the pies," she said. "You're freaking me out. Knock it off."

I took deep, calming breaths and strode past the carriage house. "Right. Right. Everything is okay." Aside from a man being murdered and me nearly getting killed.

Gordon was speaking to two uniformed officers outside the saloon. He gestured toward the opposite side of the street and at Charlene's Jeep outside the pottery shed.

The officers nodded. They walked behind the squat building and vanished into the eucalyptus trees.

I waved. "Gord . . . I mean, Detective Carmichael."

His eyes crinkled. "You can call me Gordon when I'm on duty." He eyed me appreciatively. "Nice dress."

My chest heated, and I crossed my arms in embarrassed pleasure. "Thanks. My pies. I left five on the porch, there." I pointed. "Now they're gone. Ewan said he saw a police officer taking them somewhere. Do you know where they are? We need them for the contest this afternoon."

He frowned. "It's the first I've heard of it. Wait here. I'll find out what happened to them." He strode through the swinging saloon doors.

"See?" Charlene said. "He'll take care of it." Frederick's white tail coiled around her neck.

"I know. It's fine." *Fine, fine, fine.* Worst case, I'd get new pies. So what if we ran out today at Pie Town? It could be a good thing. If people assumed we were selling out, it could make our pies more desirable. It would be like playing hard to get. With pies.

Gordon emerged from the saloon with Chief Shaw.

The chief grimaced. "Sorry, little lady. Those pies are evidence."

"What?" My hands twitched. "But they had nothing to do with the murder. The only pie with any connection to the crime is lying dead in the street." I pointed, but the box had been removed.

A portly cop waddled from the saloon and brushed golden crumbs off his blue shirt.

My eyes narrowed. Were those piecrust crumbs? They were!

"But . . ." Shaw lowered his chin. "Like your clothing, the pies could be integral to the crime scene."

"How?!"

"They're only pies, Val," Gordon said.

My eyes bulged. Only pies? *Only pies!* And I'd wanted to date the man? I sputtered.

Charlene grasped my arm. "Someone nearly killed her today, one of our pies was brutally attacked, and then she found a corpse. It's a lot for one morning. She's a little sensitive."

"I am not," I ground out.

"I'd offer to return them," Shaw said, "but I doubt they'll be much use once we're done with them."

I raised my chin. "It's all right. I understand." I whirled, crinolines swishing, and stormed to the Jeep.

Gordon trotted after me. "I'm sorry about your pies. Look, I'll make it up to you."

"There's no need," I said stiffly, and opened the rear doors. I slid a stack of boxed pies toward me. "They're only pies. I have more." Okay, there was a microscopic possibility I might be overreacting. Maybe Charlene was right. Maybe getting shot at had thrown me off my game.

I strode to the photo shop and nudged the door open with my hip. The small room was a mass of costumes, with a backdrop at the back and an antique camera on a tripod. I set the boxes on the counter beside an old-fashioned cash register.

"Are those pies really a problem?" he asked.

I turned.

He carried a stack of boxed pies and set them on the counter. His green eyes darkened with concern.

Gordon was taking this seriously. This mess wasn't his fault, and he was trying to help.

I almost smiled. It was too easy to smile around Gordon. "No. I'm stressed out because I hired and promoted staff for an expansion, and we're barely breaking even again. And finding that poor man . . . The shot at me must have had something to do with his murder."

"Let's not jump to conclusions. We need to gather more evidence. At least we've got a limited pool of suspects. And if it helps, I don't seriously consider you one of them. This is all procedure."

Gordon followed me to the Jeep, and I grabbed more pies.

"I'm glad you're in charge," I said, and meant it. "You'll figure this out."

He glanced over his shoulder at the saloon.

Chief Shaw gesticulated at Charlene, who stood, head cocked, arms crossed.

"Mm," he said. "'In charge' is a relative term." He took a stack of pies from the Jeep and again followed me into the photo shop. "But thanks. And if it makes you feel any better, after seeing you in that outfit, I'm highly motivated to clear this up so we can go on that date."

In spite of everything, a bubble of laughter tickled my chest. "You should have seen the corset."

Grinning, he swaggered to the saloon and said something to Charlene.

I shouldn't have felt a warm, fuzzy glow at a murder scene. But with my almost boyfriend in charge, I knew everything would be okay.

Charlene strolled to the Jeep and set Frederick on the dash. "Ready?"

I shut the rear doors. "I'm more than ready. I'm rough and ready."

She groaned and stepped into the car.

I slid into the passenger side. "And speaking of rough, what's up with you and Marla?"

"Oh, you noticed that, did you?"

"Kind of hard to miss the nails-on-a-chalkboard tension."

"That woman's made a point of one-upping me in everything." She started the Jeep. "Her life has been a whirl of trips to the Riviera and wealthy husbands, and she'll never let me forget it."

"Oh, come on. It's not as if you've lived a dull life. You were in the roller derby."

Charlene tore down the street, the Jeep's tires kicking up a cloud of dust in our wake. "She was in the Ice Capades."

"You're joking."

"Serious as a heart attack. It's where she met her first husband."

"He was in the Ice Capades?"

"He saw her picture in the paper and deluged her with roses and expensive champagne until she agreed to go out with him."

We careened around a bend in the road, and I clutched Frederick and the dash for balance.

"Roses and champagne?" I asked. That was old school.

"She makes sure I know every detail."

"So, she grew up here?"

"She moved away every time she got married, and then returned every time one of her husbands dropped dead. She's been married more times than Liz Taylor and not a single divorce."

"That's—"

"Suspicious."

I was going to say "tragic."

"Enough about that woman," she said. "Did Carmichael give you any clues?"

"No. Gordon said it was too soon to know anything. What about Shaw? Did he spill about the crime?"

"There's only one thing you need to know. If Shaw's in charge, we're doomed."

"Oooh! A spot on the street!" Charlene whipped the Jeep into an open space in front of Heidi's Health, a local gym and Pie Town's next-door neighbor. The uber-fit owner, Heidi Gladstone, stood on the sidewalk in her trademark green hoodie and black yoga pants. She frowned at a workman adjusting a sign behind her gym window.

"Wait here," I said. "I'll run inside and get the—"

Charlene stepped from the Jeep and stretched, her hand brushing a flower pot hanging from an iron street lamp.

I got out of the car and slammed the door on my striped satin skirt. Cursing beneath my breath, I opened the door, setting myself free.

Heidi turned, her blond ponytail bobbing. "Like my new sign?"

I brightened. "You took down the SUGAR KILLS sign?" Heidi, the health fanatic, had been at war with Pie Town since she'd moved in next door. She was also dating my ex-fiancé. I'd come to terms with their romance, but the SUGAR KILLS sign sent steam spewing from my ears.

Smiling, she stepped aside, revealing a new SUGAR KILLS sign approximately the size of a highway billboard, and complete with a skull and crossbones.

"Oh, come on," I said. "Really? Do you have to put that in your front window?"

"No time for chitchat, ladies." Charlene winked, draping the cat over her shoulder. "Got to get those pies for the pie-eating contest. Picture it, Heidi, all those people, jamming pie down their gullets as fast as they can." She sauntered into Pie Town, setting the bell above the glass front door ringing.

Heidi's nostrils flared. "I can't imagine a worse tradition. Obesity is at epidemic levels, and you only encourage—"

"Yeah, yeah, yeah." I hurried after Charlene. Pie Town did offer sugar-free, savory potpies, but Heidi wouldn't be satisfied until every pie was sugar-free and probably crust-free as well. *Yeeesh.*

I walked inside, and the tension in my shoulders released. Pie Town was my happy place, with its retro, 1950s decor and pink booths and big glass case filled with pies. Two old men—Graham and six foot six Tally Wally—sat at the counter and sipped coffee. The booths were filled— tourist families with sunburned, sticky-faced kids, and regulars from the town. A group of college-age kids, overflow from the comic shop next door, debated over a role-playing game in the corner booth.

Joy, the owner of said comic shop, swiveled on her barstool and stared, her dark brows lowering. Her silky black hair was done up in a top knot held in place by a pencil.

Normalcy. I loved it.

Joy braced her elbow on the linoleum counter. "Nice get up, Val. But it's a little early for a costume party."

Charlene stopped dead in the middle of Pie Town's checkerboard floor. She jerked her thumb over her shoulder. "The *police* confiscated her clothes."

There was a spattering of applause from the gamers' table. Diners in the pink Naugahyde booths put down their forks and stared. Looking interested, the old men swiveled on their barstools.

"Someone tried to kill Val again," Charlene said. "She had to change her knickers."

"Not my knickers—"

"I told you that gym owner was trouble," Graham said.

His rolls of belly fat swelled beneath his frayed, tweed jacket. His white hair was rumpled, the soft cap he usually wore lying on the counter beside his coffee mug.

His lanky friend, Tally Wally, cackled. "About time Val got tarted up. Get it? *Tart?* Because she's in a dress like that, and she sells 'em."

I raised my hands in a warding gesture. "It wasn't—"

"It's got nothing to do with tarts," Graham said. "She sells pies."

"What's the difference?" Wally asked.

"A tart has a more vertical crust and is thinner than a pie, right, Val?"

"They tend to have layers too," I said, drawn into the argument in spite of myself. "Such as a cream filling on the bottom and berries on top." *Mmm . . .*

"Why'd that gym owner try to kill you?" Graham asked.

"It wasn't—"

"Val's killing *me* in that outfit," joked the red-head, Ray, one of our regulars. He tossed a set of twenty-sided dice across the table. They banged into a shiny gaming book, its cover sporting a babe clad in a fur bikini and wielding a sword.

"Ignore him," said Henrietta, a fellow gamer. She brushed her sandy hair from her eyes. "He doesn't do suave or deeboneair."

"That's not how you say that word." Ray shifted his bulk.

"See what I mean?" Henrietta asked me.

"I need pies," I said, and flounced through the Dutch door by the register and behind the counter.

Petronella, my assistant manager, braced her elbow on the cash register. She was a dedicated Goth: pale face, pixie-cut hair dyed black, and cat's-eye eyeliner. "Was Charlene serious about an attempted murder?" she asked.

I hurried to a rack of pies at the other end of the counter and grabbed a cherry. "A stray bullet hit one of the pies at the Bar X. The police confiscated the other pies I was carrying at the time. I need six more cherries."

She winced, jamming her hands into the pockets of her pink Pie Town apron. "Oooh. I just sold two. We've only got five left."

"Did you say a pie was shot?" Joy asked in her rat-a-tat, just-the-facts-ma'am voice. A drop-dead gorgeous Eurasian woman, she hid her light under a bushel of gray business suits and high collars.

"Right out of her hand." Charlene sat on the vacant stool beside her. "Whiz! Splat!" She slapped her palms together.

"Then I'll take six of anything," I said to Petronella, "as long as it's fruit."

"I think we've got enough apricot to do you," Petronella said. "I'll help you box 'em. Say, do you have a minute?"

"I will after I get these pies to the Bar X." I grabbed a handful of flattened pink cardboard boxes from beneath the counter and popped them into shape. "Is it urgent?"

Petronella shrugged. "No. It'll keep."

"Why would someone want to kill a pie?" Joy asked.

"It probably had something to do with the murder," Charlene said loudly. "Val found another body."

The old men edged closer.

"Time to go," a mother said from one of the booths, looking pointedly at her three sunburnt kids. They left, trailing sand from their flip-flops.

Petronella hustled around the counter.

"You found another body?" Joy said. "That seems excessive, even for you."

"Well, who was it?" Graham asked.

"The bartender at the Bar X," Charlene said.

"Shoot, I've always wanted to go there." Wally fidgeted on his seat, and I hoped he was comfortable on the stool. He walked with a limp because he'd gotten "ass shrapnel" (his words) in Vietnam. "They've got a bar?"

"In the saloon," Charlene said.

"Who's the bartender?" Wally rubbed his ruddy nose.

"Guy named Devon Blackett," Charlene said. "New in town."

"Huh." Losing interest, the old men swiveled forward and resumed their caffeine meditations.

"If he's new in town," Joy said, "why kill him?"

I paused in the act of lowering an apricot pie into a box. "That's a good question."

"Well, he's not that new in town," Charlene said. "Devon's been working at the Bar X for the last three months, enough time to drive someone to murder."

"He'd have to be pretty irritating," Joy said. "But that still doesn't explain your cancan girl fashion."

"It's part of a, er, lady of the evening costume," I said. "You know, from one of those Wild West photo booths." Without the corset, and with the striped skirt, it did have something of a Parisian hot-cha-cha feel. I whipped a Pie Town T-shirt from beneath the counter and darted into my office to change.

Charlene walked inside as I was pulling a PIES BEFORE GUYS T-shirt over my head.

I glared. "Don't say it."

"That now you look like a bag woman who knocked over a dinner theater? Wouldn't dream of it."

"My VW's in the alley," I said, wanting this day to end. "I'll drive to the Bar X with the pies. It shouldn't take long."

"Sure you want to do that?"

"Why wouldn't I?"

"Joy was right. Shooting that pie doesn't make sense. And I'm not loving the stray bullet theory either. Anyone want you dead? Because maybe the killer really was shooting at you."

Chapter Four

I survived my return trip to the Bar X, and the next day dawned bright and sunny. Pie Town's kitchen AC fought a losing battle against the summer heat and the massive pie ovens. Charlene left after her morning shift and returned in the afternoon, by which time I was a sweaty mess.

But I was an optimistic sweaty mess. Ewan had suggested we meet again today to discuss future pie sales.

Now, Charlene and I puttered up the winding road in my sky-blue VW Bug. She hated my car for its smallness and oldness, but I was no fan of Charlene's quick-draw braking. Ignoring her running critique of my driving skills, I took my time evading potholes on the dirt road.

"Have you considered a girdle?" She stroked Frederick, puddled in her lap.

My hands jerked on the wheel. The VW bounced over a rut. "A what?"

"A girdle. For your first date."

"This is not the nineteen fifties," I said, enunciating, "and I do not need a girdle."

"It's not a matter of need," she said. "The retro-burlesque look is hot. Though now that you mention it, a little tightening up never hurt."

"No gir—"

A coyote bolted from a tall stand of dried grass and loped across the road.

I braked, startled, and it vanished into the sagebrush. "Did you see that?" I asked. It was rare to see a coyote in the daytime.

"See what? I was too busy thinking about Marla." She shifted Frederick to drape over the collar of her olive-green tunic.

Sighing, I put the VW into gear and lurched forward. "I wonder how her fundraiser went."

"It was huuuuge."

"Did Ewan tell you?"

"No one told me. It doesn't matter how the fundraiser did. That's what Marla will tell everyone."

I squinted into the afternoon sun.

"You should clean that windshield." She stroked Frederick.

"It looked fine when we left Pie Town." And I felt like a shirker for leaving. Late afternoons were always slow, mostly folks dropping by to take pies home for dinner. Petronella could handle it, but Pie Town was still my responsibility.

We rounded a bend and slowed to a halt in front of a closed, wooden gate. A sign above it read: Bar X.

"Hang on," Charlene said. "I got it." She lumbered from the VW and unlocked the gate, pushing it open and waiting while I drove through.

She closed the gate and got into the car.

"The gate was open yesterday," I said, driving forward.

"And your point is?"

"Maybe the killer *was* a hunter. There wasn't anything to stop someone from coming onto the property."

"Even if the gate was locked," she said, "the killer could have been anyone. I could jump that gate. Turn the car around. I'll show you."

"No, it's fine."

"What? You think I'm too old?"

I thought she really would try to prove her high-jumping abilities. "Of course not. I don't want to be late for our meeting with Ewan." I glanced at the backseat and the pink-and-white Pie Town box filled with hand pies. Nothing beats free samples to close a sale. I'd found recipes for hand pies dating back to the California Gold Rush, but I preferred to use my own. Besides, Charlene's crusts were amaze-ola.

We drove through the ghost town and parked in the driveway to Ewan's sunny Victorian.

I stepped out and unstuck my pink-and-white Pie Town T-shirt from my back. Maybe I wore my own tees too often. But my slogan gets smiles, and that's worth any fashion faux-pas. Besides, I was standing next to a woman wearing her cat as a stole. By comparison, I was a fashion plate.

On the porch, Ewan sat at a wicker table and frowned over an old-fashioned ledger. His white shirt looked freshly pressed, and his jeans well-faded. A pitcher of iced tea and three empty glasses sat on the table. Glancing up at us, he waved. "Charlene! Val! Come on up. Can I offer you iced tea?"

I lifted the pie box from the backseat, and we walked up the porch steps.

The silver-haired man rose, the lines around his eyes crinkling more deeply. He pulled out two wicker chairs. "Sit. Sit."

We sat, and I laid the box on the table. "I'd love some tea. Thanks. I brought hand pies." I opened the box.

He stretched a calloused hand across the table and ruffled Frederick's fur. "How can I say no?" He reached inside and took one. "How do you know what the flavor is?"

"The initials are on the crust." I pointed to the fork-tine holes that spelled BB.

"Clever," he said. "Blueberry?"

I nodded.

He took a bite, swallowed. "Perfect. I still prefer actual pie to hand pies—there's more filling to crust—but these will sell like crazy."

My heels bounced on the wooden deck. This was actually happening. My first wholesale client!

Charlene sniffed. "The crust is the best part."

"The orders will vary," he warned.

"As long as I can get at least two days' notice, we can fill them," I said. "We bake our pies fresh each morning, but I need to make sure I've got enough supplies in advance."

We talked numbers, and my skin tingled with delight. They were really good numbers.

"I think we're done here." He extended his hand. "Is it a deal?"

I shook. "Deal." A handshake deal! This was so Old West.

"Now." Charlene leaned forward and tapped the table with one gnarled finger. "Let's talk murder. Did you learn anything from the cops?"

"They're not talking to me." His ruddy face creased. "It's as if they think I'm a suspect."

"You had an alibi for the time he was killed," Charlene said. "You were with Marla and me."

"That Detective Carmichael is acting like my alibi doesn't mean much." He took another bite of blueberry hand pie.

My brow creased. Gordon wouldn't be suspicious for no reason. When exactly had Devon been killed? I'd assumed it was around the time I'd been shot at. But what if that shot had been meant to deceive, to make us think the murder had occurred then? What if Devon had been killed earlier?

A warm breeze flowed over the balcony, ruffling the tablecloth.

"What can you tell us about your bartender?" I asked.

He heaved a sigh, his muscled bulk shifting in the chair. "Unfortunately, not much. I've got his résumé if you want to see it. Devon was a recent hire. My daughter had been working the bar and doubling as our photographer. The old-time photography was more popular than we expected, so we hired Devon."

"Was he a good worker?" I asked. "Were there any tensions between him and the staff?"

"You know bartenders. He could be flirtatious with the guests, but he was always respectful to Bridget. He'd have been an idiot not to be, since she's my daughter."

I scooted the wicker chair closer to the table. "Who might have wanted to kill him?"

"Beats me. He broke up a fight a couple weeks ago. I didn't think there were any hard feelings, but I could have been wrong."

"A fight?" Charlene sipped her tea and set it down, wiping the condensation beads that had formed on the tall glass. "Not in the saloon?"

"A group of financial advisors, if you'd believe it. Someone had had too much to drink, and there was a brawl. I gave Devon hell afterward—not for breaking up the fight—but for over serving. We may not be a normal bar with normal bar problems, but they'll yank my liquor license quick enough if we serve people who are drunk."

"Who were these financial advisors?" I asked.

"A crew out of San Francisco. I'll get you the name of the company if you want it."

"I'm more interested in the guys who were in the fight," I said.

"I've got notes on that too." He gave me a hard smile. "They're banned from the Bar X."

"Now . . ." Charlene smiled innocently. "What's the story on this phantom of yours?"

Mentally, I slapped my head. I should have expected a detour into the supernatural sphere.

"Ah. That." He turned his head, staring at the western town sprawled below. "It started out as a fairy tale for the tourists. You know how it is. Everyone loves a good ghost story. And Bridget figured my fake ghost town should have a fake ghost. I didn't see the harm."

I folded my arms over my chest, relieved. See? Fake ghost.

"Started out?" Charlene asked.

He rubbed his bristly cheek. "The thing is, before I knew it, the Bar X had a real ghost."

She leaned forward, her lips parted. "Tell me."

"It's the usual haunted stuff. Doors open and close for no reason, lights flick on and off, there are strange rapping sounds. It was all harmless until someone left the corral gate open, and Moe and Curly's horses escaped. Fortunately, they didn't get far, but those two were furious."

Charlene frowned. "The corral gate?"

"Horses?" I asked. "I thought they were trick shooters."

"That's part of the trick," he said. "They shoot their targets from horseback. It's quite a show."

Face pinched, Charlene turned a quelling look on me. "Why did you blame the open corral on the ghost?"

"No one else took credit for it. I can chalk up the doors and noises and lights to natural causes. The problem is, people have actually seen the ghost."

She clasped her hands together. "What have they said?"

"A pale form," he said. "It's all vague. But I think it's a tulpa."

"A what?" I asked blankly.

Charlene pressed a hand to her mouth. "A manifestation that's imagined into existence. There was a case in England where a group of psychologists brought people into a castle and told them it was haunted. They invented an entire history for the so-called spirit. So naturally, half the group experienced the ghost. The psychologists chalked it up to the power of suggestion."

"Right," Ewan said. "Then tourists who hadn't been involved in the experiment reported seeing the same ghost. They couldn't have known the details of the story the psychologists had fabricated. Charlene tweeted about the case last year, I think. Never expected to see something like this in San Nicholas."

Oh. My. God. Ewan followed her on Twitter. They were two peas in a spacepod. And was that the scent of romance in the air? I smiled. Charlene deserved to find someone who appreciated and understood her.

"I don't like this business about the corral," she said. "Why didn't you tell me sooner?"

His face colored. "I didn't want you to think I was making up the story to flatter your interests. And I had invented the original ghost story."

She shook her head. "Ewan. I would never think that."

He rubbed the back of his neck. "Well, I guess I'd better get those files you asked for." He rose and walked into the house. The screen door banged shut behind him.

"We're in." Charlene rubbed her hands together.

"I know." I pumped my fist in the air. "Who would have guessed he'd need so many pies on a regular basis?"

"I'm talking about the investigation. I wasn't sure he'd agree to let us investigate."

"Er, did he agree to let us investigate?"

Ewan returned and handed Charlene a manila folder. "Here you go. A copy of Devon's résumé and that information on the financial planning group."

"Thanks," she said. "Mind if we nose around? Ask your staff some questions?"

"Have at it," he said.

She shot me an I-told-you-so look and rose. "We may have more questions for you later, if you don't mind."

"Try not to disturb the staff too much," he said. "Between you, Marla, and the cops—"

"Marla?" Charlene's jaw dropped. "What does Marla have to do with anything?"

"She's here at the Bar X," he said, "asking questions just like you."

A crimson wash raced from Charlene's neck to her snowy hairline.

"Okay, thanks!" I tugged lightly on Charlene's knit sleeve and led her, sputtering, to the VW.

"Marla." She clenched her fist.

"I'm sure it's nothing."

"Marla!"

Frederick raised his head from her shoulder.

"So what, if she's asking questions?" I asked, soothing. "She doesn't know what she's doing. We do. We've got experience on our side."

"Marrrrrrlaaaaaaa."

For a moment, I couldn't speak, fear locking my jaw into place. I'd always thought of Charlene as hearty, but she was old. "Are you okay? Is this a stroke? Oh, my God. It is a stroke." Heart thudding, I wrenched open the car door. "Sit down. I'll call an ambulance."

She brushed away my arms. "It's not a stroke! I told you she's always competing with me. What's worse is she always wins. Always!" Her face screwed up, childlike.

I was torn between laughter and tears, her expression recalling all my own childhood disappointments. The hand-me-down clothes. The ragged, home-grown haircuts. The missing father. And I sensed there was more to this feud than simple one-upmanship. Something in it struck at Charlene's vulnerabilities.

"Come on," I said gently. "The roller derby is way cooler than the Ice Capades."

"It's more than that." She picked at a loose thread on her tunic.

"Then what?"

Her mouth sagged. "She's always been better than me. I once blogged about a tarot reader who told me I'd live a long and eventful life."

"And you have. You are!"

"Two weeks later, Marla finagled a spot on a TV show with some famous psychic. They investigated the White Lady's ghost." She tucked her hands behind her elbows.

"A TV show I'm sure everyone's forgotten by now," I said, disconcerted. The White Lady haunted a nearby cliffside bar and restaurant. She was big news in these parts. "The White Lady's only a local ghost. Look at all your Twitter followers!"

She bit her bottom lip.

"What?" I asked. "She's got more?"

"She has her own online video channel. She puts on a life-coaching show. Professional production, soft lighting, the works. And now she wants Ewan."

"What?"

"You saw her. She was all over him like a cheap suit."

I tucked my chin. "Do *you* want Ewan?" And more importantly, had he been serious yesterday about wanting to join the Baker Street Bakers? I wasn't sure how many conspiracy-addled seniors I could handle.

"No. We've been friends for ages. I thought . . . well . . ." She shook her finger at me. "Mark my words, Marla's got him in her crosshairs only because I'm in the picture. She's going after what she thinks I want. And that isn't fair to Ewan."

"Can't you just tell her you're not interested in the man?"

"Ha! As if she'd believe anything I said." White curls quivering, Charlene slumped against my VW. "Our investigation is doomed."

I'd never seen Charlene rattled before, and I didn't like it now. "The heck it is! We solved the biggest crime to hit San Nicholas in decades. Not to mention that weird business with Old Man Rankin's missing moose head."

"Are you *trying* to be alliterative?"

"The point is, you know what you're doing. Marla is in over her head."

"You'd better watch it," she said. "If she knows you and Carmichael have a thing going, she'll be all over him too. She may be chasing Ewan now, but it wouldn't surprise me if she was one of those jaguars, on the prowl for younger victims like Gordon or that bartender, Devon."

"Women who chase younger men are called cougars. And Devon wasn't exactly a kid." By my estimate, he'd been in his midforties.

"When you get to be her age, it's a jaguar."

"I'm not worried about Gordon."

"You should be," she said.

"Let's nose around the Bar X."

"Fine."

Charlene's skin had a grayish tinge. Even though the stroke scare had been in my head, I took it easy driving down the short hill into the ghost town. I parked in front of the saloon.

Yellow police tape fluttered at the alley entrance. The saloon's batwing doors swung, hinges creaking, in the salty breeze. Remembering Devon's body, sprawled in the nearby alley, my scalp prickled.

We pushed through the saloon doors and walked inside, leaving footprints in the thick sawdust.

Cards in their hands, Bridget and Curly looked up from a green felt table.

"Hi, guys," I said. "How did the pie-eating contest go yesterday?"

"No one puked." Curly rubbed his double chin and threw down a card. The strap of his green eyeshade bit into his military haircut. "That's positive."

"Oh." Ew. I hadn't considered that possibility. Those were Class A pies, but they wouldn't taste good going the wrong way.

"The contest was great." Bridget frowned at her cards. Her long blond hair was out of its braid and cascaded over the shoulders of her blue T-shirt. "I think they were expecting whipped cream in a piecrust. Actual fruit pies classed up the event. It also slowed down the eating."

"Want to play?" Curly said. "I'm teaching Bridget poker, but it's better with more than two people."

"Poker, huh?" Charlene asked.

"I'm one of the Bar X's dealers on casino nights," he said.

"Is poker legal?" I asked.

"When it's for charity, it is," he said, "like last night."

"Deal me in," Charlene said. "What are the stakes?"

"We're playing for pretzel sticks." Curly nodded toward a small bowl by his elbow. "Grab a bunch."

Borrowing a handful of Bridget's pretzels, I joined the game too. "Curly can't be your real name."

"It used to be Charles," he said. "I legally changed it to Curly when I joined up with Moe—short for Maurice—and with Larry."

"It's amazing," I said. "You two really do look like your Three Stooges counterparts." I couldn't wait to meet Larry.

"It's the hair." He adjusted his eyeshade.

"Have the police said anything to you about the murder?" Charlene asked.

"They won't even admit it is a murder," Curly said.

"I don't see how it can be," Bridget said. "Who would want to murder Devon? He was a nice guy."

"To the boss's daughter, maybe," Curly said.

"You mean he wasn't as pleasant to others?" Charlene asked.

"He thought pretty highly of himself," Curly said. "Couldn't say a word without spinning it to make you look stupid and him sound like a genius."

"That's not fair," Bridget said. "Just because he was well educated—"

"Doesn't mean you have to jam it down everyone's throat whenever you get the chance," he said. "I raise you five pretzel sticks."

"Who was the last person to see him alive?" I asked.

"Aside from whoever killed him?" Curly's broad nose wrinkled.

"Fold." Suddenly looking every inch of her forty-some years, Bridget laid down her cards. "I was the last to see him. Devon and I were both here, in the saloon. I was setting up the food, and he was cleaning the bar. He went outside to get some supplies that weren't in the store room. If I'd gone with him—"

"You might have been shot too," Curly said. "Don't think that way. It wasn't your fault."

"When did he leave?" I asked.

"About thirty minutes before I stepped outside and saw him dead and you covered in cherry pie," Bridget said.

"Where were you when the hullaballoo started?" Charlene asked Curly.

"Walking my horse to the carriage house. It threw a shoe when Moe and I were practicing in the corral."

"Threw a shoe?" I asked. "The shoe actually flew off?"

"No, it came loose. We had to stop. You can't let a horse run around on a loose shoe. It messes 'em up."

"Anyone see you at the carriage house?" Charlene asked, subtle as a brick to the face.

He lowered his head, staring. "No. The police asked me that yesterday. And is that a cat you're wearing? No animals are allowed in the saloon."

"He's a comfort animal." Charlene sniffed.

"Oh, then you've got a license for it," he said.

"It's all right," Bridget said quickly. "No one's here but us."

"I wonder if that's true," Charlene said. "I hear the Phantom of Bar X let your horses escape from the corral. It sounds like the phantom is getting out of control."

I smothered a groan. I should have known Charlene wouldn't let anything as juicy as a local ghost story go.

"Phantoms aren't real," Curly said. "That's why they're called phantoms."

Bridget took the deck and shuffled it. "This one is. But it didn't let the horses out."

"Oh?" Charlene canted her head. "Then who did?"

Bridget flushed. "Not a ghost."

Curly snorted. "The only ghost is in the heads of a bunch of drunk tourists."

"I dunno," Bridget said. "Sometimes when I'm closing up at night, after an event, weird stuff goes on."

"Such as?" Charlene asked.

"I was in the saloon late one night, cleaning up—"

"Devon's job, wasn't it?" Curly asked.

"He had an emergency," Bridget said.

Curly raised a skeptical brow. "Right."

"Anyway, I had this feeling I was being watched, you know? And it kept growing. The saloon got really still, and then I heard a door slam in the storeroom."

"Was anyone there?" I asked, breathless. I tried desperately to get a hold of myself. Phantom, shmantom. It had probably been the wind.

"There was no way anyone could have been," Bridget said. "I closed up fast and left."

"Curly's right." Charlene shot Bridget a look I couldn't interpret. "There's no phantom. Best we all forget about it."

I gaped. No phantom? Phantoms were Charlene's bread and butter, the peanut butter to her chocolate, the cheese to her wine. "I heard Devon had only been here a few months," I said, perplexed by Charlene's change of heart.

"Yeah." Bridget tore her gaze from Charlene. "He wasn't here long, but we'll still miss him. I can't believe this has happened. Devon was sweet."

Curly plucked the deck of cards from Bridget's hands. "Are we playing or not?"

"It had to have been an accident." Bridget leaned across the green felt table. "Murder doesn't make sense. Devon hadn't been here long, not long enough to make enemies. There was no reason for anyone to kill him. We never got any complaints. He was a good person."

"If he was so sweet," Curly said, "why did someone shoot him? People don't get killed for no good reason."

"That's not fair." Bridget's nostrils flared. "You're blaming the victim!"

"Did he have any family?" I asked.

She gazed at the pretzels piled in the center of the table. "No. He told me his mother died six months ago. And now he's gone too."

"Maybe it's for the best his mother wasn't around to see this," Curly said. "There's nothing worse than losing a child."

Bridget gnawed her bottom lip. "No. No, I guess there isn't. I'm sorry. I can't . . ." She scraped back her chair and hurried from the saloon. The batwing doors flapped, stirring a breeze.

Curly's mouth twisted with disgust. He dropped the deck on the table. "Do you have to be so damned nosy?"

"I'm sorry," I said. "I didn't mean to upset her. Should I go after her?"

"Her mom died when she was young," he said. "She's a little sensitive about it. Not your fault. Best to leave her alone." He gave Charlene a hard look. "About everything."

"Someone killed that bartender," Charlene said. "And that someone may still be here, at the Bar X. Things aren't going to be right for her or for anyone else until this murder is solved."

"Well," Curly said, "I didn't do it, so you can stop looking at me." He dealt us each a hand.

"You're right," I said. "Having a murder hanging over you isn't a good feeling." I knew that sense of creeping unease, of wondering who around you wasn't who or what they seemed. I pushed my chair from the table. "I'm going to find Bridget."

The saloon doors swung open, and Marla swanned in on Moe's arm. Her diamond-spangled fingers tightened on his plaid shirtsleeve.

Charlene bolted upright in her chair. On her shoulder, Frederick rose on all fours. He hissed, his back arched.

"Well, well, well." Marla smoothed the front of her denim shirt. "Look what the cat dragged in."

Chapter Five

Charlene's lips pinched. "Marla."

Settling back onto her shoulder, Frederick growled, his blue eyes narrowing.

Marla released Moe and turned up the collar of her blue shirt. The gesture had a dual effect: flashing her rings and exposing her massive turquoise necklace. The sawdust floor muffled the sound of her high-heeled cowboy boots, tucked discreetly beneath her white-denim slacks.

The woman had style.

Curly raised his cards higher, shielding his face. He scrunched, making tires of his neck and stomach.

Marla drew a business card from her breast pocket and handed it to me with two fingers. "My card."

I glanced at it. Thick white paper stock. Matte. Elegant black print: MARLA VAN HELSING, DISCREET INQUIRIES. I choked. Van Helsing? Like the vampire hunter? And how did she get the cards produced so quickly?

Marla dropped another card on the table in front of Charlene. "I'm here to solve the crime," she said.

Charlene purpled.

"Did you know she was once on TV?" Moe grinned and smoothed his slicked, too-dark hair.

Curly peered at Marla over his cards.

"That psychic who investigated the White Lady has been thoroughly discredited," Charlene said. "She's a fraud and a charlatan, and I wouldn't be caught dead in the same city with her, much less the same TV show."

"The televised séance was awfully fun," Marla said. "And I got sooo much fan mail."

"Marla," I said, "what are you doing here?"

"Oh." Marla tapped her turquoise necklace, and her rings glittered beneath the saloon's stained-glass lamps. "I forgot you're only a pie seller, dear. I'll break down the vocabulary. 'Discreet inquiries' means I conduct personal investigations for only the best caliber of client."

I folded my arms. "I was an English major."

"Of course you were, dear. So good of you to give Charlene a job in her golden years."

"You're a year older than I am," Charlene told her.

Marla tapped her silvery head. "Age is all in the mind. It's just a number."

"And what's your number?" I asked Marla. In Charlene's job application, she'd listed her age as forty-two. I'd doubled that number, subtracted ten, and not asked any questions. Now I might finally get an answer.

Marla wagged a finger at me. "It's not polite to ask a lady her age."

Charlene flipped the business card over and scowled. "You've got an office?"

"I always have an office. You mean you don't? Where do you meet your clients? In the pie shop?" Marla laughed, the sound of breaking glass.

"Our procedures are none of your beeswax," Charlene said.

I plucked a fallen ace of spades from the sawdust. Apparently, we hadn't been playing with a full deck, which seemed somehow appropriate. "Um, Moe? Curly told us that his horse had thrown a shoe, and he had to walk it back to the carriage house around the time of the murder." I slid the card onto the green felt table.

He glared at Curly, his black eyes beady. "Yeah?"

"Is that what you remember?" I asked.

"I remember him walking the horse from the corral. I didn't examine the shoe, if that's what you're asking, but the horse was hobbling like the shoe was loose."

"And what were you doing when Curly was in the carriage house?" I asked.

He crossed his arms across his broad chest. "The police have asked me, Marla's asked me . . . I'm done answering questions."

"Why?" Charlene asked. "Talking about a murder in your own backyard can't be that boring."

He glared at me. "You were there when Devon was killed. You tell me what happened."

"I'm not sure what I saw," I said slowly. Had I seen anything? I wracked my brains. Had there been a sound? A smell? Anything? If there was some clue buried in my subconscious, it eluded me. "Maybe you can help me figure it out."

"I've got better things to do," Moe said. "What do I get out of answering your questions over and over?"

Charlene's eyes narrowed. "What do you want?"

Moe blinked. "Huh?"

"You like potpie?" Charlene asked.

His eyes narrowed, as if it was a trick question. "Who doesn't?"

"Come to Pie Town tomorrow for lunch," Charlene said. "I'll set you up with a potpie on the house, and you answer our questions."

"Whatever." He stormed out.

Marla smiled. "He already answered my questions."

"Whatever!" Charlene stalked from the saloon.

"I'm not only a pie maker, you know."

Marla shrugged. "Whatever."

I walked down the dusty street to the Bar X photography studio, a small, wooden building with a false front. In the wide, square window stood a display of two mannequins in western garb and an antique camera on a tripod.

I imagined Gordon in a cowboy hat and smiled. Confession time: I've always had a thing for cowboys. Not that I encountered many in California. But Ewan's private ghost town was the sort of cockeyed fantasy I could get behind. No wonder Charlene liked him.

I rapped on the door, and it swung open beneath my fist. *Gulp.* That was rarely a good sign.

I leaned into the room. "Hello?" The photo studio had been rearranged since I'd been inside yesterday. A dusty, oriental carpet lined the floor. Two ornate, wooden chairs and a small table sat before a changing screen with scarves draped over the top. A red velvet chaise longue pressed against one wall.

Something metallic crashed behind the screen, and it wobbled. The fringed scarf slipped to the carpet, and there was a feminine curse.

"Bridget?" I asked, hoarse. Please let it be the photographer and not a murderer, marauder, or horse thief. "Need some help back there?"

She emerged from behind the screen, her pale face taut. "No," she said, voice clipped. "Did you need something?"

"To apologize."

She tilted her head. A whorl of gray-blond hair looped across one shoulder of her T-shirt. "Oh."

"You probably heard someone died in Pie Town earlier this year," I continued, "and it turned out to be murder. The man who died . . ." I blinked rapidly, my eyes burning. "He was a good person. The investigation was rough for a lot of reasons."

She dropped onto the chaise longue. "I know. I heard."

"I'm sorry for what you're going through. And I'm sorry if I was insensitive earlier in the saloon."

She stared at the oriental rug. "It isn't right that people are trying to make this Devon's fault. He was the victim."

"People?"

"Curly and Moe. They're both acting like he must have done something to deserve getting shot. Even my father . . ." She clasped her hands between her knees. "It's like . . . If it's Devon's fault, then they're safe, you know? They didn't do anything wrong, so no one will hurt them. But it's not true. They're just slandering his name, so they can delude themselves into thinking this could never happen to them."

"Why do they think Devon brought this on himself?"

She sagged against the arm of the chaise. "Moe's been insinuating that Devon was killed over a girl. Curly thinks it's because he worked as a bartender. Maybe someone got drunk, didn't like getting turfed out by Devon, and came back for revenge."

"Is that likely?"

"No!" She grimaced. "I don't know. Devon was good-looking. I think he flirted for tips, and he might have gone home with some of the women. If my father found out . . ." She looked out the paned window.

"What?" I prompted gently.

She met my gaze. "He would have fired him. Maybe I should have told Dad, but the women were all of age. If anything, Devon tended to like the older women."

Did Bridget fall into the "older woman" category? A filmy scarf slipped from the screen. It fluttered, wraithlike, to the oriental rug. And even though there's no such thing as ghosts, I shivered.

I shook myself. "Any women in particular?"

"I didn't keep track. If I was in the saloon, I was there to work."

"Does everyone do double duty at the Bar X?" I sat opposite her on a rickety, wooden chair.

"Pretty much. Curly and Moe both work as dealers for poker and twenty-one. My dad drives the stagecoach. I'm the official photographer, but I help out wherever I'm needed."

"Who takes care of the horses?"

"We all help out," she said, "but Larry's our farrier." A shadow of uncertainty crossed her face.

"Larry . . . ?"

"Of Larry, Curly, and Moe."

"What's his connection to Devon?" I asked.

Her head jerked up. "Why do you think he has one?"

"He spent time at the Bar X. It's a small ghost town."

She gnawed her bottom lip. "Larry's a good person."

"But?"

She sighed. "I saw him arguing with Devon last week."

"Do you know what it was about?"

She shook her head.

"Larry shoes the horses?" I asked.

"Yeah, but it's not even a part-time job. Which is a good thing, because he and Curly can't stand each other anymore."

"Why not?" I asked.

She picked at a throw pillow's loose thread and didn't meet my gaze. "I don't know what happened."

I didn't believe her. "Where can I find Larry?"

"He owns a used-car dealership down the coast."

"I don't suppose he was here the day Devon was killed?"

Her blond brows furrowed. "He might have been. He's a real horse lover, stops by whenever he gets the urge, and no one except Curly cares. But even Curly admits he's good with the animals."

If he was such a great farrier, why had Curly's horse thrown a shoe? And conveniently around the time Devon had been killed? I didn't know if that meant anything, but it was another reason to chat with Larry.

"Was anyone else at the Bar X when Devon was killed?" I asked.

She shook her head. "It was still early. The event didn't start for hours. Our extra help hadn't arrived yet. So, the killer had to have been a hunter, or maybe a random shooter. Nobody here would hurt a fly."

I guess I had a darker view of human nature, but I didn't argue. Bridget seemed less depressed, so my apology mission was accomplished. Not knowing what else to ask, I said good-bye and left.

The street outside was deserted, though a police car sat parked in front of the saloon. I guessed Charlene was out detecting or had gone up to the house to keep an eye on Marla and Ewan.

At the far end of the road, the carriage house's tall doors hung open, a gaping maw. In front of the building, two black horses stamped, hitched to the stagecoach.

Even if it was a fake ghost town, the quiet was unnerving. Not even the eucalyptus leaves rustled. Unsettled, I tugged down the hem of my T-shirt and continued down the road. I peered through the windows of the pottery shop, rattled the door to the bath house. In front of the little wooden chapel, my steps slowed.

My dream of marrying Mark Jeffreys had died, a stake driven through its heart, when he'd started dating my work neighbor, Healthy Heidi. I'd gotten over our failed engagement. It was crystal clear now, that my ex and I had never been right for each other. What I couldn't fathom was why I hadn't seen it when I'd been with him. Something cold—a combination of fear, insecurity, and mistrust—quivered inside my chest. I'd tried too hard to make that doomed relationship work. How could I be sure I wouldn't make the same mistake again?

I stood rooted, gazing at the chapel. My mother would have loved it for my wedding. It was adorable, small enough to hide the fact that I didn't have any relatives to fill it with. Cancer had taken my mother over a year ago, but the realization of her death hit hard at random moments, spaced further and further apart, but no less painful. I briefly closed my eyes, the pain of that loss washing over me with a suddenness that left me breathless.

Shaking myself, I walked on.

Near the carriage house, I stopped in the street and looked around. A tumbleweed blew across the road and came to rest against the police car.

I rubbed my bare arms. Ewan had done almost too good a job creating the ghost town. It really was starting to feel haunted.

I pushed aside my dark thoughts for more prosaic ones. Firstly, what was up with the tumbleweed? They weren't native to the northern California coast. Here, blowing sand and fog ruled the day. Did Ewan import the dried scrubs? What was the police car doing here? And most importantly, where was Charlene?

There was a shout, a rumble.

I turned.

The stagecoach bore down at me, the black horses galloping, driverless.

"Val!"

I froze, my brain refusing to process the data. The horses thundered closer, their nostrils flaring.

A blur of motion. Someone knocked into me, driving me sideways, and I cried out. I hit the ground hard. Something sharp dug into my hip and elbow.

The stagecoach rattled past. Dust billowed, coating my face and throat.

Gordon raised his head and coughed.

I stared, disoriented. What was he doing here?

Fine particles of earth drifted to the ground and covered his dark hair and blue suit. "Are you okay?" he asked.

Trembling, I rolled off the rock pinching into my side. "Yeah." It was the only word I could force past my lips. I gaped, stunned, after the clattering stagecoach.

He clambered to his feet.

To my shame, a faint stab of regret pierced my chest now that he was no longer pressed against me. So, I guess I wasn't in that much shock.

Gordon brushed his hands off on his suit jacket, knocking loose clouds of dirt. "Next time, look both ways before crossing." Extending his hand, he helped me rise.

"You're a scream." It wasn't funny, but I started laughing anyway, hilarity tinged with hysteria. Legs wobbly, I brushed the dirt off my Pie Town T-shirt. "I didn't think . . . What are you doing here?"

"Work. What else?"

"Val!" Charlene trotted toward us, Ewan and Marla at her heels.

Ewan continued past and shouted after the departing horses.

"I hope you closed the front gate when you arrived," Charlene said to Gordon. "Otherwise, those horses will be halfway to San Nicholas before Ewan catches them."

"Of course, I . . ." His green eyes widened. "Oh, damn." He took off after Ewan and the stagecoach.

"You shouldn't fool around with horses if you don't know what you're doing," Marla told me and examined her manicure.

"I didn't—"

"It's not Val's fault those horses got loose." Charlene jammed her hands on her hips, rumpling her tunic.

"Well," Marla said, "that carriage didn't get loose on its own. Unless you're suggesting the phantom did it."

"Val didn't release the carriage brake, did you, Val?"

"I don't even know where it is," I said, knocking another cloud of dust off my jeans.

"Well," Marla said, "someone else could have been hurt. Bad enough about that poor bartender." She sighed dramatically. "Such a tragic life."

"Life?" I asked. "Not his death?"

Marla brushed a wisp of silvery hair from her eyes. "I meant what I said. The poor man never knew his father, and he resented it terribly. It gnawed at him like poison."

"Some fathers aren't worth knowing." Charlene's gaze cut to me. "How do you know this?"

"People tell me things," Marla said.

Bridget emerged from the photo shack and ambled toward us. "What's going on? I thought Dad was giving you both a stagecoach ride?"

"He was," Marla said, "but the coach left without us."

Bridget touched the base of her slim neck. "What?"

"Runaway coach," Charlene said. "Nearly ran down Val, then took off down the street."

"Oh, my God! The horses!" Bridget raced after the dust trail.

This was probably a perfectly sensible reaction. I was okay, and the horses were out of sight. But I couldn't help feeling annoyed. I'd nearly been smashed to a pulp.

"Of course," Marla mused, "I didn't actually see Ewan tie the coach up. Did you?"

"What are you suggesting?" Charlene's jaw jutted forward.

She shrugged. "So, you didn't see him tie it up either?"

"I wasn't paying attention," Charlene said, "but I'm sure he did. He's no tenderfoot."

Marla tapped her cheek, her diamonds flashing in the sunlight. "I suppose it could have been an accident. It's strange the Bar X has had so many disasters of late."

I shifted, uneasy. And this had been the second time I'd been the target of a near miss.

Chapter Six

Ewan led the stagecoach down the dirt road. The black horses' flanks gleamed with sweat; their heads tossed.

Gordon and Bridget walked beside him. When they reached us, Gordon halted and stripped off his navy jacket. Ewan and Bridget continued on, walking the horses toward the carriage house.

Gordon turned to me. "Got a minute, Val?"

I glanced at Charlene and Marla.

Charlene made a shooing motion.

Marla smirked.

"Uh, sure," I said, uncomfortably conscious of their scrutiny.

He jerked his head toward the saloon, and I followed him, stopping beside his police car.

"What are you doing here?" he rapped out.

I stiffened, disconcerted by his tone. "Charlene and I met with Ewan and finalized our deal with the Bar X. He said we could look around. I didn't get much chance the last time I was here."

"That's great news about the pie contract." His shoulders relaxed. "Congratulations."

My ex had only sniped and complained when I'd started

Pie Town. Gordon had been supportive since I'd opened the pie shop, and he'd barely known me then. But that was Gordon—he'd joined the police force to help people, and that commitment bled into his personal life. It was one of the reasons I admired him, even when he was asking me hard questions.

"It's more of a handshake than a contract," I said. "But thanks. This is a big win."

"You've worked hard. You deserve it." He paused, eyeing me. "What happened with the stagecoach?"

I glanced down at my filthy T-shirt and jeans. "I didn't notice anything wrong until the stage was nearly on top of me."

"Was anyone else on the street?"

I shook my head. "Not that I saw."

"Me neither. I spoke to Ewan. He swears he tied up the horses and set the brake on the coach."

My pulse accelerated. I took a step closer to him before realizing I'd done it. "So, for that stage to get loose, someone would have had to both release the brake *and* untie the horses."

"Not only that," Gordon said. "Someone or something also would have had to startle those horses. We've been looking at this case as if Devon was the intended victim. Now I'm starting to wonder if you were."

"M—me?" I stuttered. "That's . . . that's ridiculous. I own a pie shop. I've got no money, no heirs, no one hates me." Okay, Heidi didn't love me, but it was a big jump from putting a SUGAR KILLS sign in the window to attempted murder.

"What about your ex? Seen him lately?"

I grimaced. I couldn't help but see my ex-fiancé. Mark was a realtor, and his grinning mug was plastered on FOR SALE signs across San Nicholas. "Not really. I mean, he works out at the gym next door, but we don't say much to each other besides 'hello.' But Mark can't even kill spiders. He's gone New Age, which I guess is old age now, since it started in the nineteen-sixties. He does yoga!" I clawed my hands through my hair, remembering too late I was wearing my usual chignon. A twist of hair fell loose against my neck.

Gordon shook his head. "You never know what's going on inside people."

"I don't see how he could have snuck onto the Bar X, twice, to try to hurt me. There are better places for murder. My house is isolated. And I'm at work by five to start prepping. Someone could pick me off in the alley before sunrise." My hair blew into my mouth. Impatiently, I ripped it free. My how-to-kill-Val exercise was not making me feel better. "The point is, I'm pretty sure Mark's afraid of horses. And guns. I doubt he even knows how to shoot."

"It's not that hard. And figuring out that coach's braking system wouldn't take a genius either."

"If someone wanted me dead, wouldn't I know why?" Or was I falling into a blame-the-victim mentality as well? Had Devon known someone wanted him dead?

A black cat slunk down the empty street and vanished behind a rain barrel.

Gordon brushed the loose hair off my neck, and I shivered. His eyes glittered like emeralds. We stood close enough for me to smell his woodsy cologne.

The breeze dropped, the rustling trees falling silent. Time seemed to stop.

I swayed toward him. My lips parted.

"Stay away from the Bar X, Val."

Phooey. I pulled away, my breath quickening with embarrassment.

"Listen," he said, "I've got to go take Mrs. Van Helsing's statement."

I snorted. *Van Helsing.*

"What?"

"Nothing, it's just . . . Van Helsing!"

He looked at me blankly.

"The vampire hunter from *Dracula*?"

"You've been spending too much time with Charlene."

"What's that supposed to mean?"

"The Baker Street Bakers had better not be on this case."

"We're not . . ." Oh. Right. We were. My face heated.

Mouth clamped shut, I followed him to the carriage house. The coach stood outside. In the stalls, Ewan and Bridget rubbed down the horses, now freed from their harnesses. Marla and Charlene leaned over the stalls, watching.

Gordon said something to Marla in a low voice and drew her from the carriage house.

Ewan shook his head. "I'm sorry about this, Val. That coach shouldn't have gotten loose. It's a miracle you weren't hurt." He rubbed the back of his neck. "You *weren't* hurt, were you?"

"No," I said. "I'm fine. A little dusty, that's all."

"That's a relief," he said.

The doors on both ends of the carriage house were open, creating a breezeway that tickled the back of my neck.

"How did the coach get loose?" I asked.

"I can't explain it," he said. "I swear I had the horses tied and the brake on. I must have forgotten one or the other."

"You didn't," Bridget said. "No one's more careful with the horses than you."

"Obviously I wasn't careful enough." He scrubbed a broad hand across his face. "Val, how can I make this up to you?"

Bridget shot him a sharp look.

"How about a stagecoach ride at a date to be determined?" Charlene said, stroking Frederick, limp over her shoulder. "The quickest way for her to get over the trauma is to get right back in the saddle."

Since I hadn't been in the saddle in the first place, I wasn't sure the saying applied. But it gave us an excuse to return, so I smiled brightly.

He patted the horse's gleaming flank and closed the animal inside the stall. "It's the least I can do. What time do you want to come by?"

Watching us carefully, Bridget finished up. She stepped from the stall and closed its door.

"Same time tomorrow?" Charlene asked. "Late afternoons are slow at Pie Town."

He nodded. "I've got a wedding tomorrow night, but if you're here by three o'clock, it should work."

I checked my watch. Afternoons might be slow at Pie Town, but I needed to get back. "Thanks, Ewan. I'm glad the horses are okay."

We said our good-byes, and Ewan and Bridget exited from the opposite carriage house door.

Glancing over her shoulder, Charlene walked with me to my VW.

I flipped through my keys. "So. I talked to Gordon." For some reason, the admission made my heart flutter.

Charlene sighed. "I suppose he warned you off playing detective?"

I winced. "He warned me off the Bar X. He thinks . . . One possible theory is that I might have been the target all along, and Devon was collateral damage."

Making herself comfortable on the hood of my car, she adjusted Frederick over her shoulder. "That pie shooting did seem kind of odd."

I opened the car door, hoping she'd take the hint and get inside. "I don't think he's right," I said, chilled in spite of the hot air flowing from the VW's interior. "No one wants to kill me."

"No one except Heidi, but she has an alibi. She was at her gym teaching an aerobics class when you were shot at. I checked."

Charlene had considered Heidi a real suspect? I leaned against the VW, and my gaze lost its focus. "Do you think Heidi hates me that much?"

"It depends on how crazy she is."

"That's not much of an answer."

"It wasn't much of a question. What aren't you telling me?"

"Nothing," I said.

"You're not telling me something. Out with it."

"Gordon asked me if Mark might hold a grudge," I said reluctantly.

"Mark?" She burst out laughing.

Frederick slid from her shoulder and she caught him before he could slide to the ground.

The cat raised his head and hissed at me.

Charlene's laughter morphed into a coughing fit. "Mark Jeffreys thinks Frederick is his power animal." She wiped her eyes. "He has the killer instincts of Barney Fife and the same amount of bullets in his gun, if you know what I mean. Do you seriously believe he could have crept onto the Bar X at high noon, shot at you, killed Devon—"

"By accident. This isn't my theory. It's Gordon's, and it's only a theory." One I now felt guilty about revealing.

"And then returned to set a stagecoach on you? I don't think so." She angled her head. "He might have hired a hit man though. I hear they're not that expensive. And considering the results, it would be just like Mark to hire an incompetent."

My neck stiffened. "I'm just telling you what Gordon said."

"For someone to aim a runaway stagecoach at you,

they had to know horses. And that means someone at the Bar X."

"They do all seem to know horses." I draped my arm over the open car door. "Moe and Curly are trick riders, and they were both at the Bar X. Bridget and Ewan take care of the horses too."

"Ewan couldn't have done it," she said. "He was with me and Marla when Devon was killed."

"Are we sure we know when Devon was killed? Maybe someone shot at me just to set the time of death. What if someone somehow rigged a gun to go off after Devon was killed? That would explain why I was shot at. Maybe the bullet wasn't meant to hit anyone." I wished I could ask Gordon, but I knew he couldn't tell.

Charlene's eyes widened. "That would explain how Marla could have pulled it off. Or maybe she had an accomplice. A second shooter, like the grassy knoll."

We always came back to that grassy knoll. "I guess an accomplice does make more sense than someone rigging up a gun to go off at random." I shifted, impatient to go. "When did Bridget say she last saw Devon?"

A man shouted, and I glanced toward the carriage house.

"About thirty minutes before his body was found," she said. "But there were shots from the sharpshooters going off regularly. You're right. Devon could have been shot right after he stepped out of the saloon, and it took us thirty minutes to find him."

"Which leads us back to who shot at me? And why?"

"It could have been Marla," Charlene said. "She's just the type to cook up a plot that byzantine. And how does she know so much about that bartender's father? There was more between those two than she's admitting."

"Ewan did leave the carriage house when we did, didn't he?" I asked, squinting in the bright afternoon light.

"Today you mean? Yes, why?"

"Because it sounds like two men are arguing over there."

Raised voices drifted from the carriage house.

Charlene's shoulders slumped. "I'm going as deaf as Frederick." She stomped toward the carriage house.

"Wait." I lurched from the car. We needed to return to work. Or, at least, I did. "I didn't mean . . ."

Charlene kept walking.

I trotted after her.

The shouts grew louder as we approached. We paused inside the wide, open carriage house doors. I blinked, my eyes adjusting to the dim light.

"I reckon you didn't since the shoe came loose." Curly's wide face twisted in a scowl. He folded his muscular arms across his chest.

"The other three shoes are fine." The other man clenched his fists. His wild gray hair receded, leaving a high, domed forehead over a hooked nose. Of average height and weight, he looked fit in his gray business suit. He could only be Larry. He looked exactly like his Three Stooges namesake.

"That's what you say," Curly said.

"Yeah, that's what I say. I said it to you, and I said it to the police. I'm getting tired of saying it. And I told you I'd repair it free of charge. What more do you want? Blood?"

In their stalls, the horses stamped, restless.

"You're scaring the horses," Curly said.

"Me?!"

I coughed. "Larry?"

They whipped around. "What?" they asked in unison, then glanced at each other.

Curly's broad shoulders slackened. "Oh. Hi. Were you looking for me?"

"Nope. For Larry," Charlene said.

"Well, you found him." Curly strode through the open

doors on the far side of the carriage house. We watched him make his way into the corral.

"I suppose your horse lost a shoe too?" Larry asked.

"I don't have any horses," I said. They'd always scared me, an emotion amplified by my recent near miss.

He snapped his fingers. "You're the little lady who nearly got run down by the stagecoach."

"Word gets around fast," I said.

He scowled. "Curly practically accused me of releasing the brake on the stage."

Had he tampered with the coach? I stepped forward and shook his hand. "I'm Val Harris. This is my colleague, Charlene McCree."

"Of Pie Town?" he asked.

"Yeah," I said, pleased and surprised. "You've heard of us?"

He pointed at my stomach, and I glanced down at my Pie Town T-shirt covered in dust. My cheeks warmed. Maybe we should invite Larry to join the Baker Street Bakers.

"So how does a used-car salesman end up working part-time as a farrier?" Charlene asked.

He drew himself up. "Because I'm not a salesman. I'm the owner, and I'm semiretired. So, I do what I want."

"Like trick shooting?" I asked.

His expression grew wistful. "There's something about cold, blue steel. At least I get to shoot on my commercials." He mimed a fast draw. "Have you seen them?"

I shook my head. I hadn't gotten around to installing cable yet—maybe next year when Pie Town brought in a steadier income.

"Too bad," he said. "Anyway, without a live audience, it's not the same. But Ewan still lets me carriage house my horse here." He angled his head toward a tall white horse in its stall.

"Is that why you stopped by?" Charlene asked.

"That, and Ewan called me about Prince's lost shoe."

"Prince?" I asked.

"Curly's horse."

"When did you last shoe Prince?" I asked.

"About a month back," he said.

"So, it's unusual that the shoe would come loose?" I asked.

His face pinked. "I care about horses, and I'm careful with my work. I don't know what happened."

"Was there anything weird about it?" I asked.

"Weird?" He goggled at us. "What do you mean by *weird*?"

"She means, was it tampered with?" Charlene said.

"Tampered with?" He rubbed his chin. "Who would want to do that?"

"Let's worry about the *who* later," Charlene said. "Could the shoe have been messed with?"

"I checked the hoof," he said, "and I didn't see any signs of tampering."

"What would the signs of tampering be?" I asked.

A fluff of hay drifted down from the loft, and he gazed at the wood-beamed ceiling. "Since I've never seen any, I couldn't tell you. Look, a horse can be injured when it throws a shoe. It could damage the hoof wall."

I nodded thoughtfully, as if I understood what he meant.

"No one who loves horses would intentionally loosen a shoe or do anything else that might hurt the animal," he said.

"If you carriage house your horse here, you must stop by often," I said. "Were you here the day of the murder?"

"No."

"I heard you and Devon had words last week," I said.

"You think *I* killed him?" he yelped.

"Well, did you?" Charlene asked.

He rubbed his balding dome. "That bartender was under-pouring."

"What's that?" I asked.

"It's when the bartender pours the customers less alcohol than he's supposed to," Charlene said. "Then he sells the excess alcohol and pockets the money."

A piebald horse snorted.

Charlene shrugged. "I worked as a bartender once. Not that I ever underpoured. But a bartender can siphon off a lot of money that way."

"I suspect he was embezzling in other ways too," Larry said darkly. "I told Ewan, but I don't know if he did anything about it."

Ewan hadn't mentioned embezzlement or underpouring. Why? Had the suspicions been unfounded? Or was something else going on?

"That old VW parked down by the saloon," Larry said. "Does that belong to either of you?"

Charlene rolled her eyes. "Do you think I'd be caught dead driving that beater?"

"It's mine." I frowned at her.

He reached into his suit pocket and handed me a card. "If you ever want to trade it in, I can set you up with a great deal."

"Thanks." But I planned to drive that Bug until it couldn't drive anymore. It was one of the few relics of my pre-San Nicholas life. I had fond memories of that VW.

We said our good-byes, and Larry strode from the rear carriage house doors.

"So, that's the mysterious Larry," Charlene said.

"If he'd been at the ranch on the day of the murder," I said, "he would have made a nice suspect. Assuming he had a motive."

"It's down to Moe or Curly. Unless we've got the time of death wrong. Then maybe Marla did do it. She killed the bartender, and then somehow set up a later shot to give herself an alibi."

We strolled out the doors Larry had exited through and watched him walk inside the distant corral.

"We should get back to Pie Town." I pointed left, toward the ghost town, with my thumb.

But Charlene turned right, toward the winding road leading up to Ewan's yellow Victorian.

"Wait. Charlene?" I hurried after her. Where was she going?

"If Marla's the killer," she said. "I'm not leaving Ewan alone with that woman."

I trotted after my piecrust maker. "If the timing was messed with, that puts Ewan in the frame too."

"Ewan couldn't have done it."

"Why not? And why didn't he mention anything about Devon underpouring?"

"Maybe Larry was wrong. Ewan's good people. He's not a suspect."

And sometimes good people got pushed too far and did not-so-good things. "Does Marla know anything about guns?"

"She's probably a member of some elite gun club," Charlene said, morose. "I took a class once. My husband insisted when I got my peashooter."

"You have a peashooter?"

"And since *I* took a class at the local range, she probably hired a military sniper to give her lessons. Did I tell you about the time my husband and I bought our little boat?"

"I think you did mention a boat." We huffed to the top of the rise. A breeze ruffled the tall, dried grasses beside the dirt track. The corral spread below us.

Larry paced inside the corral, his head lowered. He squatted and picked something up, pocketed it.

"Marla sailed into the harbor two months later," Charlene said, "on a yacht, courtesy of husband number three. Nearly swamped us."

"Marla's not going to solve this case."

Charlene stared at her wrinkled hands. "She's beaten me at everything else."

"We can't watch her constantly."

Her eyes narrowed. "That's what you think."

Chapter Seven

I hunkered down on Charlene's floral-print couch. A glass of Charlene's signature drink, root beer and Kahlua, chilled my fingers. *Stargate* credits rolled down the flickering TV screen, which provided the room's only illumination. I'd managed to talk my crusty piecrust maker out of a showdown with Marla at the house. Now, I wondered if I'd made a mistake.

During *Stargate*, she hadn't cracked lewd jokes about sexy aliens. She hadn't made *zzzt zzzt* noises when a weapon was fired. She hadn't thrown popcorn at the buzzkill bureaucrats who plotted to shut down Earth's only defense against invasion. And she hadn't made more suggestions about risqué lingerie. Instead, Charlene had sat slumped on the couch, her expression glazed, her chin sunk to her chest.

"So, what's next?" I asked, full of false cheer. If the sci-fi show hadn't lifted her spirits, maybe detecting work would.

"Episode thirteen."

"No, I meant for our case."

"Oh. That. I suppose we sit back and let Marla figure it out. She's like *Stargate's* Captain Carter to our Rodney

McKay. He thinks he's a genius, but he's nothing compared to the captain."

It was mildly depressing that I understood the McKay/Carter reference. "So far, Marla hasn't done any outstanding detective work."

"That you know of."

"And you're no Rodney McKay."

"I am. And that would make you his loser sidekick, Dr. Zelenka."

"I am so not the sidekick."

"Whatever."

I sat forward and set the root beer cocktail on the coffee table. "I don't understand you. There's no way Marla can jump in and solve this case. Why are you worried about her?"

"She's got business cards."

"We can get business cards." I rose and flipped on the lights, turned off Charlene's TV.

"That would make us copycats."

"Charlene . . ."

She sighed. "You don't understand. You've never had a rival that beats you at everything."

"Aren't you the best piecrust maker in northern California?"

"Only because Marla's too high and mighty to get flour on her diamonds."

"You're worth ten of Marla."

"Not in financial terms."

My smile wavered. "Why don't we look at that résumé Ewan gave you?"

Charlene wandered off to another room and returned with a manila folder. "There's nothing in it. Devon's last job was in Truckee. If there's any dirt on him from his prior gig, I don't see how it can affect what happened here."

I scanned the résumé. Devon had bartended all over the

country. Six months seemed to be his max in any one place. He'd quit his last job three months ago, after his usual six-month stint. If he had been ripping off the bars he worked at, was that why he never stayed in any one place too long? Was he leaving before he could get caught? And what would Ewan have done if he'd caught Devon stealing?

"There's nothing there," Charlene said. "And why bother looking? Marla will probably use one of her high-flying contacts and get all his travel records."

"I can't believe you're rolling over for her. Did I give up when Heidi moved in next door with her SUGAR KILLS sign? Did I give up when someone dropped dead in Pie Town, and all of San Nicholas thought it was food poisoning? Did I give up when I had to tell everyone my wedding was off? Do you have any idea how humiliating that was?"

"Getting dumped at the altar must have smarted."

"It was mutual! And the reason I didn't give up, was because you and I were a team. You didn't let me quit."

"Maybe I should have."

I heaved myself off the couch. "Fine. I'm solving this case with or without you. And if it's without you, then that makes *you* the sidekick. Have a nice night, Zelenka."

She sank deeper into the sofa cushions.

I hesitated, my hand on the front door. Shaking my head, I walked outside and down the steps to my VW, parked on the dark street.

Mist sheened its windows. I flicked on the wipers and pulled away from the curb. The dash clock read eleven o'clock, and, automatically, I yawned. Bakers need their beauty sleep.

I turned left onto Main Street. With the exception of Heidi's gym, all the windows along the road were black. For once, I was glad to have the gym next to Pie Town, even if it was owned by someone who despised me. People worked out there at all hours, making burglarizing my pie shop less attractive. Not that I worried about that sort of thing in San Nicholas.

My hands twisted on the wheel. There had to be more to this rivalry with Marla than Charlene was letting on.

A sedan slid into place behind me, its headlights blinding.

Adjusting my rearview mirror, I made a left past the fire station. Before me, the low, rolling hills were dark masses in the mist and moonlight.

The car behind me turned and followed.

I shifted in my seat, my palms growing damp on the wheel.

A white rabbit hopped across my path, and I braked, watching it disappear into the tall grasses along the roadside.

Driving more slowly, I continued on, winding up the one-lane road. The car behind me flicked its high beams, no doubt annoyed by my slow pace. But there was nowhere for me to pull over so the car could pass. Finally, I reached a driveway and pulled aside to let him go by.

The car behind me drifted to a halt.

I rolled down the window and motioned for him to drive on.

The car didn't move.

Hair prickled on my scalp. I was being followed.

My heart pounded, erratic. I scrabbled in my bag for my phone. No sooner was it in my sweaty hands when it rang. Gordon!

"Gordon. I'm driving home, and someone's following me."

"Yeah. I am."

"Oh." My shoulders slumped with relief. "Why?"

"Sorry. I didn't mean to scare you."

"You didn't." I cringed. How obvious was that lie?

"I'm going to get out of my car now."

Anxious, I watched the mirror.

He exited his car and strode to my open window.

I craned my neck out. "What are you doing out here?"

"I saw you driving through town. It was late, and with everything that's been going on, I thought I'd see you home. I know you don't have an earpiece, so I didn't want to call while you were driving and distract you. I flipped my high beams at you a few times, but I guess you didn't notice it was my car."

"Um. No." At night, one set of headlights looks pretty much like another. I blew out my breath, unsure if I should be annoyed or pleased that he cared. "Well, thanks. I'm almost home now."

"Mind if I follow you the rest of the way?"

"Sure. I mean, no, I don't mind." My jaw clenched. I was acting as nervous as a girl on a first date.

I waited while he returned to his car, then I drove on, making a right at a narrow track compressed by tall eucalyptus trees. The VW bumped and wound up the dirt road. A sagebrush scraped the car's side, and I winced.

The road dead-ended at a clearing and the rectangular silhouette that was my rental. I pulled up beside the picnic table, and the automatic light came on by my front door, reflecting off the wide windows facing the ocean. Thin lines of foam, mercury in the moonlight, chugged toward the invisible shore.

Gordon parked and unfolded himself from the sedan. He squinted at the converted shipping container. "How do you live in that tiny thing?"

"It's bigger than it looks. Want to come in for a cup of coffee?" I bit my cheek, unsure where I expected this to lead.

"I'm not sure I'd fit." But he followed me inside.

I flipped on the light, illuminating the polished wood floor, the soft white walls, and the kitchenette anchoring the center of the tiny house. At the other end of the container, a wooden bookshelf shielded a sleeping area.

He pulled out a chair in the dining nook beside the kitchen, and sat, hunching his back and shoulders.

"It's not that small." I laughed.

"It feels small."

"It's better during the day, when you can see out the windows."

"Yeah," he said, wistful, "you must have a helluva view."

I brewed coffee in my French press and set two mugs on the small, square table. There was no reason to feel nervous. He was only here for coffee. This was definitely not a date, but my stomach butterflied.

"Thanks," he said.

"You're welcome." I took the chair across from him. "How's the investigation going?"

He barked a laugh. "Right to the point."

My face heated. "It's been on my mind."

"Mine too."

"A better question would have been how are you doing?"

"This is Shaw's first big case as chief. He's very . . ."

"Involved?" I turned the warm mug in my hands.

"Interested."

"And it's your first big case as a detective in San Nicholas."

"It shouldn't matter—I was a detective before, in San Francisco. And I dealt with homicides there more than I wanted to. Coming home, it's a different kind of pressure."

"Because your parents are watching?" Gordon's parents were aging poorly, and when he'd returned here, he'd initially accepted a lower rank to be closer to them.

"The whole town's watching. There's no anonymity here." He sipped his coffee. "Is Charlene okay? She seemed tense."

And that was another reason I liked Gordon. He paid attention to the details. "I'm not sure," I said. It wasn't my place to tell him about the Charlene-Marla rivalry. "We've got a theory that Devon wasn't killed when we think he was killed. Maybe someone shot him earlier, and then rigged a gun to go off later to give the killer an alibi. And my pie got in the way."

Over his mug, Gordon's gaze bored into me. "You and Charlene have a theory?"

"I sort of have a theory. More of a hypothesis. Kind of an idea we've been spitballing."

He set down his coffee. "Can I be straight with you?" His tone was coolly disapproving.

"Of course."

"Earlier this year, when you and Charlene helped solve those murders . . ."

"Yes?"

"You do know the only reason you solved it was because you irritated the murderer into trying to kill you."

"That's not . . ." Was that how we'd done it? But we'd figured out the motive and the lead suspect and everything.

"And these other so-called cases of yours are a far cry from a murder investigation. If you want to chase lost cats, that's one thing—"

"It might not have been the kind of cat burglar the police are interested in, but someone stole a prize-winning cat. You have no idea how banana-pants crazy people can get at cat shows. We diffused an ugly hostage situation."

"I read the report. I'm sure Mr. Sprinkles was grateful."

Frederick hadn't been. Charlene's cat and Mr. Sprinkles had not hit it off. The fight was the most active I'd seen Frederick since . . . ever.

"If I find out you two are investigating this murder," he said, "I will arrest you for interfering in an investigation."

I banged down my mug. A few drops of coffee splashed the slick tabletop. "I can tell you're serious by the lack of contractions in that sentence." Who said English majors couldn't make good detectives?

"I am serious."

Okay, I'd actually researched interfering with an investigation for just this reason. The police couldn't arrest us for asking questions—only for doing stuff like withholding evidence or messing with crime scenes. I was pretty sure. Mostly.

"Who says we're investigating?" I sputtered. "We were delivering pies to the Bar X, and someone nearly killed me. Of course, everyone is talking about the murder. And in the interests of not withholding evidence, we . . . I, was chatting with Larry the farrier today. He couldn't figure out why Curly's horse mysteriously threw a shoe right around the time of the murder."

"I've also spoken with Larry the farrier."

"You have?"

"Of course, I have. I spoke with everyone at the Bar X on the day of the murder."

"What?" Larry had told me he hadn't been there. Why had he lied? "You mean he was at the Bar X when I was shot at?"

A look of annoyance crossed his chiseled face. "I thought you'd spotted him that day."

"No. I was too preoccupied with the exploding pie."

"I shouldn't have said anything." He rose, his movements jerky. "Look, I like you. I think you're a good person, and you look great in crinolines. But stay out of this case. I mean it, Val."

"Mm."

He rested his hand on the doorknob. "Val?"

"What?"

"I'm not hearing you promise to stay out of the case."

"How can I? The rules are so vague. What if I happen to talk to one of the suspects in the course of doing business? And what if he or she happens to let drop some interesting information? Am I interfering? Because I'll tell you if I hear anything interesting."

He growled. "Val."

"I promise not to interfere." And my fingers weren't even crossed, because asking questions wasn't interfering.

Gordon released his breath. "Thanks. And thanks for the coffee. I'll see you around." He strode out the door.

Dissatisfied, I watched the taillights of his sedan vanish behind the tree line. Larry had been near the crime scene, and he was an ex-trick shooter. The field of suspects had just expanded.

Chapter Eight

I tried to relax into the Zen of pie making. The morning sunlight streamed through the skylight. It glinted off the industrial ovens and metal countertops and sinks. My blue antique pie safe sat opposite the door to the flour-work room. A thick, three-ring binder filled with our recipes lay atop it. Standing at the butcher-block work island, I crimped crusts and passed pie tins to our new assistant pie maker and wannabe poet, Abril.

Her long, black hair neat beneath her paper hat, Abril filled the crusts with sweet and savory mixtures. Her sensible white shoes squeaked on the rubber floor mat. The scent of baking pies filled the industrial kitchen.

But today, the work rhythm failed to calm me. The glory of pie couldn't make me forget the sight of Devon's lifeless body.

I'd called the financial planning company in San Francisco and asked about the fight in the Bar X saloon. The three financial advisors who'd been involved were currently on a company trip to Mykonos and had been gone for the past five days. At least I could cross vengeful financial advisors off the suspect list.

Other questions gnawed in my gut. If not one of the

advisors, then who had killed Devon? Who was trying to kill me? And would Gordon and I ever go on our first date?

Charlene poked her head out of the piecrust room. "What about a corset?"

I crushed a ball of pie dough. "No."

Abril looked a question at me, and I shook my head, embarrassed. At least Charlene was getting some of her mojo back.

"Retro is in," Charlene said.

"No, Charlene."

My assistant manager, Petronella, banged through the swinging kitchen doors. "Val. Someone's here to see you." She ran one finger beneath the delicate net imprisoning her spiky black hair.

I checked my watch. It was only eleven—too early for my lunch/interrogation with Moe. I washed my hands in the sink and dried them on my Pie Town apron. "Thanks. I'll be right—"

"It's Heidi from next door."

My stomach plummeted. What next? *Another* lecture on the perils of sugar? I stretched my mouth into a smile. "I'll be right out." Double checking my own hair net, I followed Petronella through the swinging doors and behind the counter.

Pie Town was surprisingly busy for a Friday morning. Cheerful voices and the clank of forks echoed off the black-and-white tile floor. A handful of shaggy-haired gamers sat in their corner booth, dice rattling across the Formica table. Graham and Tally Wally sat on pink barstools, their elbows on the counter, sipping coffee and arguing politics. They were surprisingly loud considering they both agreed with each other.

Heidi, in her green HEIDI'S HEALTH hoodie and yoga pants, loomed in front of the register. Her fingers tap-tapped the linoleum counter. Catching sight of me, she leaned over the counter. "Unbelievable," she hissed, her blond ponytail twitching. "How selfish can you be?"

A group of retirees scraped their chairs away from the two tables they'd put together. They gathered their books and purses, readying to go.

I slowed to a halt behind the register. "What?"

"A policeman showed up at Mark's doorstep this morning, asking about you."

The retirees stopped moving toward the door. Purses clutched to their chests, they cocked their heads.

I blinked. "About me?"

"The cop practically accused him of trying to kill you. I don't know what you're into, but you know perfectly well Mark had nothing to do with it. Just because he dumped you—"

"It was mutual!"

"—at the altar—"

"We were not at the altar." My hands bunched in my apron. The breakup had gone down a couple of months before the wedding.

"—does not mean he wants to kill you. I'm sure there are plenty of other candidates for that job."

Such as Heidi? I shook my head. "No one's trying to kill me. It's all a mistake. I'll call Mark and—"

"Don't you dare call him. You've done enough to that man. Leave Mark Jeffreys alone." Spinning on her workout shoes, she stormed from the shop. The bell over the door tinkled merrily at her departure.

I turned to escape.

Grinning, Charlene leaned through the open window between the kitchen and the restaurant. "Yep. She wants you dead."

"You don't need to look so happy about it," I said. "And she does not."

"Don't listen to her," Graham said. He slurped his

coffee. "No one here wants to kill you. And I'll take Pie Town over that gym any day."

"Thanks." I would have offered to top off his mug, but we were self-serve, and the coffee urn was within his reach. I nudged the tray of hand pies closer. "Another?"

He patted his bulging stomach. "I'm on a diet. Cutting back. Lost five pounds already."

"Congratulations!" My mouth quirked. I'd heard that before. "Good for you."

The bell over the door tinkled, and an elderly woman wearing a flowered hat and sagging hosiery tottered in. I slid a boxed strawberry-rhubarb pie from beneath the counter and waved. "Good morning, Mrs. Banks."

"Those damned grocery thieves are at it again," she said. "Stole a dozen eggs and a half gallon of almond milk right out of my car. I need the Baker Street Bakers."

Graham shook his head. "San Nicholas isn't what it used to be. I remember when you could leave your doors unlocked."

Mrs. Banks counted out exact change. "Someone's got to do something about these supernatural thieves. I've been turning my pockets inside out, Val, but it doesn't help at all."

I rang her up and slid the boxed pie across the counter. "Pockets?" Baffled, I scrubbed my hands in my apron.

"Char thought it would keep the fairies away, but it's not. I guess that means the disappearances might be ectoplasmic after all."

"Hm." I glanced over my shoulder at the kitchen window, but my piecrust maker had vanished. "We'll stop by soon," I promised. A spectral investigation would make a good excuse to make sure everything was okay at her home. I hoped her absentmindedness was a normal consequence of aging and not something more serious.

"That would be a relief." She turned to go.

"Mrs. Banks?" I pushed the pink and white box toward her. "Your pie."

"Oh!" Coloring, she took the box.

Graham rose from his stool. "Let me walk out with you."

Together, they moseyed from the shop, and I smiled. Graham would make sure both Mrs. Banks and the strawberry-rhubarb got into her car.

Returning to the kitchen, I removed a batch of mini pulled-pork pies from the oven. The slowly rotating racks, designed to give the pies an even bake, were mesmerizing. There was a cadence to sliding the pies from the oven on the long-handled paddles. I set the pies on metal racks to cool.

Charlene banged a stool beside the butcher-block table and sat, stretching her legs. "Nothing like putting in a full day's work to make you feel useful."

I gave her a look. Charlene only worked half-time, and her day usually ended before noon. "You should have been finished an hour ago. What were you doing in the flour-work room?" Ha! Last night's pep talk had worked. Charlene was waiting to interview Moe. She just didn't want to admit it.

Charlene straightened. "Just what are you accusing me of?"

"Nothing," I said innocently. "I'm only curious."

She yawned. "Thought I'd try a new piecrust recipe."

I froze, my heart thudding. "What?" Her piecrusts were the best in Northern California. You don't fiddle with perfection!

"What you said last night about Marla and the piecrusts got me to thinking," she said. "I've been resting on my laurels. I could do better."

"No," I said. "No, you can't. The customers love your crusts!"

"Sure, they do now, but Marla—"

"Marla, Marla, Marla! Enough is enough. Listen to yourself. She's playing you like a conga drum. You've let her get under your skin, and now you're second-guessing yourself. Change your piecrust recipe? Are you nuts?"

Wooden paddle in hand, Abril reared away from the big oven. "A new piecrust? You can't! These are pie perfection, perfect rippling spheres of crust that melt on the tongue."

Charlene's white brows rose.

"See?" I said. "Abril agrees."

Petronella wandered into the kitchen. "Agrees about what?"

"Charlene wants to change her piecrust recipe," Abril said. "But the pies won't be the same without them. Those succulent globes of tart cherries, bursting with flavor against the buttery, decadent crusts . . ."

We stared.

"This is a joke, right?" Petronella asked.

"No joke," Charlene said, eyeing Abril. "I'm changing it up."

A series of expressions—shock, annoyance, anxiety—flashed across Petronella's face. "And put Pie Town out of business? Thanks a lot. I just made assistant manager."

"You should never get complacent," Charlene said.

"But you can't just . . . change things!" Petronella said.

"Do you think Steve Jobs, after creating his whiz-bang phone, said, 'good enough?'" Charlene asked.

"You can't eat a phone," I said.

Charlene crossed her arms, her jaw thrusting forward mulishly. "You don't understand."

"I understand perfectly." She'd lost her confidence. I'd been there, done that. "The piecrust recipe stays." Abruptly, I remembered I hadn't had the chat with Petronella that she'd asked for. "Hey, Petronella, if you want to . . ." I glanced out the kitchen window. Looking lost, Moe stood in the center of Pie Town's checkerboard floor.

"What?" my assistant manager asked.

"Sorry." I shook my head. Petronella would have to wait. "Charlene, Moe's here."

"Moe?" Charlene stared, expression blank.

"Moe," I said. "You arranged for him to come here for lunch so we could talk about the Bar X?"

She sniffed. "You don't need me for the interview. What do I have to contribute? I'm old and useless. I can't do anything *new*."

"I'm not doing this alone," I said.

"Why don't you call Marla? I'm sure she could provide some insight."

"I'm not calling . . ." I exhaled heavily, exasperated. Just because I didn't want to change the piecrust recipe. "This interview needs someone with experience."

"What do I know? I'm just playing at detective. Marla's right. Meeting clients in a pie shop is unprofessional. And we don't even have business cards."

"I will order business cards tonight," I ground out.

"They won't be as good as Marla's."

"Charlene, I need you out there. I can't do this by myself."

She sighed theatrically. "Fine. If you really think you *need* me." She rose and slouched into the dining area.

Grabbing a menu, I followed.

Moe turned his cowboy hat in his hand. A line imprinted his straight, dark hair where the hat had rested. His neatly pressed white shirt was tucked into his jeans. He nodded when he saw us. "So," he said. "I'm here."

I motioned toward an empty corner booth, and we sat.

"You said something about lunch," he said.

I handed him the menu. "Take your time."

"I will." He smacked his lips. "It's been ages since I've had a decent potpie."

"Today we've got chicken curry, turkey, and beef.

There's also a mini pulled-pork pie." We'd done it as a Fourth of July experiment and gotten more interest than I'd expected.

"I'll take a mini turkey and a pulled pork."

Two five-inch deep-dish pies seemed like a lot for one person, but I didn't comment. "Anything to drink?"

"Diet cola."

"Sure thing." I went to the kitchen and plated the pies, adding a heaping spoonful of mixed salad. When I returned with the food and drink, Charlene and Moe appeared to be locked in a staring contest across the Formica table. "Here you go," I said. "Careful, they're hot." I slid the plates in front of him and set him up with silverware and a napkin.

He grunted, breaking eye contact with my partner in crime solving. "Thanks." He pierced the crust of the turkey pie with his fork. Steam spiraled into the air. Moe leaned closer, sniffing. "Smells real."

"Of course, it's real," Charlene said. "You think we serve fake pies?"

He took a bite and sighed. "It *is* real. I haven't had a pie like this since my mother died. So, what do you want to know?"

"Can you walk us through the morning Devon was killed?" I asked. "What you did, who you saw, that sort of thing?"

"I got to the Bar X around nine and checked on my horse. Curly was in the carriage house doing the same. We went to the corral and did some standing target practice—"

"Standing?" I asked.

"Without the horses," he said between bites of pie. "Around ten we brought the horses in, warmed them up in the corral, and began practicing our trick shooting on horseback." He pressed his broad finger into the tabletop.

"And let me tell you, there's no way one of our bullets could have hit anyone standing outside the saloon. Not from the corral. Not even if we were trying. There are at least three buildings in the way."

"See anyone else?" I asked.

"Bridget came by to watch for a bit."

"What time was that?"

"Around ten, I think. Oh, and Larry was hanging around. I saw him leaving the carriage house just as I walked in."

"Why did you three break up your partnership?" I asked.

"What's that got to do with anything?"

I shrugged. "Probably nothing. I'm just trying to figure out the players and their histories."

"Larry got greedy with the takings," he said.

Charlene's brow rose. "Greedy? Are you talking about embezzlement?"

He snorted. "That's too fancy a word for it. We don't make enough to steal. Gunslinging is a hobby that pays for itself. Larry figured he had bigger expenses than we did, and he wanted a bigger share for his work shoeing our horses. Words were said."

"Did Devon know anyone at the Bar X before he started working there?" I tightened the apron strings at the front of my waist.

"That's a funny question. I don't know. Maybe. He and Bridget seemed to have some weird connection."

"Weird how?" I asked.

"Not romantic, I think, but they were familiar. They acted like they'd known each other for a while, but they didn't *know* each other." He lifted his shoulders, dropped them. "Hard to explain."

"Did Devon have conflicts with anyone at the Bar X?"

He studied his coffee.

"There is someone, isn't there?" I asked.

He scowled. "Curly'd been acting closemouthed and antsy, especially around that bartender. It made me wonder if Devon had something on him."

"Had something?" I asked. "Like what?"

"Nothing I know about. I don't pry into a man's past."

"What about someone outside the Bar X?" I asked.

"How should I know?" He folded his arms over his broad chest.

I glanced at Charlene; her arms were crossed and her face shuttered. "Okay," I said, getting no help from that quarter. "You and Curly were shooting, and then his horse lost a shoe. What happened next?"

"He took his horse back to the carriage house. I kept practicing."

"Got it," I said. "Do you remember hearing any shots after Curly left that weren't your own?"

"Nah. When I'm practicing, that's all I'm paying attention to—my horse and my target. That's enough. Then I heard a woman screaming—you, I guess."

"That was Bridget."

"Then you know what happened next."

"So, you were at the corral the whole time, between nine and a quarter after eleven," I said.

"Yup."

This was going nowhere. "What did you think of Devon?"

His face darkened. "He was a smart-ass." He pointed at the remaining pulled-pork pie. "Can I get that to go?"

"Sure," I said. "Why'd you think he was a smart-ass?"

"Because that's how he acted. I'm not surprised someone offed the smug bastard."

I sat, waiting for more. When he didn't speak, I rose. "I'll get a box."

Thinking hard, I walked behind the glass counter and

pulled out a flattened pink and white box. If I were a real detective, I could drag Moe into the police station and ask the same question over and over until he cracked like an egg.

I popped the box into form and returned to the silent table. "Is there anything else you think I should know about that day that might explain what happened to Devon?"

Moe boxed his pie. "Sorry. It's a mystery."

Thank you, Captain Obvious.

Charlene and I watched him leave.

"Well?" I asked. "What did you think?"

She shrugged. "How should I know? I'm just an old woman, in over her head, alone and confused."

"Charlene, you're not alone, and—"

She raised her hand. "No, don't say it. I don't need your pity." Shoulders slumped, she walked out the door.

A sharp ache rocketed from my left eyeball to the back of my skull. Grimacing, I returned to the kitchen.

Tourists surged in and out of Pie Town like the tide. As the afternoon progressed, the waves came in longer, slower intervals.

The baking wound down, and I spent more time behind the register, greeting customers and selling pies. Baking was still my favorite part of the business, but chatting with customers ran a close second. Everyone had a story. The harried mom whose son got his arm stuck in a fence and had to be removed by the fire department. The insurance agent buying a pie for tomorrow's office party. The husband bringing home a pie for an anniversary dinner. In spite of the horror at the Bar X, life went on. So would I.

The lighting dimmed. I turned the OPEN sign to CLOSED and glanced at the gamers.

"Mind if we stay a little longer?" Ray asked, his freckles darkening.

"As long as you don't let anyone else in." I had book-keeping to do, so I'd be working late in my office. Given the recent attacks, I didn't mind having the gamers in the next room.

So people wouldn't see the gamers and think we were still open, I dropped the blinds, then walked into my office. Arching my back, I unlaced my apron and hooked it on the edge of the metal bookcase.

My office was woefully Spartan. I'd picked up the cheapest furniture I could scavenge: a dented, metal desk; bookcases jammed with cleaning supplies; a three-year-old computer.

While the computer booted up, I whipped off my hair net and scrubbed my head. It would be so easy to put the bookkeeping off until tomorrow, but it was the end of the month. Our CPA got grumpy when the numbers came in late.

I worked until my eyes blurred. Finally, I slumped in my chair and pressed SEND, relieved to have the work off of my desk and onto the accountant's. I checked my watch and groaned. Ten o'clock. No wonder my eyes burned.

Exhausted, I shrugged into a lightweight safari jacket. Grabbing my purse off the bookcase, I strode into the dining area. In their pink booth, the gamers argued over whether a spell was legal.

"I'm headed home, everyone," I said.

Ray rumpled his red hair. "Okay. Time to wrap it up, guys."

They gathered up their books and papers and dice.

I held the door as they ambled onto the sidewalk, and then I locked it behind us.

Fog brushed the rooftops. On Main Street, the iron street lamps gleamed with moisture. The shops were dark, only light from the gym and a restaurant across the street making tentative inroads on the nighttime gloom. A woman walked her white poodle. The dog's nails clicked, a hollow sound on the sidewalk. The two vanished into the fog.

"Where are you parked?" Ray asked.

"Down the street," I said, gesturing.

"I'm that way too. I'll walk you."

"Thanks."

We strolled down Main Street, passing empty parking spots and a brick hotel with Spanish arches.

"That must have been some game," I said. "How long do they usually last?"

"Until they're done, and this dungeon hasn't been solved. You should try an RPG sometime."

"RPG?"

"Role playing game." He grinned. "I know, it sounds kinky, but it's not."

We reached the end of the block.

"I'm across the street." I pointed to my Bug.

He nodded at a Ford Escort. "This is mine, but I've come this far. I may as well walk you to your car."

We stepped into the road. Lights caught us, blinding.

Ray shouted. He grabbed my jacket and yanked me backwards, pulling himself forward at the same time.

I gasped, unable to react, and stumbled toward the curb.

The car swerved toward us, too close, and there was a sickening thump. Ray careened off the speeding car and slammed against me, knocking the air from my lungs. He groaned and dropped to the pavement.

The car, a Prius, sped off.

For a moment, I couldn't speak. Then I cursed and fell to my knees. "Ray? Ray!"

He groaned, his eyes rolling up in his head. "My leg. I think it's broken." Ray went limp, his chin falling to his broad chest.

"Oh, no." Hands trembling, I pulled my cell phone from my pocket and called nine-one-one. The phone rang once, twice.

Hurry, hurry, hurry.

"This is nine-one-one, what is your emergency?"

"I'm on the corner of Main Street and Primrose in San Nicholas." My voice shook. "I need an ambulance. My friend's just been hit by a car." I swayed. It seemed impossible. But there was Ray, on the damp pavement.

Ray's eyes opened. "Don't tell them," he croaked.

"What? Don't tell them what?" The cold from the street seeped through my jeans and into my knees.

"Don't tell them I was taken out by a hybrid."

I laughed, shaky. He was well enough to make jokes. I prayed that meant he'd be okay.

The dispatcher—bless her—stayed calmer than I did. After promising an ambulance was on its way, she walked me through checking out Ray's injuries.

Firemen and paramedics arrived first; the station was only seven blocks away. Blue and red emergency lights whirled, their beams distorted by the fog. The firemen pulled me away, taking charge.

I blinked back tears. "Is he going to be all right?"

"We'll need to take him to the hospital for X-rays," a paramedic said, "but he's conscious."

A uniformed cop strode to our group and pinioned me with a glance. "Val? What happened?"

I knew the man, a muscled African-American cop named Alan. He lunched in Pie Town fairly regularly, a big fan of the pulled-pork pies. "We were crossing the street," I said, "and he was hit by a Prius."

"Where's the driver?" Alan asked.

"I don't know. He drove off."

His expression hardened. "Did you get the plate?"

"No, I'm sorry. It happened so fast, and this fog . . ." I clenched my jaw. If I'd been paying more attention, if I hadn't panicked, gone blank . . . How could I have been so stupid?

"Anything else you can tell me about the car? The color?"

"Blue! It was blue." My neck muscles bunched. Blue like every second Prius in California. So much for my razor-sharp observation skills. Thanks to me, they'd never find the driver.

"All right," Alan said. "It's okay. If you think of anything else—broken headlights, any numbers on the plate—let me know. Uh, you were part of the Bar X mess, weren't you?"

"Yes," I said, confused.

"I'd better call GC."

"Gordon? Why?" My head swam, and I pressed my hand to the hood of Ray's white Escort. Because this wasn't a random hit-and-run. Someone was trying to kill me.

Chapter Nine

"Val!" Gordon strode through the swirling mist. Blue and red lights illuminated his craggy face, creased with concern. "What happened? Are you all right?" He wore jeans and a lightweight, navy V-neck sweater over a white tee. He'd been off duty.

I glanced at Ray, who was laying on a stretcher and being loaded into an ambulance. The gamer was sitting up. "I'm fine. Ray . . ." My throat tightened. "He was hit by a car."

Gordon drew me aside. "What happened? Take your time."

I drew a shuddering breath. "Ray was walking me to my car." I nodded to the sky-blue Bug, parked across the street.

"Ray?"

"He's a regular at Pie Town, one of the gamers."

Gordon nodded.

"The Prius seemed to come out of nowhere," I said, limbs trembling. "I didn't even see it. Ray pulled me back. I think pulling me backwards pushed him forward, into the path of the car. This is all my fault."

"It isn't. Those hybrids are quiet. They're easy to miss in the dark."

I shook my head. "It was more than that. There's not

much traffic at night on Main, but I did look before crossing. Its headlights switched on at the last minute, and he or she was driving too fast."

"You think it was intentional?"

"I'd swear the car accelerated," I said. My stomach grew heavy with doubt. Was I remembering something that hadn't happened, my mind filling in the blanks? Sickened, I rubbed my arms. "With everything that's been going on, yes, I do think it was intentional. Especially since the driver took off afterward."

The ambulance drove away, its blue lights flashing.

"You may be right," he said, "but let's not jump to conclusions."

I tensed. "I'm not jumping!"

Two cops glanced toward us, and I lowered my voice. "Sorry, but three near misses in as many days? I didn't want to believe it, but I think someone's trying to kill me." Even I could hear how paranoid I sounded. Why would someone want me dead? I didn't have money for anyone to inherit. Sure, Heidi didn't like me, but I had a hard time picturing her as a murderess. And if someone was trying to scare Charlene and I off investigating Devon's death, why was I the only one . . .

My heart seized. "Charlene." Oh, God. What if something had happened to her? I pulled my cell phone from the pocket of my safari jacket and dialed. Her *X-Files* ringtone played behind me, and I whirled.

Her face pale, Charlene dug through the pocket of her purple knit jacket. Frederick burrowed deeper into her thick collar and snuggled against her ear.

Shoulders slumping as if deboned, I disconnected. "Charlene, are you okay?"

"About time you phoned," she grumped. "I had to hear about the accident over the police . . ." She glanced at Gordon, and I knew what she'd meant to say: over her police scanner. Which she wasn't supposed to have. "Over the grapevine. Social media is remarkable. What happened?"

"A hit-and-run," I said. "Ray pulled me out of the way and . . ." I swallowed, getting teary again. He was going to be okay. He had to be. And he'd been conscious, so that was a good sign, right?

Her eyes widened, and I noticed the dark circles beneath them. "Ray? Gamer Ray? He's our best customer."

"I know," I wailed. "No one eats more cherry pie than Ray. Once he found a pit in his slice and didn't even get mad. He just kept rolling those twenty-sided dice."

A uniformed officer walked to Gordon and said something in a low voice.

Grimacing, Charlene patted my shoulder. "Now, now. Tell me what happened. I take it this wasn't an accident."

"No." Fear and anger scalded my insides. "And Ray got in the way. And then I thought someone didn't like that we were asking questions, and they'd come after you as well."

"Ray made a choice to save you." Her voice hardened. "It's not your fault. And I'm sure he'll be fine."

But it *was* my fault. Ray wouldn't have had to throw himself into the path of a rampaging hybrid if it hadn't been for me.

Gordon cleared his throat. "We found an abandoned Prius out by the Half House. Want to come and take a look, see if you can identify it?"

I doubted I could tell one blue Prius from another, but I nodded.

"We'll follow in my Jeep," Charlene said. "Val's too shaken to drive."

I guess I must have been shaken, possibly even stirred, because I got into Charlene's yellow Jeep without arguing.

"Did he say Prius?" Charlene asked.

"For some reason, Ray doesn't want anyone to know he was run down by a hybrid. So, keep it quiet."

Her mouth twisted. "I don't blame him."

Frederick's white tail twitched, coiling around Charlene's neck.

We followed Gordon down Main, taking a left at Ohlone Drive and winding through the night fog. The Half House stood near the base of the rolling hills, their swells blocking the stars. The building is a historical landmark that looks like a saltbox house that someone cut down the middle, so Half House is what the locals called it. Its lights were dark at this hour.

Gordon's sedan drifted to a halt beside a waiting police car, its headlights shining across a field of dried grasses. He stepped from his car.

Charlene killed the Jeep's ignition. A dog—or maybe it was a coyote—howled a lonely lament.

We tramped along the shoulder to join the cops. Tall grasses dampened our knees.

"Ms. Harris, Mrs. McCree," Gordon said, "this is Officer Burkett."

Hands gripping the collar of his bulletproof vest, the officer nodded. When I'd first seen a cop wearing a vest in San Nicholas, I'd thought it was an over-the-top precaution. The way local crime was trending, it now seemed sensible.

Burkett led us to the edge of a gully and pointed.

A blue Prius angled nose down into the ditch, as if the driver had tried to take a shortcut to the Half House driveway and failed.

Or had tried to hide the damage from hitting Ray.

I pointed. "That yellow sticker on the rear window. I remember that."

"Are you certain?" Gordon asked.

The fog parted, and a sliver of moonlight quartered the Half House.

"Yeah," I said. "I'd forgotten it, but now that I see it . . . It was there. That could be the car."

"Could be?"

I raised my hands, helpless. "It's a blue Prius with a yellow sticker on the rear window. I didn't notice much beyond that." Honestly, I was amazed I'd remembered the yellow sticker.

"That's good enough for me. I'll ask our forensic guys to take a look. Thanks, Val."

"I wish I'd seen whoever was driving." I jammed my fists into the pockets of my safari jacket.

"This is helpful," Gordon said. "Really." He saw us to Charlene's Jeep. "Whatever's going on, it's serious. And you need to let the police handle it."

"No," I said.

"What?"

"No." My pulse accelerated. "Someone's tried to kill me. Repeatedly. I won't interfere with your investigation, but I'm not sitting around and waiting for someone to figure out who wants me dead. Not after Ray got hurt."

He ran his hand along the top of his crewcut. "Val, did you ever think the reason someone's coming after you is because you've been sticking your nose into the Bar X murder?"

"Yes, I did consider it. But if that were true, someone would have threatened Charlene as well. And someone shot a pie out of my hand before I even found the body." I turned to her, pale in the faint strip of moonlight. "Has anything happened to you?"

"Um . . ?" She looked moonward. "No."

"Val—"

"This is who I am, Gordon." And if that meant we never

had our first date . . . The thought was spectacularly depressing, but I pushed it aside. An innocent bystander had been hurt because someone was gunning for me. I wasn't backing down. "If you need to arrest me, I understand and will respect your decision. I'll probably be safer in jail anyway." I got into the passenger side of the Jeep.

"Val," he said. "I get that you're upset. Anyone would be. But you need to think this through."

Charlene started the Jeep.

I didn't want to think anymore. I was too angry. "You're probably right," I said, "but I don't think I'll change my mind. Thanks, Gordon. I hope you find something in the car."

Charlene was silent on the drive into town. She dropped me at my VW. "I'll follow you home," she said. "Just to make sure no one is following you."

Grim, I nodded. Cancel that. I wasn't grim, I was stinking mad. My knuckles were white on the steering wheel as I drove the winding road, Charlene's headlights flashing in my rearview mirror. I pulled up beside my tiny home sweet shipping container.

The automatic light by my front door flashed on. My gaze swept the lot.

My anger at the hit-and-run was swamped by a wave of apprehension. The picnic table cast long shadows, reaching for the looming rectangle that was my house. Behind it, eucalyptus trees rustled. I'd never felt creeped out by my own home before, but tonight I was glad Charlene had returned with me.

At the front door, I fiddled with the lock.

Charlene came to stand beside me. "I need a drink," she said.

I shoved open the door. "Root beer and Kahlua it is."

"Something with more heat, I think."

"Hot chocolate and that cinnamon whiskey?"

"That's the ticket." She followed me inside. "Gordon will come around," she said, making herself comfortable in the dining nook while I microwaved the milk.

"I'd like to believe that," I said. I'd meant what I'd said about continuing to ask questions. But I could see his point of view. I only hoped he could see mine.

"He can't expect you to sit on your hands while someone's trying to kill you. Not unless he's offering police protection. We both know San Nicholas can't afford that."

Rumors were swirling that the small town was on the verge of bankruptcy. With finances so tight, I was amazed Gordon had gotten his promotion to detective—a testament to the fact he really was that good. The thought depressed me even more.

Mixing the drinks, I squirted whipped cream on top, adding a sprinkling of cinnamon and cayenne pepper. I set the mugs on the square table and sat.

She frowned. "No cinnamon stick?"

I heaved myself from the chair and clumped to my kitchen, dug a cinnamon stick from a plastic container in the cupboard, and handed it to her.

She swirled it in the whipped cream and sucked on the end.

I sat across from her and sipped my own drink, getting a nose full of whipped cream. The warmth of hot chocolate and alcohol cascaded through my veins. I stretched out my legs.

Charlene stirred her drink with the cinnamon stick. "That detective of yours is right. We shouldn't *play* at investigating."

My heart crashed to earth. I'd managed to forget Charlene's loss of confidence. Her issues hadn't gone away, but after what had happened to Ray, I had to go on with or without her. And if I plowed on without her, would I make my best friend feel worse? "He's not my detective."

"You're too young to die," Charlene said, ignoring me. "And I'm too old to pretend."

"Charlene, if you don't want—"

"So, the gloves are coming off." She stabbed a crooked finger in my direction. "And Marla can suck eggs. She's always had a knack for getting under my skin. We're going to find whoever did this or die trying."

I gaped. "Well, I'd rather not die trying—"

"That yellow sticker on the Prius, did you see what was written on it?"

Tentative, I took another sip of the cocoa concoction. "Larry Pelt's Pre-Owned Cars."

"People don't drive around with a used car sticker in their window. That was fresh off the lot."

Huzzah! Charlene was back! I nodded, relieved. "You think Larry was driving? Using and abandoning his own car seems a little obvious."

"Obvious or not, tomorrow we're going to see what he has to say."

Tomorrow? Crikey. Charlene was back. "Tomorrow's Friday. It's a big day for pie sales. I can't—"

"You've got an assistant manager, don't you?"

"Well, yes, but—"

"That's why you hired all that new staff, wasn't it? So you could have more free time?"

"Yes, but it's still my business. I've got responsibilities." I *had* wanted Charlene to return to normal. But on one of my biggest sales days?

"You've got two choices. Work yourself to death at Pie Town, or get killed by a lunatic with an obsession for flattening you."

I shifted in my chair. "I'm fairly certain there's at least one other choice."

"Sure. You can step away from the oven and help me figure out who's behind this."

"Help *you* figure it out?"

"Fasten your seat belts," she said in a poor imitation of Bette Davis. "It's going to be a bumpy ride."

Chapter Ten

Charlene banged on Pie Town's front window.

A gamer at the corner booth twitched. His dice rolled off the table and scattered across the linoleum floor.

The game had gone on. Ray was in the hospital, but he'd recover, and Charlene and I would visit him this afternoon.

She pointed at Frederick, draped over the shoulder of her green, knit tunic. Raising her eyebrows, she mouthed: "Get out here."

I grabbed my purse from beneath the counter and hurried outside, glancing over my shoulder. We were in our usual postlunch slump, and Petronella had a handle on everything, even if she was looking exceptionally dark and stormy today. We still hadn't had that talk, but she hadn't pushed, and the murder had taken precedence. I'd talk to her this afternoon. Definitely.

"You shouldn't make an old person wait." Charlene's white hair tossed in the breeze. "Especially not on a hot sidewalk."

"I thought you were only forty-two," I said. And it wasn't that hot. The day was cloudless, but experience told me the breeze would bring fog tonight. "Besides, you could have come inside."

Her eyes widened. "With Frederick? And break the rules?"

I compressed my lips. She'd ignored my requests to keep Frederick out of Pie Town so often, I'd sort of forgotten. "You're right," I said. "Not everyone loves animals."

She sniffed. "They ought to. My Jeep's around the corner."

"So's my VW."

She turned and stared.

I stared back.

"Fine," she said. "Since someone tried to kill you last night, you can drive."

"Thanks!"

Charlene and I strolled into a residential section of Victorians and saltbox-style homes. I inhaled deeply, smelling salt air and the roses trailing over a nearby picket fence. You didn't get this kind of fresh air in the big city.

We got into my sky-blue VW and puttered west, turning north on Highway One.

Three miles later, I pulled into a used-car lot. A dancing balloon man flapped by the entrance, streamers of its yellow plastic hair billowing in the breeze. A giant sign rotated overhead: PELT'S PRE-OWNED VEHICLES.

Charlene snorted. "Like we don't know 'pre-owned' means 'used.'"

"It does sound nicer."

"It's deceptive advertising."

"It's not really deceptive. More manipulative."

"Why are you arguing about it?"

I sighed. "I don't know." Since I'd joined the business-owning class, I'd become more sympathetic to marketing tricks. I was even thinking of having an app made for Pie Town.

I parked beside a gleaming, flat-roofed building of glass and metal. "What if Larry isn't here?" I asked.

"Then we interrogate his staff. I'll bet they'll spill all sorts of dirt. Who wouldn't want a chance to rat out the boss?"

Uncomfortable, I shifted in my seat. *I* was a boss. And despite my running battles to keep Frederick off the premises, I thought I was a reasonable manager, and the staff liked me. But every manager probably believed that.

Charlene clambered out of the VW and arched, pressing her fists into her lower back.

Frederick woke up enough to stretch as well, his claws extending. Then the white cat returned to his favorite pose—limp around Charlene's neck.

We strolled toward the glass door.

A young salesman in a crisp white shirt and khakis intercepted us. He beamed. "Hi! My name's Greg. How can I help you today?"

Charlene angled her head at my VW. "She needs a replacement for the beater she's driving."

What? That hadn't been part of the plan.

His tanned brow creased, and I imagined him on a surfboard, his sandy hair thick from the salt water. "I can see she does. What year is that car? Seventy-two?"

"Seventy-four," Charlene said. "Larry said he'd set her up personally."

His brown eyes lighted. "You know Larry? He's my uncle."

"Good to see nepotism is alive and well," Charlene said.

"My uncle's with a customer right now, finalizing a contract on a sweet Cadillac SRX. That's an SUV."

Charlene's gaze narrowed. "I know what it is. You think just because you're dealing with women, we don't know cars?"

I hadn't known what an SRX was.

"No, no." He raised his hands in a warding gesture. "Not at all." He turned to me. "What are you looking for?"

"Something, uh, durable," I said, "and with good storage

capacity. I own a pie shop, and we're starting to deliver, wholesale." It *would* be nice not to have to depend on Charlene's Jeep, but a new car was a pipe dream.

He snapped his fingers. "Got it. Something that will double as a business vehicle. We've got SUVs that can fit the bill."

"And not too expensive," I added hastily. I couldn't afford an SUV. Then I remembered it didn't matter what he showed us. I couldn't afford a new car, period.

"I think I know what you need," he said. "While we're waiting for Larry, why don't you follow me?"

We trailed behind him, winding through the mass of shining cars.

"What are we doing?" I whispered to Charlene.

"Killing time until Larry's free," she said. "What's the harm?"

Dread pooled in my stomach. *What's the harm?* Speaking the words aloud was a sure jinx.

"It's on the other side of the building." He glanced over his shoulder.

We rounded the corner, and I stumbled to a halt.

"Oh. My. God," Charlene said.

Frederick raised his head. His blue eyes widened.

A pink Volkswagen van sat parked in the shade of the building.

Pink. *Exactly* the same shade of pink as our pie boxes.

"What the heck is this?" Charlene asked. "A Barbie Dream Van?"

Frederick blinked, winced, and buried his head in Charlene's shoulder.

"It's fifteen years old," the salesman said, "but it's only got ten thousand miles. The owner was an elderly woman who thought she'd use it for camping, but she never really took it anywhere."

"Was she blind?" Charlene asked.

"Does it . . . Does it run?" Hardly daring to believe it was real, I reached to touch it and visualized the Pie Town logo on its sides.

"Like a dream," he said. "The prior owner may not have taken it anywhere, but she made sure it went to the garage for an annual checkup. This van is in pristine condition."

It was perfect.

"It's pink!" Charlene snorted. "No wonder you've got it hidden. That thing's so bright, it'll send drivers on the highway careening into a ditch."

"The prior owner was worried about other drivers being able to see her," Greg said. "It's not likely anyone will accidentally run into you driving this gem."

"Gems aren't hot pink," Charlene said.

"How much?" I asked, my voice hoarse. I could install racks in the rear for the pies. It would be totally recognizable around town. And . . . branding!

"Nine thousand, nine hundred and ninety-nine," he said. "Plus tax."

I wanted it so badly my chest tightened, and I looked away. Too bad I couldn't have it. I was cash poor at the moment.

"Ten thousand dollars? Are you out of your mind?" Charlene asked. "For that Pepto-Bismol monstrosity? You should pay *us* to take it off the lot. Where's Larry?"

He smiled knowingly. "Think about it. I'll see if he's free." Stepping aside, he pulled out his cell phone and made a call.

"It's perfect," I whispered.

Charlene snapped her fingers in front of my face. "Perfectly loopy. We're not buying that van."

"Look at the color."

"I can't help but look at the color. It's scarring my retinas."

"It's the Pie Town color. It's our logo."

She angled her head away and squinted. "Is it?"

"I've got a pie box in the Bug. If it's not an exact match, it's pretty close."

"I guess I never noticed how awful that pink was. It's okay in small doses, but an entire van . . ." She shuddered. "Yeesh."

"Imagine our logo on the side. We could use it for deliveries." My shoulders slumped. Imagining was all I could do. Even on a payment plan, I couldn't afford this blushing beauty.

"Frederick and I will not be seen in a pre-owned vehicle the color of a vomited prom dress."

"You won't have to." I sighed. "Buying a new, used van is only a fantasy."

"Fantasy? This is a hot-pink nightmare."

Greg pocketed the phone and smiled. "My uncle's free. Would you like some coffee? We've got donuts inside."

Charlene perked up. "Donuts? Have you got any chocolate old-fashioned?"

We followed him inside the glass building.

Larry stood by the open front door. A breeze blasted through it, tossing the older man's thinning hair. He shook hands with a tall, broad-shouldered man who had his back to us.

I sucked in my breath, turned on my heel. I knew those broad shoulders and that navy suit.

"Charlene?" Gordon asked. "Val?"

I turned and pasted on a smile. "Hi, Gor . . . Detective Carmichael."

His expression hardened. "What are you doing here?"

"There is a pink van for sale that is exactly the shade of our pie boxes," Charlene said. "It's kizmet."

Gordon lifted a single eyebrow. "A pink van."

I gulped, yesterday's bravado gone with the wind.

"For pie deliveries," she said. "Now that we've got customers like the Bar X, we need a van. Pre-owned." She leaned closer and lowered her voice. "You know Val's a penny-pincher."

Frederick's ears twitched in agreement.

"I was just telling Officer Carmichael about our stolen car." Larry rubbed his broad, hooked nose. "Probably some kid looking for a joy ride."

"In a Prius?" I asked, disbelieving. There were a dozen muscle cars on the lot that I wouldn't have minded taking for a joy ride.

"Officer Carmichael told me what happened," he said. "I hear the young man who was hit is going to be fine. But if you hadn't stopped by, I would have called you, Miss Harris. I feel terrible."

Gordon made a noise. It sounded a lot like a growl.

"Terrible enough for an I-let-someone-steal-my-car-and-nearly-kill-you discount?" Charlene asked.

"Last night," Larry said, "someone broke a bathroom window and got inside the dealership. He stole one of the keys from the board and took the car. I thought we had good security, but I guess it wasn't good enough. There's some real damage to the front of the car as well."

"There was some real damage to Ray," I said, indignant.

"I know," he said. "I'm sorry. Do you think he'd mind if I sent flowers?"

A vein pulsed in Gordon's neck. "Val. Can I speak with you? Outside." He stormed out, not bothering to see if I'd follow.

Which, of course, I did.

He stopped beside a pre-owned Porsche.

A semi rumbled past on Highway One.

He rubbed his forehead. "Val?"

"Yes?"

"What are you doing?"

"Trying to find out what Larry knows about whoever ran me down, if it wasn't Larry himself. He told me he wasn't at the Bar X when Devon was killed, but you told me he was."

"Imagine that," he said. "A witness lying to a fake detective. Now why do you think he'd do that?"

"I'm not a fake detective, because I'm not trying to be a detective. And if you're worried I'm going to screw up your investigation—"

"I'm worried you're going to get hurt."

"Oh," I said, taken aback. Since I'd been shot at and nearly run over by both horse-drawn and motorized carriage, getting hurt wasn't entirely out of bounds. "Someone's been trying to hurt me from the start. The killer shot that pie from my hands before I even began asking questions. So, I may as well keep asking."

He ground his palms into his eye sockets. "I know. I know. For God's sake, Val, if you want to investigate crimes, you need to wait until you get a PI license."

Whaaa . . . ? "Wait. You mean . . . You think I *am* capable of investigating?"

"Of course, you are. You're smart, and you're driven. Why not become a PI? But, right now, you've got no training and very little clue."

"But I have *some* clue." That had to be progress.

He glared. A breeze ruffled his lapel. "Val . . ."

I scrubbed my hand over my face. "Sorry. That wasn't funny. Not after what happened to Ray. Larry may feel bad about his stolen car being used in an attempted homicide, but it's my fault Ray got hurt."

He sighed. "Will you stop saying that? There's only one person at fault, and it's the same person who decided to steal a car and rampage through San Nicholas."

"That sounds like you think it was a joy ride too."

"That would be stretching coincidence too far. Until I have more evidence, I'm not jumping to conclusions. Neither should you."

Had he just given me permission to investigate? I opened my mouth, closed it. Smiled. Ignorance was bliss. And I didn't quite believe him about not jumping to conclusions.

"No more investigating, Val. Not without a PI license." He strode through the parking lot to his sedan.

That was more definitive.

I returned inside, where Charlene and Larry were chortling as if they'd known each other for decades.

"And then he said, but I've already got a parrot!" Charlene hooted.

Larry wiped his eyes. "That's a good one."

"What did Detective Carmichael want?" Charlene asked.

"To make sure I was okay after last night," I said. "Larry, I can't help but think that the person who tried to run me over had something to do with the murder at the Bar X."

"That seems like a stretch," he said. "After all, I'm the only pre-owned car dealership in thirty miles. If someone's going to steal a car from a dealership in the San Nicholas area, it will be from mine."

"Unless someone involved in the Bar X murder wanted to frame you," I said.

He blinked. "Frame me?"

"You were at the Bar X when Devon was killed," I said. "You know horses and could have aimed that stagecoach at me—"

"Anyone could have done that," he said. "Look, I wasn't near the saloon the day of the murder. I only went to the carriage house."

"I'll take your word for it," I said. "But doesn't it seem odd that both of us have a Bar X connection to Devon's murder, and someone stole your car to try to run me down?"

"Are you sure they were trying to run you down?" He crossed his arms over his barrel-shaped chest.

"No," I said. "But what else could it have been? The car snuck up on us."

"It's a Prius," he said. "They sneak up on everyone."

"Did anyone at the Bar X have reason to want Devon dead?" I asked.

His square jaw worked. "I saw that Marla woman arguing with Devon."

Charlene straightened. "Really? When?"

The white cat raised his head from her shoulder.

"A couple nights before he was killed. I'd gone there after work to visit the horses. I won't give them up, even if I do have to run into Curly and Moe every now and then. The lights were on in the saloon. Sometimes, Ewan opens it just for the Bar X staff. We serve ourselves and have a good time, you know? So, I wandered over, but it was only Devon and that woman."

"What were Devon and Marla arguing about?" Charlene asked, breathless.

He glanced toward the glass front doors. "I don't know. I don't like confrontations, so I beat it out of there."

"Did anyone else see them?" I asked.

He chewed the inside of his cheek. "Bridget might have. I ran into her, coming around the corner of the saloon. She had a funny look on her face."

"What about Moe and Curly?" I asked. "Why did you three break up the act?"

"They started taking it for granted that I'd take care of their horses. I may love horses, but I didn't love my partners' attitudes." He grimaced. "It got out of control. We'd had a good thing going. At least it didn't bust up my friendship with Ewan and Bridget."

That tracked with what Curly had told me, though I wasn't sure if any of it mattered.

His expression softened. "Moe and Curly are good guys too. Moe's had some hard luck in his life, and it's made him a little short tempered. But we're all part of the Brotherhood of Blue Steel."

"The brotherhood?" It sounded like a secret society, which goes to show I'd been spending too much time around Charlene.

His thick fingers twitched, as if readying for a gunfight. "It's a local shooting group made up of guys who like the Old West. We only use single-action shooters. Single-action revolvers, pistol-caliber, lever-action rifles, and old-time shotguns. Since only three of us live in San Nicholas, we got pretty close. Or we were until that stupid fight."

Out of that monologue I'd understood the words "revolver" and "shotgun."

"What happened to Moe?" I asked. "The hard luck, I mean."

"His only son died," he said, biting off the words.

A heaviness centered in my chest. "That's awful."

"I don't have kids," Larry continued, "but no parent should have to go through that. As far as I'm concerned, Moe can be as big a horse's ass as he wants. He gets a pass."

Charlene looked out the tall window. She was estranged from her only child, a daughter, who lived in Europe. "No," she said quietly, "no one deserves that."

"I guess that's one of the reasons I've got so much respect for Ewan," he said. "He didn't have it easy either, raising Bridget on his own. In spite of his loss, he kept his sense of humor, and Bridget turned out well. They've been good to me, letting me keep my horse in their carriage house and come around whenever I wanted." He shook himself and rubbed his broad hands together. "So, about that van . . ."

"Sorry, gotta go and visit Ray," Charlene said, and steered me out the door.

"Nice exit," I said. "I was starting to think I'd have to buy the van."

"You do. I got him down to eighty-five hundred."

"You what?" I bit back my annoyance. "You said you and Frederick wouldn't be caught dead in a pink van."

"Frederick and I won't be making the deliveries. I'm piecrusts only, remember? The only reason I came with you to the Bar X is because Ewan is a personal friend of mine."

"But—"

"I just knocked fifteen percent off the sticker price," she said. "Do you know what a coup that is? You're lucky I was here. And you're buying that van."

I made a low noise in my throat—a whimper of despair. I couldn't afford it at eighty-five hundred dollars either.

Chapter Eleven

Charlene and I drove to a local flower farm. In its cool greenhouse, I selected a dripping bunch of lavender from a plastic bucket. I grabbed a vase off the shelf and met Charlene at the register.

The cashier packed up our bouquet, setting the vase in a box for stability.

"Marla's the killer," Charlene growled. "I know it."

The cashier, a plump woman with silver hair, shot her a startled glance.

"A killer instinct for fashion, that's for sure." Smiling maniacally, I paid for the flowers.

Charlene sniffed. "She keeps turning up in the case, and I find it highly suspicious she's now investigating." She put the last word in air quotes.

I steered her outside and into my VW. "Maybe we shouldn't accuse anyone of murder in public."

"Why?" Charlene buckled up. "She's the most likely suspect. Marla's selfish and self-centered and has no regard for anyone. She's the perfect murderer."

"Uh huh."

The Bug started with a cough, and I pulled onto the highway, looping inland. We crested a low mountain. At its top, a cemetery overlooked a series of lakes glittering in the valley below, golden with dried grasses.

"Maybe we can go to that new mall after we visit Ray," she said.

"Sure. What are you looking for?"

"I thought we could go to that fancy lingerie store."

"What do you . . . ?" Right, for my date that was never going to happen. My lips compressed. "I'm not buying a girdle."

"Who said anything about a girdle?"

"You did."

"A girdle is out. You shouldn't be physically uncomfortable on a date. Now, new lingerie—"

"Forget it, Charlene."

The modern hospital where Ray was recuperating was in a small city on the Peninsula. I found a parking space at the back of the lot, and we walked inside the blue-glass building.

Collar up to hide Frederick, Charlene skittered into the glass and tile lobby.

I shook my head. If she got caught with the cat, I would disavow all knowledge.

While she pretended to examine some lending books in the lounge, I asked at the help desk for Ray's room. A volunteer directed me upstairs.

Like a spy who'd escaped a retirement home, Charlene slunk behind me and into the elevator. On the second floor, I had to ask for directions at two more nurse's desks before I finally located Ray's room. A curtain had been drawn across the open door.

I knocked on the frame. "Ray? It's Val and Charlene. Can we come in?"

"Hey," he called. "Yeah."

I pushed the curtain aside.

Ray lay in a hospital bed, his red hair rumpled. One leg

was in a cast and raised at an angle by a complicated series of straps and ropes and pulleys. His stomach made a mountain of the beige hospital blanket, and his freckles stood out against his pale face.

Marla smiled at us from the nearby lounge chair and touched her silvery hair. She snapped shut her notebook. "Following my lead again, I see." She tightened the belt of her trench coat.

Charlene sucked in her cheeks. "You—"

"You crazy gamer," I said loudly. A hospital catfight involving an actual cat was all we needed. "How are you feeling?" I set the lavender bouquet on an empty table near his bed.

He grinned. "Sore. Did you bring pie?"

I opened my bag and pulled out a pink box and a plastic wrapped spork. "A mini cherry. I don't think it's warm anymore though."

"Gimme." He reached toward me, and I handed him the box.

"Marla," Charlene snarled.

"Charlene," she said.

"Leave your fedora at home?" my piecrust maker asked.

"I don't wear silly hats," Marla said. "Or helmets. Those things you had to wear in the roller derby looked heinous. I suppose with all those times you were slammed into metal fences though, you needed one. Multiple concussions can do long-term damage. Have you ever had your head examined?"

Charlene's nostrils flared. "What are you doing here?"

"When I heard what happened, it was obvious that the attack on Ray and Val was connected to Devon's murder."

Charlene jammed her fists on her hips, rumpling her green tunic. "How did you hear about the hit-and-run? It didn't make the morning papers."

"You Tweeted about it," Marla said.

Charlene said something unladylike.

"Mrs. McCree!" Ray's brows rose.

Charlene pinked. "Sorry, Ray."

"Sloppy work, Val," Marla said, "putting one of your own customers in jeopardy."

I shriveled with guilt. "Ray, you saved me from that car. I'm so sorry for what happened. And thank you."

"Aw." Ray made a dismissive motion, and the metal contraption holding his leg creaked. "That's okay. I walked you to your car because Mrs. McCree said someone was trying to kill you. I knew what I was getting into. And I guess Mrs. McCree was right."

Marla looked me up and down. "You might have moved a little quicker if you laid off some of those pies."

Bullpuckey. I wasn't getting fat. Was I? Forcing a smile, I turned to Ray. "How bad is it?"

"My leg's broken in three places, and my hip is cracked."

I winced. Ouchy. "Did you get a look at the driver? Because I didn't."

"Yeah, I gave the cops a sketch."

"What did he look like?" Charlene asked eagerly.

"Sort of, you know, like a dark shape."

"A dark shape," I said, disappointed.

"Kind of a blob." He unwrapped the spork. "The cops wouldn't tell me anything. What have you heard?"

"We think we found the car," I said. "It was abandoned near the Half House. The police are running tests."

"They're probably trying to pull my DNA from the grill." He nodded sagely. "Car forensics. I saw it on TV."

Charlene tugged on my sleeve and made growling noises.

"Who's car was it?" Ray asked between bites of pie.

"Someone stole it from a local dealership," I said.

Charlene's grumbles grew more insistent.

"Pelt's?" he asked.

"Larry Pelt?" Marla asked. "He was at the Bar X when Devon was murdered."

"Duh," Charlene snapped. "We already figured that out."

Marla tapped her Mont Blanc pen on the notebook— leather bound, naturally "Interesting."

"What's so interesting about it?" Charlene asked.

"That Val is at the epicenter of so many deadly events."

Charlene crossed her arms over her chest. "Obviously, someone's trying to kill her too."

"Is it obvious?" Marla asked. "Val was right there when Devon was killed. And now all these odd things are happening to her. It makes one wonder if she hasn't set up these so-called attacks in an amateurish attempt to divert suspicion from herself."

"What?!" Charlene's eyes bulged.

"I haven't," I said. Not that it mattered what Marla thought.

"The evidence suggests otherwise," Marla said. "I predict you're in for an unpleasant surprise, Charlene."

"Nice try, Wrongstradamus," Charlene said.

"Are cats allowed in hospital rooms?" Marla asked.

"He's a comfort animal," Charlene said.

"Oh?" Marla tilted her head. "Do you have a license?"

Charlene ground her teeth. "Are you asking to see it?"

"Since the license should be visible around the animal's neck, it's obvious that's no comfort animal." She rose. "I've got everything I need here. Thank you, Ray. I'm sorry Val and Charlene dragged you into a murder investigation."

"I don't mind," he mumbled between bites of pie.

She waggled her fingers, diamonds flashing, and swept from the room.

"Why did you tell him about the stolen car in front of Marla?" Charlene scowled at me. "Now she knows about Larry Pelt!"

"Ray deserves to know what happened."

"You couldn't wait until she'd left?" She thunked into

the chair Marla had vacated. "What did she want to know, Ray?"

"Same stuff the police asked—if I'd gotten a look at the driver. I didn't. All I saw were headlights. Those hybrids are so quiet. Thanks for not telling her what kind of car it was."

"Not even Val would blab about that," Charlene said.

Not even Val? Thanks a lot.

"What else did she want?" Charlene asked.

His freckled skin darkened. He swallowed. "Uh, well, she asked if Val had pushed me."

I laughed. "Seriously?"

"You heard what she said." Ray shifted the pie box on his stomach. "She's trying to pin this on you. I told her you had nothing to do with it. Like you could shove me in front of a car. I'm twice your size. Still, you'd better be careful."

"I'm not worried about her," I said. "How much longer are they keeping you here?"

"Another couple days," he said gloomily.

"How does a breakfast pie sound tomorrow morning?" I asked.

He brightened. "Better than the hospital menu."

"I'll bring one by, and a variety pack of mini pies for later in the day."

"You have variety packs?" he asked.

"Figure of speech." Though it wasn't a bad idea.

We hung out with Ray until Henrietta arrived.

She paused in the doorway, giving us time to ogle her combat boots/miniskirt combo. I'd never seen her in anything other than baggy tops and military pants; she had some killer curves.

Her cheeks turned a dusty rose. "Oh. Hi. Is this a bad time?"

"Not at all," Charlene said. "We were just leaving."

"See you tomorrow, Ray," I said.

We left the room.

In the hallway, Charlene pulled up her collar, concealing Frederick. She pushed the elevator's down button. "I'm no longer worried about Marla solving this crime."

"No kidding. If she thinks I did it, she's way off base."

"Now I'm worried about her framing you. The woman's a piranha."

"She said I was fat. Or at least she implied it." And I was not fat.

"Some older people can be critical. Don't take it personally."

Some older people? Pot. Kettle. Black. "We don't have any real evidence proving Marla was involved."

"Oh, don't you worry. I'll get evidence."

Unease rattled my bones. "I'm glad you're back in the investigative spirit, but—"

"But me no buts. If she doesn't frame you, she'll kill you. We need to neutralize her."

"Neutralize?" Maybe Gordon had a point about the perils of investigating after all.

That night, I sat on Charlene's floral-print couch and watched her pace in front of the TV. The *Stargate* credits scrolled, and I clicked on the orange, seventies-era table lamp.

"Weren't you supposed to be ghost hunting tonight?" I asked.

"Get your priorities straight. We're hunting a killer."

A bead of sweat trickled down my back. Charlene didn't believe in air conditioning. And in spite of the open windows and cool night air, the house refused to release the afternoon's heat.

"There's got to be a way to take her down," she said.

"Her who?" I sipped my Kahlua and root beer. At least the glass was still nice and frosty.

"Marla, of course! The question is, who is her accomplice?"

"Maybe we shouldn't focus only on Marla at this stage," I said, cautious. "We still don't know—"

"I'll bet Curly helped her. He's a sharpshooter, and he's got a crush on her, which proves he's mentally deficient."

Above us, a ceiling fan turned slowly, making no inroads on the heat.

I wrinkled my nose. "He does? Are you sure?"

"Oh, please. It's obvious. And Larry said he heard her arguing with the victim."

"Maybe Devon overcharged her for a drink. We don't know what their fight was about."

She shot me a knowing look. "Oh, don't we?"

"Do we?"

"Obviously, she was having an affair with Devon like one of those jaguar women."

"You know perfectly well they're called 'cougars.'" I crossed my leg over my knee. "I don't think that's obvious at all. If we focus solely on Marla, we may miss some real clues to whodunnit."

"Not if Marla's guilty. Look at how she was trying to pin the blame on you. Would an innocent person do that?"

I rubbed the bridge of my nose. "Even if she was having an affair with Devon—and that's a big *if*—why kill him?"

"For whatever they were arguing about." She snapped her fingers. "She wants Ewan. Marla knows that Ewan won't see her the same way if he finds out she's been doing the horizontal tango with his young stud of an employee."

"Devon wasn't that young." He'd been close to Bridget's age.

She ignored me. "Marla had to kill Devon to keep him

quiet. It wouldn't surprise me after all the husbands she's buried. We can't let her get her claws into Ewan."

"Uh huh. Marla's the black widow of San Nicholas. Maybe she's the Phantom of Bar X too."

"Don't be sarcastic," she said. "Or ageist."

"All right, Mulder. I'll remain open-minded," I lied and stood to turn off the TV. "But we still need more information."

"I'll get the laptop." Charlene hurried to the kitchen and returned with the small computer. She plopped onto the couch, bouncing me on my cushion, and booted up the computer.

"Fine, Marla's a suspect," I said, "but we need to be objective and look at all our suspects—Moe, Curly, Larry, Ewan—"

"Ewan's not a suspect."

"Charlene—"

"He couldn't have done it. We were together when Devon was killed."

"Yeah, you two were with Marla. If she's a suspect—"

"A good investigator looks at everyone." She pouted. "And we can't ignore Marla, even if we can't figure out how she did it. Yet."

The bulb in the table lamp popped and went out; now our only illumination was Charlene's computer screen.

"Great," I said.

"We'll start with the obituaries."

"Maybe we can start with a new lightbulb. Where do you keep them?"

"Hold on. I'll get it. Take a look at this."

A floorboard creaked, and I looked up, my scalp prickling. The furniture made odd shapes in the gloom. "What was that?"

"Frederick. He's more active at night."

He had to be. The cat was comatose for most of the day.

"Here we go," she said, and pulled up an obituary. "Marla divorced her first husband. Here's husband number two—heart attack."

"So. Natural causes."

"Well, write it down," Charlene said.

"Fine." I stomped to the kitchen, banging my thigh into an occasional table on the way. Limping, I turned on the kitchen light.

Frederick lay coiled in his cat bed near the modern, brushed-nickel refrigerator.

"Are there any lightbulbs in here?" I called.

"Forget the lightbulbs!"

I rummaged through my purse, laying on the butcher block work island, and found a pen and battered notebook. Returning to the living room, I flipped on the overhead lamp and sat.

"Did you turn off the kitchen light?" she asked.

I got up, trudged to the kitchen, turned out the light, and returned.

"Did you write it down?" she asked, staring pointedly at the notebook clenched in my hand.

"If we had more light—"

"Don't be such a baby."

She looped a pair of reading glasses on a chain around her neck, and adjusted the glasses on her nose. "Husband number three died in a skydiving accident."

"Ouch."

"And number four had a heart attack too."

"How old was he?" I asked.

"Seventy-three."

"And the second husband?"

"Sixty-eight."

"So, they were in the normal age range for natural deaths," I said.

"Sixty-eight? Are you kidding me? He was practically a

baby. Now, husband number five had a stroke at seventy-four, and husband number six . . . another heart attack, this time at ninety-two."

"I'm getting the feeling Marla's into older men," I said, "not the younger ones."

"She marries the old ones and toys with the young ones, like a jaguar with its prey."

"Cougar."

"Don't you think it's a little odd that nearly all her husbands died on her?"

"Not if she was marrying older guys."

Charlene's snowy brows drew downward. "Now you're being stubborn."

"Statistically, the deaths do seem odd. But . . ."

A floorboard squeaked, and I looked over my shoulder. We were alone in the living room.

I shook my head, pushing away my disquiet. It was an old house and was only settling. I didn't know why I was spooked.

"But what?" she asked.

"But all her husbands' deaths seemed natural—or at least accidental. Devon's death was murder. Someone shot him. Even if Marla was a ruthless killer, that's not her MO."

"Unless she got one of those sharpshooters to help her. Plugging people full of lead is their modus operandi."

"They shoot tin cans and paper, not people," I said. "But let's take a look at them."

Impatient, I shifted on the couch while Charlene surfed the Internet. She turned up a slew of articles mentioning the three sharpshooters as party entertainment, but nothing nefarious. Larry was all over the web advertising his used cars, but we didn't find any personal information.

Charlene gave a low whistle. "Take a look at this." She handed me the laptop.

On the screen was an article about a late-night attack on

a donut shop in central California. Curly had gotten drunk, tried to shoot through the hole of the giant rotating donut sign, and missed. Repentant, he'd waited in the parking lot to get arrested.

"He's got a drinking problem," she said.

If I kept imbibing Charlene's "special" root beer, I was going to have a drinking problem. "Do you think Ewan knows about the arrest?"

"If that bartender did, he could have been blackmailing Curly."

"I thought you were convinced Marla did it."

She raised her nose. "I am. But it gives Curly a motive to work as her accomplice."

Riiight. "Gimme." I took the laptop from Charlene and typed in Ewan's name.

"What are you doing?" Charlene asked.

"Seeing what I can find on Ewan and Bridget."

She slammed shut the lid of the laptop, plunging us deeper into darkness.

I yelped and yanked away my fingers.

"He didn't kill that bartender, and neither did Bridget." She removed her glasses, letting them drop to her chest.

"We can't be sure," I said. "Bridget was right there in the saloon. And if Marla could have used an accomplice or rigged a gun to go off to make her look innocent, Bridget and Ewan could have done the same. I'll bet they know their way around a handgun."

She snatched away the laptop. "It's a waste of time. The killer was Marla, working with one of those three sharp-shooters."

My gaze flicked to the front window. Light from the street lamp filtered through the curtains, turning the living room gray. "I know you've got some hundred-watt bulbs stashed away. Where are they?"

"I'm saving them."

"For what?"

"You never know."

I stretched, pressing my body deeper into the flowered sofa cushions. "Fine. You know Bridget and Ewan better than I. What makes you so sure they're innocent?"

"I was friends with his wife before she died," she said in a strained voice. "Poor Ewan raised Bridget alone. Ewan's a straight arrow. He had some wild days in the military, before he married, but that's what you get for stationing men in a beach town."

"Beach town?"

"San Diego. Once he met Beth though, he flew straight."

"Did he marry late in life?" I asked.

"Why?"

"Bridget's what? Late thirties? Early forties?" Ewan had to be in his seventies.

"Ewan and Beth married in their midthirties, and Bridget came along not long after."

Midthirties seemed awfully late to figure out it was time to stop catting around. But what did I know about the transformative power of love?

"How did Beth die?" I asked.

"Cancer," she said shortly.

My limbs grew heavy. Unwanted images flashed in my own head of my mother's failed battle with cancer. Her confusion. The pain. Her body shrinking, collapsing into the bedsheets, even while the tumors grew. "How old was Bridget when it happened?"

"She was only a little girl, but old enough to realize what she was losing." She grimaced. "Bridget and my daughter used to play together. Looking back, I wish I'd done more for them."

And I wasn't sure if she meant more for Ewan and Bridget, or more for Bridget and her own daughter. But I wouldn't ask. Charlene rarely spoke about her daughter.

Yawning, I rose. I'd had enough root beer and speculation for one night. "I'm going to drive home and hit the hay." And maybe do some more Internet research on my own. I hoped Charlene was right about Ewan and Bridget—she obviously cared about them both. But we had a limited pool of suspects, and the Bar X owner and his daughter were in the mix.

Expression taut, Charlene trailed me to the door. "It can't be Ewan or Bridget, don't you see? If it was one of them, it would kill the other."

Or kill Charlene.

Chapter Twelve

Charlene closed the door behind me, and I walked slowly down her three porch steps. Wraiths of ground fog twisted through Charlene's darkened garden, twined through her picket fence. I couldn't see a reason why Ewan or Bridget would have killed Devon—at least not yet. I hoped they were innocent, but I wasn't willing to rule them out as suspects.

Stars glittered in the night sky, and in the distance the mountains loomed, black waves of earth. A night bird skimmed the rooftops.

Yawning, I placed my hand on the gate.

A shriek broke the stillness, and my hand clenched on the damp wood.

I whirled, heart slamming against my ribs. The shout had come from Charlene's house.

I raced down the brick path and leapt the steps to the porch. I rattled the knob.

Locked.

I pounded on the door with my fist. "Charlene! Are you all right?"

A crash. A woman's scream. A gun blasted, rattling my eardrums. Glass shattered.

"Charlene!" Black fear swept through my veins. I grabbed a flower pot from the porch railing and hurtled it through the front window. "Charlene! I'm coming!"

Breaking out the shards of glass in the sill, I clambered through the filmy curtains.

Frederick streaked past, a blur of white.

"Charlene!"

"In the kitchen!"

Mouth dry, I raced through the living area and into the homey kitchen. Charlene sagged against the black granite countertop, a shotgun in her hand. Shards of glass and pottery lay scattered on the tile floor. A splintered hole yawned in one of her white-painted cabinets.

"What happened?" I asked. "Are you okay?"

"Someone broke in." Hand shaking, she set the shotgun on the granite counter. "Frederick cornered him in the kitchen. I took a shot at him, and he ran off."

"Him? You saw *him*?" I moved toward the kitchen door to give chase, then jerked away. What was I thinking? I licked my lips, tasting sweat and fear.

"The light was off. I only saw the back of him, running through the door." She pointed to the door, open to the yard. "He was all in black, like a cat burglar." Charlene gazed mournfully at the cabinet. "I'm going to have to get that replaced."

If she'd only seen the rear of the intruder, that meant she'd taken a shot at him when he was running away. Not exactly sporting, but she'd shot wide. Besides, when an intruder's in your house, all bets are off.

She braced both hands on the counter and lowered her head, exhaled. "We should call the police before the neighbors do."

"Charlene, this can't be a coincidence." I gripped the edge of the work island. The attacks on me, Ray's hit and run, a break in . . . We were being targeted. The root beer concoction I'd drunk threatened to reverse its course.

She walked to a seventies-era, wall-mounted phone—jarring in the otherwise modern kitchen—and dialed. After a muttered conversation, she hung up.

"We need to find Frederick," she said. "I think I scared him with the gun."

"I thought he was deaf," I said, trying to shake my anxiety by switching to a topic I could understand. I was pretty sure Frederick's hearing was fine, but I didn't want to upset the applecart. The cat had done a maestro's job wrapping Charlene around his paws.

She raised her chin. "He felt the vibration."

"Oh, that makes sense." In a comic-book universe.

We found Frederick cowering beneath the coffee table in the living room.

Charlene pulled the white fur ball from his hidey-hole. "Oh, you poor . . ." She gaped at the shattered front window. "What the hell?"

"Um. Sorry." My fingers curled. "The door was locked and—"

"You broke my window? Do you have any idea how much those cost?" She petted Frederick with quick, hard strokes. "It's double paned!"

"I'm sorry," I said. "I'll pay for it."

"I'll add it to your rent. What were you thinking?"

"You were screaming! There was a gunshot—"

"And so, you came barreling into a gunfight? What if the burglar had been the one with the gun? And I wasn't screaming. I told you, Frederick attacked the burglar."

A siren wailed in the distance.

She set her reading glasses on her nose. Walking to a table lamp near the kitchen door, she extended one of his paws beneath the shade. "Look! DNA evidence!"

Relieved she'd been diverted from the broken window

(what *had* I been thinking?), I drew closer. There was a trace of red on Frederick's extended claws, and a tiny piece of black fabric.

"Have you got a pair of tweezers?" I asked. "We should get those threads before Frederick loses them."

"Upstairs, in the bathroom's medicine cabinet."

I hurried up the narrow steps to the antique bathroom and returned with tweezers. Carefully, I collected the threads and deposited them in a plastic baggie from the kitchen.

"You're right," Charlene said. "The burglar had to have been our killer. This is a good neighborhood. A break-in at my house is too much of a coincidence." Gleeful, she hugged Frederick to her chest. "Someone's trying to kill me too."

"And that makes you happy?"

"Don't you see? The reason someone's been going after you isn't because of you. It's because of our investigation. We're getting close." Her voice lowered dramatically. "Too close."

A stiff ocean breeze flowed through the broken window, and I shivered.

A sedan pulled up to the sidewalk, and a black and white squad car stopped behind it. Gordon stepped from the sedan.

"He must get a call every time one of our names comes through the dispatcher." My face warmed.

"I'll deal with this." Charlene opened the front door and disappeared onto the porch. "Detective Carmichael! What a lovely surprise."

I sank onto the saggy floral-print couch. Oh, boy.

His rumbly voice floated through the broken window. "Hi, Charlene. Frederick. I heard you had some trouble out here."

"Can I make you some cocoa?" she asked him. "I have a special recipe."

"I've heard about your special recipes. Maybe some other time. What happened?"

"A break-in. Frederick and I scared him off with my shotgun."

"Where?"

"The kitchen."

"What happened to the window?"

"Val."

A masculine sigh. "Where is she?"

"Inside. Come in, come in."

She walked into the living room pursued by Gordon and two uniformed officers I recognized as customers from Pie Town.

I waved limply. "Hi."

Gordon turned to Charlene and pulled a notepad from the inside pocket of his navy suit jacket. "All right. Tell me what happened. Step by step."

"We'd been watching *Stargate*, like we always do," Charlene said. "Season five. Teal'c has a new haircut. I don't like it, even though his skin is less shiny."

"And then?" Gordon prompted.

"Val had just left. I was returning to the kitchen when I heard someone yell and Frederick howling. I grabbed my shotgun—"

"From where?" Gordon asked, taking notes.

"From behind the couch cushions."

I jerked forward. "You keep a loaded gun here?" I'd spent a lot of time on that couch.

"A gun's no good if you can't get to it fast," she said.

He nodded. "Okay. So, you got your shotgun, and then what?"

"Then I ran into the kitchen. It was dark, but I saw him, a tall figure in black." She frowned. "At least I think it was black. It was dark, like I said. And Frederick was all over him. I couldn't shoot the burglar, because Frederick was in the way. So, I aimed high, to scare him. He took off through the kitchen door and into the yard."

"Were you able to get a sense of his build?" he asked.

"Big."

"Big tall? Big wide?"

"Tall. And wide. Or maybe not. Sort of average. Maybe on the thin side. Things moved very quickly."

"How did he compare to Officer Barry?" he pointed to a bulky officer.

"Maybe a little bigger," she said. "Or smaller."

I cradled my skull in my hands. Charlene's description was little better than Ray's.

"The kitchen's that way?" Gordon asked, pointing.

"Yes," she said, "right through there."

"Go ahead, guys," he said to the two officers.

They nodded and strode into the kitchen.

"Did Ray give you a description of the scoundrel who tried to run Val over?" Charlene asked. "Maybe it's the same person."

Gordon stared at her. One beat. Two. He reached into his inside pocket and pulled out a folded piece of paper. "He drew me a picture." He handed the paper to Charlene.

Her brow crumpled. "This is it?"

"What?" I asked. "What is it?"

She passed me the paper.

I cocked my head. The drawing was a circle and a line—the top half of a stick figure. But it was more detailed than the "blobby" description he'd given us. "Seriously?" I asked.

"Ray drew it himself," Gordon said. "The department can't afford a sketch artist."

"So basically, all you know is the driver has a head," Charlene said.

Expressionless, he turned to me. "Can you confirm the head?"

"I think I'm detecting a touch of sarcasm, but . . . no-o."

"So, the driver may or may not have had a head," Gordon said.

"Hey, all I saw were headlights." I noticed Gordon wasn't taking notes.

"Right." He turned to Charlene. "How exactly did your window get broken, Mrs. McCree?"

She gestured halfheartedly. "Val panicked. The front door was locked, so she broke the window and came inside that way."

He rubbed his forehead. "Val, of all the idiotic—"

"Charlene was in trouble!"

"Why didn't you call the police?" he asked. "You have a cell phone."

"Things were happening kind of fast," I mumbled.

"Have you got any plywood or sheets of plastic?" he asked Charlene.

"In the garage."

"Why don't you show me? I'll help you clean this up." The two walked outside, leaving me by my lonesome.

The cops in the kitchen gave me permission to remove a broom and dustpan, and I got to work sweeping the broken glass into a pile. Did I say pile? I meant mountain range. I swept the hardwood floor and vacuumed the living room rug. Charlene and Gordon returned, the latter carrying two large, square pieces of plywood. Charlene held a roll of thick plastic beneath her arm, and carried masking tape and what looked like a nail gun.

"Can I help?" I asked, meek. After refurbishing Pie Town, I well knew the cost of windows.

Gordon pressed one of the plywood boards over the hole, adjusted it, and cocked his head. "Yeah. Hold this."

I pressed the board against the wall, and Gordon shot nails through it into the window frame. He took the second board and laid it over the first, covering the remaining gap along the left side, and we repeated the process.

One of the cops, Officer Barry, emerged from the kitchen. "We took prints around the door, but we'll need Mrs. McCree's and Val's prints for comparison."

"No, we don't," Gordon said, taping the plastic around the plywood. "We've already got their prints at the station."

I hunched my shoulders. Having prints on file at the local cop shop just wasn't normal.

"Sure thing," Officer Barry said. "Then I think we've got everything we can. We checked the backyard. It's pretty dry out there, so we didn't see any footprints. The gate is open though. Looks like whoever broke in might have run out that way."

"Did you notice any vehicles driving away?" Gordon asked us.

We shook our heads. I'd been too relieved Charlene was alive to notice much beyond that.

"Okay, guys," Gordon said, "why don't you do a sweep of the neighborhood, and we'll call it a night. Val? A word?" He jerked his head toward the front door. I followed him into the garden. We watched the two officers cruise off in their black-and-white.

He blew out his breath.

"Okay," I said. "Running into Charlene's house might not have been the smart thing, but she could have been bleeding out for all I knew. I should have called nine-one-one first, and *then* jumped through the window."

Gordon raked his hand through his thick hair and growled. "That's exactly what I'm talking about. Do you have any idea how terrifying you are?"

"Terrifying?"

He grasped my shoulders, and I caught a faint whiff of his cologne. My stomach fluttered.

"What do I have to do to keep you safe?" he asked. "Arrest you?"

"Your cousin Petronella would kill me if she got stuck managing Pie Town on her own."

His arms dropped to his sides. "I give up. You and Charlene are out of my control. I've said what I have to say. You know what the dangers are. You're both adults."

Well, *I* was. Sometimes I wasn't sure about Charlene. "Gordon—"

A muscle spasmed along his jaw. "Not. Another. Word." He stalked to his car, got in, and slammed the door.

I winced.

Gordon drove off, his taillights vanishing around the corner.

Charlene strolled onto the porch. "That went well."

I squeezed my eyelids shut and took a calming breath. "Were you eavesdropping?"

"It's not eavesdropping when the conversation's happening in your own garden."

"I think I can safely say my dating life is DOA."

"What are you talking about?"

"You heard."

"I heard a man who is concerned for your well-being, but thinks enough of you to let you make your own choices."

Charlene was in think-positive mode. I was not. "How's Frederick?"

"Oh! They didn't swab for DNA. Let's bag his paws."

I arched a brow. "Do you think he'd let us do that?"

"Mm." She rubbed her jaw. "You could bag his paws."

"No way."

"At least we have that thread from the burglar's clothing."

Which I'd forgotten to give to Gordon. I slapped my forehead and groaned.

She walked down the steps and clapped me on the shoulder. "We're shaking things up, my girl. The killer knows we're getting close, and he wants to silence us."

She rubbed her wrinkled hands together. "At last, our case has got some direction."

"It does?"

"It's time we Baker Street Bakers channel Sherlock Holmes. The game is afoot!"

"Holmes never said that, you know."

"No one likes a know-it-all. Now, off to bed. We've got a lot to do tomorrow."

"Aside from bake pies?" She had something in mind, and my nerves hummed with anxiety. Charlene's plans always seemed to end up with me injured or covered in mud.

She gazed at me over her reading glasses. "I have a plan."

Fantabulous. "What's your plan?" I asked, unenthusiastic.

"Just you wait and see." She jogged up the steps and slammed the door shut.

I stared at it, dismay puddling in my stomach. Charlene with a plan. Now that was terrifying.

Chapter Thirteen

We made it through Saturday without any disasters. Sunday, a suspiciously smug Charlene vanished into the flour-work room. She churned out a slew of piecrusts and disappeared at the end of her shift without saying a word.

Certain she was up to no good, I spent the rest of the morning filling pies at the work island and waiting for the other anvil to drop.

I finally emerged from the kitchen to help Petronella with the Sunday lunch crowd. The tourists were out in full force. Families with overexcited and overtired children swarmed the booths. A long line stretched from the counter for takeaway.

I worked the register, spitting out orders, boxing pies, and delivering plates of salad and mini pies to their tables. The counter was an oasis of calm, lined with friends and regulars—Joy from the comic shop, and the retirees, Tally Wally and Graham. The three sat and sipped coffee in a silent meditation.

Watching me box a peach pie, Joy brushed back her curtain of silky black hair. "How's the investigation going?"

"I'm sure the police have it well in hand," I chirped.

Wally chuckled. "Or Charlene does."

I knotted my hands in my apron, mirroring the knot twisting my stomach. What *was* Charlene up to?

Graham leaned across the counter, nudging his tweed flat cap off the ledge.

I caught it before it hit the linoleum floor and returned it to him.

"Thanks," he said. "I hear someone broke into Char's place last night."

"Word gets around fast." Small town fast.

"And I heard she took a potshot at the guy," Wally said.

"With what?" Graham asked.

"A gun, what do you think?" Wally said.

"Knowing Charlene, it could have been a blow dart." Graham cackled, and Wally joined in.

I whirled to the cash register and handed over the peach pie.

Henrietta, in a swingy green skirt and blouse, hurried into the restaurant and looked around. Seeing the gamer booth full to the brim, she hustled to the counter and squeezed between Joy and the two men. "I saw Ray in the hospital," she said breathlessly. "He says thanks for the pies."

"He saved my life." I swiped a damp towel over the counter. "Pies are the least I can do."

"I heard he saved you from a runaway dump truck," Graham said.

"No, it was one of those foreign sports cars," Wally said. "A Maserati."

"It was a Prius," Henrietta said. Brown eyes widening, she clapped her hands to her mouth.

"A Prius?" The old men hooted with laughter.

"Is it even possible to kill someone with a Prius?" Graham asked.

"Oh, sure," Wally said. "You could kill someone with anything. See that pie tin over there? I could kill someone with it."

"Last I checked, you were in the Air Force just like me," Graham said. "Not some super-secret special forces ninja school."

"The car was going really fast," Henrietta said earnestly.

"It snuck up on us," I agreed.

The men laughed even harder.

"Quit while you're ahead," Joy said in her monotone voice and took a sip of her coffee.

"Who was driving it?" Graham asked. "The ghost of Bar X?"

The two roared. Even Joy cracked a smile.

Looking abashed, Henrietta slunk to the gamers' corner.

I sidled down the counter. "You two know about the Phantom of Bar X?" Strange that Charlene hadn't yet roped me into a ghost-hunting adventure. Maybe she was learning to prioritize.

"Well, sure," Tally Wally said. "I told Ewan to put the phantom on his website to drum up more tourists, but for some reason he hasn't."

Hold up. Charlene had acted surprised when she'd heard about the ghost. Not only was she paranormal central, but she was also good friends with Ewan. She *had* to have known about it. A dark suspicion formed in my mind.

"When did you learn about the phantom?" I asked.

Wally rubbed his bristly chin. "Not so long ago. A few months, I guess. Why? Do you think the ghost killed that young fella?"

"No," I said, "that doesn't seem likely. Do you know Ewan well?"

"A bit. He's a good guy, even if he is a little nutty about the Old West."

"What ghost?" Joy asked.

"The usual sort of haunt," I said. "Opens doors. Leaves cold drafts and eerie feelings in its wake."

"That ghost town isn't even real," Joy said. "How can it have a ghost?"

"Exactly," I said, and went to take a customer's order at the register.

By three o'clock, the crowd had thinned, and the decibel level dropped. With only the gamers and a few tourists nursing coffee in the pink booths, I turned to Petronella.

"Hey," I said, "we never had that talk."

"Oh." She bit her bottom lip, a very un-Petronella-like gesture, then straightened. "So, I started mortician training. Online."

"Congratulations!" Becoming a mortician had been a long-time dream of Petronella's. She was fantastic with our customers, especially the older ones, and I knew she'd do a great job working with families during their darkest hours.

"Riiight." She tapped her booted foot.

I blinked. "Oh! Do you need to change your hours for your studies?"

Her delicate nostrils flared. "No, it's online." She stared intently at me, as if willing me to . . . Actually, I had no idea what she wanted.

"Well, I'm really happy for you. I'll support you in any way I—"

"Don't you want me to stay?"

"Well, yes, sure. But—"

She sighed heavily. "Never mind. It's cool."

Tally Wally ambled to the counter, and she turned to chat with him.

Baffled, I ducked into my barren office.

I woke up my computer and dropped into the rolling chair behind my battered, metal desk. Charlene had been reluctant to dig up background information on Ewan and Bridget. I wasn't confident I'd discover anything online, but the Friths were suspects, and my detecting options were limited.

Bridget's social media pages were set to private. Aside from a website for her photography business, I couldn't find anything about her on the web. There was a bit more on Ewan—an article in the local paper about the grand opening of the Bar X and a few mentions from clients. Not really expecting to learn anything, I searched their names in the local court records, and Bridget's popped up.

Startled by my success, I clicked the case record number and a gray report lit my screen: DEVON BLACKETT vs. BRIDGET FRITH. Whoa. What?

I combed through the report—dates and titles of hearings with the occasional, sparse minutes. Last month Devon had started a lawsuit against Bridget.

For stalking.

My stomach curdled. Had Charlene known? Had Bridget's father?

I leaned back in my chair, and it emitted a grating screech. Court cases took time to get rolling. Devon had only worked at the Bar X for three months. Bridget would have had to put in some serious stalking time soon after Devon had arrived.

From the court filings, it looked like Devon had acted as his own attorney, so maybe that had sped the legal workings. And he'd only got as far as filing the complaint, so they weren't deep into the suit.

But *stalking*? I looked up the California stalking laws. Apparently, stalking was both a civil and a criminal offense. Why had Devon decided to go the civil route rather than press charges with the police?

I checked the court websites of other towns where Devon had worked but didn't find any similar suits. So, he wasn't one of those serial-lawsuit people.

Glancing at the clock, I realized I'd left Petronella alone longer than I'd meant to, and I hurried into the restaurant. I needn't have worried; a hoard of customers had not stampeded into Pie Town. A young couple exited, the bell above the door jingling in their wake.

Petronella reached for a plastic bin from behind the counter.

"I'll clear their table," I said. "You take a break. Sorry I was away so long."

She raked a hand over her hairnet, nearly invisible against her spiky black hair. "No problem." Yawning, she clomped into the kitchen.

I walked to the table and piled the bin with dirty tableware, then wiped the Formica.

A shadow passed in front of the window blinds, and I glanced up.

On the sidewalk, Heidi stood with her hand on Gordon's arm. The gym owner leaned closer, wrinkling his navy suit. Her head tilted coquettishly, a plaintive expression on her face.

My eyes narrowed. What the . . . ?

I shook myself. Ha. I wasn't jealous. Gordon wasn't my boyfriend. I had nothing to be jealous about. Nothing. At. All.

Gordon smiled at her. Disentangling himself, he nodded, patted her arm, and walked into Pie Town.

The bell jangled.

He stopped in the center of the checkerboard floor and frowned at the near-empty counter.

I cleared my throat and tried to ignore my internal lurch of excitement. "Hi."

He turned. "There you are. How are Charlene and Frederick recovering after last night?"

"Well, I think." She'd either spent the afternoon getting window replacement estimates or plotting revenge. "Speaking of Frederick, there were threads caught in his claws. We put them in a baggie in case you want them for evidence."

Gordon looked less than enthusiastic. "Sure. Drop them

by the station. But don't expect hot shot forensics like you see on TV."

We stared at each other.

I shuffled my feet.

"So. Heidi!" I said brightly. "I saw you talking outside. Is everything okay? She's not having trouble at the gym, is she?"

"In a manner of speaking. She's made a complaint about the dumpsters. Says you've been using hers."

I felt a quick stab of panic, then I shook my head. "What? Seriously?"

"Seriously. Have you been using her bins?"

"I have not." I gripped the plastic bin more tightly, its edges digging into my palms.

"Could one of your employees be dumping without you knowing?"

"No. They know better than that."

"They probably don't think it's that big a deal. Anyway, I told her I'd talk to you about it."

My brain throbbed. "We are not dumping in Heidi's bins." That woman wouldn't quit! I took a slow breath, counted to ten. "Sorry. I appreciate you talking to me about this instead of filing a formal complaint."

He shifted his weight. "Uh, by complaining to me, Heidi has filed a formal complaint. I have to submit a report."

"Oh." I forced a smile. "That's all right." That wasn't Gordon's fault either. He had to go by the book. It was one of the reasons I liked him. Though now that I thought of it, he'd been giving Charlene and I a lot of leeway with our "investigation."

He peered at me, his jade eyes intent. "How would it look if I neglected to file a complaint right before we went on a date?"

A date was still on the table? Huzzah! "Then, formally, I deny all charges. And if Heidi wants to go dumpster diving to try and prove her case, I'd love to see her try." The thought of Heidi covered in banana peels brought a half smile to my face.

His mouth quirked. "I'll make a note of it. Of your denial, not the suggested dumpster diving. About last night, I was a little hard on you—"

"No." I grimaced. "It's okay. You weren't wrong."

"Look. The first thing to do when entering a potentially dangerous situation is to assess the environment. That's true even when you're going to help an injured person. You need to identify any potential threats before acting."

Normally, I hated being told what to do. But his look of concern stopped me cold. "And I didn't do any of that." Even if I had, I still would have gone in for Charlene.

He glanced around the near-empty restaurant. Stepping closer, he lowered his voice, and it rumbled through me. "I really would like to go on that date sometime. So, don't get yourself killed. Or arrested."

"Okay." Yay, me. Queen of witty repartee. "Want some pie?"

"I can't today, but thanks." He patted his trim stomach. "I'm teaching a dive class tonight."

Petronella appeared in the window between the kitchen and the counter area. "Hey, cuz!"

He waved. "See ya, Pete!"

I watched him depart, and an odd twinge of disappointment shivered through me.

"So?" Petronella asked. "Are you two going to go on that date or what?"

My cheeks warmed. Did *everyone* in San Nicholas know about my thwarted love life? "Maybe. Probably."

"Better do it soon," she said.

"Why?" I wrung my hands in my apron. Did he have a better offer?

"Because someone's trying to kill you again, remember?"

Heidi strode past the window. Tossing her blond ponytail, she shot me a triumphant look. She'd had her bit of revenge with the dumpsters. If only the murderer at Bar X had taken such a simplistic approach.

I frowned, reflecting on that. Why had I connected revenge with the bartender's murder? I didn't have enough evidence to theorize on the killer's motive.

But it was time I got some.

Chapter Fourteen

I closed Pie Town and drove to my container on the bluff. Watching thin lines of waves power across the Pacific, I barbequed a burger and skewered veggies. A warm, twilight breeze caressed my bare arms. The scent of barbeque mingled with that of sagebrush and eucalyptus.

I ate, my plate balanced on the wide arm of my Adirondack chair. Beneath a sky slowly turning pink and tangerine, I read my new mystery novel. The evening darkened to cobalt, and then to an ebony sheen, my e-reader casting an eerie glow. A waning moon rode low on the horizon, and its silvery trail rippled across the ocean. My home might be cramped, but I knew people who'd kill for the view.

The night cooled, and I shrugged into one of Pie Town's, EAT PIE, NOT CAKE hoodies, unwilling to leave my chair.

My cell phone buzzed. I set my book on the broad arm of the chair and checked the screen. Charlene.

"Charlene, did you know that Devon was suing Bridget for stalking?"

"Shhh! You've got to help me," she whispered.

I sat up, knocking the e-reader to the grass. "What's wrong?"

"I'm trapped at Marla's house."

My brow wrinkled. "Trapped?"

"Trapped upstairs," she hissed. "I broke in . . . well, I didn't *break* in. I found her spare key. Now she's come home early, and the only way out is past her. You need to get over here and distract Marla, so I can sneak out. If she catches me, she'll have me arrested."

I rubbed my eyes. *Unbelievable.*

"Are you still there?" she asked.

"I'm here," I ground out. "Where are you?"

"I told you! At Marla's."

"I mean, what's her address?"

"Twenty-three-oh-four Cypress. And hur—"

The phone disconnected.

Because it wasn't a Sunday unless I was an accessory to one of Charlene's crimes, I grabbed my purse and keys.

Stomach burning with worry, I raced through town in my VW and crossed to the residential section beside the ocean. I should have seen this coming. Charlene had been obsessed with the idea of Marla as the killer. And in her mind, burglary didn't count if you could get your hands on a key.

Cypress Street ran along an ocean cliff lined with cypresses, twisted by the wind and creepy as all get-out in the darkness. I spotted Charlene's yellow Jeep, parked beneath a tree, and I slowed.

Outside the iron-gated driveway to 2304 Cypress, I whistled. The narrow drive sloped down to what looked like a private beach. Holy moly, Marla must be loaded.

Cranking down my window, I pulled up to a squawk box and pushed the yellow button.

After a moment, Marla's voice trilled over the intercom. "Yes? Who is it?"

"Hi, Marla. It's Val Harris from Pie Town."

"Yes?" she asked, her voice several degrees chillier.

I shifted beneath my seat belt. The gate was a problem.

I'd figured I'd be able to walk up to her front door and keep Marla busy there, not have to talk my way through a barricade. "I've discovered something in the course of our investigation, and I wanted to talk it over with you."

She laughed. "You mean you want to know what I know. Forget it. You and Charlene are going to have to do your own work."

My muscles relaxed. If she'd discovered Charlene, she'd have mentioned it by now. "I'm worried about Charlene," I said. "She's getting older, you know, and she's been behaving a little . . . um, erratically. You've known her for such a long . . . um, longer than I have." I made a face and sent a mental apology Charlene's way.

"Oh, she's definitely gotten crazier."

"I'd really like your advice." I waited, biting my bottom lip.

The intercom buzzed, and the iron gate swung open.

My shoulders sagged. I'd done it!

I inched the VW down the steep, winding driveway, my foot heavy on the brake.

At the base of the drive, I parked in front of a storybook-style house with gabled slate roofs and an actual turret. Lights glowed through diamond-paned windows. I imagined Charlene shimmying through them like an aged Rapunzel and shook my head. The place was no mansion, but it was big. It had to have tons of escape hatches and hiding places. I gnawed my bottom lip. How had Charlene gotten trapped?

I walked to the front door, intricately carved in a peacock design. An all-seeing eye had been cut over the peep hole. I guess it was meant to be a visual pun, but my flesh pebbled.

I knocked. Waited.

In the darkness below, the ocean waves crashed dully. To

my left was another iron gate, protecting a swimming pool lit Mediterranean blue.

I tapped my foot.

A seagull fluttered onto the Spanish tile roof and squawked.

I rubbed my arms beneath my hoodie. What was taking so long? Had Charlene gotten caught before I'd had a chance to—

The door swung open, and Marla looked down at me with a self-satisfied smile. She adjusted the collar of her long-sleeved blue turtleneck. In her wide-legged white pants, she looked like she was ready for a spin on her yacht.

"So, you're worried about Charlene," she said. "Poor dear. She's had such a difficult life. Come inside." She stepped aside, and I walked into a tiled foyer. A chandelier glittered from the arched, high ceiling. An air conditioner hummed, and I shivered.

"What a lovely home," I said, glancing at the curving staircase leading to the second floor. Was that where Charlene was trapped?

"I knew I'd return to San Nicholas someday, and I'd always wanted this house. Fortunately, when I did come back, the owners had just put it up for sale."

"You returned to San Nicholas? From where?"

Her laughter tinkled. She turned and walked through a wide archway and into a living room with floor-to-ceiling windows facing the ocean.

White lines of foam crept across its dark surface, and in spite of the tension twisting my gut, my heart hitched with joy. The ocean always had that effect on me.

"It's a lovely retirement community," she said, "but San Nicholas is not the sort of place one *stays*. There's simply nothing here. I'm sure you've noticed."

"My pie shop's kept me too busy to think about it."

"Oh, yes. Pie Town." Her lips curled, and she sat in a fat white chair facing the archway and the staircase. She pulled down the hems of her sleeves to cover her knuckles. "And poor Charlene is breaking her back in the kitchen. At her age, she should be retired and on a cruise."

A soft, high-pitched wail floated from the upstairs, and my neck muscles bunched.

Frowning, Marla sat forward.

"Yes, about Charlene," I said quickly, and sat opposite her on a cream-colored divan. "She's gotten more obsessed than usual about this case at the Bar X. Do you have any idea why that might be?"

"Why doesn't matter. It never matters."

"Motive kind of does in a murder investigation. Not that Charlene's—"

"That's wrong thinking." She tossed her well-coiffed hair. "People are always looking for excuses. Why, why, why. My mother was mean to me, so I can't help it if I stuff my face with candy every day. My father was distant, so it's not my fault if I can't maintain a decent relationship. It's enough to know you've got the habit to break it."

I shrank into the soft cushions. My father had been so distant, I hadn't seen him since I was three. Was that why . . . ?

I got a grip on myself. "And you think that applies to Charlene?" I had to get Marla's focus away from the foyer stairs. Rising, I edged to the window overlooking the ocean. A trail of moonlight lit a path to Marla's porch. Pots of geraniums sprouted from the wooden deck. "What a great view. Oh, hey, is that a whale?"

She didn't take the bait, sticking like a barnacle to her seat. "You have good eyes if you can see one at night, but it's possible. It's the right time of year."

"Sorry, it's a pod of dolphins," I lied, my voice strained. "Wow. It's huge. There must be hundreds."

"That's the ocean, dear. Now I believe you had a point in coming here?"

"Right, yeah. I was asking about Charlene."

"Oh, Charlene! Where to start?"

"It might be easier if we started with the relationships at the Bar X," I said.

She wagged a bejeweled and bedazzling finger at me. "If you're trying to get me to divulge my investigation findings, naughty, naughty."

"I'm only trying to understand why Charlene is so passionate about this case."

She sniffed. "Well, there's that silly ghost story. She's always been gullible when it comes to the paranormal."

The stairs creaked.

Her expression sharpened, and she turned toward the sound.

My heartbeat accelerated. "I wouldn't exactly say she's gullible."

"Wouldn't you?" She relaxed in her chair and again tugged down the sleeves of her navy turtleneck. "But if you want to know about the Bar X, I suppose her obsession boils down to, well, me. We've always been rivals, and I've always beaten her, and it drives her crazy. What am I supposed to do? Not live up to my full potential to make Charlene feel better? It isn't my fault her life is pathetic."

I scrunched my face, hoping Charlene wasn't listening. "Would you mind if we go out on your deck? It's such a gorgeous night." I touched the brushed-nickel latch on the glass door.

"A little cold, if you ask me."

"You think?" I asked, desperate. What would it take to peel the woman away from her staircase view?

"About Charlene," she said, "do you really believe she's gone senile?"

"Well . . . uh . . . mm," I stammered. The only thing that interested the woman was dissing Charlene. Charlene, who at this moment was creeping down the curved stairs. Charlene, Charlene. I pointed at the cliffs. "Oh, my God! Is that someone on the cliffs?" I pressed my face to the cool glass. "It looks like Charlene!"

Marla leapt from her chair and hurried to join me. "Where? Where?"

"On the left and up, in that strip of moonlight." I tugged on the lock. Why wouldn't the stupid handle budge? "It's hard to see from this angle." Finally, the lock flipped up, and I slid open the glass door. A draft of cool, salty air flooded the living room, and I strode onto the wooden deck. I leaned over the railing and pointed. "See? Over there?" There was no one on the cliffs, but if I looked stupid, so be it. If Charlene was where I thought she was, sneaking into the foyer, it shouldn't take long for her to reach the front door.

Marla squinted. "Oh, my goodness, yes. Is that Charlene?"

Brow furrowing, I pulled slightly away and glanced at her, then at the cliffs. I didn't see anyone. "Yes! By that cypress with the exposed roots sticking out of the cliffs. Am I imagining a person there?"

"Goodness, no. We should call the police. I can't believe Charlene would be so—"

From behind us came a thunk, a crash, a howl.

Her eyes widened. "What on earth?" She raced inside.

Dreading what I'd find, I raced after her.

Charlene lay sprawled in the foyer rubbing her ankle. By the closed front door, Frederick arched his back, his snowy fur standing on end. He yowled.

Marla grasped her wrist and cowered against the wall. "That cat! Get that animal out of here!"

Frederick hissed and spat like he'd spotted the neighbor's dog. Granted, Frederick had just gone ass over teakettle with Charlene—unsettling for any cat. But I'd seen him take worse and slide into a nap. He only went after people he had a real grudge against. And I didn't believe for a second he was merely picking up on Charlene's animosity.

I looked from Marla to Frederick to Charlene, and the pieces clicked into place. All that business with the long sleeves now made sense.

"Forget the cat." Charlene grimaced, rocking on the tile floor. "I think I sprained my ankle."

Marla stared at my piecrust maker as if seeing her for the first time. "You. You! You're like the mark of doom I can't escape. Everywhere I go, everything I do, you're there! I can't catch a break! Is this payback for last night?"

Bingo! "You were the one who broke into Charlene's house last night," I said.

"And look what that animal did to me." She jerked up her sleeve, exposing deep red scratches on the back of one hand. "What if I get cat scratch fever?"

Charlene shook her finger. "I hope you do."

"I should sue! That animal belongs in the pound."

"I should sue you for twisting my ankle on your stupid staircase," Charlene said. "It's a hazard!"

Marla sneered. "Do you really think your lawyer is better than mine?"

A headache flared at the front of my skull. "Ladies, you each broke into each other's houses. There will be no suing."

"Why not?" Marla said. "Two wrongs don't make a right."

"Because you'll both look ridiculous," I said. "Do you think the press won't pick up the story?" I was fairly certain they wouldn't, but I was betting the two women were egotistical enough to assume they were newsworthy.

Marla turned on Charlene. "What are you doing in my house?"

"Looking for evidence, you dolt," Charlene snarled.

"Trying to steal my work?" Marla asked.

"Your work? You killed that boy, and I'm going to prove it." Charlene jut her chin forward.

Marla's face reddened. "I *killed* him? *I* killed him? You're insane!"

"Go ahead," Charlene said. "Call the police. It will just give them an excuse to search this overblown bordello."

I helped Charlene stand and wrangled Frederick. He went limp in my arms, feigning sleep. "Okay, Charlene, why do you think Marla killed Devon?"

She shot me a look of annoyance. Then her expression cleared, and she nodded. "Marla was with Ewan and I when Devon was presumably shot." She grasped the wrought-iron bannister for balance. "Marla knows her way around a gun. She joined a fancy gun club and did a photo shoot for one of those gun magazines back in the seventies. She could have killed Devon earlier, then rigged a gun to go off at a later time, giving her an alibi."

Marla folded her arms. "And exactly where was this mythical rigged gun?"

"After the gunshot," Charlene said, "you didn't follow Ewan and I right away to see what had happened. You lagged behind, because you already knew."

"Of course, I didn't go after you two," she said. "Only a complete idiot would run into a gunfight."

My cheeks warmed.

"You went to get your rigged gun, and then hid it," Charlene said.

"I waited where you two *abandoned* me," Marla said, "by the carriage house. That trick shooter, Curly, was leading his horse back, and we stopped to talk. You can ask him."

"How do we know he's telling the truth?" Charlene hopped forward, using the bannister as a crutch. "He could be your accomplice. Maybe he loosened his horse's shoe as an excuse to leave target practice."

"Which direction was he coming from?" I asked, determined to be the voice of cool reason.

"How should I know?" Marla asked.

"You're a detective now, aren't you?" Charlene said. "What was your relationship with Devon Blackett?"

"I didn't have a relationship with him," she said.

"Someone told us they saw you arguing," Charlene said.

Marla huffed. "That stupid bartender refused to infuse the *mezcal* with bacon fat. What sort of bartender at a western-themed event venue would refuse to do that? He said he didn't know how, but all he had to do was go online to figure it out. I took it up with Ewan, and he said he'd infuse the *mezcal* himself. For me." She stroked the hollow of her neck and smiled. "Problem solved."

"You can infuse alcohol with bacon fat?" I asked, intrigued. Nearly everything was better with bacon. But booze?

Charlene's fists clenched. "Why did you break into my house?"

Marla clamped her lips together.

"Tell me," Charlene said, "or I will call the cops, consequences be damned."

Marla looked away. "I wanted to see your notebook."

"My casebook? You wanted a look at the notes on our investigation! You cheat!"

"All's fair in love and murder."

"But you didn't find the book." Charlene raised a self-satisfied eyebrow. "I keep it hidden."

"If it hadn't been for that stupid cat, I would have. I knew it was in the freezer. That's where you keep all your important documents."

Charlene's face sagged, her mouth gaping. "It's not . . . You don't know anything!"

"Okay." I shifted Frederick over my shoulder. "This sounds like a simple misunderstanding. We'll be laughing about it over drinks next year."

"Oh, no, we won't," Charlene said darkly.

"If you think I'd slug down Moscow Mules with her," Marla said, "you've got another think coming."

I tugged Charlene toward the arched front door. "This is a tempest in a teapot. Much ado about nothing. All's well that ends well." Bustling my limping piecrust maker outside, I closed the front door with my heel.

I helped her into my VW, and we puttered up the driveway, the engine wheezing and straining.

She plucked a snoring Frederick from my shoulder and draped him across hers.

We crept toward the iron gate. Would Marla keep us locked inside? Call the police? But when we neared, the iron gate opened automatically. I pushed my back deeper into the car's seat, flexing my hands on the wheel.

On the street, I pulled in behind Charlene's Jeep, a silhouette hunched on the side of the narrow road. "Charlene, what were you thinking?"

"I'm thinking Marla's a big fat liar."

"You can't go breaking into people's houses!"

"It wasn't a person's house. It was Marla's."

"She had every right to call the cops."

"I'm sure your Detective Carmichael would have smoothed things over."

My nostrils flared. "I'm not. Heidi complained to him

that Pie Town was using her dumpster. He had to file a formal complaint."

"Meh." One corner of her lips curled. "They'll never prove it."

"What do you mean prove it? Charlene, did you use the gym's dumpster?"

"I had to get rid of my brush clippings somewhere. My cans were full."

"Charlene—"

"Wait here." Limp gone, she sprang from my VW and strode to her Jeep.

Perfect. Just perfect. Now I had to apologize to Heidi the Horrible. I slammed my palm on the wheel and pain shot through my arm. "Ow." I couldn't even lose my temper without hurting myself.

Opening the Jeep's rear door, Charlene pulled out an expensive-looking camera and returned to my car.

"Now I have to apologize to Heidi," I complained.

"Why would you do that?"

"Because—"

She pulled a camera memory card from the pocket of her black tunic.

I groaned. "Don't tell me you got that from Marla's house."

"Stole it out of her camera. Don't you remember? She was taking pictures the day of the murder. I'll bet there's something incriminating on here."

Charlene!!! I struggled for calm. "If Marla was the killer, she'd hardly take pictures of herself committing murder." But I flipped on my overhead light for a better look. What was done was done. It would be silly to ignore potential evidence.

She slipped the memory card out of her own camera and replaced it with Marla's. "Right. Hers isn't the sort of camera that works with a selfie stick. She may have captured other evidence from that morning."

Turning on her camera, Charlene leaned across the seat and held it so we could both view the small LCD screen. She flipped through the photos. The most recent ones were indeed from the ranch.

I squinted. "If there's anything here, it's too small for me to see."

She pressed a button and another picture flickered onto the screen. Devon grinning from a bed. Thankfully, he was clothed.

She laughed. "Hoo hoo! That's Marla's bed! I recognize the duvet."

"You went into her bedroom?"

"How do you think I got trapped upstairs? This proves there was more between Marla and Devon than just a bad cocktail."

Unfortunately, it did. "Can I see the camera?"

"Don't accidentally delete anything," she warned.

I clicked through the pictures, returning to those from the ranch and a wide shot of its "main" street.

I gasped. There I was, leaning inside the Jeep for the pies. Was my butt that big? Maybe I really had put on a few pounds.

I shook my head. *Focus*. Because on the same image, a man walked into the passage between the saloon and the bath house next door. "There's someone by the saloon— a man—but I can't make him out."

"You can zoom with these cameras." She snatched it from me and pressed another button. The image of the man enlarged.

"Larry," we said simultaneously.

"He lied," I said. "He told us he was nowhere near the saloon that day. Are you sure these were taken the day of the murder?"

"Sure, I'm sure," she said. "There's a time stamp. Plus, look, the picture right before it is of me and Ewan, and then the picture afterward is of Ewan in the carriage houses."

"Larry lied," I repeated.

"Well, he is a used car salesman. What do you expect?"

"I expect . . . we need to talk to him tomorrow and get the truth."

Chapter Fifteen

Master of avoidance, I shilly-shallied on the sidewalk outside Heidi's gym.

A Monday morning of freedom stretched before me. Pie Town was closed today, and normally, I'd spend Monday running errands and/or sprawled in my Adirondack chair. But I had to talk to Heidi, because *someone* had decided to use her dumpster without permission.

Bracing myself, I walked past the SUGAR KILLS sign and into the gym.

A smiling twentysomething in a green HEIDI'S HEALTH AND FITNESS golf shirt looked up. She splayed her hands on the frosted-glass counter. "Hi! Welcome to Heidi's Health and Fitness! Would you like to learn about a gym membership?"

I tried not to roll my eyes. The clerks asked me this every time I came in here. Not that I came in that often. "No, thanks. Is Heidi here? It's about the dumpsters."

The woman's expression soured, her lips pinching. "I'll check." She whisked through a door behind the counter and into a back room.

A few minutes later, Heidi emerged. "Yes?"

My heartbeat grew loud in my ears. "Morning, Heidi. How's it going?"

Her blond ponytail twitched. "I'm teaching a yoga class in ten minutes."

"Okay. I'll get right to it then." I shuffled my feet. "So, it seems I have to apologize. It turns out that someone on my staff did use your dumpster without permission."

"Who?"

"I don't think that's important."

"Was it that batty Charlene?"

I gripped the counter. "The point is, I've spoken to the staff, and it won't happen again."

"And how are you going to compensate me?"

"Compensate?" Did she want me to pay her by the square foot? Had she weighed and measured the felonious garbage?

"Compensate."

Somehow, I didn't think she'd accept a pie. "I . . . what exactly were you thinking?"

She leaned closer, her blue eyes narrowing. "Fifty."

"Dollars?"

"Pushups."

I looked at the green-carpeted floor and brushed a loose hank of my hair over one ear. "You want me to do fifty pushups?"

"Are you deaf *and* out of shape?"

"I'm not doing pushups."

"Scared?"

"I'm not scared." I regularly lugged around fifty-pound sacks of flour, though I lived for the day I could hire someone to do that for me. "I'm just . . . This is ridiculous. It's a silly . . ." I puffed out my cheeks. "Look, I'm sorry about the dumpster. It won't happen again."

She walked around the counter. "And how will you compensate me?"

"I don't—"

"Your employee jammed my dumpster full of tree limbs, and I had to pay to get them carted away."

"How much did it cost? Of course, I'll repay you."

"I don't care about the money. I want fifty, or I call the cops on Charlene."

"You wouldn't." What Charlene had done was annoying and wrong, but the cops?

"Try me."

"Fine." I huffed. "I'll do the pushups, but only if you promise that the next time you've got an issue with Pie Town, you come to me before the police."

She sneered. "Done."

Maybe Heidi had a sense of humor after all. Pushups wouldn't be so bad. It had been a while since I'd done any, but I had great muscle tone.

"Drop and give me fifty!" she bellowed.

"What? Here?"

"Move it!"

"Can't we do this later? Don't you have a yoga class to get to? I wouldn't want to—"

"Shall I just call Detective Carmichael now about the dumpsters?"

Mentally cursing Charlene, I scrambled to the carpet and got on all fours.

"Get off your knees!" she shouted. "What are you? A girl?"

A cluster of well-clad gym rats gathered in the entrance to the weight room and stared.

"ONE!" she roared.

I did a pushup.

"What is that?" she asked. "Your arms should be at a ninety-degree angle! TWO!"

I dipped.

"Get your ass out of the air! THREE!"

I panted, my stomach going rock hard. Cripes! Apparently, pie lifting didn't build pushup muscles. By number fifteen, I was panting. My movements slowed, but I closed my eyes and kept going.

"TWENTY-FIVE!"

My arms trembled. I blinked sweat from my eyes.

"FORTY-FOUR, FORTY-FIVE, LOWER!"

A group of weightlifters cheered. "You can do it!" someone shouted.

Heidi spun on her expensive exercise shoes and glared at the offender. My cheerleader cringed and drifted into the weight room.

"Forty-seven," I gasped.

"Forty-six," Heidi said.

Hells bells. I lowered myself toward the ground. Forty-seven!

It was only fifty pushups. No problem-o. But the carpet looked soft, inviting. It smelled good too. They'd recently vacuumed it and must have used one of those lavender-scented powders. All I wanted to do was drop and stay down.

"Forty-eight," she said, "forty-nine . . . forty-nine . . . forty-nine . . . I said a ninety-degree angle!"

"Come on," I muttered, and forced myself lower. And up.

"Fifty," she said reluctantly.

I collapsed onto the carpet.

There was a smattering of applause.

"So," I panted. "We're good?"

Her mouth twisted. "For now."

I staggered outside and leaned against Pie Town's cool, brick wall. My knees buckled, and I bumped to the sidewalk. Spent, my arms flopped to my sides.

"You look like something the cat dragged in." Charlene

strode down the sidewalk, Frederick draped over her shoulder. She wore a violet tunic, brown leggings, and matching violet sneakers. "What are you doing on the ground?"

"Resting."

"Why do you need rest? You never do anything that works up a sweat."

I compressed my mouth. *Ignore it. Ignore it.* "Are you ready?" Charlene's theft of the memory card and my discovery of Devon's lawsuit had finally given our case direction. At least today, I could investigate without stressing over Pie Town.

"My car's around the corner."

Stumbling to my feet, I followed her to the sunshine-yellow Jeep and got inside.

We drove down Main Street and turned onto the One.

I braced my rubbery arm on the Jeep's open window, adjusted my sunglasses, and inhaled. Eucalyptus and ocean and a cool breeze on my damp skin. Heaven.

We dropped by Larry's car lot and met a wall. His nephew informed us that Larry'd taken the morning off to go riding at the Bar X.

So, there we headed in Charlene's Jeep. She tore down the winding track. California poppies clustered along the side of the dirt road, their petals tossing in our wake.

The Jeep roared through the open gates to the Bar X. In my lap, Frederick's ears twitched, his eyes firmly closed.

"How'd you break into Marla's house anyway?" I asked.

She accelerated over a pothole, and I bounced in my seat. Frederick dug his claws into my thighs.

Wincing, I disentangled them from the fabric of my jeans.

"I told you, breaking in would be illegal," she said. "I found her spare key under a rock."

I imagined Marla's front yard. There'd been a lot of rocks. And flower pots. "How did you find the right rock?"

"When I realized her key wasn't under the doormat or any of the flower pots, I used the hose." She cut a tight turn, hurling me against the side door.

"The hose," I repeated. Was that a code?

"It was on one of those wheely things. I pulled the hose straight out until it reached a rock and checked beneath it. Sure enough, that was the rock with the key. People use the hose so they can remember where they've hidden their spare." Her lip curled. "Marla may know my freezer trick, but I've got her number."

"When she figures out where her camera's memory card went, she'll have yours."

"You want evidence, don't you?"

I gripped the seat belt. What I wanted was an ejection seat with a parachute attached.

We screeched into the ghost town. The street was empty, the buildings shuttered.

"Don't be such a worry wart," she said.

"Whenever you tell me not to worry, is exactly the time I should be."

"Worrying is a waste of time. Marla won't notice the card's gone for a while. Those cameras have internal memory, you know."

She pulled up beside the cutesy wooden chapel and parked. Our dust cloud settled around the Jeep.

Resolutely, I turned my head away from the narrow, clapboard church. "I thought we were meeting Ewan at his house?" I stepped from the Jeep. A warm breeze blew the dust into my face. Faintly, the church bell clanged.

"That coach ride is only an excuse." She slammed her door. "It's Larry we want."

"And Bridget," I said. Charlene might not want to hear it, but Ewan's daughter remained a suspect.

She adjusted the collar of her violet tunic. "I don't care

what the court website said. She's no stalker, and she had nothing to do with that bartender's death."

"Maybe." I walked toward the carriage house. Its doors hung open, so presumably Larry was inside. "But Devon accused her of stalking, and we need to know why."

"Just don't say anything in front of Ewan."

"I won't." If Bridget was keeping the lawsuit quiet, I wouldn't blow the whistle. But I didn't see how she could keep the secret from her father . . . short of killing Devon. I twisted my watch, its band damp against my skin.

We strolled inside the carriage house. The scents of warm hay and fresh manure twined around us, and I sneezed. Horses whickered in their stalls. The coach sat in its place, but the carriage house was otherwise empty.

Returning outside, I stared down the dirt road. The door to the photography shack stood open.

"What?" Charlene asked.

"I'm going to talk to Bridget."

She lowered her head and stared at me, her voice hardening. "Bridget is no stalker. And she's not a killer either."

"Then she won't mind answering some questions."

"We'll talk to Bridget together."

"Fine," I said.

"Fine."

I strode down the road.

Charlene speed walked, edging ahead of me.

I sped up.

She quickened her pace.

"What are we doing?" I asked, passing a stand of eucalyptus trees.

"I'm going to talk to her first."

I panted. "Seriously? We're doing this?"

We lurched through the photography shop's open door. Our shoulders collided in the narrow entry.

Bridget raised her head from an old-timey camera on a

tripod. She squinted, deepening the lines around her eyes. "Hello?"

I smoothed my Pie Town T-shirt: WHEN IN DOUBT, EAT PIE! "Hi, Bridget. How's—"

"What's with the lawsuit?" Charlene said, and glared at me.

Flushing, Bridget drew her hands through her loose, blond hair. "I don't . . . you . . . How did you find out?"

"Nosy Nancy here found Devon's suit on a court website." Charlene jerked her thumb at me.

Someone knocked on the door, and we turned to look.

Marla glowered in the open doorway, hands on her slim hips, diamond rings flashing. "Where is it?"

Charlene's eyes widened, innocent. "Where's what?"

"You know what!"

Charlene smirked. "And I know what's on it too, so you'd better keep a civil tongue in your head, little Miss Jaguar."

"You . . . you . . . ," Marla spluttered.

"What's going on?" Bridget's gaze ping-ponged between the two older women.

"Dementia, I suspect." I angled my head toward the door. "Have you got a minute?"

We walked outside, leaving Marla and Charlene to argue about memory cards and criminal behavior.

"Are they okay?" Bridget edged into the shade of the eucalyptus trees.

"It depends on how you define 'okay.' I don't think they'll break anything or each other, if that's what you're worried about."

She folded her arms over her white blouse. "So. What did you want to talk about?"

"The lawsuit."

"Look, it was a mistake." She jammed her hands into the rear pockets of her jeans. "I wasn't stalking anyone. I mean,

Devon and I worked together, so we saw each other a lot, and he somehow got the wrong impression."

Why didn't I believe that? I had a hard time picturing Bridget as a stalker, but I didn't know any stalkers to compare her to. "How would Devon get that idea?"

"I don't know. He was just weird."

"How was he weird?"

"I don't know." She motioned helplessly. "He just was!"

Her denials were less and less convincing. "I'm surprised he stuck around the Bar X if he thought you were harassing him."

"He said he didn't want to lose a good job. And like I said, I wasn't harassing him."

A crow settled on a branch above us. A eucalyptus leaf drifted from the swaying branch and landed on Bridget's shoulder.

"Did your father know about the lawsuit?" If he had, could Ewan have given Devon a pass on his shenanigans with the liquor as a way to soften Devon's attitude toward the family, and maybe drop the lawsuit?

"No!" Her face paled. "You can't say anything. Look, if you found out about the suit, I'm sure the police know as well. There's no reason to tell anyone, especially not my dad. It would only upset him."

"How do you know Devon didn't say anything to your father?"

She bit her lower lip. "Because he . . . He wouldn't. It would make working together even more uncomfortable."

"It sounds like you weren't very worried about the lawsuit."

"No one likes being sued. But I talked it over with Devon, and we cleared the air. He was going to drop the complaint. And then he died."

How convenient for Bridget. "Did he have conflicts with anyone else?"

A shot cracked, and I flinched. Bridget didn't respond to the sound, so I figured Curly or Moe was practicing.

"Other stalking lawsuits you mean?" Her pale brow furrowed. "I don't know. I guess you could find out about others the same place you found out about mine."

"I did check and didn't find any other suits he'd filed."

Marla stormed from the photography studio and headed down the dirt road. She disappeared behind the carriage house. A minute later, she reemerged on the hillside road to Ewan's house.

Charlene banged open the door to the photography studio and glowered at me.

What had *I* done?

Bridget shrugged. "Well, there you go. He didn't have any other lawsuits. Listen, I've got to get back to work. Okay?" She walked into the photography studio.

Harumph. She was so lying.

"Marla is impossible," Charlene said. "You would not believe what she had the gall to say to me."

"What did she say?"

"She said . . ." She breathed heavily. "Never mind what she said!"

"Did you return her memory card?"

"Can you believe she wanted my fingerprints?"

I wandered toward the carriage house. "She knows you broke into her house."

"That's not the point, and I didn't break in. I told you, I had a key. What did Bridget say?"

"That Devon was crazy, and there was no basis for the lawsuit."

"See? I told you it was nothing."

"I don't think she was telling the truth." A trickle of sweat dripped down my back. It was going to be another hot one, and I looked forward to San Nicholas's natural AC—the ocean fog—kicking in.

"If she said he was nuts," Charlene said, "then he was nuts."

"She also said that if I'd found out about the lawsuit, then the cops must know too. She's right. And she's going to need a better answer for them than she gave me."

A breeze rustled the treetops, scenting the air with eucalyptus.

Charlene's forehead creased. "She wouldn't stalk someone. She's a good girl."

"She's no more a girl than I am." Bridget had to be fifteen or so years older than me.

The carriage house doors stood open, and I detoured inside. Something clunked, metallic.

"Hello?" I called. "Larry, is that you?"

Moe backed from an empty horse stall, his checked shirt-sleeves rolled to his elbows, his face pink with sweat.

"Oh, hi." I edged past the coach. "I heard Larry was going riding today. I thought he might be here."

"Answer an argument for us," Charlene said. "Was Devon the nutty sort who might think a girl was obsessed with him when she wasn't?"

He blinked. Rubbing his hand over his head, he knocked his cowboy hat to the straw-covered floor. "What?"

"Devon, the bartender," Charlene said.

"He's dead." Moe grasped the low wall of one of the stalls and sagged sideways.

"No kidding," Charlene said. "We know he's dead."

Moe's legs folded beneath him, and he thudded to the ground. "Oh, my God."

"Are you all right?" I approached him slowly. Moe didn't look good; his chin sunk to his chest.

He bowed forward, his stomach bulging beneath his blue, checked shirt.

"I've seen this before," Charlene said. "He's left the denial stage about the murder. Funny, it usually doesn't take this long for reality to set in, but everyone reacts differently to tragedy."

Curly led his horse into the carriage house. Between his bulky form and sunburned face, he looked like a fireplug in cowboy boots. "Larry finally shoed Prince, and we're back in business." He stopped short, staring at his partner. "What are you doing on the floor?"

Moe pointed a shaking finger toward the open stall.

Frowning, I walked to the compartment.

Inside it, Larry lay on the straw. He stared, open-mouthed, at the beamed ceiling. Blood covered his face, darkened the hay.

"Charlene!" Shaky, I dropped to my knees and grasped Larry's wrist. The flesh was warm, but I couldn't find a pulse. *Not again.* I swayed, dizzy, and rose, backing from the horse stall and bumping into Charlene.

"What happened?" Curly rubbed his broad hand across his jowls.

"Another man's been murdered." Charlene pulled a cell phone from the pocket of her violet tunic and dialed. "I'm calling the police."

"What? But . . ." He looked to Moe. "What happened?"

Moe shook his head. "The stall door was open," he croaked. "I looked in and saw him. I thought Larry was alive, messing around, but he's not."

Charlene walked past the coach to the open carriage house door and spoke low into the phone.

"Curly," I said, trying to get a grip, "why don't you go to the main house? You can tell Ewan what's happened, and that Charlene is calling the police."

"Yeah," he said. "Yeah. Moe, are you all right?"

Moe swallowed. "I'm fine. Go ahead. I'm fine."

Curly didn't budge.

Charlene returned with a checked, wool blanket. "You're

in shock." She draped the blanket over Moe's shoulders. "The police will be here in fifteen minutes."

Another body. Another murder. My breath turned shallow. Larry had been near the saloon when Devon had been killed. He must have seen something.

I'd also been near the saloon, near enough to get a pie shot out of my hands. Did the killer think I'd seen something too? "But I didn't see anything," I blurted.

Charlene patted my shoulder. "It's okay. I didn't see Larry either when we first looked into the carriage house. We didn't search the stalls. Why would we have? Larry was probably lying here the whole time. If we'd noticed sooner . . ." She sighed. "No, it's no use thinking that way. This isn't your fault, Val."

"Maybe it was an accident," Moe said. "That was his horse's stall. The horse could have kicked him in the head and bolted."

"Under the circumstances, I doubt that's likely," Charlene said. "Don't you?"

"I should find his horse." Moe rose, and the blanket cascaded from his shoulders to the straw. "It's got to be panicked. Could be hurt."

"Curly, go with him," Charlene said, stern. "Then get Ewan."

"Right," Curly said. "Sure." He and Moe wandered from the carriage house.

"Do you think Moe's okay?" I asked.

"Quick, search for clues before the cops arrive." She snapped pictures of the body with her cell phone.

"I don't think so," I said. "We shouldn't go inside the stall. We'll contaminate evidence."

"You've already been in the stall," she said.

"Because I'd thought he might still be alive." I rubbed the back of my neck, my muscles jumping. If I'd really been thinking, I would have known immediately he was dead.

"Fine. We'll play it your way." She raised her camera high over her head and shot down into the stall, then paced the carriage house, taking more photos.

I walked to the open wooden doors and leaned heavily against their rough frame. Another man dead, and someone I slightly knew. I tried to swallow, couldn't. A breeze tossed the tops of the eucalyptus trees in a silent wave.

"Is it a coincidence," I said, "that all the suspects are at the Bar X again? Marla, you, me, Ewan, Bridget, Curly, and Moe?"

"And Larry." She glanced at the body. "Don't forget him."

Forget Larry? The image of his broken body was burned into my brain. I couldn't forget if I wanted to.

And I wanted to.

Chapter Sixteen

Gordon strode into the carriage house. A phalanx of uniformed police officers followed, their movements quick, decisive.

Relief unspooled inside me. Though it had only taken him ten minutes to get to the Bar X, it had seemed an eternity. I had to force myself not to hurtle into his arms for a comforting hug. Someone had killed again, killed someone I *knew*, and a sick, creeping malaise hung over us all.

Gordon stopped short and stared.

Moe held the bridle of a palomino mare. Ewan stood, expression grim, one hand braced on the coach. Marla peeked over the ghost town owner's left shoulder, her hands clamped on his arm. Curly slumped against a closed stall. I tried to look inconspicuous and edged behind Charlene.

One of us was a killer.

Gordon zeroed in on me. "Why aren't I surprised? Wait, let me guess." He raised his index finger. "You thought a stroll through the carriage house would be fun and just happened to stumble across a body. No, hold it. You were on the hunt for the Bar X Phantom, and a corpse threw itself into your path."

I winced. It wasn't as if we'd been looking for a body.

Charlene stuck her nose in the air. "We were invited here for a carriage ride."

Ewan cleared his throat. "I did invite them both. I'd meant to give them a ride the other day, but then the coach got loose and, uh, nearly ran down Val." His gaze cut sideways.

"Where is Mr. Pelt?" Gordon asked.

Ewan nodded toward the open stall door.

Gordon stalked to it and studied the corpse. "Someone's missing."

"Pardon?" Ewan asked.

"It looks like everyone's here but—"

"What's going on?" Bridget halted inside the carriage house's tall, open doors, her eyes wide. Backlit by the sun, her long shadow writhed across the straw-covered floor.

"And now we've got a full house," Gordon said. He jerked his chin toward the uniformed officers. "Secure the scene. Separate the witnesses. You know the drill. Miss Harris, you're with me." He walked into the sunlight without waiting to see if I followed.

After a worried glance at Charlene, I trotted after him. We stopped in the shade of the carriage house.

Gordon stared down the dusty street. "Why does it always have to be you?"

"I didn't find the body. Moe did. Charlene and I walked into the carriage house right after he found Larry."

"What were you doing here in the first place?"

"We really were invited for a coach ride."

His gaze turned flinty.

"And I might have asked Bridget about Devon's lawsuit," I admitted.

"So, you found out about that, did you?"

"It must have been uncomfortable for them both, with Devon suing the boss's daughter for stalking. Do you think her father knew?"

A muscle jumped in his jaw.

I jammed my hands in my jeans pockets and told myself to shut up. But the words kept flowing, a nervous prattle. "It sounds bogus to me. Outside of *Fatal Attraction*, I can't imagine there are a lot of women stalkers."

He rolled his eyes. "You have no idea. Women do it all the time, and it's even easier now with the Internet."

"Seriously?" My muscles relaxed. We were talking again. I couldn't blame him for being irritated, but it wasn't an emotion I'd hoped to evoke.

"I worked a case recently where an old girlfriend went after her ex's new girlfriend. She messed with her college application, the works. It wasn't hard to catch the stalker, but it made a mess of the new girl's life."

"That's terrible," I said. "Is the world getting stranger, or am I imagining things?"

"Definitely stranger." He ran his hand over his crewcut. "Are you all right?"

I nodded, a long way from all right.

"What happened here?" he asked, all business.

I could be professional too. "I can't tell you much beyond what I already have. Charlene and I did look inside the carriage house when we first arrived, around ten o'clock. We didn't see anyone, but we only stuck our heads in. If Larry was already lying dead in that stall, we wouldn't have noticed his body."

"What were you looking for in the carriage house?"

"The doors were open, and we'd planned a coach ride." I nodded toward Charlene's yellow Jeep, parked beside the chapel. "We thought Ewan might be inside," I fudged.

"Was anyone hanging around the carriage house?"

"No," I said, determined to be helpful. And not just because of the promised date, which I really shouldn't have been thinking about at a murder scene. In my defense, there was something appealing about Gordon's take-charge attitude. "Bridget was in her photography studio." I pointed down the road to the small, wooden shack. "Marla showed up there as well, and Bridget and I stepped outside to chat while Charlene and Marla, er, caught up. I didn't notice anyone going into or out of the carriage house." I bit the inside of my cheek. "But there are two entrances—front and back—and both were open. I only had a view of the former." The carriage house was a big, two-story building that housed horses and a coach. Someone could have easily entered and exited through the rear, and I would never have noticed.

"Did you see anyone else around the Bar X?"

"No, only the people you saw in the carriage house."

"What time did you and Charlene find Moe and the body?"

"I guess about twenty minutes ago." A good detective wouldn't have to guess, because she'd have checked her watch.

"What was Moe doing when you found him?"

"Hyperventilating. He seemed stunned, disoriented."

Gordon drew a notepad from the inside pocket of his suit jacket. "That's to be expected. He and Larry knew each other well, didn't they?"

"They'd had a falling out, but I guess you already knew that. According to Larry, it was a misunderstanding. Curly's confirmed that."

"Did you go inside the stall?" He made a notation.

I tugged at the collar of my T-shirt. "At first, I wasn't sure if Larry was dead or hurt, so I went inside to check his pulse. Aside from that, I didn't touch anything."

"Then what happened?"

"Charlene called the police from her cell phone. Moe looked shaky. Curly showed up—"

"Did either of them go inside the stall?"

"Not that I saw," I said. "Anyway, Moe was worried

about Larry's horse, because it was missing from its stall. So, he and Curly went to look for it. They must have found it, because Ewan, Moe, and Curly led that palomino into the carriage house right before you arrived."

"How did Ewan come on the scene?"

"I'm not sure. We'd asked Curly to let him know what had happened and that Charlene was calling the police. Then Curly and Moe went off to search for the horse."

"Anything else?" he asked. "Anything that struck you as odd or interesting?"

I shook my head. "I was too focused on Larry's body, and then on Moe." In spite of the summer warmth, I shivered and rubbed my arms. Poor Larry. He'd seemed like a decent guy, and I wondered if he had any family aside from his nephew.

"All right. You can go. If I have any more questions, I'll be in touch."

I nodded and went to lean against the Jeep and wait for Charlene.

White cat draped over her shoulder, she emerged from the carriage house fifteen minutes later.

I straightened off the car. "How'd it go?"

She raised a finger. "Not here."

I zipped my lips and got into the passenger side of her Jeep.

We drove out of the Bar X. I rolled down the window. We passed a long ridge of high, brown grasses, and I held out my hand, letting the fronds tickle my palm. There was something strangely comforting in their feathery touch.

Charlene leaned forward, peering over the steering wheel. "Now we know who Marla's accomplice was."

"Who? You mean Larry?"

"That's why he was at the saloon—to kill Devon. Marla took the photo of him for blackmail purposes. And then when he pointed out that she had as much to lose if the truth came out, she killed him."

"Maybe," I said, noncommittal, and adjusted the Jeep's sun visor. The road dipped down, coiling through the hills, and my shoulder grazed the car door. "Did you ask her about her photographs with Devon?"

"What's to explain?"

"Maybe she cared about Devon. Maybe that's why she's investigating."

Charlene shot me a look, and the Jeep swerved toward a barbed wire fence.

"Watch it," I said.

She yanked the wheel, and we hit a pothole.

My skull banged the roof. "Ow!" I bent double, elbows on knees, and gripped my throbbing head.

"Whoopsy-daisy!"

I breathed through the pain and straightened up. "We know Marla had a relationship with Devon. Maybe she has some insight into who might have wanted him dead."

"We know who wanted him dead. Marla."

"We've got no evidence. I think we should return to Larry's car dealership tomorrow."

"Why?" she asked.

"Because the police will be all over it today, and because Larry was killed for a reason. Maybe there's a clue why at his office. Unless you know where he lives?"

She shook her white curls. "That's no good. I've been doing research too. He lives in a condo up the coast. I'll never be able to get my hands on his spare key."

"A condo? Did he live there alone?"

"Yep. Never married."

Somehow, that made me feel worse about his death.

After Charlene dropped me at the car, I spent the rest of the day running errands and laying low at home. I tried not to think about Larry, his life cut short. I tried not to think about the fact that someone at the Bar X was a killer. I tried not to think about Gordon. And I failed on all counts.

When Tuesday morning finally rolled around, I immersed myself in baking. Berries were in season, and today I was experimenting with a ginger-lime peach and blueberry pie. Ginger seemed to work with both peaches and blueberries, and I'd found a recipe for a ginger-lime peach and blueberry crisp. It was easy enough to convert to a pie recipe. Besides, my customers seemed to enjoy my experiments. I promoted them as "limited-time-only" specials and gauged the reactions. The winning recipes got a regular spot on the menu.

At the metal counter, I grated ginger into a giant metal bowl piled with sliced peaches and blueberries marinating in sugar.

While I worked, Abril deftly removed steaming strawberry-mascarpone hand pies from the big oven using a long-handled paddle. You *could* turn off the oven's rotating racks to remove the pies, but Abril didn't bother. She was that good.

Light streamed through the skylight, sparkling off the industrial refrigerator and countertops. The kitchen smelled of baking fruit, and I hummed to myself, the horror of Larry's murder dissipating.

Then I realized I was humming an old western song and clenched my fist. The peeled ginger shot from my fingers like a wet bar of soap, struck a ceramic stand of kitchen utensils, and came to rest on the counter. Abashed, I picked up the ginger, washed it, and set it aside. I shifted gears and zested a lime.

Charlene emerged from the flour-work room and stretched, reaching for the white-painted ceiling. "Done!" She sniffed, peering at the tray of circular hand pies Abril slid onto a cooling rack. We'd used a cookie cutter to punch little stars out of the top crust, and the effect was *très* patriotic. "What did you add to those strawberry hand pies?"

"Mascarpone and a hint of lemon." Abril adjusted the net over her knotted black hair. "It's the perfect ménage à trois of flavors."

Charlene eyed her askance. "I meant those star holes in the crusts. How much of my crust was wasted?"

"None," I said, nodding to a stack of piecrust stars. "We're layering the stars on the top crust for these new ginger-lime peach and blueberry pies."

Charlene shook her head. "Awfully fancy for San Nicholas."

"A little egg wash," Abril said, "and they'll be a sensual, succulent Nirvana."

"Abril, you need to get a boyfriend." Charlene drew me into the hallway between the kitchen and the restaurant. "And you should ask her to write our next menu," she said to me in a low voice.

"I just printed new menus!"

"What's going on with that girl? Is she boy crazed?"

"She's a poet." I'd mainly hired her because I'd been bedazzled by her vocabulary.

"A poet? How do you know? She didn't say anything to me."

"She asked if we could host a poetry slam next month."

"Why didn't you tell me?"

"It doesn't affect you. You're usually gone before noon, and the slam will be in the evening."

"Well, I hope it's bakery themed. There once was a pie from Nantucket—"

"Family restaurant, family restaurant!" I angled my head toward the dining area.

She harrumphed and exited out the front door, her shift over and out.

I returned to the kitchen. Adding vanilla and cornstarch to the peaches and blueberries, I mixed the filling and loaded it into prepped pie tins. I folded the top crusts over the fruit, cementing the stars with the egg wash. Abril loaded the pies into the ovens, set the timer, and I cleaned up. Then I restarted the process, switching to savory and mixing the fillings for chicken potpies.

By noon, I was a sweaty, but satisfied, mess. I dried my hands, switched to a fresh Pie Town apron, and turned to Abril. "Can you manage in here? I'm going to help out in the dining area."

She slid unbaked pies onto the wooden paddle. "No problem. I just need to slip these beauties into the oven."

Smiling, I walked through the swinging doors and behind the long counter.

Petronella manned the cash register, her black hair like an angry rooster's crown. She was in full goth mode—wearing all black except for her Pie Town apron. I wasn't sure how she managed to spend so much time on her feet in those motorcycle boots, but to each her own. Petronella made change and handed two burly farmers a white-and-black plastic number tent.

The restaurant was hopping, voices a dull hum. Forks and glasses clanked. Tuesday lunchers packed the tables and tackled potpies—chicken curry and beef—and traditional shepherd's pies.

My heart lightened, and not only because the business I'd poured my entire life into was popular. The place had a *feeling* to it. Maybe I was imagining it. Maybe it was just me. But whenever I walked through the door, I felt like I'd come home to family.

The bell tinkled over the glass front door, and I glanced up.

Ray struggled inside, his crutches banging into the slowly closing door.

I hurried from behind the counter, but two gamers and a harried-looking mother beat me to it, holding the door for him.

"You're out of the hospital," Henrietta exclaimed, helping him into their corner booth. She was back in her usual shapeless gamer-wear: baggy olive pants and a loose T-shirt that disguised all her assets. Her happy, eager look brightened her appearance.

I walked to their table. Normally, people ordered at the counter, and we brought them their food if they were dining in. But the poor guy was on crutches, and he *had* saved my life.

"How are you doing, Ray?" With the gamer back at Pie Town, life really was returning to normal. Inexplicably, a chill ran down my spine.

"Better," he said. "No more murder attempts?"

I lowered my head, my good mood evaporating. "I guess you didn't see the morning paper."

"There's been another murder at the Bar X." Henrietta yanked a canvas backpack wedged between her hip and the wall and pulled out a cell phone. She tapped the keypad and aimed the screen at me. It displayed an article from the local paper. "Larry Pelt, the used car guy."

"What?" Ray's eyes widened. "I bought my car from him. It runs like a dream."

"What'll it be, Ray?" I asked. Suddenly, talking about the murder was the last thing I wanted.

"Vegetarian potpie," he said.

I dropped my pencil. Vege-whaaaa?

"A nutritionist dropped by my room," Ray said. "She convinced me I should give greens a chance."

I stooped and grabbed my pencil off the linoleum floor.

One of his fellow gamers chortled. "She? What'd she look like?"

Ray's freckles darkened. "I've heard the veggie pie is good, okay?"

The other guys ribbed him. Henrietta shrank into her seat.

Sympathetic, I smiled at her and whisked to the kitchen window.

Abril grabbed the new ticket, nodded, and a minute later slid a warm, mini potpie through the window.

"Thanks." I grabbed a bundle of wrapped utensils from the bin and hustled it to the gaming table.

A fixed smile on her face, Henrietta rolled a set of dice across the table.

Since I couldn't figure out my own love life, much less sort Henrietta's, I dropped off the pie and turned to go.

Gordon strolled into the restaurant in his dark-gray suit, and I stopped short.

Marla clung to his arm, and I couldn't help but remember Charlene's warning. My jaw tightened. Marla was probably only trying to Mata Hari information out of the detective. Still, this was the second woman dripping off Gordon in a week. Had it always been like this, and I hadn't noticed?

The two stopped in the center of the checkerboard floor, and Marla murmured something in his ear.

My eyes narrowed.

Or maybe she wasn't whispering sweet nothings. Maybe she was shouting in his ear, forced to get close because of the noise. The decibel level had risen now that the gamers were in full swing.

Jaguar. I almost turned, imagining Charlene's voice in my head.

I strode to the counter, grabbed an empty plastic bin, and cleared a table. When I returned to the register, Gordon waited there alone.

And I felt that same, stupid smile Henrietta had worn creep across my face. "Hi," I said. "What can I get you?"

He rummaged in the inside pocket of his charcoal-colored suit jacket. "I've got a list. I'm supposed to bring these to the station." He passed me the rumpled paper.

I raised a brow. It was a delightfully long list. I jammed the paper into the wheeled ticket holder and spun it to face the kitchen.

Abril peeked through the window.

"Those are all to go," I said.

She nodded and disappeared.

I returned to the register. "So," I said. "Marla."

"Mm, hm," Gordon said.

"I suppose you gave her the same warning about not interfering in an investigation."

His dark brows slashed downward. "Interfering?"

"In the murder investigation. She and Charlene have a competition going."

"Over what?"

"Marla's asking around about the Bar X murder. Murders," I corrected.

Gordon burst into laughter. "Is that what she wanted? You three are too much."

"Hey, Marla's not on our team. She's a lone wolf." And was I imagining a jagged-knife edge to his chortles?

"What next?" he asked. "Are you going to recruit the local senior center as Baker Street Irregulars?"

My mouth compressed.

"Order up," Abril caroled.

I grabbed the tray sticking through the kitchen window and boxed the pies. Thinking hard, I tied the pink boxes into two stacks and slid them across the counter. "Color me confused. Earlier, you thought I was going to get myself killed. Now you act like the Baker Street Bakers are a joke."

He sobered and counted a handful of bills, laid them on

the counter. "No, you getting killed would not be funny. And I still wish you'd steer clear. But I've decided to take a Zen approach to things I can't change. I've got two senior citizens and a pie maker playing amateur detective in a murder investigation. Last week I was called out to investigate a suspicious coin. It was a quarter. That wasn't half as annoying as the drunken interpretive dance that followed. The week before, I was brought in on a bird-napping case. The bird in question—a cockatoo—was found dead at the bottom of its cage. By me. And don't get me started on the dog park."

"Are the fairies back?"

He stared, expressionless.

"Or space aliens. I heard someone saw something strange," I finished weakly.

"It's just kids fooling around, but now it's my job to catch them in the act."

"You're a detective. Why isn't someone else chasing kids and bird nappers?"

He scrubbed a hand over his dark hair. "Town politics have gotten tense. It's made its way into the department. Chief Shaw's worried he'll lose his job, since he only got it because the old chief of police was arrested."

"Oh," I said in a small voice, and made his change. "You were joking about the interpretive dance, right?"

"Was I, Val? Was I?" He gripped the counter, his knuckles whitening. He picked up the boxes. "Take care of yourself, Val."

More confused than ever, I watched him leave. I no longer worried about solving the case in time to get a first date with Gordon. Now I worried about getting that date before San Nicholas turned him banana-pants crazy.

Chapter Seventeen

Lights gleamed through the narrow windows of Ewan's cheerful Victorian as Charlene and I climbed the steps to the front porch. In a suicidal frenzy, moths batted themselves against the lamp beside the white front door.

I shifted the boxed boysenberry pie in my arms and smothered a yawn. For a Tuesday, the day had been strangely tiring. "Are you sure they want to see us?" Ewan had invited us both to dinner, but I wasn't sure how much of it had been his idea and how much was a put-up job by Charlene.

"We're bringing pie," she said in a low voice. "And I told you, he invited us. I think he needs a distraction. These murders are weighing on him."

I knew the feeling. The death in Pie Town earlier this year had left me with a sickening, creeping sensation and the knowledge that someone close could strike again. It had been a bad time, and had nearly sunk my new business.

Charlene knocked on the door.

After a moment, the door creaked open and Bridget stood, her blond-gray hair haloed by the light from the foyer behind her. She glanced at me, and her expression faltered. Bridget plastered on a smile. "Hi! My dad told me you were coming for dinner. Come on in. Is that pie?"

"What else?" Charlene asked.

Bridget led us through the foyer and into the living room. The paneled walls were painted off-white and the hardwood floor was stripped to a rustic finish. A brick fireplace stood unlit on the opposite wall. A longhorn skull hung above the cream-colored couch.

I walked to a white-painted shelf and studied its books and western artifacts: a gray feather in a bottle, a railroad spike, a lasso.

Bridget plucked a bottle of wine from the low, natural-wood coffee table. "Zinfandel?"

Charlene collapsed onto the ivory couch. "It's too hot for red wine. Got any beer?"

"Always." Carrying two frosty brown bottles, Ewan strolled into the room. The lines beneath his eyes had deepened and turned cavernous. A tuft of his silver hair stuck out from behind one ear. "That kind of day?" He patted her shoulder, and she laid her hand atop his.

A look passed between them—fondness, admiration, relief.

"Thanks," Charlene said.

He hitched his jeans and handed her a bottle. "Val? What about you?"

"I'll try that Zin," I said.

Bridget poured a goblet. Forehead creased, she handed it to me.

"Thanks." I shook my head slightly. I wasn't going to rat her out about the stalking lawsuit.

Charlene took a swig of her beer and made a face. "Blech. Tastes like hippy."

I choked on my wine, trying not to laugh.

Bridget snorted.

"Has it gone bad?" Ewan passed her his bottle. "Here,

take mine." He sat in a wide, leather chair angled to face the couch. Ewan stared into the bottle's amber depths. "We were supposed to have a wedding here tonight. They canceled."

I grimaced and sat beside Charlene. "Because of the murder?" *Murders*, I mentally corrected. Plural.

He nodded. "They were up front about the reason for the cancellation. This was supposed to be a joyous occasion, and they didn't want it ruined with blood and police tape. And they aren't the only cancellations. If I get another wedding party at the Bar X, it will be a miracle. How did you deal with it?" he asked me.

"Me?" I straightened on the couch.

"The death in Pie Town last spring," he said. "I read the papers. It was initially blamed on your quiche. That couldn't have been good for business."

"No." I turned the goblet in my hands. "Eventually the truth came out, and the customers returned. The same will happen here." I tried to inject confidence into my voice.

"Will it?" he asked. "Do you have any idea how hard it was to get this place rolling? A fake, Old West ghost town as an event venue? Everybody thought I was nuts to do it. If I lose the Bar X—"

"You won't lose it," his daughter said fiercely. "They'll find out who killed Devon and Larry, and this will be over."

He shook his head. "I don't know. It's one thing to have a phantom haunting the premises. Two murders are something else. There aren't many people who'll rent a place with that kind of history."

Charlene banged her beer bottle on the table hard enough to rattle the cheese platter. "Enough with the pity party. No one ever pulled out of a slump by sitting around and feeling sorry for himself."

"That's not fair." Bridget's eyes flashed.

"Fair's a carnival," Charlene said. "We live in the real

world, and we need to deal with the truth. The only way you're going to get your business back on track is if you focus on what you can do to make it work, not on all the reasons why it won't."

Bridget flushed. "You have no right—"

"No," Ewan said. "She's right." He rose and paced before the cold fireplace. "I never got anywhere in a funk. We need to figure out who's responsible and finish this. And I need to get back to basics. I've been letting the business ride on its reputation. When I started the Bar X, I had to build that reputation. I had to do footwork, bring people in. I can do that again."

"Of course, you can," Charlene said.

Thoughtful, I slipped a piece of Irish cheddar onto a cracker. Two murders in one place . . . Could the killer have a grudge against Ewan? Or were the murders a kill-two-birds-with-one-stone scenario? Get rid of people you don't like *and* destroy Ewan's ranch?

"Do you have any enemies?" I asked him.

"Me?" He tucked his chin, his grizzled brow furrowing.

Charlene nodded. "You're thinking the harm to Ewan's business might not be an unintended side effect."

"You believe it's intentional?" Bridget asked.

"I don't know," I said. "We need to explore all the possibilities."

"If someone wanted to hurt me . . ." He glanced at Bridget then looked to the darkened window. "I can't imagine who would. I wasn't the best person when I was young. The Navy eventually straightened me out, but there were a dozen men who wouldn't have minded taking a swing at me. But that was a lifetime ago, and none of them are in San Nicholas."

"What about this property in general?" I asked. "Was anyone upset about how you developed it?"

"There was a local environmental group that wanted to

buy the property and keep it as an open space," he said, "but I outbid them. They weren't happy, but they were never threatening."

"What about Marla?" Charlene asked.

I schooled my expression.

"Marla?" Ewan's ivory brows lifted. "What about her?"

"She was on the scene," Charlene said. "Rumor has it she was close to Devon."

"To Devon?" Ewan asked. "Curly's not going to like that. He's got a big crush on her."

"So, she has been spending more time around the Bar X than your average client," Charlene said.

"What do you mean?" Ewan asked.

"I mean enough time to get to know both Curly and Devon," Charlene said.

"She's held several events here," Ewan said. "Private parties, things for charity. We've all gotten to know each other."

"I also heard that Devon might have been underpouring drinks," I said.

Charlene shot me an irritated look.

"I heard that too," Ewan said, "but I never saw any evidence of it."

A timer pinged from the kitchen.

"That's dinner," he said. "Come on, folks."

They led us into the dining room. The walls were painted deep red, setting off the rustic wood table and chairs and the wagon wheel on one wall. On the opposite side of the room was another cold fireplace.

She and her father moved back and forth between the kitchen and the dining room. They loaded the long table with lasagna, sourdough bread thick with garlic, buttered asparagus, and a green salad.

"More wine?" Ewan asked, extending the bottle toward me.

"She can't. She's driving," Charlene said. "But I'll have another beer."

I made a face. So *that* was why Charlene had agreed so easily to let me drive. "By the way," I said, "where did they find Larry's horse?"

Ewan topped up Bridget's glass and sat at the head of the rustic table. "Tied up at the corral."

So, the animal hadn't kicked him in the stall and bolted. "Why would Larry leave his horse there?"

"The corral's not far from the carriage house," Charlene said. "Maybe he tied the horse up, saw something or someone in the carriage house, and decided to walk over."

"I suppose that makes sense," I said, but it seemed odd he'd leave his horse. Or was I getting as superstitious as those partiers who'd canceled?

During dinner, we made small talk, and Ewan regaled us with tales of the Old West, which was wilder than even the movies painted.

"Can you imagine striking out like that for unknown territory?" Ewan asked. "Being completely on your own— just you and your wits and your horse? The hope and dread and excitement?"

"And the manual labor." Charlene raised her beer. "I'll take this century, thank you very much. I like my indoor plumbing and antibiotics and washing machines."

"Who knows?" Ewan's eyes twinkled. "Maybe what they say about reincarnation is true, and we get to experience it all."

The conversation turned to the metaphysical and paranormal. Half listening, I watched the interplay between Ewan and Charlene. Was he winding her up, or did he really share her interests? I turned the wine goblet in my hands. If the latter, why hadn't he told her about the Bar X phantom sooner?

"Any more phantom sightings?" I asked, studying Charlene.

"None," Bridget said sharply.

"I've been researching tulpas," Charlene said. "And I have to say, I'm concerned. If that's what you've got, they can get nasty."

Ewan's brow creased. "What are you thinking? An exorcism?"

Bridget scraped her chair away from the table. "Val, do you want to show me how to warm that pie?"

"Right," I said, reluctant to leave. I'd need to head this exorcism business off at the pass. Charlene's occult escapades had gotten me into more trouble than I wanted to admit. It's all fun and games until someone nearly wanders over a cliff while hunting UFOs.

I followed Bridget into the kitchen, which was one hundred percent modern. Its metal countertops would have fit right in at Pie Town.

"So . . . three-fifty?" she asked.

"What?"

"The oven temperature for the pie."

"Oh," I said, "right. Yeah."

She pushed buttons on the stove then lifted the pie out of its pink and white box and set it on the counter.

"Is the Bar X in as much trouble as your dad thinks?" I asked.

She slumped against the counter. "We've had five cancellations this week. At least we get to keep the deposits, but if people stop wanting to come here . . . This will kill my dad. He put everything he had into the Bar X. This is his retirement."

And Charlene would do everything in her power to save him. Worried, I rubbed my hands on my jeans. "Then the sooner we figure out who killed Devon and Larry, the sooner the Bar X can move forward."

She gnawed her bottom lip. "I get that, but I don't know anything that might help."

"You know the truth about Devon's lawsuit."

"I didn't kill him," she said, her voice low and intent.

"Then tell me what the lawsuit was really about, so we can focus on other things."

"You're not the police. Why tell you, when I can tell them?"

My neck stiffened. Telling the police did make more sense. At least she'd sort of let slip there was more to the story than she'd admitted. "You should tell the police. But Charlene wants to clear the Bar X, and so do I."

"You don't understand." She blew out her breath. "I wasn't *stalking* stalking him."

"What does that mean?"

She flushed. "I was sort of checking him out."

"Checking him out? Why?"

The oven beeped, and she slid the pie inside. "How long does it heat for?"

I fought my rising impatience. "Fifteen minutes."

She set the timer. "I think we've left Charlene and my dad alone long enough."

"Bridget, why check Devon out? This is important."

"Don't you see it's embarrassing?"

I crossed my heart. "What's said in the kitchen, stays in the kitchen."

Her lips quirked. "Devon said . . ." She stared at the glass-fronted cupboards. "Well, he hinted . . . I thought he might be my half brother," she blurted.

My stomach capsized, sank. "Oh." Did Ewan know? Did Charlene know? "That must have been a shock."

She laughed hollowly. "You have no idea. My dad's made no secret of the kind of man he was when he was young. He was stationed in San Diego and had a slew of girls. And that's when and where Devon was born."

"What exactly did Devon tell you?"

"That he wasn't at the Bar X by accident," she said. "That it was fate he'd heard about the Bar X when he was working at a bar in the Sierras."

"How did he hear about it?" I asked.

She massaged her forehead. "That's the weird thing. He said . . . well, he seemed to think I'd sent him a newspaper article about us."

"You? Why would he think that?"

"Someone anonymously mailed him a newspaper clipping from San Benedetto."

"He told you this?"

"He smirked about it, thought I was trying to lure back my big brother."

"But . . . if he knew that you knew he was your brother, why would you stalk him? I mean, can you stalk a relative?"

"According to my lawyer, yes, you can. Anyway, he was curious about the clipping—who wouldn't be? When he looked into it, he read about my family. And then he started telling me about his family—about his single mother who'd gotten knocked up and abandoned by a sailor in San Diego. About how hard their lives had been, while mine had been so easy. He kept drawing parallels without coming out and saying he was my father's son. Their names are even similar—Ewan and Devon. He brought that up too."

Stranger and stranger. "Who else could have known that Devon was Ewan's son?"

She laughed harshly. "I didn't even know it until he turned up."

"And so, you started digging."

"And he caught me."

"Did you tell him why you were looking into his background?"

Head bowed, she turned to the stove and fiddled with

the digital timer. "How could I? But I think he knew. He had to know. And then he brought that damned lawsuit. I think he was taunting me, trying to force me to ask my dad if it was possible Devon was his son."

"You mean your dad still doesn't know?" I asked, appalled.

She shook her head, her long, blond braid swinging against her back. "And you can't tell him. If he found out, especially now that Devon's dead, it would kill him."

"Are you sure Devon didn't say anything to your father?"

"If he had, my dad would have told me."

"Why do you think Devon didn't ask your father? Why harass you?"

"I don't know." A muscle jumped in her jaw. "I think he wanted money."

That would explain why Devon had filed a lawsuit rather than going to the cops about the stalking. My stomach burned. "Did he ask you for money?"

"Not in so many words. It was all innuendo." Lightly, she grasped my wrist. "Please, don't tell my dad."

"I won't, but Bridget, I think you need to tell him."

"Why? Devon's dead. It doesn't matter anymore. And my dad didn't kill him. If he had any idea who did, he'd tell the police. He's got no reason to hide anything."

Unless he did know and feared his daughter had committed the crime.

Chapter Eighteen

In my empty restaurant, I swept the dining area. The glass cases, empty of pie, sparkled. The checkerboard floor gleamed. My neon TURN YOUR FROWN UPSIDE DOWN AT PIE TOWN sign glowed pink above the window to the kitchen.

On the not-so-good side, Charlene had once again avoided me all day. Now suspicion wormed in my gut that she was up to something I wouldn't like.

Last night, when we'd driven home from dinner at the Bar X, I'd told her about Bridget's confession and the mysterious clipping that had brought Devon to the Bar X. My piecrust specialist had looked thoughtful but remained uncharacteristically silent. When I'd dropped her off at her Victorian, she hadn't quite banged the door in my face, but it had been a close call. She hadn't been happy that I'd interrogated Bridget.

I leaned on my broom. The restaurant seemed almost too clean. Without customers, it was empty to the point of void. I shook myself.

Of course, it was empty; we were closed for the evening, and I was wrung out. But things were looking up. Ray was on crutches but in good humor. Wally and Graham had been in fine form, cracking jokes and chowing down on discounted hand pies. And a fraternity had stopped by and bought out all of our banana-butterscotch cream pies. I assumed they planned on eating them, but you never knew what went on in frat houses. Life was good.

I knit my lip. But a killer was still out there. Was it possible Ewan hadn't known about Devon's claim he was his son? Who at the Bar X could have known about the possible connection between the two men aside from Bridget and Ewan? Could Bridget have killed Devon to protect her father? Was Ewan protecting her now? And why the heck hadn't Charlene known about the Bar X Phantom earlier? She lived for the weird and paranormal. She should have told Curly about that bit of San Nicholas trivia, rather than the other way around.

I stuffed my hands into my apron pockets. Something was rotten in the town of San Nicholas.

There was a metallic clank from the kitchen. I whipped toward the noise.

Gripping the broom, I crept toward the kitchen door, sidling past the register. My heart thumped unevenly.

The swinging door banged open, and I leapt away, banging my hip on the counter.

Charlene stormed into the restaurant. In lieu of Frederick, she'd wrapped a fuzzy violet scarf around the neck of her lime-green tunic. "Get your coat. We've got a mission, and the fog's in."

My broom clattered to the linoleum. "Charlene!"

"What? Better not leave that broom laying on the floor. Someone might trip."

"What mission?" I smiled. We were co-detectives again. "Marla."

My smile turned upside down. "She's going to sue you for stalking if you're not careful."

"We know she was doing the jaguar with Devon."

"Will you stop calling it that?" I asked. "I used to like jaguars."

"It's time to confront her over her crimes."

"Crimes? We don't know—"

"Marla's on the verge of snapping. She's at the Main Street Bar now. We strike while she's drinking, in *vino veritas*."

"I prefer *cogita ante salis*," I said. Determined Charlene was a welcome improvement over depressed Charlene, but this did not seem like a good idea.

"Look before you leap? We're going to a bar. What can go wrong?"

Alarm bells rioted in my mind. What *couldn't* go wrong? But I couldn't let Charlene tackle Marla on her own. There needed to be at least one adult in the room. "I'll get my coat."

I locked up, and we walked down Main Street. Baskets of impatiens, their moss and wire baskets glistening with dampness, hung from iron street lamps, which lit the fog with a beery glow.

"Have you been tailing Marla?" I asked.

"What kind of person do you think I am?"

Dangerously obsessed. Delightfully looney. Devilishly erratic. "I think you're on a case."

"You *think* Bridget and Ewan are involved in the murders. I *know* Marla is."

"Without evidence, we don't know anything."

"We'll see who's right."

If we don't get arrested for stalking first.

We walked into the bar. It was surprisingly crowded for early Wednesday night. A baseball game flickered on the three small TV screens. The Giants' batter struck out, and moans of despair echoed across the dark, wooden walls and the sticky floor.

Charlene pointed at the bar. Rows of bottles lined its

mirrored shelves. "There she is, cozying up to that young bartender. It's a pattern."

"Or she wants a drink."

Charlene wedged between Marla and a beefy guy in an orange and black jacket. "So."

"You." Marla's silvery brows slashed downward. "I know you took my camera's memory card. Give it back, before I call the police."

Charlene sneered. "Do you really think the police are going to bother with a memory card worth only a few bucks?"

I pursed my lips. They might. Gordon had gotten called out over a suspicious quarter, and he was a hotshot detective with a badge on his belt.

"What do you want?" Marla asked.

"What do you think?"

Marla rolled her eyes. "Fine. I was having an affair with the bartender. Happy?"

"I already knew that," Charlene said. "A picture is worth a thousand innuendoes."

A man bumped me from behind. "Sorry," he said.

I nodded and smiled and tried to edge closer to Charlene and Marla. But there was no more wedge room.

"What else can I tell you?" Marla smirked.

"Why Devon?" I asked. "What kind of person was he? You were having an affair. You must have learned something about the man."

Marla's smile broadened, coy. "Nothing that could go in a police report."

Ugh. She hadn't told us anything, and we'd already wandered into the TMI zone.

"You've been spending a lot of time around the Bar X," Charlene said, "and that started before the murders. What are you up to?"

"Nothing. I have a passion for the Old West. Is that a

crime?" She ran her fingers along a pineapple-topped swizzle stick.

"We'll figure out what you're up to," Charlene said.

"I've already told you what I'm up to. I intend to solve the crime."

"Fat chance of that," Charlene said.

"I do know things," Marla said. "Things you'd like to know."

I was getting flashbacks to high school. "Marla, if you know anything important, tell the police."

She arched a brow. "I suppose you're handing the handsome Detective Gordon Carmichael everything you learn?"

"I am." Mostly.

"Of course, we could always help each other out," she said. "Pool our resources?"

Charlene snorted.

"How?" I trusted Marla even less than I trusted Charlene, but I was curious.

"No," Charlene said. "No way. She's trying to trick us into giving her information. That's not the way blackmail works, Marla. We've got the goods. You tell us what you know."

"Blackmail?" Marla's lip curled. "Is that what you're attempting? Darling, for blackmail to work, you'd have to have something over me I wanted kept secret. As far as I care, you can post those photos on your ridiculous Twitter feed."

"I have ten thousand followers!"

"Of course, you do."

"I do! It's right there on my—"

I touched Charlene's arm. "Let's hear what she has to say."

Marla swiveled on her barstool and faced me. "Curly."

"The sharpshooter?" I asked. "What about him?"

"I have reason to believe he's a vampire," Marla said.

Charlene folded her arms. "A vampire," she said. "What do you know about vampires?"

"Devon, no doubt, learned the truth," Marla said, "and he had to be done away with."

I burst out laughing. I couldn't help it.

Charlene frowned. "I'll bite. Why do you think he is a vampire?"

I laughed even harder.

"Because unlike you," Marla said, "I've been following actual suspects."

"And you saw Curly doing what?" I wiped my eyes. "Wearing a satin cape and flapping around the Bar X?" I laid my palm on the wooden bar, and it came away wet. Surreptitiously, I dried it on my jeans.

"I saw him going into the woods above the tide pools wearing dark robes," Marla said. "At night. I've seen him in that weird cape at the Bar X at night too."

"So, of course, he's an immortal creature of darkness," I said, an overdose of sarcasm in my voice. "What other possible explanation could there be?"

Marla tapped her swizzle stick on the cocktail glass. "He's not a real vampire. He's one of those weirdos who *thinks* he's a vampire."

Charlene gnawed her bottom lip. "She could be on to something, Val."

Moe had said Devon might have been holding something over Curly. Could this possibly be it? Still, I trusted Marla about as far as I could shot put her. I jerked my head toward the ladies' room. "A word?"

I pushed through the crowd, and Charlene followed me to a dark corner by the juke box. "We need to follow up on this," she said.

"No," I said. "We don't. Vampires aren't real."

She rolled her eyes. "Duh. Even Marla admitted that. If Curly is holding occult ceremonies in the woods—"

"Who said anything about occult ceremonies?"

"Everyone knows the woods above the tide pools are used for secret rituals."

"What? I walk that trail all the time!" I wasn't sure which was more startling—that Charlene didn't believe in vampires or that there might be occultists in the woods. Sure, the rows of dark cypress trees with their weird orange growth could be eerie, but it was a short, easy hike along the ocean cliff. "Everyone uses that trail!"

She raised her brows. "Exactly. Don't you see? That could explain the tulpa."

"The tul . . . what? How?" I sputtered.

"It makes sense," Charlene said. "It takes a lot of psychic energy to create a thought form like a tulpa. I figured the phantom had come into existence because so many visitors believed in it. If an occultist at the Bar X was involved, then it wasn't my—" She coughed. "My goodness. We should check this out."

"There's no tulpa in the woods."

"Of course not." She rolled her eyes. "The tulpa's at the Bar X."

"Forget the phantom. Marla's playing you. She knows you're interested in the paranormal. She's admitted she reads your Twitter feed. She's trying to trick you into helping her."

"Why would she?" Charlene asked. "She doesn't want me . . . I mean us, to solve this crime. Besides, she thinks she's the bee's knees when it comes to crime solving."

"Do bees even have knees?"

"The only reason she'd ask us for help is if she was really stuck. The paranormal is my field of expertise. Little wonder she needs my assistance."

I wrinkled my brow. Why would Marla even hint she couldn't do something as well as Charlene? "This doesn't smell right."

"That's just Rick." She motioned toward a skinny man slumped beside the juke box. Beer dribbled from the glass he held loosely atop his thigh. "He only bathes on Sundays."

"How do you even know that?"

"There are strange doings at the Bar X. We need to follow every lead, including Curly's occult trips into the woods."

"Maybe he's role playing a wizard, or—"

Ignoring me, my piecrust maker strode to Marla and tapped her shoulder. "All right. We're in."

Marla slid off the barstool. Dropping some bills on the bar, she slung her Chanel bag over her shoulder. "No time like the present. Let's go."

"Go?" I yelped. "Go where?"

"To Curly's house, of course," Marla said.

"Do you have a key?" Charlene asked excitedly.

Marla turned to stare down at her. "Why on earth would I have a key?"

"It's not breaking and entering if you have a key," Charlene said.

Marla strode out the door and onto the fog-shrouded sidewalk. "Is that how you justified breaking into my home?"

"I told you," Charlene said, "I didn't break in."

"You did steal my property."

"Semantics." Beads of moisture glittered on Charlene's white hair. "And you were in my house too, don't forget."

Marla's nostrils flared, and she paused beneath a street lamp. "You have no proof—"

"So, what's the plan for Curly's house?" I asked, before the argument could go nuclear.

"We will *not* be breaking in," Marla said. "Private detectives aren't allowed to break the law, you know."

Business cards or not, Marla couldn't possibly have gotten her PI license this quickly.

"Then what are we talking about?" I asked. "Surveillance?"

"In a manner of speaking," Marla said.

My eyes narrowed. "In what manner of speaking, exactly?"

"He's got a big yard," Marla said. "It backs onto the creek."

"And?" Charlene asked.

"And he's got a mother-in-law cottage that he doesn't rent out."

Charlene stopped on the brick sidewalk. "Are you sure?"

"I did say I was surveilling him," Marla said.

"That *is* fishy." Charlene rubbed her chin. "A cottage would be hot property in this market. Maybe he turned it into a temple for his occult rites."

"Or maybe," I said, "he stores equipment in it. Or uses it as an artist's studio." I'd been down Charlene's supernatural mazes before—Bigfoot hunts and ghosts and UFOs. The UFO hunt was the worst, because they may actually exist. I don't care what people say about the impossibility of interstellar travel. Just because we haven't figured out how to zip to other planets, doesn't mean a more intelligent race bent on experimenting on hapless humans hasn't. I shivered in the fog.

Marla stopped beside a green Mercedes roadster. "We'll take my car."

"We'll follow you," I said.

"This is a small town," Marla said. "People will notice a caravan. And I wouldn't be caught dead in either of your jalopies."

"She's right," Charlene said. "One car's better. Besides, Curly's place isn't far." She sneered at Marla. "I've been investigating too."

I crammed into the backseat of the sports car. Knees to my

chest, I muttered a prayer of supplication, and we rocketed down the dark street.

The two women bickered up front, and I watched Main Street speed past. We veered east, past the nineteenth-century jail. Marla turned the Mercedes into a residential area of looming trees, white picket fences, and tumbled gardens.

She parked in front of a low, white-painted adobe with a tiled roof. A cinderblock wall enclosed it, the only entrance either over the wall or through its iron gate. A trellis tangled with heavy-scented jasmine arched above the gate, and a bell dangled from its apex. In the nighttime fog, the house looked like a haunted Spanish prison.

"Is there a basement?" I whispered.

"In California?" Marla asked. "We don't do basements. Why do you ask?"

"I was wondering where the dungeon was."

Marla creaked open the iron gate and stepped through. "All right," she whispered. "You two go around the left. That's where he keeps the garbage. Grab the bags and take them to my car."

"What?" Charlene hissed, striding into the yard. A dim light above the front door made crags of her face.

"Garbage duty," I whispered. "So that's why you wanted us to come along." Closing the gate behind me, I followed them into a neat garden of brick paths and lavender bushes. The night turned their stems and blossoms the silver of dull knives. A fountain in the center of the garden trickled spookily, and I repressed a shiver. "I'm not dumpster diving so you can keep your hands clean."

Marla raised her nose. "It's basic private detecting. If you think you're too good for it—"

"We'll do it," Charlene growled.

"Good." Marla nodded toward the adobe house. "I'll

circle around the right side and check out the mother-in-law cottage."

"No, you won't," Charlene said. "I'm going with you."

"We need to move fast," Marla said. "And that means two people on the garbage. Besides, this is my operation. I invited you along. You wouldn't even know Curly thought he was a vampire if it hadn't been for me."

Charlene's nostrils flared.

"We're going to get caught if we don't move fast," I said, wanting to get this over with. I've watched crime TV. Searching garbage was a legitimate PI technique, even if it was gross.

"Fine," Charlene huffed, and headed left.

I scuttled after her.

On the left side of the house stretched a narrow gravel path. Bins for garbage, recycling, and yard clippings sat against the adobe wall. The stench of rotting things coiled around us. She pointed to a large, plastic box. "Compost," she whispered, her nose crinkling.

"I'm not touching that," I said in a low voice.

She nodded, jerking her chin toward the garbage bin.

Tiptoeing across the gravel, I lifted the green lid and tried not to gag. Most of the garbage was contained in plastic bags. Most. Not all.

Making a face, I brushed past a damp and stained cloth and grabbed a bag. I walked it out to Marla's car. What were we even looking for? Plastic fangs? Empty bags of blood?

But I was impressed Marla was willing to put the garbage in her sleek sports car. Maybe she really was serious about this investigation.

Wiping my hands on my jeans, I leaned the bag against the rear wheel and trotted back to Charlene.

She handed me another bag, and I delivered it to the Mercedes.

I dropped off a bag of recycling and again crept inside the gate, edging toward the left side of the house.

Something metallic crashed.

I raced around the corner.

Charlene stared, openmouthed, down the narrow gravel path. "Marla!" she whispered.

A side door to the house crashed open. The unmistakable *clack-clack* of a racking shotgun froze me in place.

A flashlight beam blinded me. My heart rolled over, played dead.

"You two!" Curly roared. "What the hell are you doing here?"

Charlene slowly raised her hands. "Mar . . . we . . ."

"Citizens recycling police," I said, thinking fast.

"What?" he snapped.

"You put paper towels in your garbage bin," I said. "They belong in the recycling bin. We won't fine you this time, but—"

He lowered the flashlight, and I blinked. Slowly, my vision returned.

Curly stood barefoot on the red, concrete step, a shotgun in one hand aimed squarely at me. A pair of suspenders dangled from his broad hips. His jowls quivered with indignation. "Recycling police? We don't have that San Francisco nonsense here. Now, what are you really doing? Talk quick before I call the cops, because you're both trespassing."

A Mercedes engine started and roared down the street.

I ground my teeth. *Marla.*

Charlene dropped her hands and glared at me. "And I'm no garbage snitch. We know you've been prancing around the Bar X in a cape, and you've been spotted on the cliffs performing occult rituals. Spill it, Curly."

I gaped. We only had Marla's word for any of that, and her clues were worthless.

He lowered the shotgun.

No longer staring down its double barrels, I sagged against the recycling bin and started breathing again.

"So what?" he asked. "You think that gives you the right to dig through my garbage for evidence?"

"Exactly," Charlene said. "Now, what's going on, Curly?"

His mouth compressed. "Come inside. And wipe your feet on the mat. You two stink. I don't want you tracking trash inside my house."

We followed him inside to a circa 1972 kitchen: green linoleum floor, dark wood cabinets, and a white linoleum countertop flecked with bits of gray and gold. He set the flashlight on the green stove and ran his hand over his buzz cut.

With his bare foot, he nudged aside a chair at a round, wooden kitchen table and sat. "Talk."

I took a chair.

Arms folded, Charlene sat across from me. "Certain ignorant people think you're one of those modern-day vampires. I, however, think you're an occultist. Which is it?"

He sat between us. "And so, you went through my garbage?"

"I imagine neither rumor will do your reputation a bit of good," Charlene said. "You being a rootin' tootin' gunslinger."

"Oh, for Pete's sake." He leaned the shotgun against the table.

"Does Ewan know you've been sneaking onto his property at night?" Charlene asked.

He blew out his breath. "Yes, he does."

"He . . . what?" I asked. Was Curly actually admitting this? "What's with the cape?"

"I'm a druid. Ewan knows. Moe doesn't." He glowered. "And he'd better not find out, either."

"You worship trees?" I asked, bemused.

"I revere all nature, and people are a part of nature, even if they do act like horse's behinds most of the time. I had nothing to do with Devon's death."

"Did Devon know about your, er, practices?" I asked.

He grimaced. "Yeah. He followed me one night. Thought I was the phantom, and he was going to catch me."

"Followed you where?" Charlene asked.

Curly smiled. "Ewan's got an amazing oak tree on his property. I've never seen an oak that big, and some of its branches twist low to the ground. It's like Mother Earth's temple. I like to go there to meditate."

"In a robe," Charlene said, voice thick with disbelief. "At night."

He colored. "It's quieter at night."

"And the robe?" Charlene asked. "You must have known people would think you were the phantom."

"Why? The phantom's not known for floating around in a robe. It opens doors, makes weird sounds, moves stuff around."

"And the robe?" Charlene insisted.

"I know it seems silly," he said. "And sometimes it feels silly, but that's the point. Sometimes you've got to get out of your comfort zone, make the ritual a bigger risk, to really feel the magic you're doing."

"Wait a minute," Charlene said. "Don't druids run in gangs? Who else is in your club?"

"No one," he said. "I'm a solo practitioner."

She harrumphed. "That's it? That's your big secret?"

"If Moe and the other guys in the Brotherhood of Blue Steel found out," he said, "they'd laugh me out of the society."

"All right," I said. "So, Devon knew your secret. What was he threatening to do with it?"

Curly shifted in his wooden chair. "Aside from give me a hard time? Nothing."

"He gave you a hard time?" I asked. "What did he do?"

"You know, called me a tree hugger. Told druid jokes in mixed company—"

"There are druid jokes?" Charlene asked.

He sighed. "What do you get when you cross a Zen Buddhist and a druid?"

"No idea," I said.

"Someone who worships a tree that's not there."

"This is fascinating," Charlene said. "Unfortunately, it doesn't get us any closer to figuring out who killed Devon and your ex-partner, or what's behind the Bar X Phantom."

"I can answer the last question," Curly said. "It's a tulpa."

Charlene bolted upright in her wooden chair. "That's what I said! Did you generate its spectral form in a magical ceremony?"

"Nope," Curly said. "Wasn't me."

"Rats." Her shoulders slumped.

"But a tulpa's the only answer that makes sense," Curly said. "There's no history of anyone dying at the Bar X." His expression darkened. "Until now."

Right. Sure. Tulpa. "Larry must have known or seen something," I said. "He was near the saloon when Devon was killed. What I don't understand is why he didn't tell anyone what he'd seen." Unless he was protecting someone. Someone he cared for. Someone like the Friths.

"So, that's it?" Charlene said. "You're a druid?"

"Well, there is one other thing." Curly's broad face turned the color of a brick.

"What is it?" I asked.

"So . . . about Marla."

I tensed and glanced at Charlene.

She clamped her lips together. Whatever else she might be, Charlene was no snitch. Even on Marla.

"Yes?" I asked.

"You three are friends." He shifted in his seat and blushed more furiously. "Has she said anything about me?"

Chapter Nineteen

I opened the big oven, and a blast of heat scorched my face. A turkey potpie glided into view, and I slid it from the oven with a long, wooden paddle. We had a fan and the AC humming, but there was only so much I could do to keep cool in the kitchen on a San Nicholas summer day.

A bead of sweat trickled down my spine. I loaded potpies onto the cooling rack and checked the clock above the window to the dining area. It was nearly noon.

I didn't know what to make of Curly's admission. With San Nicholas being not that far from freewheeling San Francisco, I doubted nature worship would make Curly an outcast. But he was of a different generation and worked in a macho, gunslinging culture. Had Devon really stopped at druid jokes? Or had he tried to blackmail Curly, pushing him too far?

I rubbed my eyebrow. The bartender had certainly sent Bridget over the edge with that lawsuit.

Charlene, perched on a stool by the industrial dishwasher, had her own ideas. "You never should have listened to Marla. Vampires!?" She smoothed her burnt-red tunic over her thighs. "What were you thinking?"

"*I* shouldn't have listened to her?" I wiped my hands on my apron.

"I told you she couldn't be trusted. She knocked over that pile of junk on purpose last night, so we'd get caught."

Marla had certainly made a racket, but she'd put herself in jeopardy as well. "Why would she do that?"

"Because she'll do anything to get one over on me. Plus, look at the way she drove off and left us. She even took the garbage we'd collected!"

"She's welcome to it."

"She'll probably try to talk us into digging through it for evidence," Charlene said darkly.

"Here's a wacky thought. Let's say *no*." I replaced my flour-dusted apron with a fresh one and whisked through the swinging doors into the restaurant. Most of the tables were full. My Scrooge-like heart glowed, profits dancing in my head.

Abril handed a plastic number tent to a customer, and he wandered to an empty table. She pushed a strand of dark hair over her ear and turned to me, a look of panic on her face. "Can you take over?"

"Sure." Abril was an introvert. She'd rather work in the kitchen than deal with customers, and I felt a twinge of guilt for asking her to work the register. But it was Petronella's day off, and Charlene was piecrusts only. Besides, if Abril was going to read poetry in front of a crowd next month, she needed to step outside of her comfort zone.

Abril scuttled through the swinging door, nearly colliding with Charlene.

My crusty piecrust maker poured herself a mug of coffee from the urn and found a seat at the counter within earshot of the register.

Beside her, Wally rose to top off his cup, his gait uneven. "I hear you went dumpster diving last night, Char. The ingredients in these pies had better be fresh."

"We were set up," she groused.

His graying brows rose. "Set up to dumpster dive, or set up to get caught?"

"Both. By that harridan—"

Marla sailed into Pie Town, setting the bell over the door tinkling. She posed in the center of the checkerboard floor and fluffed her silver hair. Her diamonds flashed in the overhead light. She wore a navy, short-sleeved knit top and white jeans.

Wally and Graham eyed her appreciatively.

"There you are," she said, shifting the purse over her shoulder. "I've been looking all over for you, Charlene. I thought your shift at Pie Town ended in the morning."

The plot curdled. Had Charlene been loitering in Pie Town to avoid her nemesis?

Charlene sucked in her cheeks. "Go. Away." She turned to face the kitchen window. Her jaw set, mulish.

Marla minced toward us on high, white heels. She dropped her navy purse on the counter. "I see you weren't arrested, even if you were caught stealing garbage like a homeless person. Did you play the pity card? In your shoes, I would have." She glanced at Charlene's sneakers. "Are you really wearing those?"

"Since they are on my feet, yes, I am wearing them. What do you want?"

"I'm here to gloat. Thanks to you two, I uncovered some fantastic leads."

"You found something in the garbage?" I asked.

"I haven't checked it yet, but when I was in the yard . . . Well, let's say mysteries were revealed. This case will be sewn up in no time." She raised a finger in the air and caught my eye. "Coffee?"

I pointed to the urn. "Self-serve."

"How quaintly trusting."

"That'll be a dollar in the coffee jar," I growled.

Wally held the oversized jar in his wrinkled hand and rattled it. "In it goes, or no java."

She rummaged in her purse. "Whoops. I don't have any dollar bills." She tossed in a fiver, and Wally carefully counted out her change. Marla poured a cup of coffee from the urn. "What about you two? Did you learn anything interesting?"

"Forget it," Charlene said. "The détente is over. You want clues, go excavate them yourself."

"So, you didn't learn anything." She sipped her coffee and shrugged. "Too bad. For you." Flashing a wintery smile, she sidled to the end of the counter and took a seat.

Watching Marla from the corner of my eye, I rang up a customer.

Abril dinged the bell in the kitchen window, and I whisked two breakfast pies—aka quiche—to a table. On an aromatic cloud of cheesy-bacon goodness, I returned to the register. "What's Marla really doing here?" I asked Charlene. "Because it feels like we're being surveilled."

"Yup." Charlene slurped her coffee and slid off her stool. "I guess I'll take one for the team and lead her away. Don't worry. If you never hear from me again, point the cops in Marla's direction. The ocean currents are strong around her house, but I hear CSI can figure out where bodies were dumped, even if there isn't much left of the corpses. Water does terrible things to a body. I'll bet Carmichael could tell you all about it." She wandered out of the restaurant.

A few moments later, Marla followed.

Figuring Marla was in more danger from Charlene than vice versa, I repressed my instincts to follow them both. Besides, I had a pie shop to run.

The customers kept me hopping. I swished between

counting change at the register and delivering mini potpies to the tables.

Marla had been every bit as nasty as Charlene had warned, but I wondered about the relationship between the two. That sort of intense rivalry didn't just happen. Something had gone down between the women. Did I want to know what it was?

Who was I kidding? I was dying to know.

Ray limped into the restaurant on crutches. He tossed a wobbly wave in my direction and swung into the corner gamers' booth.

I waved back and wondered how to show him my appreciation for saving me from that Prius. Free pies for life would induce coronaries in us both.

The lunch crowd faded, and I switched to worrying about the murders and dreaming about a giant pink pie-delivery van. It could be like the Mystery Machine. With pies. And let's face it—pretty much everything is better with pie. And bacon.

Gordon walked into Pie Town. He approached the register, his expression wary.

"Afternoon, Detective Carmichael," I said, warming. I hoped he hadn't heard about our misadventure in garbage collecting. "What can I get for you?"

"Got any more of those mini cauliflower pies—the ones with the blue cheese?"

"Yep. How many, and for here or to go?"

"One. For here."

My skin tingled. I wasn't sure what was going on in our relationship—or even if we actually had one—but it was a good sign if he wanted to eat in.

I rang him up and handed him one of our plastic number tents.

He poured himself a cup of coffee from the urn, then

strode to an empty corner table and sat facing the door, presumably in case Pie Town was attacked by marauders. Or by Marla.

I leaned through the kitchen window. "Cauliflower and Blue pie."

Abril nodded, plated a pie with greens, and handed it through the window. "This is the last of them."

"Since it's past noon, that's okay." Our savory pies and quiches were doing well. We even had a low-cal, goat cheese, spinach, and zucchini quiche for the waistline-watching crowd. It didn't taste at all healthy, which was probably why it was so popular.

I crossed the CAULIFLOWER AND BLUE CHEESE pie off the chalkboard menu behind the counter and carried the plate to Gordon's table.

"Thanks," he said. "Have you got a minute?"

"Sure." Smiling like an idiot, I slid onto the bench opposite.

"There's a rumor going around town that you and Charlene were caught dumpster diving." He wrapped one strong hand around his coffee cup and took a sip.

"Dumpster?" I laughed. The sound had a raw, hysterical edge.

Outside, Heidi stopped to look in the window. She caught my eye and smirked, then moved on. I could guess who'd ratted me out to Gordon. But who had Heidi heard the story from? "Ick. No way."

"Mm. So it's not true?"

"I have never removed trash from a dumpster." That, at least, was true. Curly owned plastic bins.

"Good. I'd hate to think you were still investigating these murders. San Nicholas is weird enough without you crawling through garbage."

"Yeah." I propped my chin on my fist and struggled

for a change of subject. "It's strange, when I first moved to San Nicholas, I only thought it was a cute beach town."

"And now?"

"The yoga instructor next door has declared war on my pies. Her boyfriend, my ex-fiancé, thinks Charlene's cat is his power animal. And someone tried to run me over with a stagecoach in a not-haunted, fake ghost town. By comparison, the fantasy gaming going on in the corner is passé." I nodded to the gamers. "What's slaying a few imaginary trolls in the grand scheme of life?"

He glanced at Ray and friends. "They're the normal ones, aren't they?"

I steeled myself. In the interests of solving the crime, I'd promised myself I'd never withhold evidence from the police. "There is something I should tell you. It turns out Curly is a member of an alternative religion. Devon found out, and Curly doesn't want anyone else to learn his secret. He said Devon wasn't blackmailing him, just making his life uncomfortable. I'm not sure I believe him, not after what Bridget told me."

"That Devon was suing her for stalking?"

"That he hinted he was Ewan's illegitimate and unknown son. Bridget said he was applying some pressure, though no overt blackmail. I think she was trying to protect her father."

"I know. She admitted the same to me."

So, she'd taken my advice after all. That was a relief.

Gordon frowned. "What's Curly's alternative religion?"

"He's a druid."

"A druid," he said, face impassive. "And he confided in you because . . . ?"

"He was seen flitting around the Bar X and other, er, places, in a suspicious robe."

"A suspicious robe?"

"I meant, it was suspicious he was in a robe. Not a bathrobe. A cape."

"Sighted by whom?"

My English-major heart warmed at his proper grammar usage. "A confidential informant." I wasn't going to give Marla the credit. Not after she'd left us holding the garbage bags.

He buried his head in his hands.

I winced. "And I should also mention that Marla had a romantic relationship with Devon."

He didn't respond.

"Gordon?"

"I'm having an aneurism. Pay no attention. And please stop playing detective without a license. I can't date a jail-bird."

I slithered from the booth and returned to my station behind the counter.

Graham jerked his thick thumb toward Gordon. "What's with Grumpy Cop?"

"Oh," I said vaguely, "you know. What have you heard about the murders? Any idea who did it?"

The two elderly men glanced at each other, shrugged. "I heard the Phantom killed 'em."

Ugh. What was with this town's obsession with the paranormal?

I must have looked skeptical, because Wally continued. "Well, it's got something to do with that ranch."

"What do you mean?" I asked.

"There's a lot of money in it."

"Is there?" I asked.

Graham set his cab-driver's cap on his head and adjusted the soft, checked fabric. "The price of Ewan's land has sky-rocketed. I heard some Silicon Valley tech billionaire made a multimillion-dollar offer."

"Multi?" I asked. "How multi?"

Graham named a figure.

I whistled. Now that was money worth killing for. "What did the tech guy want with it?"

"Heard he wanted his own private cowboy ranch here on the coast. It would have put those sharpshooters out of a job— a lot of the other artisans who work there too."

"But Ewan said no?"

"Ewan hasn't said anything yet," Wally said. "I hear the offer's still on the table."

"I should talk to some of the other artisans," I said, more to myself than to Graham. I hadn't seen any around whenever I'd visited the Bar X. "They must come to the ranch just before the events start," I muttered.

Graham shifted his bulk. "You could try the gal who sells pottery. Most days she works out of the garden center on Main."

Wally rubbed his pink nose. "And that Indian feller who sells the whatchamacallits—dream catchers and sage and stuff. You can find him working the bar at the White Lady most nights."

"You don't call 'em Indians anymore," Graham said. "They're indigenous peoples. Get with the times."

"The guy's from New Delhi," Wally said. "His last name's Patel. I suppose you'd call someone from Ethiopia an African-American?"

"No, I'd call him an Ethiopian."

I cleared my throat. I knew Arjun Patel well enough to say hello, but I hadn't known he'd been moonlighting at the Bar X. "Anything else?"

"Follow the money," Graham said. "When it comes to murder, it's usually jealousy, greed, or revenge. With all the money tied up in that ranch, I'm betting these murders were fueled by greed."

"That's a good point," I said, thoughtful, and went to clear a table.

If Devon really was the blackmailing type, could he have squeezed Ewan to keep their secret from Bridget? And assuming Devon really was Ewan's long-lost son, his appearance would cut into Bridget's inheritance.

Absently, I dried my already dry hands in my apron. Had she been protecting her father? Or herself?

Chapter Twenty

The downside of being a baker? Feet.

I still hadn't found a pair of truly comfortable shoes. By the end of the day, my dogs were barking.

After closing, and in spite of my swollen toes, I forced myself to walk down Main Street toward the Garden Shop. Let no one say San Nicholas is subtle with its business names.

I crossed the bridge, pausing at the center to lean on the concrete railing and watch the creek trickle past. It was after six o'clock. The summer sun was a white disk behind the fog, which hovered over the town in a cooling embrace.

Straightening off the concrete balustrade, I zipped my Pie Town hoodie to the collar and jammed my hands in its pockets. I strolled across the bridge and stopped in front of a barnlike building surrounded by a tumble of flowers. A CLOSED sign hung from the Garden Shop's rolling wooden doors.

I made a face. Of course, the nursery was closed. Aside from restaurants and Heidi's torture gymnasium, most shops on Main Street closed at five or six.

Turning, I made my way back to my VW, parked in the alley behind Pie Town. I squeezed inside, and in a fit of paranoia, locked the doors before I dug out my cell phone and called Charlene.

"It's about time you called," she said. "Marla's still skulking behind me. I could have been dead!"

"I've got a new lead. Do you think you can lose Marla and join me?"

She chuckled. "I've lost her twice already. Now she's parked outside my house."

"Where are you?"

"Inside my house, but she didn't follow me here. She must have figured this was where I'd end up. I lost her at the beach, and I can do it again. Trust me."

"The bartender at the White Lady sells Native American crafts at the Bar X. He wasn't around at the time of the murders, but—"

"Who? Patel? He might have some good dirt. I'll meet you at the White Lady. *Without* Marla."

I drove to the two-story restaurant and bar built into the cliffs. Fog drifted above the Spanish tiles lining its slanted roof. A sign in its white, adobe wall proclaimed it a historic landmark. During Prohibition, smugglers had hauled booze up from their boats and into the restaurant and speakeasy. I couldn't imagine lugging a crate of alcohol up the steep cliffs, but the profits must have been ginormous.

It wasn't the history that made the White Lady Charlene's favorite hangout. The restaurant was also the source of a ghost story. Since the nineteen-thirties, a spectral lady dressed in white had been seen in the restaurant and wailing along the cliffs. One of those ghost hunter reality TV shows had even done a special on the restaurant.

I found Charlene in the bar on the top floor, sipping a hot cocoa spiked with peppermint schnapps. Her brown, knit jacket bunched around the hips of her burnt-red tunic.

A youngish, dark-skinned man in a white apron polished a glass behind the bar. Couples sat at tables scattered throughout the bar area. In the restaurant, a crowd of diners ate a late dinner, their voices a gentle murmur. Through the windows, the setting sun turned fog and ocean into an impressionist painting of blurred pinks and blues. And this was why the White Lady was also one of *my* favorite spots, though I usually sat on the breezy patio below.

"Hi, Arjun," I said.

"Hey, Val. What can I get you?"

"Whatever Charlene's having."

"Sure thing." He grabbed a mug off a hook and got busy.

"Looks like you managed to shake Marla," I said to Charlene.

She snorted. "That wasn't hard. She's got as much chance of tailing someone as Frederick."

Her cat was absent his usual spot over Charlene's shoulder. The White Lady didn't allow animals inside. This was why we usually wound up on the outside patio.

"Have you asked him yet about the Bar X?" I nodded toward Patel, spraying whipped cream into my mug.

She straightened on her barstool. "You think I'd investigate without you?"

I smiled, pleased and a little guilty. "No, but I confess I did some investigating without you. Graham and Wally were in Pie Town today—"

"They're in Pie Town every day."

"And they mentioned someone had made an offer on the Bar X." I named the figure.

Charlene whistled. "Tempting, even for Ewan. But I can't imagine he'll sell. He loves the place too much. Besides, the Bar X is his home. If he sold, where would he live?"

"For the amount he was offered, he could go a lot of places."

"And build another Bar X?" She shook her head. "Never.

They'll be carrying him out of the Bar X feet first." Her expression shifted. "Though I hope they don't."

I slid onto the stool beside her. "But . . ." I trailed off. The money in the Bar X gave Bridget a motive. Ewan's daughter might not like having her inheritance split two ways. But I knew how Charlene would react if I suggested Bridget could have killed Devon. "Graham and Wally also mentioned a potter."

Charlene nodded. "Sarah Onaka. She works part-time at the Garden Center. We can catch her there tomorrow."

Patel slid my mug across the damp, wooden bar. "Here you go."

"Thanks," I said. "Hey, I hear you sell Native American crafts at the Bar X."

He shrugged. "Sure. Why not? The dream catchers were a hobby, but Ewan convinced me I could make some money off them."

"How'd you get into that?" I asked.

"An ex-girlfriend dragged me to a dream catcher workshop." He leaned his elbows on the bar. "Making them relaxes me. Still, I needed more inventory for the Bar X Trading Post, so I've been buying turquoise jewelry and pottery from a guy I know in Arizona."

"When do you find the time to work two jobs?" Charlene asked.

"It's a portfolio economy now," he said. "Haven't you heard? Lots of little part-time jobs instead of full-time work. I'd rather have taken another bartending job at the Bar X, but Devon beat me out." His skin darkened. "I wasn't happy at the time, what with his reputation and all. Now I'm relieved I didn't get the job."

"His reputation?" Charlene asked.

"Devon overserves people. Sorry, *served*, past tense."

"I thought he underpoured," I said, confused.

"He might have been doing that too," Patel said. "It's

possible to water down the drinks and still serve too many.
You can get in real trouble if the customer leaves drunk.
Ewan knew about his reputation, but I guess he figured
everyone needs a second chance. Ewan's a good guy that
way."

But Devon *had* done it again, getting a group of financial advisors drunk enough to brawl. And Ewan hadn't
fired him.

"Was Ewan good to you?" Charlene asked.

"Ewan did me a real favor," he said, "and he doesn't
charge for me to sell at the Trading Post. Dream catchers
and turquoise jewelry may not seem like much, but it beats
being an unemployed lawyer."

"You're a lawyer?" I asked.

"I passed the bar exam and got my license, but there's a
glut of lawyers. Turns out I wasn't the only one whose parents pushed them to go into law." His mouth turned down.
"It was either law or medicine, and I can't stand the sight
of blood."

"Do friends ask you for legal advice often?" I asked.

He wiped a damp rag across the bar. "You have no idea."

I swiveled toward Charlene. "Didn't Bridget mention
getting good advice from Patel?" It was a stab in the dark,
but maybe Bridget had asked Patel for advice on the stalking lawsuit on behalf of "a friend."

His dark brows slashed downward. "Did she? I don't—"

"There you are!" Marla swanked into the bar. She tightened the belt on her trench coat and strode toward us.

Charlene clutched the bar, her knuckles whitening. "I
lost her. I swear I lost her."

"I thought we were partners." Marla leaned an elbow
against the bar. "And here you are, interviewing a suspect
without me."

"Suspect?" Patel yelped.

She thrust a finger at him, her diamonds blazing. "Where were you the morning Devon Blackett was murdered?"

"I don't know," he sputtered. "At home, I guess. Probably making a dream catcher."

Marla sneered. "A dream catcher? Do you expect us to believe that? And I suppose you were alone."

"Come on, Marla," I said, "he's not a suspect. Take it easy."

"Take it easy?" She quivered, indignant. "Two men are dead. And this . . . *bartender* just stands there, polishing that beer glass like nothing's happened."

Charlene groaned and braced her head in her hands.

"What's wrong with being a bartender?" Patel asked.

"Ask Devon Blackett," she said. "Oh, right, you can't, because he's dead."

"I don't need this." Patel's jaw tightened. "Are you ordering or not?"

"You were jealous," Marla said.

"Marla," I said. "No. Patel's got nothing to do with—"

"Admit it," she said, her cheeks flushing. "You were jealous because Devon got the job bartending at the Bar X, and you didn't. And so, you killed him."

He folded his arms over his chest. "The three of you need to leave." His voice rang across the bar area. "Now."

At their tables, customers turned to stare.

My face went hot. "The three of us? We're not—"

"I should have guessed you two were trying to make me a patsy in one of your stupid cases," he said.

I pressed a hand to my heart. "I wasn't! We weren't!"

"Our cases aren't stupid," Charlene said.

"Patel," I said, "this is all a misunderstanding. Right, Marla?"

"Wrong," she said. "Patel knows what he did, and I won't stand for it."

"What is this?" he asked. "Good cop, bad cop? I don't

have to answer your questions, because here's a news flash. None of you are cops. Now get out, all of you, before I call the real police."

I stammered. "But . . ."

Charlene threw some bills on the counter and grabbed my arm. "Come on."

A waitress walked into the bar and glowered at us. "Is there a problem in here?" She shifted her tray beneath her arm.

"No," I said. "But—"

"Let's go," Charlene said.

I'd never been thrown out of a bar before in my life. Red-hot mortification flooded every single one of my cells. "But—"

"No buts," Charlene said, "you heard the man. We'll clear up this misunderstanding later."

"This isn't over," Marla shouted at him.

Chin to my chest, I trudged into the sloped parking lot. The fog swirled around us, providing welcome cover for my shame.

Charlene glowered at Marla. "Nice job, Columbo."

"I suppose you think you could have done better," Marla said.

"He was giving us real information," I said. "If you hadn't started hassling him, we might have learned more."

"More information you weren't going to share with me," Marla said. "I thought we were partners."

"Partners?" Charlene scoffed. "After you hung us out to dry at Curly's?"

"I had to," she said. "If I hadn't caused a distraction, I would have been caught. And then how could I have saved you?"

"You didn't save us," Charlene said. "You ditched us."

"Only so I could get away with the garbage bags." She

raised her eyebrows, her gaze questioning. "I don't suppose you want to help go through them?"

"*No*," Charlene and I said in unison.

"Did you learn anything from Curly?" Marla asked.

"Yeah," Charlene said. "He owns a shotgun. We're lucky he didn't fill us full of lead or call the cops."

"I don't see what you're so upset about," Marla said, "since neither happened. Besides, thanks to me, you now know that Patel person is a suspect in Devon's murder."

"He's not." I pulled my Pie Town hoodie tighter. It wasn't made for frigid ocean breezes. "He wasn't at the ranch when Devon or Larry were killed. And I really liked that bar." I wasn't much of a bar person, so it was pretty much the *only* bar I liked. Now I couldn't imagine returning. This was worse than getting caught by Curly.

"Yes," Marla said, "Patel is a suspect. Devon confided that Patel was jealous he'd beat him out for the job at the Bar X. Did you know Patel once let the air out of Devon's tires?"

Charlene squared her jaw. "Devon caught him at it, did he?"

"No," Marla said, "he didn't, but who else could it have been? The tires were flattened at the Bar X, and on a night when Patel was running his silly Trading Post."

"A night when you were there?" Charlene asked.

Marla drew herself up. "Just what are you implying?"

"Anyone could have let the air out of Devon's tires," I said. "If Devon didn't see who did it, then you can't assume it was Patel."

"And you see only what you want to see." She tossed her silvery hair and stormed to her Mercedes. Slamming the door, she roared out of the parking lot.

"I think she's really upset." I rubbed my face. "Maybe she did care for Devon."

Charlene snorted. "Marla cares about one person, and that's Marla."

"I dunno." I watched the roadster's taillights disappear over the rise.

"She's only on this case to beat me."

"You think so? Because there seems to be more motivating Marla than a simple rivalry."

"Do you remember my trip to Oregon, and that Bigfoot photo I snapped?"

How could I forget? She'd taped the blurry picture to the back of the cash register until customers complained. "Yes," I said, my head cocked.

"Two weeks later, Marla went to Scotland. *Scotland*," she said significantly.

I blinked. "You don't mean—"

"She shot a video of the Loch Ness monster. It was obviously only a floating log, but it got picked up by the Paranormal Travel Channel and Cryptozoologists International. Do you know where my Bigfoot photo went?"

"Your Twitter feed?"

"Into the local Bigfoot museum."

"We have a Bigfoot museum?"

"Not here. In Oregon."

A crow settled on the White Lady's tile roof and clicked its beak in reproach.

I pulled my hood low over my head. "I've never been thrown out of a bar before. Do you think they'll let us come back?"

"Cheer up," Charlene said. "The humiliation can't have been as bad as getting dumped at the altar."

"For the last time, I wasn't at the altar."

She patted my arm. "Of course, you weren't. Sorry. Marla makes me crazy. She's just . . ." She pinched her lips together. "She's Marla!"

"Yeah. Marla." There didn't seem any more to be said.

The sun vanished beneath the horizon, the thick fog hurrying the rush of night. I waved good-bye to Charlene and watched her drive off in her Jeep.

I took one last peek over the cliff. A dull, rhythmic roar greeted me, the waves invisible in the deepening dark.

I slid into my VW, turned the heat on full blast, and puttered down the coastal road, past beach homes and colorful Victorians. Trails of mossy old man's beard dripped from the dark cypress trees. If I was a kid, I'd trick-or-treat in this neighborhood in a heartbeat.

Two headlamps flashed on behind me. Wincing, I adjusted my mirror.

Instead of heading toward Highway One, I took a back road. Closer to the ocean, it wound past hillocks covered in sagebrush and tall grass. On a warm day, the place smelled divine, but tonight all I could smell was the musty scent from my heater. I needed to take my VW to the garage for a tune-up.

What if I did buy that van? Could I trade in my VW and get the price knocked down? I shook my head. Even if I traded in my ancient Bug—and I couldn't do that—the van would be out of my budget.

I glanced in my rearview mirror, and unease whispered up my spine. The car was still behind me. I accelerated—not exactly speeding, but getting close.

The other car increased its pace to match.

I bit my bottom lip, my glance flicking to the rearview mirror. Behind me, the car's headlights were set wide apart, probably a sedan.

I smiled.

Gordon's sedan.

Digging my cell phone from my bag, I clicked it on. "Call Gordon," I ordered. "Speaker."

There was a beep, and the phone rang.

"Val?" Gordon asked. "What's going on?"

I smiled harder. "You tell me."

"What do you mean?"

"I see your car behind me. You really don't have to follow me home tonight. I'm pretty sure I can make it there safely."

"Uh, Val. I'm at my parents'."

My mouth slackened. "Oh. Sorry. My mistake."

"Is someone following you?"

"No. I mean, I thought it was you. It's probably nothing." The road twisted into an industrial area of fishing supply companies and tumbledown shacks. Faded fishing floats and worn nets hung like Christmas ornaments from a chain-link fence.

"Where are you?" he asked.

My grip tightened on the wheel. "I'm driving toward the American Legion from the coastal road."

"Okay, make three lefts. See if he follows you."

I turned left, and left, and left again, circling a wine tasting room in a corrugated iron building.

The sedan followed.

My stomach twisted into my throat. "Ah, I've made the turns. The car's still there."

"Okay, Val, listen. I want you to drive to the police station. I'll meet you there. And stay on the line."

"Sure." My voice cracked. I glanced in the rearview mirror. In the dark, all I could make out were those rectangular headlights.

The car accelerated and slammed into my rear bumper.

My VW fishtailed sideways. I shrieked and hit the accelerator, zipping forward and narrowly avoiding a dumpster.

The phone skittered to the floor.

I wrenched the wheel to the right. Tires screeching, I whipped around a corner, barely missing an ancient pickup on cinderblocks. I veered onto a narrow road lined with unlit warehouses.

Panicked, I floored it, but my VW was outmatched by the sedan. It roared forward and slammed into my bumper again. The VW jolted.

Tinny shouts drifted from the floor of my car.

My pursuer edged to the left, as if to pass.

"Oh, no, you don't," I shouted. I'd seen enough TV car chases to know what came next. He'd slam me sideways, try to ram me into one of the corrugated buildings I was flashing past. Or worse, he'd cut me off and box me in.

The industrial area vanished, giving way to a farmer's field. I wove drunkenly, blocking the other car from getting around me. The car thunked me from behind, snapping me forward.

I shrieked like a five-year-old girl.

A ribbon of moving lights stretched before me. Highway One.

My shoulders tightened. "Come on, Bug. You can do it. You can—"

The car rammed me again. My seat belt caught me hard across the stomach, and I gasped with pain.

The red and gold lights zipping along the highway grew closer. Closer.

Ahead, the road sloped sharply upward before a stop sign. I didn't slow, didn't think. On the One, the line of cars magically parted. I could see my way into the flow of traffic.

I sped up, hit the rise. The VW went airborne.

"Huzzah!"

The car landed with a hard bump, lurching forward. I wrenched the wheel hard to the right. The VW skidded.

I wedged myself into traffic and vaguely registered a hubcap flying into a field.

A horn blared, but I laughed out loud. I was alive! I was Mario Andretti! And the police station was less than two miles away.

Red and blue lights flashed behind me. Like that was going to stop me. For all I knew, my pursuer had fake police lights.

At the turn into downtown, the stoplight's arrow turned green, the traffic gods giving me their blessing. I hung a left, then a right, crossing the bridge and screeching onto Main Street. The siren behind me howled, but I was closing on my target.

In front of the police station, I jammed on the brakes. The car skidded sideways, out of control. The VW hit something hard, flinging me into the door. There was a rending sound, a tearing, the VW wailing in agony.

And then all was silent.

Hands trembling, I stepped from the car.

A blaze of light blinded me. "Don't move!"

Chapter Twenty-One

So. I got arrested.

How was I to know that was a real traffic cop behind me? And, of course, whoever had been chasing me had fallen back as soon as I got on Highway One.

Fortunately, Gordon, chiseled and serious, arrived at the police station about fifteen minutes after I did. Unfortunately, Chief Shaw was there too.

"I'm sorry, Miss Harris, your pies are excellent, but the law's the law." Shaw stared down his hawk nose at me.

I perched uncomfortably on the edge of a plastic chair, my hands cuffed.

"Chief," Gordon said, "she called me, and I told her to drive straight here. And there is rear-end damage to her car. I was on the phone with her the entire time—"

"And talking on your cell phone while driving?" Shaw asked. "Do you have any idea how many laws you've broken?"

"I was on speaker phone," I bleated. "It's voice activated."

"Between that, the reckless driving, the damage to that light pole—"

"Sir," Gordon said, "may I have a word?" He shrugged his shoulders in his motorcycle jacket.

"I suppose there's no harm in it." Shaw moved away.

"Um, Sir, I meant with you." Gordon trotted after him, and they disappeared into an office.

The arresting officer loomed over me. "You should have pulled over."

"I know, Officer Perkins." Double embarrassment. Perkins was a regular at Pie Town. "All I could think was to get to the police station. Someone really was chasing me, and I was so close."

"Close only counts in horseshoes and hand grenades."

I lowered my head and stared at the linoleum floor. How apt. Because it felt like I'd stepped on a grenade. I wasn't sure which was worse. Getting thrown out of a bar or getting arrested for reckless driving.

"You do have good pies though."

"Thanks."

"The department went nuts when all those cherries came back from the Bar X. Really, excellent work, Val."

"What?!" I knew those cops had snaffled my pies to eat!

Chief Shaw stuck his narrow face out of the door. "Perkins?"

The officer nodded and strolled into the office.

Fuming over the pies, I rolled my shoulders and waited. For the record, handcuffs are not comfortable. Unless you're a yogi, they bite into your wrists. And the longer you're in them, the more painful they become. Maybe I should have requested waist shackles instead.

The cops emerged from the office. Gordon and Chief Shaw ambled toward me.

"Stand up," the chief said.

I rose.

"Turn around."

I did, and he uncuffed me. Relieved, I rubbed my wrists.

"What you did was foolish, young lady," Shaw said.

I bit my tongue. *Young lady?* He wasn't that much older than me. Ten years, tops. Maybe fifteen. Possibly twenty.

"We'll only be charging you with speeding," he said, "and you'll have to pay for any repairs to that light pole."

I released a gusty breath. "Thank you, Chief Shaw."

He preened, seemingly pleased with the "Chief." "Don't thank me," he said. "Thank Detective Carmichael and Officer Perkins. I think Perkins has a soft spot for you." He winked and wandered down a rear hallway.

"See ya, Val," Perkins said, and he left too.

"How are you feeling?" Gordon asked.

"Humiliated, but grateful. Thank you."

"I meant physically." His jade eyes darkened with concern. "That sort of crash can do a number on your neck."

I rubbed my muscles. "I feel okay."

"You might not tomorrow. Put some ice on it. Come on, I'll drive you home."

"I don't want to ruin any more of your evening. I can drive myself."

He held the front door open for me. "No, I don't think you can."

I walked outside and stopped short at the top of the brick steps.

An iron lamp post was embedded in the side of my blue VW. My car was half up the curb, its wheels at an odd angle.

I tried to swallow, couldn't. In all the excitement of being arrested, I hadn't really noticed the damage to my vintage car.

"Have you got Triple A?" he asked.

Numb, I nodded. Pointed. "My wallet is in the car."

I stumbled down the three brick steps to the sidewalk. My Bug. Squashed. I suspected the insurance company's verdict: totaled. The repairs would likely cost more than the old car's value, and my throat thickened. I'd had that VW since college. It was one of the few souvenirs from my old life, my pre-engagement life, life with my mom.

Gordon opened the driver's side door and leaned in, extracted my purse. He strode to the sidewalk and handed it to me. "Here you go."

"Thanks."

His green eyes darkened with concern. "Are you all right?"

Unable to speak, I motioned toward the Bug.

He gave me my cell phone. "I found it on the floor. The good news is, I don't think you've damaged the light pole. Some scraped paint, but that's it. All you'll get stuck with is the speeding ticket."

I nodded and tried to feel grateful. I was alive. I wasn't under arrest. And I had friends like Gordon and Officer Perkins to help me out of a jam. But all I felt was awful.

Swallowing, I pulled myself together and dug through my wallet for my membership card. I called, explaining the situation, and requested a tow truck.

"Are you in a safe place?" the dispatcher asked.

I glanced at Gordon, then at the police station, its windows glowing amber through the fog. "Yes."

"We'll get a tow truck to you in fifteen to twenty minutes," she said.

"Thanks." I hung up. Maybe Gordon was right. Maybe I had gotten in over my head. Maybe Charlene and I had gotten lucky in our first murder investigation.

"It's not that bad," he said.

I forced a smile. "Any day above ground is a good one, right?" It was one of Charlene's favorite sayings.

"What can you tell me about the car that was following you?"

"It's probably got my blue paint on its front fender. It looked like a sedan. The headlights were spaced wide apart. That's why I thought you were behind me. But I couldn't tell you the car's make or color. Oh." I remembered. "And the headlights looked rectangular." I shivered and hugged myself.

"We can wait inside." He nodded toward the police station.

"No," I said quickly. "That's okay." I'd rather not spend any more time in the police station than I had to.

"You've attracted the wrong person's attention."

"You warned me about asking questions." I'd already nearly gotten Ray killed. How many hard lessons did I need before I learned? "I should stay out of this," I said dully.

"I think it's too late for that. This is the third attempt on your life. Fourth, if you count the pie incident."

Surprised, I looked up at him. "Then what—"

"I'll come up with something."

Heat bubbled in my chest, my rotten mood evaporating. I had friends. I was unhurt. And whoever had tried to run me off the road had picked the wrong pie maker to bully.

We waited on the sidewalk.

He shrugged out of his jacket. "Take it." He handed it to me, and our fingers brushed.

A shiver of energy tingled through me. Swallowing, I slithered into the jacket and was enveloped in Gordon's woodsy scent.

A few minutes later, the tow truck rumbled up the road.

The driver lumbered out of the yellow truck and stared at my crushed Bug. Shaking his graying head, he removed his cap and laid it over his heart. "I used to own one of these. Good car."

He promised to tow it to my regular garage, and we left him muttering and clucking over the patient.

Gordon drove me home, staying to check out my hobbit-sized house for intruders. He glanced at the kitchenette, stuck his head in the bathroom, and peered around the bookcase that blocked off the sleeping area. No attackers lurked in the shadows.

Seemingly satisfied, he said, "Where's that ice pack?"

"Um. Freezer." I grabbed a bag of frozen peas.

Whipping a dish cloth from the oven handle, he wrapped it around the peas. He turned me around and lifted my hair, pressed the peas lightly against the back of my neck.

I drew in a quick breath—from the cold or from his presence, I couldn't say.

"I don't like leaving you here alone," he rumbled behind me. "Is there anyone who can stay with you?"

"I'll call Charlene." She'd want to hear about the car chase, but she wouldn't want to spend the night. And I wouldn't ask her to.

He stepped to the door and smiled, lopsided. "Tell her to bring Frederick." Gordon brushed a kiss across my forehead and left.

In spite of the frozen peas, I had a whacking-big neckache the next day. The sunlight streaming through the blinds at Pie Town assaulted my eyes. The chatter of diners and clatter of plates and rolling of dice battered at my ears. Not even the scent of baking fruit and sugar cheered me.

My VW was dead, and I was in mourning. The garage thought they could get a hundred bucks out of it for scrap.

Scrap!

Moving stiffly, I cleared one of the tables. "It was vintage," I muttered.

"You okay, Val?" Henrietta called from the gamers' booth. Beneath her mop of sandy hair, she beamed.

Balancing the plastic bin full of dishes on one hip, I turned my body to smile at her. "I'm fantastic."

Ray's crutches leaned against the gamers' table. He'd

draped his arm along the back of the booth, and his fingers grazed Henrietta's shoulder. A casual gesture? Or something more?

Enough with feeling sorry for myself. Poor Ray had suffered multiple breaks, and he was moving on. "Can I get anything for you?" I asked.

"Not me," he said, glancing at Henrietta.

She shook her head. "I'm good."

Ramrod straight, I delivered the bin of dirty dishes to the kitchen and set them beside the dishwasher. When I returned to my post behind the counter, Charlene had materialized on one of the pink counter stools.

She eyed me sympathetically and raised her mug. "Looks like you need an aspirin."

"An aspirin, a heating pad, and a vodka tonic."

"What's the word on your car?" she asked.

I shook my head, and hot pain streaked up my neck. "Totaled." I rubbed the heel of my palm against my chest, as if to ease the ache.

"You know what this means, don't you?"

"I'm screwed?"

"We've got a real excuse to return to Larry's Pre-Owned Vehicles. You need a new car. I can't drive you to work every morning."

Cautiously, I leaned my hip against the counter and it didn't hurt. As long as I kept my spine arrow straight, my lower body could do the merengue, and I'd feel no pain. "Do you think it's odd that this is the third time someone's tried to kill me by vehicular homicide? Devon was shot. Larry was bashed in the head."

"You know what they say. The definition of insanity is doing the same thing over and over again and expecting different results."

"Meaning?" I asked.

"Meaning whoever's trying and failing to kill you is a lunatic."

"In San Nicholas, that doesn't narrow the field by much."

"Or it means the third time isn't the charm." She slurped her coffee. "The good news is, I've put the word out on the Internet and have gotten some intriguing responses."

"Word out?" I asked.

"About whoever was chasing you. Turns out a sedan's gone missing from Larry's lot."

"Really?"

"One of the salesman is a follower of mine on Twitter." She tossed her sleek white hair and checked her watch. "I'll return to Pie Town at six, and we can car shop together."

"Six is when I close. I need a little more time to clean up."

"Do it later. The car lot's only open until seven."

"But—"

She swiveled off the stool and marched out, the bell over the door jingling.

I made a noise of despair. She was right. I needed a new car now. I couldn't exactly walk to work, and there wasn't any bus service in the hills where I lived. So, I kept calm and manned the register, doling out pies.

Graham and Wally ambled in. Pouring themselves coffee, they took up positions at the counter.

I sidled over to them. "You two are usually morning visitors. What gives?"

Graham removed his soft cap and took a sip of his coffee. "What? We can't switch things up every now and again?" He glanced at Wally, and they roared with laughter.

I didn't get the joke.

"He's fooling with you," Wally said. "We're early risers and will always be morning guys. We stopped by because we heard about your car chase. Word is, you took out a lamp post."

"I didn't take it out," I said. "I only scratched the paint."

"Get a good look at who was chasing you?" Graham asked.

"Aside from Officer Perkins, no."

"Too bad," Graham said. "We didn't hear anything either."

Since they didn't seem to have more to add, I wandered to the register. A harried-looking, middle-aged man rushed to the counter and ordered four mini potpies and four mini assorted fruit pies. "Wife's out of town." He gulped. "The kids had pizza last night."

"Good luck," I said, making change.

And so it went until six o'clock. I shooed the gamers out of Pie Town and was turning the sign to CLOSED when Charlene appeared on the doorstep.

She leaned inside. "Ready?"

"I guess." I looked around. The kitchen was clean, but the tables and counter needed wiping, and the floor needed mopping and . . . I'd do it later.

We piled into Charlene's Jeep and drove down Highway One. In the west, the sky glowed tangerine and rose. The car lot's balloon man flapped morosely. I wondered who was running the lot now that Larry was dead.

A salesman pounced before I'd gotten the Jeep's door open.

"Welcome! How can I earn your business today?" He smiled, his teeth flashing white in the darkening twilight.

My brows lowered. "Um, we're looking for Larry," I lied. Charlene and I had planned our approach. I didn't think it was a very good one, but I couldn't come up with anything better.

The salesman's expression turned solemn. He lowered his voice. "I'm sorry, but Mr. Pelt has passed."

"Then who's running the place?" Charlene braced her elbows on the hood of her yellow Jeep.

"Mr. Pelt's nephew, but I'm sure I can help you. What sort of vehicle are you looking for?"

"We're looking for Pelt's nephew," Charlene said.

"We've got some great new Jeeps. And if you're interested in an SUV, we've got some real beauties. Now, I can tell you ladies are looking for something to run around town in."

"No," I said, "we're—"

"Oh, you two are distance drivers?"

"The only distance she drives is between her home and Pie Town," Charlene said.

"Pie Town?" He snapped his fingers. "The van, of course. I heard you were interested. Came back for another looksie, did you? We've got another customer who wants it, but he had to talk it over with his wife. If you act fast, I can sell it to you."

My chest tightened. Someone else wanted the van?

Charlene crossed her arms, rumpling her loose, green, knit jacket. "That's the oldest line in the car salesman handbook. What man would want that pink monstrosity?"

"It wasn't that bad," I said. It was fantastic—a perfect, pie-box pink.

"He's planning on repainting it in camo," he said. "He's a duck hunter. And for the price that van is selling at, he can repaint it any way he wants, and it's still a deal."

"Where's Greg?" Charlene asked.

"This way." He strode around the side of the building, and we followed.

Charlene pinched my arm.

"Ow!"

"What are you thinking, acting interested in that van?" she whispered.

I rubbed my sore arm. "If I have to buy a car, I may as well get the van. It's perfect for pie transport."

"Don't let him know that. My deal on the price was with

Larry, and he's dead. If Salesboy thinks you want it, he'll never drop the price."

"If that duck hunter buys it, it won't matter anyway."

Charlene snorted, weaving between a Porsche and a Ford Escort. "There's no duck hunter."

"Here it is," the salesman said, stopping in front of the pink van.

I sighed. The pink van, my blushing beauty, gleamed dimly in the twilight. And I still couldn't afford it.

"We asked to see Greg, not the van," Charlene said.

He grinned at me. "I can tell you're considering this van, and you can imagine how nice it would be to drive home in it. Greg will be happy to help with the paperwork."

Charlene swiveled on her heel. "Come on, Val."

Neck aching, I trotted after her.

"Wait!" the salesman shouted. "Don't you want to take it for a test drive?"

Charlene lengthened her strides. "If Greg's available to help with paperwork—and right now I don't trust a word out of that salesman's mouth—he's in the showroom."

The salesman hurried after us. "I can see you're used to playing hardball."

"We're used to talking with Greg," Charlene said, pushing through the glass doors. She cupped her hands to her mouth and shouted, "Greg! Get your butt down here!"

Her voice echoed off the shiny pre-owned vehicles, the tile floor, the chrome staircase.

I winced.

An upstairs door popped open, and Greg hurried down the sleek metal steps, a black armband around his crisp white shirt. "Mrs. McCree! Ms. Harris! It's great to see you both." He nodded to the other salesman. "I'll take it from here, Ron."

Ron's face fell, and he slouched from the building.

Greg grimaced. "Sorry. Ron can be a little overeager. But thanks for coming. You saw my Tweet?"

Charlene quirked a brow. "You're @GregorianChant something something?"

"That's my Twitter handle. I'm the one who sent you that tip about the stolen sedan."

"Why?" I lowered my head and studied him.

His tanned face grew somber. "Because I liked my uncle. And I don't think it's a coincidence that we've had two stolen cars in a week—the same week he was murdered."

"Did you report the theft to the police?" I asked.

"How else would we claim the insurance?" He and Charlene shared a knowing look.

"What can you tell us?" I asked.

"Same as last time," he said. "Someone stole the car's key off the board. Whoever killed my uncle must have stolen his keyring. This time, they got into the dealership without having to break in."

"Must have?" Charlene asked. "You mean, you don't know for sure?"

"The police haven't given me his effects, and they haven't told me what was or wasn't in his pockets. Why would they? I'm only a nephew. I'm also heir to Larry's vast pre-owned car fortune." He slumped against a blue Mustang convertible. "They think I have motive."

Charlene patted his shoulder. "I doubt that. It is a nice car dealership though."

"It's an amazing dealership. Larry built it from scratch. I didn't mean to sound ungrateful—I'm thrilled he left it to me. I just didn't want it to happen so soon. He was a good guy." He swallowed, his Adam's apple bobbing.

I pretended not to notice his brown eyes had grown watery. "Did Larry say anything to you in the last week about the murder at the Bar X?" I asked.

"No. And believe me, I asked. I think he was shaken by the murder. He seemed off."

"Off how?" I asked.

"He was always a happy guy. I know car salesmen have a reputation for being fakes, but Larry really enjoyed cars, and he enjoyed people too. But this last week, I could tell he was forcing it. He wasn't himself."

"I heard there was a falling out between him and the other Blue Steel guys about a horse," I said.

Greg choked back a laugh. "About a horse? It was over a woman."

My brows rose. "A woman? Who?"

"Some rich lady who's got a place on the beach."

"Not Marla Van Helsing?" Charlene asked.

"That's the one," he said. "I've seen her in action. She flirted with all of them, but my uncle ended up dating her until she found someone better. That's what broke up the team."

"Why did Larry tell us their falling out was over money and the time he was putting in taking care of the horses?"

"Code of the West," he said. "You don't speak badly about a lady."

I folded my arms. Of all the reasons to lie during a murder investigation . . .

"We'd like to take a look at Larry's papers," Charlene said. "He might have left a clue to his murderer."

"The police have already been here," he said, angling his head toward the upstairs office. "So, if you want to take a look at what's left in his desk, I guess that's okay. Come on. I'll show you."

We followed him up the stairs to the office. It was painted white, with windows overlooking the showroom and the darkening sky. Two rolling chairs sat on one side of a black, curving desk, and a matching chair was on the other.

Greg watched us rifle the desk. "Say, I can always rent that van to you, let you get a feel for it before you decide to buy."

"I'll think about it," I said, thumbing through a stack of envelopes.

We didn't turn up any incriminating photos or secret reveals to the murderer's identity, so we moved on to the filing cabinets.

After an hour, Charlene rolled back her chair and shook her head. "There's nothing."

I shut a cabinet drawer. "Same here."

"Sorry," Greg said. "The police didn't seem to find anything either. At least, they didn't take anything away."

"Why doesn't that make me feel any better?" Charlene asked.

"Because you want the killer caught as badly as I do," he said. "If you find anything, would you let me know?"

"After we tell the police," I said.

"Right," he said. "And, uh, Mrs. McCree?"

She looked up. "Yes?"

His smooth cheeks reddened. "Is it true about the fairies in the dog park?"

Chapter Twenty-Two

Pie Town's Saturday afternoon crowd was buzzing. Balancing a tray of pies, I sped to a booth full of surfers near the front window.

Heidi walked past outside and paused to scowl at me.

I wasn't going to let her bother me. So what if I could barely manage fifty pushups? I got plenty of exercise, even if my jeans had seemed a little tight this morning.

White cat draped over her shoulder, Charlene breezed into the pie shop and poured herself a cup of coffee. She lounged against the counter and eyed the restaurant. Gamers in one corner. Surfers in the opposite. Couples in between with sunburnt noses and salt-tangled hair.

"You take a break yet?" she asked.

"What?" Frowning at the cat, I whizzed past her into the kitchen. I set the tub of dirty dishes beside the dishwasher, and returned to my spot behind the register.

"I said, have you had a break yet?" She sipped her coffee.

"Sure, I . . ." My stomach rumbled, and I glanced at the clock. Two-thirty, and I hadn't eaten lunch. Had I taken a break at all today?

Expression shuttered, Petronella leaned through the

kitchen window. "No, you haven't had lunch. Go ahead, Abril and I have got this."

"You sure?" I shifted my weight, rolled my shoulders. It was busy today, and Petronella was still acting stiff around me. Somewhere, I'd wrongfooted it, and dumping more work on her couldn't help things.

"You think I don't know what I can handle?" Petronella asked sharply. "Everyone out there's already been served. We're past the lunch rush. They've already paid the bills. All I've got to do is clean up when they leave and deal with anyone picking up pies. Go."

She was right, and I was starving. Besides, I lived in a beach town, and I was spending most of the glorious California summer indoors. I untied my apron and hung it on a peg behind the counter. "Thanks."

Charlene raised her hand, palm out. "Hold up."

I waited while she finished her coffee.

She sighed. "That does the trick."

Together, we strolled onto the sidewalk. A balmy, ocean breeze caressed the bare skin of my neck and arms. I longed to loosen my chignon, let the wind play with my hair. But then I'd just have to put it up again. Loose hair does not go together with food service for oh-so-many reasons.

"What's up with Petronella?" Charlene asked.

"You noticed too? I'm not sure. She started taking those mortician classes she's always been talking about. Maybe she's feeling overwhelmed?"

"She's working and going to school? I'd have thought you'd be a little more sensitive."

"I offered to change her hours," I said, defensive. "She said 'no.'"

Charlene harumphed. "That pottery gal is at the Garden Center today. Let's head over there."

Pleading starvation, I talked Charlene into stopping at

the deli. I bought an egg salad sandwich, and we continued down Main Street. I paused at a corner park beside a mosaic statue of a mermaid. "Do you mind?"

She shrugged and sat on the green bench.

Perching beside her, I unwrapped my sandwich. A twentysomething walked past in one of my PIES BEFORE GUYS T-shirts, and I nearly dropped my egg salad. "Charlene! She's wearing one of our tees." We were getting popular!

"Well, you're selling them, aren't you?"

"Yes, but only to tourists." I'd never seen someone around town wearing one. Pie Town *was* cool!

Frederick lifted his head, sniffing the egg salad.

"The killer must think we know more than we do," Charlene said. "Or he wouldn't have tried to run you off the road, and I wouldn't have had to play taxi for you again this morning."

"Thanks for that." I took another bite and swallowed. The sandwich was a little dry, and I wished I'd gotten something to wash it down with. "I called Greg. I'm going to take him up on his offer to rent me the van until I can figure out what I'm going to do." I'd have to buy something, but I wasn't going to car shop while desperate.

"Ah, so the mythical duck hunter bowed out," she said triumphantly. "I'll tell you what you should do. Just buy that van. I saw the way you were ogling it."

"I don't have the cash."

"There is such a thing as a payment plan," she said.

"I'm kind of already on one," I mumbled between bites, feeling my cheeks flush.

"What do you mean?"

"Starting up Pie Town cost more than I expected." I cleared my throat. "And then we lost all that money after the murder earlier this year, and then I got the bright idea of hiring more staff—"

"Who we needed. Pie Town's doing well. And you're not headed to Heart Attack City from overwork."

"Profits are moving in the right direction," I said. A Ferrari rumbled down the street. It probably belonged to one of those Silicon Valley billionaires. "Things are coming together. And now with the opportunity to sell pies outside the shop, business is looking up. It's just . . . the thought of taking on more debt right now turns my stomach." Maybe I should have been a business major instead of earning an English degree.

She patted my knee. "You can't sell pies wholesale without something to deliver them in. Every leap forward is a risk. But the universe will provide, you wait and see."

"Have you been reading those self-help books again?"

"Maybe."

"You know they give you heartburn." I finished the sandwich, crumpled the wrapper, and tossed it into a nearby bin.

The afternoon sun glinted off the shop windows. We continued down Main Street and crossed the short bridge over the creek. The water trickled faintly, low in the summer. I reached up, brushing my fingers along the bottom of one of the flower baskets hanging from the iron lamp posts.

On the other side of the bridge, we crossed the street to a barnlike structure surrounded by pots of young trees and shrubs. The ground was lined with tanbark, and it crunched beneath our shoes. I took a step, and something slithered beneath my sneaker.

I shrieked and leapt into the air. A red snake with an ivory stripe on its back darted between two miniature lemon trees.

I clutched my chest, my blood pounding.

Charlene laughed. "It's only a garter snake. They're harmless."

Graham waddled out of the sliding barn doors, a floppy fisherman's hat on his white hair. "Was that a scream of delight?"

"Graham!" I wheezed. "What are you doing here?"

"I can't spend all day at Pie Town," he said. "I was looking for a new rhododendron bush. The neighbor's dog dug up mine."

Charlene stroked Frederick, who didn't deign to open his eyes. "I know that dog. He and Frederick don't get along."

"Really?" Graham raised a brow. "I didn't think he was smart enough to know he's not supposed to like cats."

"That's the problem," she said.

"So, what are you two doing here?" he asked.

"Interrogating a witness," Charlene said.

"Who?"

Charlene jerked her head toward the barn. "Sarah Onaka."

"The pottery gal? She's inside. Come on." He walked into the barn.

I rubbed the back of my neck, not liking that our chat with Sarah had turned into a group interview. But I couldn't object when Graham was one of my favorite customers.

We walked down an aisle fragrant with flowering plants. The barn's high roof was made of glass, flooding the wide building with light and warmth. Keeping an eye out for snakes, I brushed past a hydrangea bush.

Graham turned right through a display of flowering, pink bromeliads and stopped in front of a tall counter made of distressed-wood boards. A young Asian woman paused in the act of rearranging a shimmering bowl the color of the Mediterranean Sea, and I gaped.

I have a weakness for pottery. Maybe it's because pottery

is aligned with the kitchen. Maybe it's because it's one of the few forms of handmade art I can afford. I gave myself a mental head slap. Maybe I like pottery because I have nowhere to put it. I always want what I can't have.

"Hi!" She smiled, tucking her long black hair behind one ear. "How can I help you?" She glanced at my TURN YOUR FROWN UPSIDE DOWN T-shirt. "Pie Town! Hey, you're going to be selling at the Bar X, aren't you?"

"Actually, Ewan will be selling our pies," I said. "But, yes."

"They're investigating Devon's murder," Graham said.

"The police are investigating," Charlene said. "But someone's tried to run over Val three times since Devon was killed, once with a stagecoach. We're being proactive."

"With a stagecoach?" Sarah asked. "That really happened? I thought it was a new urban legend. What with the Bar X Phantom—"

Charlene braced her hands on the counter and leaned forward. "The phantom? What have you heard?"

"Um, Charlene." I tugged at the hem of my pink T-shirt. "I think—"

Charlene shushed me. "You were saying?"

"It turned everything upside down in my pottery shop. Fortunately, nothing was broken."

"When was this?" Charlene asked.

"A couple months ago. When I locked up the pottery shed, everything was fine. I came back two days later for an event, and—"

"Your pottery was upside down?" Charlene asked breathlessly.

"Not just the pottery," Sarah said. "The phantom had even turned over my pottery wheel."

I checked my watch. It was time I returned to Pie Town. "About Devon—"

"About the phantom," Charlene said, "when did you first learn about the ghost?"

"That was when I learned about it. I thought someone was pranking me, but then Bridget told me about the phantom."

"Did she?" Charlene asked. "Interesting."

"The phantom seems harmless," Sarah said. "And my pottery sales went way up afterward. People heard about what had happened, and came to check out the site of the haunting. A lot of them ended up buying. So, as far as I'm concerned, the phantom can make a return visit any time he likes, as long as nothing's broken."

"You must have been relieved," I said. "Now, Devon—"

"What sort of stories did Bridget tell you?" Charlene asked.

"The phantom's made a mess of her photography studio more than once. And I guess there've been some sightings in the saloon."

"Did Devon see the phantom in the saloon?" I asked, trying to get this interview on track.

"If he did," Sarah said, "he wouldn't admit it. He thought the whole thing was ridiculous. For a bartender, Devon could be a little snarky, but the customers liked him."

"Snarky," I said, "how—"

"What did the phantom do in the saloon?" Charlene asked, breathless.

My lips compressed. *Oh, come on!*

"Once, when Ewan opened up the saloon, all the chairs were stacked to the ceiling. And doors have opened when no one was there."

The phantom's antics sounded suspiciously like the haunting at the White Lady. I remembered our recent banishment from the bar, and my temperature rose. "Who do you think killed Devon?" I asked.

The three stared at me.

"What?" I asked.

Charlene patted my shoulder. "She's distraught. It's all the murder attempts. You understand."

"I am not distraught," I said.

Graham shook his head. "It's a strange feeling when someone's trying to kill you. When I was in the war—"

"No one wants to hear your war stories," Charlene interrupted. "Now, about the phantom."

I made a noise somewhere between a groan and a whine.

"Is that your stomach?" Graham asked. "Have you eaten?"

"She's digesting," Charlene said. "I've never heard louder intestines."

Frederick raised his head and meowed in agreement.

"You should try green tea," Sarah said.

"Two people have been killed at the Bar X," I said. "Aren't you worried about working there?"

"Why should I be?" Sarah asked. "I haven't done anything wrong."

"Did Devon do something wrong?" I asked.

"He was a man-slut," she said. "And he had a thing for older women." Twin lines appeared between her brows. "What was it he said about them? Something by Ben Franklin."

"In all your Amours you should prefer old Women to young ones . . . They are so grateful!!" Graham quoted.

Charlene glowered at him. "Says you."

"Said Ben Franklin," Graham said. "Hey, I'm a history buff. Franklin had a lot of better reasons too—like older women being more intellectually interesting. He practically wrote an essay on the topic."

"He would." Charlene sniffed. "Ben Franklin was a rogue."

Sarah grinned. "At least Franklin was a gentleman. Devon broke up with his girlfriends by text."

Charlene and I both hissed an indrawn breath. There was

no easy way to break up with someone, but a breakup text was lowdown. And how did Sarah know he broke up with women by text? "Did someone complain to you?"

Her cheeks flushed crimson. "Ah, no. I got one of those texts."

"So, it wasn't only older women he liked," I said.

"No, but he preferred them. He said they were less demanding."

"That's what Franklin said," Graham said.

Charlene's eyes bulged.

His head turtled between his round shoulders. "Well, he did!"

"So angry women or angry husbands are our suspects?" I asked. "No other people who might want to kill Devon?"

"Isn't that enough?" Sarah asked. "There were a lot of angry women."

But none had been spotted at the ghost town the day of Devon's murder. And I couldn't imagine why one would want to run me down.

We thanked her, and Charlene and I walked back toward Pie Town.

"This isn't getting us anywhere," Charlene said.

I gave her a look. It was hard to make progress on the murder when we were distracted by the phantom menace.

"Greg told us that his uncle seemed upset about something before he died," I said.

"Larry must have seen something, or guessed something, about the killer."

"And that made him the next victim. The way I figure it, either he wasn't sure about what he'd seen or believed, or else he didn't want to believe what he'd seen. Otherwise, he would have gone to the cops."

"You think he confronted the killer?" she asked.

"Maybe. So, who at the Bar X would Larry want to protect?"

"Oh, I see. We're back to Bridget and Ewan again," Charlene snapped.

"You think he'd protect them?"

"No," she said, "because they're innocent. Bridget wouldn't hurt a fly, and Ewan had no reason to kill Devon."

"Bridget did admit Devon was putting pressure on her. Maybe he was putting pressure on Ewan as well."

"If Ewan knew he had a son—and we can't be sure Devon was his son—he would have embraced him, no question."

"Maybe Ewan was trying to protect Bridget from the truth," I said. "The way she was trying to protect him?"

Charlene shook her head. "That makes no sense. Ewan's made no secret that he was out of control before he met Bridget's mother. He didn't betray his family. If Devon was his son, he would have welcomed him with open arms, and so would Bridget. Besides, she's no kid to be sheltered. She's an adult."

We crossed the concrete bridge. A woman pushing a stroller came toward us, and we stepped off the sidewalk to make way.

"So that leaves Moe, Curly, and Marla," I said.

"It's got to be Marla. Larry was protecting her, and she killed him."

"I dunno." I sidestepped a yellow fire hydrant. "If all three of the gunslingers had the hots for Marla—enough to break up their friendship—Moe or Curly might have killed Devon out of jealousy. We need to confirm that what Greg told us about Marla breaking up the sharpshooters was true."

Charlene snorted. "Who do you expect to confirm it? Code of the West, remember? Do you think Marla will tell us the truth?"

I rubbed my chin. "Under the right circumstances, yes."

"And what circumstances are those?"

"You need to make up with her."

Her mouth pinched. "Forget it."

"Hasn't this feud been going on long enough? Who does it benefit?"

"Me, because I don't have to deal with Marla." She lengthened her strides, and I trotted after her.

"Come on, Charlene. Unforgiveness is like drinking poison and expecting the other person to die."

"Who said that? The Dalai Lama?"

"I don't know." And I was fairly certain I'd screwed up the quotation. "But it's true."

"Don't push me, Val. You don't know what you're talking about."

"But—"

She spun and raised a finger. "Not another word, or I won't drive you to the car lot tonight for your pre-owned van."

I zipped my lips.

My piecrust maker was as good as her word. She drove me to collect the big pink van after Pie Town closed.

Charlene waited around for me to sign the stack of rental forms, and then sped off, claiming she couldn't be seen driving in the same zip code as a pink piñata.

The sky was darkening, rose and gold streaking the western clouds. I ran my hand over the broad steering wheel and told myself not to get too used to the van, even if it was awesome and could probably transport a hundred pies.

Wanting to share the good news with Gordon, I dug in my purse for my cell phone. It wasn't there. I turned my purse upside down; mint tins and receipts and lipsticks spilled onto the seat beside me. No phone.

"Rats!" I must have left it at Pie Town. So, I drove back

into town, parking in front of Heidi's gym. Hurriedly, I unlocked Pie Town's front door and ran inside.

When I returned, Heidi paced the sidewalk, her blond ponytail swishing behind her. "Is that thing yours?"

"Not yet. I'm borrowing—"

"You're not supposed to park on the street. Employees and owners of the buildings are supposed to park in the alley, so as not to take street parking from paying customers."

"Yes, but it was only for a min—"

"You are so selfish!" She stormed into the gym, the glass door banging behind her.

I groaned and shoved up the sleeves of my Pie Town hoodie. Would the gym owner believe me if I said I was sorry?

A black Cadillac cruised past on the street, a bag of groceries balanced on the roof. Mrs. Banks peered over the steering wheel, her gray curls quivering.

"Mrs. Banks!" I shouted. "Your groceries!"

She continued on, oblivious.

I chased after her, waving my arms in the air. "Mrs. Banks! Mrs. Banks! Stop!"

The Cadillac whipped around a corner, and the groceries went flying. The paper bag hit the pavement and split. Oranges, cans of soup, and a cauliflower tumbled into the street.

I grabbed the torn bag. Cradling it awkwardly, I scooped up the wayward groceries and kept a wary eye out for runaway Priuses.

I checked what was left inside the bag. At least she hadn't bought eggs.

Returning to my pie shop, I slid the groceries into a Pie Town bag, locked up, and got into the van. Mrs. Banks would wonder where her groceries had apported to if I didn't return them to her soon.

Slowly, still getting used to the size of the van, I drove through town and on to Mrs. Banks's house. She lived in the same neighborhood of rundown Victorians as Charlene. And though it had no view of the ocean, the rolling hills, darkening to cobalt, almost made up for the lack.

I parked in front of Mrs. Banks's purple two-story, and hopped from the van.

Somewhere nearby, something mechanical whirred.

I carried the groceries past the Cadillac in her driveway, through an overgrown garden, and up the front steps. Balancing the bag on one hip, I rang the doorbell.

The door opened, a man's tall figure silhouetted against the screen.

I took a step back.

"Val?" Gordon pushed open the screen door. The sleeves of his navy fisherman's sweater were pushed up to his elbows.

I snapped my mouth shut.

"What are you doing here?" he asked.

"Mrs. Banks lost her groceries." I raised the Pie Town bag in explanation. "What are *you* doing here?"

He flushed. "Cooking dinner." Gordon stepped close, lowering his head. In a low voice, he said, "Last time I was here, she didn't have any groceries. Come in."

Grinning, I followed him inside. I'd caught him cooking dinner for an elderly lady once before. He'd been worried that she hadn't been eating. Honestly, could he be any more perfect?

"The last time?" I asked.

He grimaced. "Grocery thieves."

Mrs. Banks hurried into the entryway, cluttered with knickknacks and shoes. She clutched a flowered hat to her chest. "Val! How lovely! I was just telling Officer Carmichael that those fairies are at it again. They took another bag of groceries."

"I've got them," I said.

She stopped short, her loose gray skirt swaying around her knees. "You got the fairies?"

"No, your groceries."

"But how?" she asked.

"They were on top of your car. You must have forgotten to load them into the backseat. I saw them fly off on Main Street."

She froze, pink creeping across her powdered cheeks. "Oh." She plucked at the hat's silk flowers. "Oh, dear." Abruptly, she sat in a cane-backed chair. The hat dropped to the parquet floor. "I forgot all about them."

"Is it possible that you forgot about the other missing groceries?" Gordon asked. "Maybe fairies aren't responsible."

"Oh, this is embarrassing." She pressed her wrinkled hands to her face. "You must think I'm an utter fool."

"No," I said quickly. "Of course not. We all forget things from time to time."

She lowered her hands to her lap and met my gaze. "But we don't all blame our forgetfulness on the fairies. The worst of it is, I'll probably forget we even had this conversation tomorrow!"

"I don't think you're that bad off," Gordon said. "Come on, Mrs. Banks. Help me set the table. Val, the kitchen's back there." He nodded down a hallway. "Why don't you take in the groceries?"

"Val, you should stay for dinner," Mrs. Banks said. "It's the least I could do after you salvaged my things."

I glanced at Gordon, and he nodded.

"I'd love to," I said. "Thanks."

I found my way to the kitchen, tiled in an unhappy, speckled brown and smelling of lasagna. The oven light was on, foil folded neatly on the counter, and I guessed Gordon had prepared the food in advance. I removed the groceries and found places for them inside the green, nineteen-seventies-era refrigerator.

The kitchen door opened and Tally Wally sloped inside, an electric weed cutter slung over his shoulder. "I finished with the backyard . . ." He stopped short. "Val? I didn't expect to see you here." He leered. "Or are you chasing down that young policeman?"

Tingling spread from my chest to my face. "I'm returning Mrs. Banks's groceries."

He whistled. "Brought 'em back from fairyland, did you?"

Gordon walked into the kitchen. "Hey, Wally. Thanks for taking care of those weeds."

"No problem. How's dinner coming?"

"Fifteen minutes," Gordon said.

Wally rubbed his broad hands. "Just in time."

"I didn't realize you both knew Mrs. Banks," I said.

Gordon leaned one hip against the counter. "She reported some fairy thieves last week. I was nearby, so I took the call."

Wally snorted. "Ever since the dog park, there's been a fairy epidemic. Did you know that if you compare reports of fairy sightings from hundreds of years ago to UFO sightings today, they're nearly identical?"

"Did Charlene tell you that?" I asked.

"Who else?" Wally leaned closer. "I saw one, you know, when I was in the Air Force. It buzzed our plane and then took off, straight into the atmosphere. No Russian bird could do that."

Presuming he meant UFOs rather than fairies, I glanced toward the open kitchen door. "I'm a little worried about Mrs. Banks," I said quietly.

"Does she have any relatives?" Gordon asked.

"Nope," Wally said. "And I don't think she's quite ready to condemn herself to a home."

"Is anyone else checking in on her?" I asked.

"Graham comes by every now and again. He lives just up the street. But I don't like the situation much either. This afternoon when I stopped by, there was a puddle of water on the kitchen floor." He pointed to a spot on the stained linoleum. "She could have slipped and cracked her head."

"Maybe we should . . ." I trailed off, unsure. "I don't know . . . set up a check-in schedule? I'm in this neighborhood often enough. It doesn't make sense for us to all show up at the same time like tonight."

"Good idea." Wally rubbed his drink-roughened nose. "Graham will go along with it. If we all stop by once a week, maybe rope in some of the neighbors, she'll get daily visitors."

I nodded, relieved we had a plan.

Mrs. Banks tottered into the kitchen. "What can I do next?"

We joked, fixing dinner, then migrated to the dining room. Gordon sat beside me, his hand occasionally grazing mine as we passed each other food. And even though this hadn't been the evening I'd planned, I was content.

Chapter Twenty-Three

My fingers flexed, getting used to the feel of the rented van's wide steering wheel. The van was pink perfection, and it handled like a dream. Sunlight glinted on the windshield, and I flipped down the visor.

We rolled over a pothole on the dirt road, and the pies stacked in the back barely jiggled.

Beside me, Charlene harrumphed. "That car salesman is trying to suck you in, trick you into buying."

"I thought you said renting the van was a good idea."

She crossed her arms. "I don't like being manipulated."

"I told you, I can't afford to buy it right now anyway," I said, and pulled up in front of the Bar X's closed gates. "Just a minute."

I went through the process of opening the gates, driving through, and closing them behind us.

"The step is too high," Charlene said. "It's hard to get in and out of this pink monster."

"It's no higher than your Jeep."

"I beg to differ."

"You? Beg?" I grinned. It was another great day of pie sales. Not only was Pie Town hopping, but Ewan had put in a big order for an event later this afternoon. I knew it was wrong to depend on one person's business. Don't put your eggs in one basket, etcetera. But if Ewan kept up these orders, and I got a few more wholesale clients, maybe I *could* afford to buy the van. And I liked that it was a VW. It seemed a fitting successor to the Bug.

We drove down the ghost town's Main Street. A tumbleweed rolled across the road, and I slowed near the saloon.

Craning her neck, Charlene stared out the front window. "What are all those cars doing up at Ewan's house?"

I looked up the hill. In front of the Victorian, a cluster of vehicles glinted in the sun. "Could those belong to the people here for the event?" I clutched the wheel more tightly.

"Too early. And we already passed the event parking lot."

"They could be the organizers." But something gleamed blue and red atop one of the sedans. I sucked in my breath. "Those are—"

"Police cars," we finished in unison.

"Keep driving," Charlene said, her expression grim.

We wound up the road to the yellow Victorian, and I parked behind a black-and-white.

Ewan's front door opened, and a police officer emerged leading Bridget, her hands cuffed behind her. Chief Shaw followed.

"Oh, no." My limbs turned leaden. I'd been right. Bridget was the killer.

Charlene slid from the van and hurried up the rough slope to the front yard.

Ewan stormed from the house and gesticulated toward Bridget.

Leaping from the van, I chased after Charlene.

"Don't say a word," Ewan shouted after Bridget. He ran down the porch steps. "The lawyer will meet you at the police station."

Chief Shaw stopped in front of me, and I braced myself for a lecture.

"Miss Harris, it looks like we have you to thank for another hot tip," he said, jovial.

My stomach tightened. "I . . . What?" I asked, flummoxed.

He clapped me on the shoulder. "No need to be modest. We always appreciate citizens coming forward."

"But, I didn't." I turned to Charlene and Ewan. "I had nothing to do with this. What's going on?" Had I said something to Gordon that had gotten Bridget arrested? I cudgeled my brains. I hadn't told him anything he didn't already know. At least that's what he'd said. Had he been faking me out?

Charlene's skin faded to paper white. Ewan's face flushed red with anger. And Gordon . . . Where was Gordon?

"No need to say any more, Miss Harris," Shaw said. "I'll see you in Pie Town." The chief got into his police car, and the cavalcade drove down the hill.

A muscle pulsed in Charlene's jaw. "What did he mean?"

"I don't know," I said wildly. "Ewan, I don't know what Shaw was talking about. I didn't give him any tips."

"What about Carmichael?" Charlene asked.

"Well, sure, I told Gordon everything I knew," I said. "I had to. But the lawsuit wasn't a secret. The court system was probably the first place he checked."

"What lawsuit?" Ewan barked out.

"Oh." My stomach plummeted. "You didn't know about Devon's lawsuit against Bridget?" I asked in a small voice. "But it was all a misunderstanding."

"You should go," Charlene said quietly. "Just go."

I stepped back, struck. "Charlene, you can't think I had anything to do with this. We're partners."

She clasped her hands together. "We'll talk about this later. Go."

Swallowing hard, I trudged to the van and drove off, dazed. It wasn't until I'd arrived at Pie Town that I realized I still had a van full of pies. A more cutthroat business woman would have called Ewan and asked what to do with them. But I couldn't bring myself to pick up my cell phone.

I parked beside our dumpster in the back alley and slunk into the kitchen.

Abril set a mini potpie on a plate and handed it through the window to Petronella. Our new dishwasher, Fernando, stacked plates in the industrial cleaner.

"Hi, Val," Abril said. "How did it go at the Bar X?"

"It didn't," I said, my voice flat. "The police arrested Bridget Frith."

"Oh, no," she breathed. "Tragedy."

"The pies are still in the van." And I should start unloading them.

"What are we going to do with them all?" she asked.

The rusted gears in my brain ground into motion. "We'll freeze them if we don't hear otherwise from the Bar X. Charlene is there now. I'll get the pies."

"Well, that's all right then," Abril said. "Charlene will take care of everything. Are you sure you want to unload the pies?"

Since I preferred lurking in the alley to faking a smile in the kitchen, I nodded. "Don't worry about it. I got this." I trudged to the van and unloaded the pies, carrying them in six at a time and stacking the boxes on an empty cooling rack in the kitchen.

Charlene *couldn't* believe I was responsible. She knew I wouldn't make a police tip without consulting her, not on one of our cases.

Once the pie transfer was complete, I went to my office

and plucked my favorite apron off the corner of the metal bookshelf. My fingers fumbled as I tied it on, and I fought the urge to hide in my office. But that wouldn't be fair to Petronella, despite my strong urge to cower.

I reached for the doorknob, and the door slammed open.

I yipped and jumped backwards, narrowly avoiding a collision.

Petronella, dressed in her usual black, colored. "Oops. Sorry."

I clutched my heart. "That's okay. What's wrong?"

"Nothing's wrong." She closed her eyes. "No, that's not true. I love Pie Town."

"That's great." I liked having happy employees, but Petronella looked far from happy.

"And I really, really love the courses I've been taking."

"Well, that's great too."

She leaned against my metal desk. "No, it isn't. How can I leave Pie Town? You just made me assistant manager, and I'm going to have to go." She raked her hand across her spiky black hair.

"Not right away. I'm assuming you don't earn mortician credentials overnight."

"No, it's a two-year degree and then an apprenticeship, but I'm still leaving. I feel terrible."

I reached for her hand, then thought better of it. "Petronella, Pie Town was my dream. You need to follow yours. Of course, we'll miss you when you leave, but everyone understands you need to do what's best for you."

She blew out her breath. "You think?"

"I know."

Knowing it was hard for Petronella to leave made me feel better. I got back to work in the pie shop, but I couldn't stop thinking about my blowup with Charlene. I'd suspected Bridget might be guilty. Now, her arrest would destroy Ewan.

Selfishly, all I could think about was Charlene's reaction. I kept glancing at the door, expecting her to storm inside.

She didn't.

The day sputtered to an end, and I drove home. The pink van that had once seduced me now seemed an ugly reminder of all my half-baked ideas.

I poured myself a Kahlua and root beer and sat on the picnic table, staring out at the ocean. The sky turned a deepening shade of blue in that not-quite-sunset hour, and a warm breeze caressed my cheeks. I tried to focus on those things, but all I could think about was my friendship with Charlene, and about Bridget and Ewan.

And why the bleeping blue blazes had Shaw gone on about me being the tipster?

A dark sedan crunched up the road and parked beside my converted shipping container.

Gordon stepped out, the cuffs of his white sport shirt rolled up, his dark hair sleek. "I heard," he said.

"What happened? Why weren't you there?"

"Shaw wanted to make the arrest himself. I didn't know about it until they brought Bridget into the station."

"But you're—"

"Off the case. It's Shaw's now."

I handed him my Kahlua and root beer. "Your need is greater."

His forehead rumpled. "Root beer?"

"And Kahlua. Unless you're on duty?"

"No." He gulped it down, made a face, and handed me the empty glass. "And if you tell anyone I drank that stuff, I'll deny it."

"No one would believe me anyway. Why did Shaw say I tipped him off? I didn't. Everything I heard, I told you, and you said you already knew about it. You did, didn't you?"

"I didn't lie to you, Val."

"I didn't think you lied, but what was Shaw talking about?"

"All I know is he got a tip—a call directly to his desk. Word is, it came from you."

Horrified, I turned to him. "Gordon, there's no way I would call Shaw. You were the investigating officer. We have a relationship." My cheeks warmed as I realized how that sounded. "I wouldn't do that to you."

He grasped my hand and released it like it burned. "I know."

My shoulders slumped. I zipped my Pie Town hoodie higher. "So, you didn't come here to tell me off?"

"You being the tipster didn't track. How's Charlene taking this?"

"I don't think she's speaking to me." Unseeing, I stared at the horizon of deep and deeper blues. "She and Ewan basically threw me off the Bar X, and I haven't heard from her since." I gestured at the dark ocean. "I just don't understand what happened. Did someone call and pretend to be me? Did Shaw make the whole thing up?"

Gordon shook his head. "And give you credit for no reason? I don't think so. What you need to ask yourself is, who benefits?"

"A lot of people knew Charlene and I were close to the Bar X. Maybe someone thought the so-called tip would be more believable coming from me."

"Maybe." Doubt threaded his rumbly voice.

I shook my head. "I'm sorry. Getting the case snatched out from under you must have been a kick in the teeth. And it was your first murder case as a detective in San Nicholas. Want another root beer?"

"Can't. Shaw's put me on dog park detail later tonight."

My eyebrows pulled together. "He didn't demote you?!

Hold on . . . Isn't the dog park closed after six o'clock? What's going on?"

"More reports of aliens—the extraterrestrial kind—at the dog park."

My blood chilled. It's not that I've got full-fledged alienophobia. Aliens probably don't exist, but why take chances? "I thought it was fairies?"

"It's kids," he said. "But you and Charlene are the paranormal specialists."

"Charlene is."

"And now that the case at the Bar X is over, I thought you might want to join me in a ride along?"

"No!" I jerked away and tumbled off the table.

He sprang from the table and helped me up.

"Sorry." Heart thundering, I brushed the loose dirt from my jeans. "It's just . . . I don't do aliens."

"They're not really aliens."

"I know, but they kind of freak me out."

"The not-aliens?"

"Because a small part of me believes that whatever's there might actually be from outer space."

"Val, for aliens to have visited Earth, they'd have to have mastered faster-than-light travel. That's impossible."

Annoyed by his cool reasoning, I raised my chin. "Just because *we* haven't figured out how to do it, doesn't mean some aliens who are smarter than us can't. From a scientific history perspective, people have thought all sorts of things couldn't be done."

He grimaced. "Is this really about aliens, Val?"

"It really is. I've had this stupid fear of being taken by aliens since I was a kid. I know it's irrational, but knowing that doesn't help. Charlene tricked me into an alien hunt once, and it did not go well."

"You weren't probed, were you?"

"That is so unfunny." I worked to calm my breathing.

"I'd love to go on a ride along with you. Or even an actual date. But if aliens are involved, neither of us will have any fun."

"Okay, I'm sorry. I'll go to the dog park by myself, catch whoever's doing whatever the hell they're doing, and prove to you San Nicholas is UFO-free. If I return with any strange implants, I'll let you know."

"You're as hilarious as a root canal."

"See ya, Val." He got into his car and drove off.

I watched the taillights of his sedan vanish between the eucalyptus trees.

I buried my head in my hands. He'd finally asked me out on a date, and not only had I declined, but I'd gone funky monkey and ranted about UFOs. No wonder I'd once gotten engaged to a man who thought a deaf, narcoleptic housecat was his animal totem.

My eyes burned. Frederick and Charlene. She was my best friend, and she thought I'd betrayed her and Ewan. We were a team, both in and out of Pie Town. Would she ever speak to me again?

I'd hit bottom. On the bright side, things could only get better.

Right?

Right?

Chapter Twenty-Four

A week had passed with Charlene barely speaking to me. I stumbled through another Sunday lunch. Sunburnt diners packed the booths. Their chatter ricocheted off the linoleum floor, Formica tables, and shiny windows. Pie Town was full, but I felt hollowed out. Sunday was Charlene's day off, so she had no reason to be here. But I'd hoped she'd stop by, let me know everything had been cleared up, all was forgiven.

She didn't.

And Heidi had put an even bigger SUGAR KILLS sign in her window, with one fateful addition: SUGAR KILLS . . . YOUR BEACH BODY.

I'd almost stormed next door to have it out with the gym owner, but I never got the better of our encounters. And at least the sign didn't seem to affect business.

The afternoon wore on, and the tide of Sunday beach-goers ebbed from the restaurant. My movements became less frantic. I began to breathe normally again.

Marla waltzed inside, brushing past an exiting family of five. Beaming, she ordered a mini curried chicken potpie at the register, took a plastic number card, and claimed a table.

I brought her the pie, garnished with salad, raspberry vinaigrette dressing on the side. "Here you go, Marla. You're looking well."

She stretched, her diamonds flashing. "I feel well." She wore a knit, blue-and-white striped top and white denims. *Très* nautical.

"That's good." Puzzled, I returned to my station behind the register. What did Marla have to look so pleased about? She hadn't beaten Charlene and solved the crime. And if she was interested in Ewan, he'd taken a bad blow. Word on the street was that Bridget was stuck in jail at least until the courts opened on Monday—assuming Ewan could make her bail. If his money really was all tied up in the Bar X, that might not happen right away.

I frowned. Were the murders a way to force Ewan to sell? I couldn't imagine anyone would want the land that badly unless there was an oil well or a diamond mine beneath. Neither were likely in coastal California. And even if they were, any drilling or mining would be tied up in decades of environmental reviews.

The front door bammed open, rattling the windows. Charlene strode to Marla's central table and pointed a quivering finger. "YOU!"

"*Moi*?" Marla blinked lazily.

Frederick raised his head from Charlene's shoulder and hissed.

Charlene's white curls trembled, her face pink with emotion. "You low-downed, yellow-bellied, snake in the grass!"

Diners swiveled in their seats to watch. Rattling dice silenced at the gamers' table.

I hurried from behind the counter. "Um, Charlene—"

"It's been Marla all along," she said. "She's the one who called Shaw. She talked him into keeping her role in the matter quiet. Three guesses why!"

I couldn't imagine, but Charlene was working up to a full-fledged scene with a capital S. Now, there's a lot I can tolerate. Being called fat. Charlene "accidentally" nailing me with her garden hose. Being dragged into Bigfoot hunts. But Pie Town was my line in the sand. These two lunatics were not going to disrupt my fledgling business. "Let's talk about it in my office."

"So she could comfort Ewan and slither into his good graces," Charlene snarled. "She's even offered to help with the bail money! Of course, Ewan turned her down."

Shut up, shut up, shut up! "Office," I hissed.

Marla set down her fork and swallowed. "Prove it."

"I already have. Unlike you, Miss Jilly-Come-Lately, I have a contact in the SNPD who overheard your phone call with Shaw."

"But . . ." My mouth flopped open and stayed that way. "Why would the chief go along with telling everyone I narced on Bridget?"

Charlene canted her head, making a face. "He thinks he's doing you a favor, boosting your reputation as a crime buster."

Marla draped an arm over the back of her chair. "And this contact of yours . . . I suppose she'll come forward?"

"My contact, whose gender shall remain unknown, doesn't need to say another word. *I* know the truth."

"And I suppose you've already run to Ewan," Marla said.

Charlene blinked. "Snitches get stitches. I'm taking this to you."

And to Pie Town's customers. The news would be everywhere in a San Nicholas minute. My jaw tensed. "You two, we need to talk about the case. In private." I turned on my heel and strode to my office, hoping they'd follow.

To my amazement, they did.

Charlene slammed my office door behind her and opened her mouth.

"No," I said. "Button it. You two are old enough to be grandparents, and you're both acting like children."

"I'm forty-two," Charlene said.

"Forty-two hundred," Marla said, propping one elbow on the rickety bookshelf.

"Enough!" I banged my fist on the battered metal desk, and they jumped. "There will be no fighting or discussing active murder cases in Pie Town. Agreed?"

Meekly, they nodded.

"I'm sorry you got burned by Marla," Charlene said. "I should have known having her around would spill over onto you."

Marla's nostrils flared. "Thanks a—"

I shot her a look, and she subsided.

"I can't believe you ever thought I would run to Shaw without talking to you first," I said to Charlene. "I'm really hurt."

Charlene winced. "I know. I realized the truth after you left the Bar X, and have spent every minute since, working to prove your innocence."

I sat against my battered metal desk. "Thanks, but we've got bigger problems. I'm not sure Bridget is guilty." She had means, motive, and opportunity, but so did a lot of other people. Something didn't feel right about her arrest. There was something I'd overlooked, or seen and forgotten.

Marla snorted.

"Oh, *now* you're not sure," Charlene said.

"You are not in a position to criticize," I said. "Look, we had to consider everyone a suspect, and both Bridget and Ewan were on the scene when both murders occurred." And who else could have known about Devon's possible parentage and sent the newspaper clipping that had lured the bartender to the Bar X?

Marla covered a yawn. "Ewan was with Charlene and I when Devon was killed. Bridget has no alibi, and Devon was blackmailing her. She agreed to pay up, and he dropped the lawsuit."

"How do you know?" I asked.

"Curly overheard them, and Bridget was perfectly positioned to kill Devon."

"I don't believe a word of it," Charlene said. "You couldn't think of anyone better to pin it on. And then, like a weasel, you blamed your mistake on Val."

"It's not a mistake." Marla straightened, her eyes flashing. "I had to tell Shaw."

"Why have him tell everyone Val was the tipster?"

"Because . . ." She blinked rapidly. "I didn't want to take the credit."

"Take the credit?" Charlene said. "You're all about the limelight. You constantly try to one-up me. I can't Tweet a thing without you trying to outdo me with an Internet video. Have you got a full-time videographer on the payroll?"

"If you want to go big," Marla said, "you need to play big."

I shifted against the desk. "Is it true you were dating all three of the Blue Steel gunslingers?"

"Well, not at the same time!"

"Is there any man in this town you haven't dated?" Arms folded, Charlene stood in front of my office door and barred the way.

Marla's eyes narrowed. "And what is that supposed to mean?"

"It means," Charlene said, "you could have sweet-talked one of them into being your accessory to murder."

"I had no reason to kill Devon." Marla deflated. "He was a sweet, charming man. Even if he wasn't the sharpest knife in the drawer, he was fun."

Charlene strolled behind the desk. She leaned forward,

pressing her fingers to the metal and narrowing her eyes. "And how will Ewan feel when he learns—"

"Ewan is business," Marla said quickly. "Don't you dare say a word to him about my relationship with Devon."

"Business?" I asked.

She adjusted a navy purse over her shoulder. "Ewan assists with my charity works. He's a good man. I am sorry his daughter turned out to be a killer, but—"

"But you need his money," Charlene said. "That's why you gave Val the credit for the tip. If Ewan knew you'd ratted out his daughter, he'd never be with you. Dating bartenders and gunslingers is all well and good, but you only married down once, and that was the first time."

The muscles jumped beneath Marla's skin. "That is low, even for you, Charlene."

"The truth hurts," Charlene said. "You're greedy, and Ewan's easy on the eyes."

I studied Charlene's arch nemesis. Her cheeks were pink. Her eyes glistened. Her diamonds trembled. "Marla, do you *need* money?" I asked.

She tugged her fingers through her silvery hair. "Everything's so expensive! The property taxes. The videographer. The yacht—do you have any idea what it all costs to maintain?" She shook her purse at me. "This cost eight hundred dollars! On sale." Her voice hitched. "Everything was fine until April."

I felt the blood drain from my face. April. The cruelest month. "Not—"

"Tax day," Marla said. "I had my regular meeting with my accountant, and . . ." She paled.

Charlene gaped. "You're broke? Why didn't you say anything?"

"I didn't say that." Marla raised her chin. "It's not as if I'm poor. I'm not poor. Everything's fine. I'm as successful as I ever was. More successful than you."

"Everyone goes through ups and downs," Charlene said. "Why, when my husband and I were first married—"

"I am not poor!" Marla slammed out of the room. My American Legion wall calendar slipped off its nail and fluttered to the floor.

On Charlene's shoulder, Frederick arched his back, claws digging through her knit tunic. She winced.

"This is bad." Charlene sank into my executive chair and set Frederick on the desk. He wandered to the computer, coiled on top of the keyboard, and fell asleep.

"She seemed pretty upset," I said.

"That's an understatement. For her to let that slip to me, her finances must be in the crapper."

I leaned my hip against the metal desk. "It can't be that bad. She's got that amazing beach estate."

"Probably mortgaged to the hilt."

"And all that jewelry."

"Don't you know that diamond rings depreciate faster than cars? There's no resale market for used diamond jewelry. Contrary to the song, they are not a girl's best friend, even if they are sparkly."

I hoped my ex was able to get a refund on my engagement ring. In fairness to Mark, he hadn't stinted on the carats.

"What about her Internet empire?" I asked. "Isn't she a big deal with her videos?"

"She mustn't make any money off of them."

"Really?" Nudging Frederick aside, I woke up my laptop and surfed to her website. Lots of videos, lots of comments from adoring admirers, but Charlene was right. Nothing seemed to be for sale. It was a vanity site. Was it possible that Marla's battle of one-upmanship had bankrupted her?

"She's a life coach without a life," Charlene said. "If

her fans find out she's broke, she's done for." Her brow furrowed. "Why does that bother me?"

"What started your feud?" I asked, thinking of Heidi. Surely, we weren't doomed to follow in Charlene and Marla's footsteps?

"I can't remember. We were best friends as girls. And then we discovered boys and drifted apart. At some point, things got nasty."

I stooped to retrieve the fallen calendar and rehung it on the white wall. Even though I'd only recently met Heidi, there was something about our squabbles that felt like the conflict between Marla and Charlene.

"If Marla was desperate to keep her affair with Devon secret from Ewan," I said, "she has motive. And with all the time she's spent at the Bar X, she's been ideally placed to gather evidence against other suspects and throw them Shaw's way."

Charlene pursed her mouth. "I don't believe it."

"What?"

"I will not let my feelings for Marla get in the way of this investigation anymore."

"She might actually be guilty. The only way she'd get her hands on Ewan's money is if he sells that ranch." Could this entire business have been a sick plot to force the sale?

"No. We need to find the real killer. No more fooling around. No more distractions. You talk to Gordon and find out what he knows."

"I can't. He's off the case."

She stared. "What?"

"That's why he wasn't at Bridget's arrest. Shaw pulled him from the case."

"That idiot!"

"Gordon was cool about it, but I think he was disappointed."

She brightened. "At least you two can finally have your first date."

I gnawed my bottom lip.

"What?"

"He kind of asked me out."

"And?"

"And I said no."

"Why the hell would you do that?"

"He wanted me to go to the dog park and help look for aliens." I adjusted a book on salesmanship on the metal bookcase. The shelf needed dusting. "Not real aliens, he knows they're not aliens. It's only kids messing around. Still . . . aliens," I finished weakly.

"You need to get over your UFO phobia."

"It's not a phobia."

"You mean it's not *the* phobia."

It'd been a few years since I graduated with an English major, but I was pretty certain I'd said what I meant.

"Your phobia isn't the problem," she said, "it's the excuse. You and Carmichael have been doing this dance for months. And what do you do when he finally asks you out? You say no. There's a word for people like you—"

"Commitment-phobes?"

"Ass hats." She braced her elbows on my desk. "Look, Val, I get it. You were dumped at the altar—"

"I wasn't at the altar."

"And your ex was probably cheating on you the whole time with the yoga instructor next door. But how could you compete with her? Imagine how flexible Heidi must be."

I stiffened. "I'd rather not."

"It's enough to shake any woman's confidence. It would have to make a woman wonder, what have I done? Is there something wrong with me? Am I doomed to pick cheating losers?"

"In fairness, I'm not sure he was cheating on me. He and Heidi said they started dating after we ended our engagement." But I *had* wondered. What frightened me was the thought my judgment had been so poor. I'd made so many excuses for that jerk.

"Val, love is risk, and not every risk you take turns out to be a winning lottery ticket. But if you stop taking those risks, what's the point?"

"Look, everything you say may be true—"

"It's exactly true."

"But UFOs—"

"No buts! Carmichael's a good man. And if you don't get your butt back on that horse and start riding, then you're not the woman I think you are. Besides, there aren't any UFOs in the dog park. I've changed my mind. That park's got a fairy problem."

Was Charlene right? Was the real problem that I was gun-shy?

She rubbed her chin. "That said, fairies are known to kidnap people. In fact, that whole probing business started centuries ago with the fairies. Of course, the victims didn't call it probing . . ."

"Charlene?"

"Yes."

"You're not helping." And I still wasn't hunting UFOs.

Chapter Twenty-Five

Monday morning, we drove into the Bar X in my perfect pink rental. The van's tires crunched past the saloon, and my hands clenched on the warm steering wheel. Even though I hadn't sicced the cops on Ewan's daughter, I felt weirdly guilty.

"Don't worry," Charlene said, a sure prelude to me freaking out. She stroked Frederick, purring in her lap. "I'll smooth things over with Ewan."

A gunshot cracked, and I flinched.

"Relax," she said. "That's only the Blue Steel Boys."

I drove past the chapel. "What's left of them. Why don't I have a chat with Moe and Curly while you're talking to Ewan?" Even though I hadn't gotten Bridget tossed in jail, I dreaded facing him. "Are you sure he's here and not at the courthouse?"

"Bridget's preliminary hearing is set for the afternoon. Ewan wasn't able to scrape together the bail money at the arraignment, but he's got it now, and he plans to get her out. He's here."

I braked, the van drifting to a halt beside the carriage house.

"You're going to make me walk up that hill in this heat?" Charlene pointed through the windshield.

Sighing, I turned onto the winding road and drove to the yellow Victorian. I slithered from the van and glanced at the empty porch. Ewan was nowhere to be seen.

Charlene climbed the porch steps and rapped on the door.

Turning in the opposite direction, I followed the sound of gunshots to the corral. At one end of it stood wooden targets. Painted like evil-doers, they wore real black cowboy hats and kerchiefs over their faces. I marched up the steps into the U-shaped stands.

On horseback, Moe and Curly raced around the inside edge of the corral fence, their pistols raised high.

"Watch out!" Moe shouted, and he pulled up his piebald horse. It tossed its head, stamped its hooves. He trotted toward me. "You can't sit there. You're in the line of fire."

"Sorry," I said. "Is there a place I can sit and watch until you're done?"

He jerked his head toward the bottom end of the U.

I walked to that section of stands and sat, smoothing the front of my blue tank top.

Leaning from his horse, Moe set green apples atop the targets' heads.

Then the sharpshooters were off, hooves thundering, guns blazing, apple guts flying. In spite of the murder of some perfectly decent baking apples, I was enthralled. Moe and Curly were amazing. If one of those two had aimed to shoot me, I couldn't imagine them missing.

I clutched my hands between my knees. So, who had shot the pie out of my hands? Had it been a misfire or a staged shot? Or had someone else intentionally taken a shot at me? Or . . .

The practice session ended, and the two men walked their horses from the corral.

Dusting off the seat of my jeans, I followed them into the carriage house and watched them remove the saddles and brush down the horses.

"You want something?" Curly asked me.

"There were two shots when Devon was killed," I said. "One of them hit a pie I was carrying."

"And the other shot killed the bartender," Curly said.

"There's been speculation that Devon was killed earlier," I said. "Could someone have rigged a gun to shoot later and confuse the time of death?"

Moe patted his horse. "Anything's possible, I suppose, but it doesn't seem likely."

"Why not?"

"I've never tried it," Moe said. "You're talking about one of those setups from the movies? Where someone opens a door and doesn't know there's a string tied from the knob to the gun's trigger? I don't see how you could pull off two shots that way. That said, someone could have gotten near the scene of the crime and discharged their weapon twice to make a ruckus."

"You think the cops got the wrong person?" Curly asked.

"I don't know," I said. "Something doesn't sit right. I have a hard time picturing Bridget killing Larry."

Moe blinked rapidly. "Larry was . . . He was a good man. We never should have . . ." Clearing his throat, he turned away and brushed his horse more vigorously.

"I heard the real reason you three fell out was over a woman," I said.

Curly pinked and cut a sideways glance at his partner. "Marla Van Helsing. She's quite a woman, but we sure made fools of ourselves over her. I'm only sorry it took Larry's death for me to see it."

I bit the inside of my cheek. When he'd cornered us rooting through his garbage, he hadn't seemed to have given up his dreams of romance. But I let it lie. "Why did you tell me your argument with Larry was about money?"

Curly's mouth twisted. "I guess I was embarrassed. And a gentleman doesn't drag a lady's name through the mud. Marla didn't do anything wrong."

"Hm." I was all for personal responsibility, but trouble seemed to follow in Marla's wake. "Well, thanks. And that was some shooting."

Moe grunted.

I hesitated, wanting to say something comforting about Larry. But I sensed the kindest thing would be to leave Moe to mourn in peace. So, I left and walked back up the hill to Ewan's Victorian. The sun beat on my shoulders, and I twisted my hair into a knot, hoping for an ocean breeze.

Charlene and Ewan stood on the porch, Ewan casting increasingly desperate glances toward the white SUV in the driveway.

I slowed, my footsteps dragging, then forced myself to smile and wave.

Charlene returned my wave, and I relaxed a little. She must have cleared things up with Ewan.

I climbed the porch steps. "Hi, Ewan. Is there any word on Bridget?"

"The preliminary hearing's at one." He glanced again to the SUV and coughed. "I'm sorry I jumped to conclusions last week. Charlene explained the caller pretended to be you. It made the tip more believable, given your past history of detecting."

Charlene's mouth compressed, and she gave a slight shake of her head.

So, she hadn't finked out Marla. I confess, a small, dark part of me wanted to drop the dime on the Internet video maven. But good for Charlene. She was taking the high road.

Ewan grimaced. "All those pies—you must have lost money on them. I'll make it up to you. But I'm sorry, I've got to go now."

"Wait," I said. "One question. Did you send Devon a newspaper clipping about the Bar X before he applied for a job here?"

His brow creased. "No. Why would I?" He brushed past me and hurried to the SUV, roaring off in a cloud of dust.

Charlene shook her head. "He's not thinking straight."

"And you didn't tell him about Marla."

"What's between him and Marla is their business, not mine."

"Are you sure about that?"

"What's that supposed to mean?" she asked.

"I just thought . . . maybe you and Ewan . . ."

Her gaze sharpened. "I don't need romantic advice from you, Missy."

I raised my hands in a warding gesture. "No argument there."

"I married the love of my life."

"I know."

"Well, then . . . one day, you will too." She walked to the van and clambered inside.

Smiling, I drove her home and returned to my own tiny house. It was a perfect beach day, but I was happy to sit at my outdoor picnic table with my laptop.

We were missing something. I wasn't sure the answers were online, but I didn't know who else to talk to. So, I broadened my search parameters.

There were a lot more Curly Nottinghams in the US than I'd expected. I scanned the first five web pages. My heart caught—a Yelp review by a customer who claimed Curly had seduced his wife and shot his hound. My chin fell. It was a Curly Nottingham who owned a carpet-cleaning business in Dubuque.

A seagull fluttered onto the picnic table and squawked. "Forget it. I'm not feeding you."

Indignant, it flapped away.

Next, I ran a deeper search for Moe/Maurice Elliot. My web research went quicker without sass-master Charlene demanding the laptop every one-point-five minutes. I found a Maurice Elliot who was a fisherman in Alaska. A guy with a cooking blog. A kid who'd been killed driving drunk in Truckee seven months back . . .

I paused over that article. This Maurice Elliot had left a bar, driven off a road and into a ravine, and been killed instantly. He was survived by his father, Maurice Elliot Sr., of San Nicholas, California.

Moe.

Larry had told me Moe had lost his son recently, but I hadn't realized how recently. Saddened, I rubbed my temple. It had only been a couple of years since my mother had passed, and her death still hit me hard at odd moments.

Even though Larry was the victim and obviously not the killer, I ran another online search for Larry/Lawrence Pelt. There's also a surplus of Larry/Lawrence Pelts in the US and Canada, and I wasted a good hour running through the various articles, blogs, and blurbs before giving up. Another search on Marla and Bridget didn't uncover anything new.

I checked the local newspaper online. If Gordon had caught whoever was doing whatever at the dog park, it hadn't made the news.

Grimacing, I shut my laptop, dissatisfied.

Chapter Twenty-Six

Stumped on next steps, and with a sunny Monday afternoon before me, I took my rental van for a spin. I drove south on the One, my gaze flicking restlessly to the rearview mirror. If someone wanted to tail me, I'd made myself a lot more conspicuous in the pink van. But I didn't spot any tails as I sped down the winding highway, the ocean playing peekaboo between sandy cliffs.

The light on the Pacific shifted golden, inviting, but the perfect weather thwarted me. Every single beach parking lot was packed with teenagers on their summer break.

Defeated, I turned the van around and returned to San Nicholas. Parking at the far end of Main Street, I window shopped, lusting after glass pumpkins and distressed chairs and fringed shawls.

I paused, staring into a gallery window filled with paintings of ocean and fog. A spot between my shoulder blades burned, as if I was being watched. I broadened my gaze, trying to catch reflections in the window. No one seemed to be watching me.

Shrugging, I strolled to Pie Town. The tension in my muscles released as soon as I stepped onto its linoleum floor and locked the door behind me. Even when closed, Pie Town was my haven.

In the industrial kitchen, I made myself a fat omelet stuffed with cheese and greens and a side of hash browns. Just because I could, I fried up some bacon too. Hot damn, cooking in a ginormous kitchen felt awesome. Also, if someone tried to break in, I had an arsenal of cast iron pans, hot oil, and knives at the ready.

I set a frozen pie in the oven to reheat, then noticed a pie sitting in the blue-painted pie safe. Had Charlene stored it there for later?

Too late, I realized I'd automatically filled the coffee urn. It percolated, popping and bubbling, the rich scent of java competing with cheese, bacon, and eggs.

"Darn it." As much as I love coffee, I couldn't drink an entire urn.

I grabbed my omelet and mug and sat in a booth. Opening a paper napkin with a flourish, I admired my pie-selling empire. Black-and-white tile floor. Pink booths. A neon, TURN YOUR FROWN UPSIDE DOWN AT PIE TOWN sign above the counter. I rose and turned on the sign because I liked the look of it, and returned to my omelet. It was a broken mess—I'd never really mastered flipping omelets—but it tasted fantabulous.

The front door rattled, the bell above it jingling faintly.

My head jerked upward. I froze, staring at a tall silhouette behind the blinds.

The door rattled harder.

Movements jerky, I stood and peered through the plastic blinds.

Heidi. Her blond hair hung loose about her shoulders. The gym owner's green, HEIDI'S HEALTH hoodie clung tight to her super-fit body.

Bracing myself, I opened the door. "Hi, Heidi. We're closed today, but is there something—"

"I need pie. Now." She pushed past me and strode to the counter.

Baffled, I stared after her and shut the door. "Are you okay?"

"Do you give all your customers the third degree?" She drummed her fingers. "I want a damn pie. Is that too much to ask?"

"We didn't bake any today." I folded my arms. "We're closed."

Her eyes widened, reddening. Her face paled.

The woman really needed pie.

I relented. Maybe this could be the start of us not hating each other quite so much. "I'm reheating a strawberry-rhubarb, but it's got another ten minutes to go."

"I'll wait. Where's the coffee urn?"

"In the . . . I'll get you a cup." I walked to the kitchen and returned with a full mug of coffee. "The cream and sugar . . ."

She scowled.

Cream and sugar were two items that would not pass her lips. So why did she want pie? Something was seriously wrong. "Heidi—"

"Go away."

Fine by me. I returned to my booth. Darting glances at Heidi, slumped at the counter, I resumed eating. Only something truly awful could have driven her into the pie shop of her enemy. I could be the bigger person.

When the oven timer dinged in the kitchen, I rose. "That's the pie. Do you want your slice à la mode?"

"No, and I don't want a slice. I want the pie."

I stopped in my tracks. "What? You mean the whole pie?"

"That's what I said, isn't it?"

Biting my tongue, I retrieved the pie from the oven. It was warmed through but not super-hot, so boxing it wouldn't be a problem. I carried the pie to the counter and slid a folded pink box from beneath the register.

Heidi grabbed the pie and slid it toward her. She jabbed a fork into the center and took a bite. Her nostrils flared. "That's good."

"Thanks." Leery, I watched her polish off the equivalent of two pieces. I confess, in my dark nights of the soul, I was capable of eating an entire pie. But I'd trained for that.

She rolled her shoulders and plowed onward for a third.

"Heidi, is something wrong?"

She slammed down her fork and glared. "Mark Jeffreys is what's wrong."

My ex? "Uh, you two had a fight?"

She drew a shuddering breath. "He said I should loosen up, be more like . . ." She pressed her lips together.

"Like what?"

"Like you," she spat. "Of course, I care about health and fitness. I own a gym for Pete's sake! Do you think this body came by accident?"

I edged away. "You look good."

"Good? I can bounce a quarter off my ass!"

I couldn't even bounce a quarter off my mattress.

"He said I was obsessive," she said. "As if he's any better! I can't walk into his house without tripping over his realty signs."

"He does have lots of signage," I said, sympathetic. I'd been through the Mark Jeffreys's wringer myself.

"But to compare me to *you*?" She sobbed. "I mean, look at you!"

"Hey!"

"I mean, no offense—"

"Taken!"

"But owning a pie shop has had an obvious effect on your physique."

"I may not spend my evenings doing pushups, but

I've got muscle tone in my legs from being on my feet all day—"

"It'll lead to varicose veins."

"And in my arms from lifting pies out of the oven and mixing and chopping, and—"

"I'll bet you can pinch more than an inch, can't you?"

"Everyone can!" Okay, maybe I can pinch a teensy bit more than an inch, but I am not fat. I'm not even pleasingly plump. True, I'm not one of those wafer-thin supermodels, or even Miss Yoga Body seated in front of me with pie dripping down her chin like Dracula's girlfriend. But I'm normal. "And for your information, I don't eat pie all day." I think about pie a lot more than I eat it. "And I certainly don't eat half a pie at one sitting. This is emotional eating, Heidi, and you're going to regret it in the morning."

"Mark's a jerk."

"But he's your jerk," I said gently. "And pies are not meant to be used for evil. You're in a dark place, Heidi." I pulled the pie away. "And this isn't healthy."

"This is your fault."

"I didn't force you to eat all that pie."

She blinked, her mouth working like a goldfish's. "You're right. I've spent years helping people realize they shouldn't stuff themselves with food as a way of stuffing emotions. Pies aren't meant for this. They're . . ." She trailed off. Her lips parted. Heidi's eyes gleamed, fierce and fervid and frightening.

I edged away. "Heidi? What's wrong?"

"I need another pie."

"We've been over this. The store's closed. I don't have anything fresh, and I'm not going to bake you a pie. Not after the pushup incident."

"You were kind of a good sport about that."

"Thanks." I crossed my still-aching arms.

"I wouldn't have really called the police."

I wish I'd known that sooner.

Her look turned cunning. "If you sell me a pie, I'll make it worth your while."

"No, you won't. A full-sized pie is fifteen dollars, but everything I've got is in the freezer. Well, there is a pie in the pie safe—"

"You have a safe for pies?"

"It's not really a safe. It's an antique pie cabinet. I found it at—"

"I'll take that one."

"I'm not sure how old the pie is."

"Doesn't matter." She dug some bills out of her hoodie pocket. "Gimme."

I studied her. Maybe now was my chance to derail our Marla-Charlene pattern. She'd been opening up, even showing a glimmer of humanity. "Heidi, if I sell you a pie when you're in this condition, you're going to hate me even more tomorrow than you do today."

"I doubt that's possible."

I ground my teeth. "You're not yourself."

"You're fat."

"I'm a size ten! What is wrong with you? You're only saying that to—"

"No wonder Mark dumped you at the altar."

I grabbed the money, counted it, and stuffed what she owed in the front pocket of my jeans. "To go, then?" Not waiting for an answer, I returned to the kitchen and removed the pie from the cupboard, sniffed it. It smelled and looked okay—probably one of yesterday's pies, a blackberry. Not something I'd normally sell to a customer, not at full price, at least, but caveat emptor. I'd warned her it wasn't fresh-baked.

I brought it to the counter, and she watched, fidgeting, while I boxed it.

She snatched the pink box from my hands before I

could tape the end shut. Heidi stormed from the restaurant, banging into Charlene, who was on her way inside.

Charlene paused in the open door. Her eyes widened. "Was that Heidi? With a pie?"

"Yep. That was Heidi." I nodded toward the remnants of the strawberry-rhubarb, still in its tin on the counter. "And that was Heidi's pie."

"She ate all that? Great Ganesh, we've got to stop her."

"Stop her from what? Driving while pie-eyed?"

"I'll bet that's the most sugar she's had at one sitting in years," Charlene said. "She's not herself."

A green SUV with HEIDI'S HEALTH plastered on the side blasted past. A screech of brakes. The blare of a horn. The SUV roared down the street.

"Too late," I said, uneasy. Heidi had reminded me of something or someone, something important. Out of reach, the memory tickled the back of my brain. "Best to let her just work it off. What are you doing here?"

"I always check the lock when I walk by. Someone might have broken in. I didn't expect it to be Heidi. Why are you here? Monday's your day off."

"I stopped in to make . . . uh, to check the mail." I didn't want Charlene to think I'd been too unnerved to return to my solitary home on the bluff. "And then I got hungry."

"I left a blackberry pie in the safe. I'll go get it."

"Sorry." I cringed. "That was the pie Heidi bought."

She goggled at me. "You sold her my pie?!"

"I didn't know it was yours."

"Who else would have left a pie in that safe?"

"I'm sorry." I flipped my ponytail over one shoulder. "I'll reheat a frozen pie for you."

"Damn skippy, you will."

Shoulders hunched, I trudged into the kitchen.

"Blackberry!" she shouted after me.

Fortunately, Heidi had thrown me off my game so

badly I hadn't turned off the small oven. I slipped a frozen blackberry pie inside and set the timer.

The front bell jingled.

I straightened from the oven. "Charlene?"

No answer.

Chest tight, I hurried into the restaurant.

Marla and Charlene squared off in the center of the checkerboard floor like two gunslingers.

I canted my head. "What's going on?"

"You saw him," Marla said, not taking her gaze from my piecrust maker.

"Ewan isn't your personal property," Charlene said. "I can see him whenever I want to."

"And you didn't tell him." Marla circled.

"I'm no rat fink." Charlene lifted her nose. "Unlike some people."

"Why didn't you tell him?" Marla's voice rose to a wail.

"Was I supposed to?" Charlene planted her hands on her hips.

"Tell him what?" I asked.

"That I was the one who called the police about Bridget," Marla said. "Why didn't you tell him?"

"I told you," Charlene said. "I don't rat people out, even if they do deserve it."

Marla sagged, bracing her hand atop a square table.

"What?" Charlene asked, defiant. "Did you *want* me to tell him?"

"Of course not," Marla said. "It would have ruined everything."

"So, what's the problem?" Charlene snapped.

"I've been pacing my balcony, unable to eat, unable to . . . You had the perfect chance to wreck everything. Why didn't you?"

"Why would I need to?" Charlene asked.

Marla laughed, a choking sound. "No, you don't need to, do you? You always win. You always get everything exactly the way you want it."

Charlene's snowy brows rose. "*I* always win?"

"You married Ben!"

Charlene took a step backward and touched the base of her throat. "Ben? You were in love with Ben?"

"And he only had eyes for you. Because of you, I married that idiot, Paul."

A love triangle? That's what had started the feud? And now Heidi and I and Mark . . . No. No way. We were *not* the same.

Charlene shook her head. "Marla—"

"And everything that happened afterward was your fault," Marla said. "You had a child! A daughter!"

"Marla—"

Marla raised her hand. "Do you know what I would have given for a daughter?"

"A daughter I haven't seen in five years," Charlene said bleakly and looked away.

My heart twisted.

"Marla," she said, "no life is perf—"

"Oh, stop it. Just stop it!" Marla stormed out the door.

Gordon leapt aside. "Whoa." Staring over his shoulder at the closing door, he walked into the restaurant. It must have been his day off, too, because he wore jeans and a worn, blue T-shirt that showed off his muscular arms and chest. Gordon worked out. A lot. "Everything okay in here?"

Charlene looked like she was chewing on something. "Pie Town's a revolving door today," she said, gruff.

I drew him away from Charlene. "Gordon. I'm glad you stopped by."

His eyes narrowed. "Why? Did something happen?"

"No. I mean, yes. How did it go at the dog park?"

He lifted his T-shirt, exposing washboard abs. "No implants, scarring, or lost time."

Now he was just showing off. "I guess I deserved that."

"I'm going to check on that pie," Charlene said loudly and vanished into the kitchen.

"I take it you didn't catch whoever's haunting the dog park," I said.

"No. And I'm sorry I made fun of your UFO issues."

"Why?" I asked, bitter. I hated my lame phobia. "Who wouldn't make fun of them? They're ridiculous."

He rested his broad hands on my shoulders. "There's nothing funny about a phobia. Besides, you're brave about so many other things—stupidly brave, if you ask me. I'll give you UFOs."

"Stupidly brave?" Hope, dread, and confusion heated my chest.

"The way you charged in to help Charlene. I wish you hadn't, but I'm glad you're the kind of person who would."

"I'll go to the dog park with you," I said quickly.

"You will?"

"I mean, not tonight. I promised Charlene I'd watch *Stargate* with her. We're on season five. But, it's time I got over my fear of little gray men."

"Is that the only reason?" His voice lowered, and he stepped closer, forcing me to look up.

My heartbeat accelerated. "And, I guess you have a lot of qualities I like too." He was tough and honorable, and kind and patient. And he looked *really* good in that T-shirt.

His arms went around me, his broad hands locking against my spine. He pulled me closer.

My knees trembled. Oh, God, he was going to kiss me. And his hard muscles—

"Don't mind me." Charlene leaned through the kitchen window and propped her head on her hands.

Releasing me, he stepped away. "So." His Adam's apple bobbed. "Friday night. I'll pick you up at your place? Seven o'clock?"

I nodded, breathless, no longer caring if I was kidnapped by aliens. A night with Gordon might be worth an abduction.

Chapter Twenty-Seven

Tires crunched over loose earth. Headlights swept my front yard, illuminating the wooden picnic table.

Wary, I stepped out of my house and shielded my eyes. I was supposed to go to Charlene's and wasn't expecting anyone tonight. And I didn't exactly live in a location you just happened to drive past. Whoever was here, was here for a reason.

Charlene's Jeep glided to a halt. She hopped from the car and adjusted Frederick over her left shoulder. My friend raised a shopping bag. "I thought we'd mix things up, watch *Stargate* here tonight. I've got root beer."

I released a huge breath. "I've got Kahlua," I said, more pleased than I wanted to admit. I loved my tiny home, but the seclusion was starting to get to me. Last night, I'd barely slept, twitching whenever a tree limb brushed against the metal sides of the shipping container, or a squirrel scampered across the roof. "Come on in."

She climbed the two steps and came inside, closing the door behind her. Charlene glanced at the tiny kitchen, the fold-up desk, and the wooden bookshelf that blocked off the sleeping area. "It seems smaller."

I motioned toward the tall windows, black against the night. "Being able to see the ocean opens up the space. What's going on? Is something wrong?"

She pulled out one of the chairs in the dining nook and sat. "Bridget's out of jail." Charlene shrugged out of her green knit jacket and dumped it over the back of the chair.

"That's great news." I set two glasses and a bottle of Kahlua on the small table between us.

"She says she's innocent." Charlene lowered her chin. "And I want to believe her."

"Want to?" I unscrewed the top of the bottle and poured, then added the root beer. "I thought you were sure she was innocent."

"That's the problem. I can't believe either of them had anything to do with Devon and Larry's deaths, because I care about both Ewan and Bridget. I've been letting my prejudices blind me, just like they did with Marla."

I sat beside her. "Have you spoken with Bridget?"

"No," Charlene said. "I haven't had a chance, and she and her father have things to discuss."

A branch cracked outside, and there was a soft, shuffling sound, like the rustling of leaves. Hair lifted on the back of my neck. I shook myself. I couldn't freak out every time a raccoon sniffed my garbage bins.

"All right." I crossed my legs. "Here's what we've got. You, Marla, and Ewan were together at the time of the two gunshots, just before I found Devon. Let's assume the gunshots were a diversion to make us misjudge the time of death, because that might explain why I got shot at. A coroner would have been able to figure out time of death within an hour or so, but a few minutes could make a difference to an alibi. Moe and Curly told me they didn't see how someone could have rigged a gun to go off twice. So, that means if Marla or Ewan were involved in said diversion, they had an accomplice."

"Not Bridget."

I took a sip. Maybe the alcohol would stimulate my creative brain. At least, it might calm my jitters. "No, not Bridget. She was right on the scene, inside the saloon, and could have fired those shots and taken out my pie. The gunshots implicated her, so there's not much point to her being the accomplice to make us think the time of death was wrong."

Charlene ruffled Frederick's fur. "This is getting confusing."

"I think we're getting too Agatha Christie about the gunshots. It's more likely one of those two shots killed Devon."

Tiny feet scampered and scratched across my roof. Involuntarily, I glanced at the ceiling.

But the local wildlife held no interest for Frederick. He didn't budge from his limp position across Charlene's shoulder.

"Why shoot at you?" she asked.

"Maybe there was a struggle between Devon and the killer," I said, "and the gun went off. Or maybe the killer did see me, and sent a warning shot my way to give him or herself time to escape."

"If one of those two shots killed Devon, that leaves us with three real suspects: Bridget, Curly, and Moe." She took a slug of her drink. "Curly had supposedly returned to the carriage house, but he could have faked the thrown shoe, tied up his horse, and shot Devon. Or Moe could have taken the opportunity to kill the bartender while Curly was away. If Larry was Marla's accomplice, maybe she killed him to keep him silent."

"Do you still want the murderer to be Marla?"

She blew out her breath. "Not as much as I used to."

Something niggled at me. Something to do with Heidi. Was the gym owner my own, personal Marla? At any rate, Heidi definitely was not involved in the murders. There was no way she could have gotten to the Bar X to shoot Devon and take a shot at me without being noticed. Besides, she might have wanted to kill me, but I couldn't see her murdering an innocent bartender just to muddy the waters.

The refrigerator hummed. I glanced at the kitchen island, as if I'd find the answers there.

"Okay," I said. "Motive. Bridget might not have liked the idea of having to share her inheritance with a new half brother."

"Or she might have been a stalker, and she went too far," Charlene said, her expression doleful.

"Someone who knew about the possible relationship between Ewan and Devon sent Devon that news clipping."

Frederick purred and burrowed his head in Charlene's fluffy white hair.

"I don't see who could have known aside from Ewan or Bridget," she said. "Unless it was Marla."

"She did need money. Forcing Ewan to sell the ranch while sending his lone heir to jail puts her several steps closer."

"All three of the gunslingers were in love with Marla, bizarre as that may be." She folded her arms over her nubby green tunic.

"Right. One of them could have killed Devon out of jealousy." None of them struck me as hotheads though, and I rubbed my palms on my jeans. I didn't like this explanation. "Larry must have seen or known something, and that's why he was killed."

"Maybe that's why the killer's been so intent on squashing you flat. You were close to the scene of the crime—close enough to get shot at. Maybe he believes you saw something that would implicate him? Or her."

I stretched out my legs. "It's the only thing that makes sense. Though if I had seen anything, I'd have told the cops by now."

"The killer might not know that." She shifted on her chair.

"Whoever killed Devon and Larry has been changing up their methods," I said. "First a gunshot, then a blow to the head, and then lots of attempts to run me down. Don't killers usually stick to the same tactic?"

"Maybe the gun was used on Devon to implicate the gunslingers. Or maybe the killer figured no one would notice the shot because of all the racket from the corral."

"Or one of the trick shooters killed Devon."

Something rustled behind the house.

We jumped in our chairs.

Frederick's ears twitched.

"What was that?" Charlene asked.

I swallowed, my heart rabbiting. "Only an animal." The hills were raccoon and coyote central, but I glanced toward the window anyway. I couldn't see anything except for my tiny house/trailer reflected back at me, but my hand crept toward my cell phone on the table.

Charlene rubbed her ear. "What if Larry was clubbed to make it look like an accident with his horse?" she asked.

"But his horse wasn't in the stall." I strained my ears, but the outside was quiet.

"Maybe the killer went to get the horse after killing Larry, but Moe discovered Larry's body before he could return the horse to the stall."

"It makes sense," I said.

"The killer could have been any of them. Whoever killed

Larry took his key and used it to steal the cars from the dealership, then followed you and tried to run you off the road. And speaking of bad drivers, have you heard from Heidi?"

"She despises me. We're not exactly checking in on each other." But I felt a twang of guilt. I hoped Heidi hadn't eaten the entire blackberry pie in one sitting.

"You shouldn't have let her drive off in that condition."

"I'm sure nothing worse happened to her other than indigestion or the sugar shakes after too much pie." Something teased my mind, out of reach, and I frowned.

"Feeling guilty?"

"No. She was a customer. I served her. As long as she doesn't get food poisoning, I'm not responsible for what happens next."

"Maybe Heidi went crazy and bludgeoned him. She's got the upper body strength."

"Bludgeoned whom?"

"Your ex, Mark Jeffreys."

"More likely she . . ." My breath caught. Oh, no. She wouldn't. Because there was another American tradition of good, messy fun with pies, and—

Something cracked outside the trailer, and I stiffened.

Frederick raised his head, ears swiveling. I was more certain than ever that he wasn't really deaf. But my heart was banging so hard, it seemed a moot point.

"Did you hear that?" Charlene rose. "Someone's out there."

Footsteps crunched behind the trailer, and I stopped breathing.

"Where's your shotgun?" Charlene whispered.

"I don't have a shotgun."

"What?"

"No shotgun!"

"Taser?" She laid her palm on the table. "Mace? Tire iron?"

"I had a tire iron in my car, which is now sitting at the garage, waiting to be scrapped. If the van has a tire iron, it's parked outside."

"Oh, for Pete's sake," she hissed. "Whatever happened to the modern woman? I thought you were all about empowerment and self-defense."

"I'm calling Gordon." I grabbed for my cell phone on the small table and knocked my empty glass off the edge. It fell to the laminate floor, shattered.

"Brilliant," she said. "When seconds count, the police are only minutes away. Lights off."

I reached behind me and flipped off the lights, letting my eyes adjust to the darkness.

The sound of the footsteps slowed.

I stared out the window, my eyes straining. The picnic table and Charlene's Jeep were dim shapes. I dialed. "If someone walks around front, the automatic lights will come on. So, no one's—"

The lights flicked on, flooding the uneven lawn with illumination.

"There," I finished, my voice cracking.

"I don't see anyone," Charlene said softly. "Do you?"

I shook my head, widening my eyes in an attempt for better night vision. "Maybe the light scared him off."

"Val?" Gordon's voice drifted through the phone. "Is that you?"

"Ah . . ." I pressed the phone to my ear. "I don't think we're alone."

"Is that a UFO joke?"

Something bammed against the side of the trailer, and I shrieked.

"Right," Charlene said. "That does it." She rose and

yanked open the door. "I've got a shotgun, and I'm not afraid to use it!"

The sound of running footsteps, the crashing of underbrush, the start of a car engine. The car roared off, the sound fading.

"Val?" Gordon asked. "Val!"

"Someone was here." My voice trembled. "Outside my house."

"*Was?* Is he still there? Are you alone?"

"I'm with Charlene. I think she scared him off."

"Coward!" Charlene shook her fist at an invisible opponent and slammed the door.

"You *think*?" he asked.

"She scared him off."

Charlene leaned close. "Don't worry," she shouted into the phone. "It's not one of those dog-park aliens. Whoever was here had a car."

"I'll be right there." He hung up.

"He coming over?" Charlene asked.

"Yeah."

She waggled her brows. "An old woman's not much protection." She reached for the door. "Maybe I should just leave you two—"

"No. Stay." Sagging in my chair, I pressed my palms to my eyes and discovered I still held the phone. I set it on the table. Whoever had been here—and someone had definitely been here—was gone. But I wasn't thrilled with the idea of being alone. "Gordon will want your statement too."

"Still can't get your nerve up, can you?"

"What does that mean?"

"You don't want to be alone with tall, rugged, and handsome."

"Actually, we have a date. Friday night. Seven o'clock."

"Where?"

"The dog park."

"You're going alien hunting with him, but you won't come with me? Thanks a lot. Maybe I'll just ask Heidi to come with me next time."

In a blazing flash, I remembered what I'd been forgetting all day. Kahlua really did help me think, and we'd been wrong on so many things. "Forget the UFOs. I know who killed Devon."

Chapter Twenty-Eight

I closed the wooden gate behind us and climbed inside the pink rental van.

A wind shivered the dry grasses, presaging an ocean fog. The afternoon heat was oppressive, smothering.

But it wasn't the weather that had set me on edge. I knew who wanted me dead, and I couldn't do much about it. My skin twitched, my nerves bunched, and sweat dampened my Pie Town T-shirt.

I cleared my throat and glanced at Charlene, dressed in a violet tunic and matching linen slacks. "It feels weird to be here."

Blue eyes wide, ears twitching, Frederick lay draped over her shoulder.

Neither responded.

"Given what we know," I continued.

"What we suspect," Charlene said. "As your boyfriend pointed out, we don't have any actual evidence."

"He'll get the evidence, and he's not my boyfriend." The van hit a pothole, and I winced, angling the rearview mirror toward the pies on racks in the cargo space. They hadn't shifted. For an old van, it had excellent shocks, and

I wondered again if there was any way I could buy it. Maybe lease to own?

She adjusted the seat belt over her violet tunic. "You heard him. He has to work this through Shaw. What are the odds our new police chief will admit he made a mistake? And while we wait on the politicking, everyone suffers."

Something in her tone made me glance at my piecrust specialist. She stared blandly out the windshield. "Marla called last night."

"What did you tell her?"

"I told her we'd given everything we knew to the police. I don't think she believed me."

My hands flexed on the wheel. "At least the event at the Bar X tonight didn't cancel," I said. The murders hadn't completely wrecked Ewan's business.

"It's a western-themed murder mystery dinner. Haunts and murders are a bonus."

"Oh."

"Do you know how often Ewan books western-themed murder mystery dinners?"

"No."

"Almost never." Her gnarled fingers tapped her knee.

We rounded a bend, and the faux ghost town spread before us. I parked the van in front of the saloon. "I'll unload . . ." I stumbled over my words, my hands falling to my lap.

Chic in jeans and a pressed, white blouse, Marla stormed from the carriage house and stalked toward us.

"What's she doing here?" I unbuckled my seat belt and wiped my damp palms on the front of my Pie Town apron.

Charlene grimaced. "Here we go." She opened the van door and hopped to the ground.

I leaned across the seat. "Just follow the—"

She slammed the door.

"Plan." Ears ringing, I stepped from the van and went to stand beside Charlene.

"It's only because of the work *I* did that you figured out who killed Devon and Larry," Marla shouted.

"What exactly did you tell Marla?" I asked, horrified. Gordon had ordered us not to tell anyone what we'd discovered.

Marla planted her diamond-studded hands on her hips. "You'll do anything to make me look bad. This is low, Charlene, even for you."

"We did the same thing you did." Charlene grinned. "We gave everything we knew about the murders to the police. Unless there's something you didn't tell the police?"

"I don't believe you," Marla said. "This is all a scheme to draw out the killer. Why else would you two be back at the Bar X?"

"Because we owe them pies for tonight's event," I said, exasperated. "Why are you here?"

"Because you two aren't going to beat me."

"Beat you?" Charlene asked. "This is a murder investigation! There's no winner."

"There's a loser." She pointed to Charlene and mouthed, "That would be you."

I groaned. "Oh, come on." They were worse than fifth graders.

"Since I've returned to the Bar X," Marla said, "I've learned some new things about the killer."

What. The. Hell. I rubbed my temple. This couldn't be happening. Marla was going to get herself killed.

Charlene's face sagged. "Tell me you haven't been revisiting the crime scenes and trying to figure out where you went wrong?"

And blabbing to all the suspects. "We've told the police everything," I said weakly.

Marla shook a glittering finger. "I don't know what cockamamie scheme you've got going, but I'll figure it out." She stalked toward the road leading to Ewan's house.

"We need to do something," I hissed. "You don't think Marla told people we've got some scheme cooked up to catch the killer?"

"She might have." She opened the van door. Rummaging in her purse on the seat, she drew out a fat pen. "Put this in your apron pocket."

"What is it?"

"Spyware."

"Isn't that for computers?"

"It's a wire. You know, a recording device."

"A wire? Why would I need . . ." Understanding cracked over my head like a rotten egg. "You're trying to provoke the killer." This was not the plan!

Her jaw set. "Fair's fair. The killer's provoked me."

"We had a plan! What did you tell Marla?"

"I didn't tell her anything. You know how she is."

"Then why did you bring a secret pen recorder?"

"I always carry one."

I blew out my breath. "We're dropping off the pies, we're getting Marla, and then we're leaving."

"That's the plan."

"No visits to Ewan's house," I said. "No interviewing our murder suspect. Leaving."

"Of course," she said reasonably. "You can't leave Petronella in charge at Pie Town all afternoon, even if she is on the high end of a mood swing."

I swallowed, my head spinning. "Wait here." Feeling exposed, I opened the van's rear doors, hopped in, and unstacked pies. I dug my cell phone from the pocket of my jeans and called Gordon.

"Hey," he said, his voice warm.

"Gordon, we've got a problem," I whispered, so Charlene wouldn't overhear. "Charlene might have told Marla that we know who the killer is."

Silence.

"And Marla's at the Bar X trying to unearth the truth," I said. "It's become a twisted contest of wills between these two. Charlene and I are here too, delivering pies."

"I'll be there in ten minutes." He hung up.

Okay. So, our plan had been blown to perdition. New plan: we'd keep Marla from getting herself killed, grab her, and get out. If my brain hadn't been stunned stupid, I would have come up with this strategy sooner.

In a louder voice, I said to Charlene, "We need to get Marla out of here, even if that means throwing her in the back of the van."

I turned, and yelped.

Bridget, wearing a plaid blouse and jeans, stood framed outside the open van doors. Her long blond braid cascaded over one shoulder. "Hi."

"Hi." Had she heard that? She must think we were plotting a kidnapping.

"Can I give you a hand?"

"Uh . . . Sure." I grabbed some pies and handed them to her.

She didn't budge. "Marla told me you know who killed Devon and Larry."

Silently, I cursed. "That's not quite true. We found some evidence and turned it over to the police." *So, there's no reason for anyone to kill us.* "Who knows? It all may be nothing. Probably nothing. What we learned most likely won't lead to the killer after all. Marla was exaggerating."

Her face crumpled. "I hope you're wrong. This has been a nightmare. I had to tell my father . . ." She swallowed, looked down the dirt road toward the chapel, its doors shut fast. "He didn't know that Devon might have been his son. But he said it's possible. He's devastated. And there's no one he can ask for the truth. Devon's mother is dead."

"I'm sorry." I thought of my own wayward father, who'd abandoned my mother and I when I was too young to remember. If Devon had only said something to Ewan, maybe none of this would have happened. But, if I met my father tomorrow, how open would I be to an honest conversation? Grimacing, I duckwalked to the open van doors.

Bridget stood aside, and I hopped to the ground. Stomach bottoming, I circled the van. Charlene was nowhere in sight.

"What's wrong?" Bridget asked.

"I told Charlene to wait here." I should have known better. When had Charlene ever followed my orders? Answer: only when they fit in with her own plans. She'd even insisted on using her own piecrust recipe in Pie Town. Granted, her recipe was better than mine, but that wasn't the point!

Fuming, I grabbed more pies from the van and thrust them into Bridget's arms. "I have to find Marla and Charlene."

"But—"

I hurried down the street. Charlene wouldn't be in the photo shack, because the photographer was standing next to my van in front of the saloon. I popped my head into the bathhouse/bathrooms and checked beneath the ladies' room stalls. "Charlene!"

No dice.

That left the carriage house, the corral, and Ewan's house.

The odor of horses and fresh hay blew through the breezeway created by the carriage house's two open doors. I whipped through the carriage house, passing the coach, glancing in the stalls. Horses whickered, but no Charlene.

I walked outside and continued down the dirt road to the corral. The arena was empty, but a piebald stood tied to the wooden fence. It flicked its tail as I strode past on the narrow road to Ewan's yellow Victorian.

Pausing, I turned. At the far end of the corral was a small outbuilding behind the wooden "bad guy" targets. I imagined they kept supplies there. Odds were that no one lurked in the shed, but . . . I glanced at the horse. Was its owner nearby?

I opened the corral gate and strode inside. If I'd felt exposed standing beside my van, it was a gazillion times worse inside the empty corral.

My stomach churned. I hurried across the corral to the painted wooden figures, mustaches curling, black hats broad.

"Don't look at me," Marla's voice carried from inside the shack. "I had nothing to do with it."

"This isn't the time," Charlene snapped.

I breathed a sigh. It was only Charlene and Marla, arguing per usual.

And then annoyance reared its tricksy head, and my fists clenched. After everything that had happened, those two were *still* at each other's throats. There was a killer on the loose, and all they could think of was their petty personal problems.

Plus, I'd asked Charlene to stay by the van! All we had to do was act like everything was normal and then go. Simple. Easy. But when you're dealing with an eighty-something going on thirteen, nothing was easy.

I stormed inside the shack. "Enough! What is wrong with you two?" The small, dark room was cluttered with cardboard boxes. Thin beams of light filtered through the wood slats and the high, narrow windows.

Charlene's jaw dropped.

"Oh, that's helpful," Marla snarled.

Someone grabbed my chignon and yanked me backward. Cold steel pressed beneath my chin.

"Moe?" I gulped.

"Thanks for joining us," he said.

Chapter Twenty-Nine

The barrel of the revolver pressed into the soft skin beneath my jaw. My breath came in quick, dusty gulps.

Charlene and Marla crowded together at the opposite side of the compact shed. Stripes of light made prison bar shadows across their faces.

"You don't need to do this," Charlene said.

"I didn't mean to do any of it," Moe shouted.

The revolver jammed into my flesh, and I winced, standing on my toes to escape the pressure.

"You're saying Devon's murder was accidental?" I gasped. Maybe if he thought we believed it, he'd let us go. "That Curly's horse throwing a shoe was a coincidence? And then you took the opportunity to talk to Devon, and things went wrong?"

"I only wanted to scare him," Moe said.

"And Curly's horse?" My heart thundered, determined to beat itself free of my chest.

"I loosened the shoe to get rid of Curly," he said. "I feel terrible about putting the horse at risk, but I didn't mean to kill Devon."

"Balderdash," Marla said. "You knew Devon was going

to die, and you made sure your partner wouldn't have an alibi."

"That bartender deserved to die!"

"No," Charlene said. "He didn't. He made a mistake, and so did you. We can fix this."

He laughed, a harsh sound. "Fix it? You can't fix it! My son would be alive today if it weren't for that bartender."

"What are you talking about?" Marla asked.

"Moe's son died in a drunk-driving accident in Truckee after leaving a bar," I said.

"Devon worked in Truckee," Marla said.

"As a bartender," Charlene snapped. "Do we need to connect the dots for you?"

"Little wonder you blamed Devon for your son's death," I said.

Dust tickled my nostrils. I scrunched my face, working not to sneeze, imagining Moe's finger jerking on the trigger.

"That bartender overserved my son," Moe said. "And he hadn't learned a damn thing. He was still serving too many drinks here at the Bar X. He didn't care! My son's death meant nothing to him. Nothing!"

"So, you confronted him," I said, "and things got out of control."

"I only wanted to scare him," he pleaded.

Even if I believed it, and I didn't, it didn't explain what had happened to Larry, or all the attempts on my life. But as long as I had a gun pressed to my neck, I was willing to go along for the ride.

"So, why did you shoot at Val?" Marla asked. "To scare her away?"

"Devon and I struggled with the gun," he said. "A shot went off before I got it away from him. Your near miss was an accident."

So, he'd gotten the gun away first and then killed Devon, an unarmed man. I'd suspected as much—the bullet that had blasted the pies from my arms had been followed by a second shot. "And then you killed him," I said.

"It was in the heat of battle!"

"You'd gone there to kill him," Marla said. "You'd planned it out. Why kill poor Larry?"

"Larry suspected the truth," I said. "We'd asked Larry if the horseshoe could have been tampered with, and he denied it, Later, we saw him in the corral looking for something—the nail, I'm guessing. What did he find on it? He knew about your son's death. He knew about Devon's role in it too, didn't he?"

Moe's breath was hot against my neck. "I didn't mean to kill Larry," he said.

"And he didn't want to rat you out," Charlene said. "Larry felt sorry for you. He suspected what had happened, but he couldn't believe it was intentional."

"Larry was near the saloon that morning," I said. "Did he hear you and Devon arguing?"

"He told me he had." His voice trembled. "Larry was a better friend than I deserved. He wanted me to explain what happened, tell him I was innocent. I couldn't. We argued. I pushed him away, and he fell. He must have hit his head on something. His death was an accident."

"And then you dragged Larry's body into the horse stall," I said,."trying to make it look like a horse had kicked him. But his horse was tied up and couldn't have done it."

"You two walked in on me. I had to pretend I'd just found him."

"You're not a murderer," Charlene said smoothly. "Everything happened in the heat of the moment. It wasn't your fault."

The gun moved fractionally away from my jaw.

"Of course, it was his fault," Marla said. "The murder of Devon Blackett was premeditated."

The gun barrel again pressed into my flesh, and my eyes widened. *Marla!*

Charlene stepped on her foot.

"Ow!" Marla glared. "What was that for?"

A vein pulsed in Charlene's temple. "You're *wrong*, Marla. Weren't you listening? They struggled over the gun. Devon goaded him into it."

"Unbelievable," Marla said. "You will say anything to get one over on me!"

"Will you put our differences aside for *one* minute," Charlene snarled. She turned to Moe. "You're no killer, and hurting us or Val will only make things worse. The police have all the information we do. There's no sense in adding three more bodies to the stew. It's over."

"I'm not going to jail." Moe walked backwards, dragging me outside. He kicked the shed's door closed. A wooden beam dropped into place, locking Marla and Charlene inside.

I gasped, knees wobbly. At least they were safe. "What are you going to do?" I squeaked.

"Keep walking." He pressed the gun into my spine and marched me across the corral.

"Not to make this all about me," I said, "but why try to run me down? And why were you lurking around my house last night?"

"It was a misunderstanding," he muttered.

"Misunderstanding?! You hospitalized one of my customers!"

"I thought you were trying to blackmail me."

"Blackmail?" I asked, my body heat rising. "I never blackmailed you."

"Not in so many words. You were like that bastard, Devon, always hinting around that you knew something."

Hinting around? "What are you talking about?"

"Oh, I'm not sure what I saw," he said, mimicking me.

"What was I supposed to think? That's why I agreed to come to your pie shop for questioning, to figure out what you knew. Your pie was pretty good."

"Thanks."

"And then I overheard just enough of you and Charlene talking in that trailer of yours to believe I was right."

"Believe? You mean you don't think so now?" I breathed in quick, shallow gasps.

He laughed hollowly. "You tricked me. Or I tricked myself. Guilt will do that to a man. If I'd kept my mouth shut, played it cool, none of this would have happened. Then that Marla started shooting her mouth off, and I figured you three were in on it together." He pushed the corral gate open with his hip, and his horse whickered.

"You panicked," I said. "Totally understandable." *Now let me go.*

I glanced up the hill. No one raced down the slope from Ewan's house to rescue me. The carriage house blocked the corral from view of Main Street, where Bridget, and I assumed other workers, might be. Only Marla and Charlene knew what was happening, and they were locked in the shed. "But you know we're not trying to blackmail you now, right? It was all a stupid misunderstanding. And the police really do know everything we do. There's no point in hurting anyone."

"Maybe the cops do, and maybe they don't." He stopped beside his piebald horse and edged to my side, aiming the gun at my ear. "I'm going to let you go, but I've got my gun on you, and you know what kind of shot I am. So, don't try anything funny. I really don't want to shoot you. I only want to get away."

"Okay," I said fervently.

Gordon strode through the rear carriage house doors.

My kidnapper froze.

Gordon whipped back his blazer and reached for his gun.

"Don't!" Moe's voice whip cracked. "You can't draw faster than I can blow her head off."

Gordon's hand hovered over his holstered weapon.

I fought a wild urge to laugh. A gun fight at the Bar X corral? Really? And for the second time in a year—one year!—I was being held at gunpoint like some marshmallow fluff damsel in distress. I might as well be back in that prostitute's costume and . . .

And I wasn't helpless. And I sure as heck wasn't a damsel. What I was, was mad.

I grabbed Moe's gun arm and shoved it away. Stomping his boot, I dove for the ground.

There was a shout, a gunshot, a cry.

I looked up.

Bent double, Moe rubbed his hand. His revolver lay in the dirt.

"Hands on your head!" Gordon barked. "Hands on your head!"

Hands trembling, Moe interlaced his hands on his head.

"On your knees!"

With two fingers, I plucked Moe's revolver from the dirt. There was an indentation on the side where Gordon's bullet had hit. I tossed the gun under the corral fence. My stomach contents threatened to reverse course, and I swallowed hard, sickened. I staggered to my feet.

"Are you all right?" Gordon asked me.

"Yeah." I gulped. "Yeah."

Someone banged on the shed door.

"Let us out!" Marla screamed.

"Charlene!" I ran to the shed and lifted the wood beam, releasing the two older women.

Charlene grasped my shoulders. "What happened? I heard a shot."

"Gordon." Holy moly. Had Gordon actually shot the gun out of Moe's hand? I'd only seen that in the movies.

I looked toward the men. Moe lay on his stomach in the dirt. Gordon squatted beside him, his knee pressed against Moe's shoulder blades, and cuffed him.

On watery legs, I walked to them.

Gordon hauled Moe to standing.

"That was some shooting," Moe said.

"I wasn't aiming for your hand," Gordon said.

Chapter Thirty

"What do you think?" Gordon asked. He wore that blue sweater I liked, but in the darkness, it looked black.

"This isn't the dog park," I said.

Gordon and I stood in the parking lot of the White Lady, the ocean crashing faintly beneath us. The restaurant's adobe walls glimmered, pale white, in the moonlight.

"No," he said. "The park didn't seem like the best spot for a first date, especially since you're a UFO-phobe." He placed his hand on my elbow.

I hesitated, pulling the fringed shawl Charlene had insisted I buy, closer. "Um. Charlene and I were recently thrown out of here."

"For what?"

"Marla upset the bartender, and we were in the line of fire."

"No problem. I'm friends with the owner. Besides, I broke up a fight here last month. He owes me."

"There are fights at the White Lady?" It didn't seem like that kind of place.

Arm in arm, we walked up the red-tiled steps.

"It's got two bars," he said, as if that explained everything.

"What happened?"

"Two women got into an argument about whether they'd seen the ghost or not. Words were said. Hair was pulled."

"You really do see the darker side of human nature."

"I wasn't the one who had a gun aimed at them." He looped an arm across my shoulders and opened the heavy, wooden door.

My anger at Moe had faded. In spite of everything, a small part of me felt sorry for the man. His son's death had driven him over the edge, and I believed that he hadn't meant to kill Larry. That didn't excuse the murder of Devon, or his attacks on me. And hitting poor Ray with a stolen Prius was just wrong.

A waitress escorted us to a table overlooking the ocean, and Gordon pulled out a chair for me. Through the glass, the moon spread its mercury trail across the water.

He sat across from me, and we bumped knees.

Electricity jolted me.

"Can I get you anything from the bar?" the waitress asked.

We ordered drinks, and the waitress departed.

"Has this finally convinced the Baker Street Bakers to retire?" Gordon asked.

"First, never say the word *retire* when Charlene's involved. Second, I made the mistake of telling Charlene we were going to the dog park. Now she's insisting I help her hunt UFOs," I said glumly. "She wants us to drive to Area 51."

He grinned. "There was something supernatural about your last intuitive leap. How did you figure out Devon had overserved Moe's son?"

"Heidi. She came into Pie Town so upset, that she scarfed down half a strawberry-rhubarb pie. Then she took a second pie to go." I had it on good authority (Graham and Tally Wally) that she'd hit my ex in the face with it. It seemed like a waste of pie.

"I'm not seeing the connection."

I unwrapped the white, cloth napkin and laid it on my lap. "Charlene thought we shouldn't have let her leave. Heidi's not used to that kind of sugar high. And then Heidi drove away, too fast, and I started making the connections. I'd been told that Devon was loose with the drinks and had a tendency to overserve. He'd been working as a bartender in Truckee at the time Moe's son, Maurice, was killed."

"Still," he said, "there's more than one bar in Truckee."

"Which is why I did more digging into Maurice's death." It felt good to hash it out with Gordon. Maybe I really could be a detective. "Once I knew what I was looking for, it wasn't hard to confirm that, on the night of his death, Moe's son had left the same bar Devon worked at."

"Careful, you'll put me out of business."

Happiness overflowed inside me. "I lack your combat skills. I still can't believe you shot Moe's gun right out of his hand."

He grimaced. "I've got to put in more hours at the range. I wasn't kidding about not aiming for his hand."

"Speaking of guns, I assume Moe used a different gun when he killed Devon, or the ballistics would have implicated him."

"Yep. Moe's got an entire arsenal." He reached across the table and gently gripped my hand. "Now, maybe for our second date—"

"What a week!" Charlene materialized beside us. She grabbed an empty chair from a neighboring table and wedged it next to mine. Setting her glass of red wine on the white tablecloth, she plopped into the chair. She unbuttoned her soft, bourbon-colored jacket, revealing a splashy yellow tunic. "Since that newspaper article came out about Val's heroics, Pie Town's been packed. I thought you two were going to the dog park."

Seriously? She knew how much this date meant.

Charlene ignored my glare.

"I don't need to spend any more nights at the dog park," Gordon said, smug. "I solved that case."

"Oh?" Charlene asked.

"Our alien was a local ghost hunter, a guy who works at Larry's car lot."

"A ghost hunter? Not Greg?" I turned to Charlene. "Why would he think the dog park was haunted?"

Charlene sank lower in her seat. "I might have mentioned it on Twitter. Before the fairies showed up, of course."

"Greg *was* the fairies," Gordon said. "Or the aliens."

The waitress set our drinks on the table. "One more for dinner?"

Gordon's phone chimed. He pulled it from his pocket and checked it, frowned. "Damn."

"What's wrong?" I asked.

"There's a major pileup on the One."

"Oh, no," I said.

"They're calling everyone in." Hurriedly, he rose. "I've got to go. Sorry. Rain check?"

"Sure," I said, dazed.

He dug out his wallet and handed the waitress his credit card. "This one's on me, Pam." He jogged from the restaurant.

Charlene shifted onto his chair. "Well, I won't say no to a free dinner." She sipped Gordon's beer and sighed. "At least he's got good taste. We'll need a few more minutes to decide, Pam."

The waitress nodded and walked away.

Charlene clapped my shoulder. "Don't look so sad. So, you didn't get your first date. It'll happen."

"I might have, if you hadn't crashed the party."

She unfurled a napkin. "Hey, I wasn't responsible for the accident on the highway. You should be grateful I wasn't in it."

"At least I would have had more alone time with him," I groused.

"No use crying over spilled milk."

"Right. How's the Bar X doing?"

"The weddings are staying canceled," she said, "but there's been a surge in mystery dinners. Ewan and Bridget will be okay, now that they don't have a double homicide hanging over their heads. It's not knowing whether Devon was Ewan's son that's killing him."

"I don't think Devon was," I said. "Moe had done his research on Devon. He knew about the missing father, and that he'd been born in San Diego. And he knew that the timing fit for Ewan's service in the Navy. He was careful to send Devon a newspaper clipping that mentioned Ewan's Navy days, suspecting that would lure him to the Bar X. But he had no real evidence of Devon's parentage. And there were lots of sailors in San Diego at that time. Odds are low there's a real connection."

"I hope you're right. The past never goes away, does it?"

We sat for a moment, silent.

Not liking the table's new somber tone, I cleared my throat. "There is one mystery that we never cleared up."

She blinked innocently. "Oh?"

"Why you claimed to know nothing about the Phantom of Bar X until Ewan told you about it," I said. "And why you peppered our suspects with questions about it, but never called for a stakeout."

"I've learned to prioritize. There was a killer on the loose. No time for phantoms."

"Or," I said, "you're the phantom. You knew that pottery had been turned upside down before Sarah Onaka told us."

Charlene coughed. "Well, that's what phantoms do, isn't it? Besides, I don't have time to flit around haunting the

Bar X. And if someone had seen me, the gig would have been up."

"No, you would have needed an accomplice. Like Bridget. She'll do anything to help out her dad."

Charlene winced. "I might have given her a few tips on hauntings. I should have known better."

"Why?" I asked. "It worked."

"Because now we've created a tulpa." She gestured, splashing red wine across her wrinkled hand. Snatching the napkin from my lap, she brushed off the stain. "Bridget swears she hasn't been responsible for the stuff that's been going on lately. And I've no idea how we're going to get rid of the thing. Probably have to hold some sort of ritual."

"Of course, we will."

Charlene hunched her shoulders. "My involvement was that obvious?"

"Simple psychology," I said, modest.

"What do you know about psychology?" Charlene asked. "You were an English major."

"I know that you were suspiciously uninterested in staking out the phantom, which meant you already knew what it was."

"Hm, I almost forgot." She reached into the pocket of her soft jacket and pulled out a key on a ring, handed it to me. "Here you go."

Puzzled, I stared at it. "What's this for?"

"It's the key to your new van."

"My what? Charlene, you didn't—"

"No, I didn't. Larry's nephew is giving you the van as thanks for solving his uncle's murder."

"Charlene, I can't accept this. That van is worth ten grand."

Charlene laughed. "No one wants that hot-pink van.

Larry might have been trying to sell it for ten thousand, but it isn't worth half as much."

"But—"

"I'm only the delivery woman. If you've got a beef with the van, take it up with Greg."

"I will. Thanks." I rubbed the key between my thumb and forefinger and wondered. It didn't feel right to keep the gift, but after wrecking my bug, I needed wheels. Maybe I could work out a discounted payment plan.

"Now," Charlene said, "about that ritual to get rid of the tulpa at the Bar X. We're going to need lots of salt . . ."

I sipped my Chocolatini and smiled.

RECIPES

Abril was given the job of typing up the pie recipes for Pie Town's giant 3-ring recipe binders and got a little colorful with the language.

PEACH-BLUEBERRY GINGER PIE

Ingredients:

1 package premade pie dough (2 rounds), chilled

A small handful of flour (for rolling out the lattice top)

4 C peaches, peeled and sliced into ¼" wedges (about six medium peaches)

1¼ C blueberries

⅓ C + 2 tsp granulated sugar

¼ C cornstarch

1 T shredded fresh ginger

¼ tsp salt

1½ tsp lemon juice

1 T heavy cream

Turn up the heat to 375 degrees.

Coax one piecrust along the smooth bottom of a 9" pie tin and pinch the dough along the top edge of the pan. Snuggle parchment paper into the bottom of the piecrust and fill the tin to the brim with dried rice or beans. Bake until a sensuous golden brown, approximately 20–30 minutes.

Carefully remove from the oven and turn the heat down to a balmy 350 degrees.

Tenderly mix blueberries, peaches, ⅓ C sugar, cornstarch, ginger, salt, and lemon in a generously sized bowl.

Remove the beans and rice from the baked piecrust. Gently tumble the fruit ménage into the tin.

Unroll the second piecrust, and with a pizza cutter or sharp knife, cut the dough into ten lattice strips, approximately ¾" to 1" in width.

Lay five lattice strips vertically across the top of the pie. Place the other five strips horizontally across the first. Snip any excess dough or press it into the piecrust. Brush the strips with the cream and drizzle with the last two tsp sugar.

Bake approximately 60 to 90 minutes, until the filling is thick and bubbling.

APRICOT PIE

Ingredients:
   4 C sliced apricots
   1 C sugar*
   1 T lemon juice*
   3 T minute tapioca
   Pinch nutmeg
   ½ tsp cinnamon
   1 package premade pie dough (2 rounds), chilled
   1 T butter
   3 T milk
   *Use less lemon and/or more sugar if the apricots
      are particularly sour

Turn up the heat to 425 degrees.

In a large bowl, mix the sliced apricots, sugar, lemon juice, tapioca, nutmeg, and cinnamon in a wanton tumble. Let stand for an achingly long 15 minutes.

Line a 9" pie pan with one crust and pour the fruit filling into it. Dot the succulent mound of apricots with butter. Cover the pie with the second crust and crimp the edges together using fork tines or your fingers. Cut three vents into the top of the crust. Using the milk, brush the crust to create a lustrous glaze.

Bake until the pie is a luscious golden brown, approximately 35–40 minutes.

CAULIFLOWER-BLUE CHEESE PIE

You will need an 8" springform pan

Ingredients:

1 medium head of cauliflower, sliced into small florets
2 T olive oil
Coarse salt
Freshly ground pepper
2 T butter, unsalted
2 leeks, thinly sliced
2 cloves garlic, chopped
3 large eggs
1 C milk
1 package premade pie dough (2 rounds), thawed
2 oz mild blue cheese
Egg wash: 2 T water beaten with 1 egg

Turn up the heat to 375 degrees.

Tumble cauliflower florets in oil, sprinkle with pepper and salt, and spread on a large, rimmed cookie sheet. Roast for 35 to 45 minutes, until the cauliflower is brown. Allow to cool for fifteen minutes.

Over medium-high heat, melt the butter in a saucepan. Add the sliced leeks. Cook, stirring often, for approximately ten minutes, until the leeks wilt and begin to caramelize. Add the fragrant garlic and cook for another minute, stirring frequently.

Allow to cool for five minutes.

Vigorously whisk the eggs and milk in a bowl. Season with pepper and salt.

Unfurl one of the piecrusts and fit snuggly into the springform pan. (If the dough tears, just mush it together to patch it.)

Sprinkle blue cheese over the bottom of the dough. Add the leeks and cauliflower. Lavish the egg mixture over everything.

Blanket the mixture with the second crust, pinching the edges together.

Lightly brush the top of the crust with the egg wash mixture to add a slight sheen.

Delicately cut a slit in the center of the top crust to vent.

Bake until the crust is evenly browned, approximately 45 minutes to 1 hour. A tester inserted into the center should come out clean.

Allow to cool for ten minutes.

Remove the springform pan's outer ring and serve, to cries of rapturous delight.

BANANA-BUTTERSCOTCH CREAM PIE

Ingredients:

1 round of premade pie dough, chilled

½ C packed light brown sugar

2 T granulated sugar

¼ C cornstarch

⅛ tsp salt

4 egg yolks (large)

2 C whole milk

½ vanilla bean, split lengthwise

4 T unsalted butter, melted and cooled

2 tsp dark rum

3 medium ripe (yet firm) bananas, unpeeled

1 C heavy cream

2 T sugar

1 tsp vanilla

Toasted coconut

Turn up the heat to 350 degrees.

Unfurl one piecrust along the smooth bottom of a 9" pie tin and crimp the dough along the top edge of the pan. Snuggle parchment paper into the bottom of the piecrust and fill the tin to the brim with dried rice or beans. Bake until a pale, golden brown, approximately 20 minutes.

Combine ¼ C brown sugar, 2 T granulated sugar, cornstarch, and salt in a small bowl. Beat the egg yolks into submission, until they are smooth and supple. Add ¼ C milk and stir.

In a 1½ quart saucepan, mix the remaining milk and brown sugar, and the vanilla bean over low heat. As the mixture begins to simmer, carefully extract the vanilla bean. Scrape the seeds from the strip and add them to the milk mixture.

Remove rice and beans from the baked crust.

When the milk mixture comes to a boil, take it off the heat and pour approximately ⅓ of the steaming liquid into the bowl of sugar and cornstarch mixture.

Stir, and then pour it all back into the saucepan, returning it to the heat. For approximately 3 to 5 minutes, continue cooking and stirring and cooking and stirring and cooking and stirring until the mixture feverishly thickens and bubbles. If you have a digital thermometer, the mixture should read 160 degrees.

Take care not to overcook, as the mixture will then separate when it cools, and that is bad.

Remove the saucepan from the heat and pour the contents into a big bowl. Fold the butter into the mix. Add the rum and stir until the filling is smooth. Set aside and allow to cool for ten minutes.

Cut the bananas diagonally into ¼" slices. Lay them along the bottom of the piecrust. Cover with the cream filling, being sure to get an even layer. Lay plastic wrap right on top (yes, right on top!) of the filling. This will keep an unpleasant crust from forming on the cream. With a fork, pierce the plastic wrap several times.

Allow to cool for 20 minutes, and then refrigerate.

One hour before serving, whip the cream into a frenzy with sugar and vanilla until soft peaks thrust skyward. Lavish the cream across the top of the pie. Sprinkle with toasted coconut.

Love spending time with
Val and Charlene in the tasty world of *Pie Town*?

Then check out this sneak peek for

PIE HARD,

coming soon from
Kirsten Weiss
and
Kensington Books!

It began with a rumble in the dark. Objects clattered on the nearby bookshelf. Silverware and window blinds rattled. Cupboard doors bumped against their frames.

My alarm clock shimmied across the low, end table. Four AM.

Never my best at that hour, I sat upright on my futon, my bare feet on the laminate floor, and held my breath. Was this as bad as the shaking was going to get in my tiny house, or would the quake worsen?

Light flared, blinding, and I staggered to my feet.

Ribbons of light streamed through the front blinds. I turned my head, shielding my face. The glare shifted downward. Something crashed, shattered.

I couldn't breathe, couldn't think. I seemed to split, to become both the watcher and the watched. I saw the clock plummet to the floor and break into two pieces. I saw the bookcase shadow lengthen. I saw myself hunched and cowering, my shoulder-length hair tousled like a mad woman's. Not liking the image, I forced myself to straighten.

It was happening again. It was—

Bam! Bam! Bam!

I shrieked. Careening backwards, I crashed into the bookcase that walled off my bedroom from the rest of the tiny home.

"Yurt delivery!" a man bellowed.

What delivery? Heart still rabbiting, I grabbed my kimono robe off the coat hook on the bookcase. I shrugged into the kimono, hurried to the door, and threw it open.

Backlit by the headlights of a semi stood a middle-aged man wearing jeans and a plaid shirt rolled to his elbows.

A truck. It had only been a truck. A big truck, with more effect on my tiny house, up on blocks, than it should have. But why was a semi on my lawn?

Baffled, I stared at his sun-roughened face. I'm five-foot-five and stood two steps higher than him in my tiny house, but our eyes were on the same level.

He consulted his clipboard. "You Charlene McCree?" His semi's headlights cut the fog. They illuminated my pink Pie Town van and the picnic table, glittering with dew.

"No. What?" I scraped one hand through my brown hair. It figured Charlene was behind whatever was going on. "Yurt?"

Two men clambered from the passenger side of the truck and walked to the rear of the trailer.

"Then who are you?" he demanded.

"I'm Val. What's this about? It's four in the morning! Who are you?" I shivered, yanking my kimono belt tighter. It was August in sunny California, but San Nicholas had its own weather patterns, and the flowered robe was thin.

"It's about the yurt delivery." He frowned, studying his clipboard. "I swear this was the same place as last year."

"Same place as what?" I flipped on the indoor light.

Two more headlights swung up the drive. A yellow Jeep scraped past the eucalyptus trees that lined the dirt and gravel road. It screeched to a halt beside the picnic table. My elderly piecrust maker flung open its door and stepped out.

Charlene blinked, her blue eyes widening. Her curling loops of marshmallow-fluff hair stirred in the breeze. Then she strode to my doorstep. "Forgot you were coming today," she said to the delivery man.

"You Charlene McCree?" He thrust the clipboard at her.

"The one and only. You need me to sign?" She reached into the pocket of her green knit, tunic-style jacket. Charlene looked remarkably put together for the hour, not a white hair out of place. She was even wearing lipstick, a bright slash of salmon.

"At the X's," the man said.

"Charlene, what's going on?" I asked.

She squinted at the board. "I can't read this out here. I'll sign inside."

Annoyed, I stepped aside, and she climbed into my tiny home-sweet-shipping container. Since she was also my landlord, she had certain privileges.

I struggled for patience. "Charlene, what's going on?" I repeated.

"Yurt delivery for the goddess circle," she said. "Sorry I forgot to tell you about it, Val."

"Goddess circle?" I bleated. "What does that have to do with a yurt? And it's four AM.!"

"Four-oh-six," she said. "You'd better get cracking if you want to get to Pie Town by five."

"What goddess circle?" I asked.

"They come here every year." She drew a pair of reading glasses from her pocket and set them on her nose. "I forgot to mention it to you. It's only for the week."

"What's for the week?"

"The circle." She sat at the tiny table between my kitchen and living area and signed the papers.

"This one of those tiny homes?" The delivery man stood

in the open doorway and scanned the miniature kitchen, the fold-up table, and built-in desk.

"Yes," I said, and turned to Charlene. "But why is he delivering the yurt here?" My lips flattened. "At four in the morning!"

She sighed with exaggerated patience. "Because this is where they have the circle."

"Here? In my yard? At four?" I blew out my breath and tried for some Zen. Charlene was more than my employee/landlady. We were friends. It wasn't her fault my rude awakening had sent me into a freaky panic spiral. And Charlene's zaniness was a part of her charm.

When I didn't want to throttle her.

"I don't know why you're so obsessed with the time." She peered over her glasses at me. "And I couldn't cancel. The goddess gals booked it before you moved in. But I am sorry I forgot to tell you."

I gaped. Charlene had apologized twice this morning. She *never* apologized. "But—"

"You'd better get dressed."

Confounded, I stumbled to my sleeping area and grabbed a Pies Before Guys T-shirt and pair of worn jeans from the closet.

Hidden behind my bookcase partition, I shuffled into the clothes. What the Hades was a goddess circle? It was probably totally normal for freewheeling Northern California, and I didn't think Charlene would plant a pagan cult on my lawn, but . . .

I'd find out soon enough. Plus, I was embarrassed by my overreaction to the truck's arrival—first thinking it was an earthquake and then thinking . . . I didn't know what I'd been thinking, only that I'd been in the throes of a full-blown anxiety attack.

In my defense, it *had* been four AM, a confusing time under the best of circumstances.

The rumbling from the truck engine stopped. Blessed silence fell.

I twisted my hair into a bun and dashed on some light makeup. Slipping into my comfy tennis shoes, I edged around the bookcase.

Charlene stood, arms akimbo, in front of the closed front door and frowned. "You're wearing that?"

I looked down at my T-shirt, jeans, and tennies. "I always wear this."

"You can't wear a PIES BEFORE GUYS shirt to work."

"Why not?" Pie Town was my bakery, and traditionally, the owner got to set the rules. Besides, we were selling the PIES BEFORE GUYS tees, so wearing it was free advertising.

"Because it doesn't say Pie Town."

"It does." I pointed to my left breast. "Right here, like I've told you over and over again."

"That's too small to see," she said.

I covered my breasts defensively. "They're not too small."

"Not your boobs, the logo! I don't know why you made it so tiny. Don't you have any earrings?"

"Why would I need earrings to bake pies?"

"And there's a stain on that shirt."

"There is?" I stretched the bottom hem forward and examined the shirt. It looked fine to me.

She brushed past and rummaged through my tiny closet. "You must have something besides T-shirts."

"Tank tops."

"Wear this." She tossed a pink Pie Town T-shirt to me, and I caught it one handed. "I'll wait outside."

I gave up looking for the stain and changed my shirt. Since it was chilly outside, I slipped a Pie Town hoodie over it. I grabbed a banana for breakfast and joined Charlene beside the picnic table.

Three men set out long, curving red poles near the cliff.

My face screwed up. If Charlene had forgotten the yurt delivery, why had she appeared on my doorstep at this hour? "Since when do you care about how I look?" I tugged my hood, which had gotten folded beneath the back of my collar.

"A lady should take care of her appearance," she said.

My cheeks warmed with realization. Was Gordon Carmichael back in San Nicholas? The detective and I had had a series of dating misfires. Then he'd been sent to Wyoming for some Homeland Security training. Was he going to surprise me at the restaurant? Maybe I *should* wear earrings.

"You're the owner of Pie Town. If you don't care about how you look, why should your employees?" She opened the door to her yellow Jeep. "I'll meet you there."

Something was definitely up. Resigned to whatever romcom Charlene had planned for Gordon and me, I climbed into my Pie Town van. It was ancient in car years, but it was the exact color of our pie boxes, and it had been love at first sight.

I followed her taillights down the narrow track to the main road. We wound through the hills, cobalt in the predawn light, and sped onto Highway One, deserted at this early hour. A few minutes later, we cruised into San Nicholas.

Main Street's iron street lamps were dark, and my van swept through tendrils of delightfully creepy ground fog. I loved San Nicholas at this hour, when the beach town was hushed and the morning full of possibility.

I drove into the brick alleyway behind Pie Town and frowned. Charlene's Jeep was parked in her spot. An unfamiliar white van sat in mine, which left me having to circle the block. Clearly, the rocky start to my morning had been a bad omen. I only hoped a stolen parking spot would be the least of my worries.

Scowling, I drove around the brick building and found a spot on a nearby street.

I strode down the alley to Pie Town's rear metal door.

Charlene clambered from the Jeep and arched her back, stretching. "You ready?"

I thumbed through my keys. "Ready for what?"

"Another day of making the best pies on the Northern California coast!"

I yawned and fitted the key to the lock. "Golly gee, yes!" As much as I appreciated Charlene's enthusiasm, it was five in the morning. Yawning, I pushed open the door to my industrial kitchen.

A silhouette shifted in the darkened room.

I gasped, rearing backward, and a hand grasped my arm.

Connect with U s

Visit us online at
KensingtonBooks.com
to read more from your favorite authors, see books
by series, view reading group guides, and more.

Join us on social media
for sneak peeks, chances to win books and prize packs,
and to share your thoughts with other readers.

facebook.com/kensingtonpublishing
twitter.com/kensingtonbooks

Tell us what you think!
To share your thoughts, submit a review,
or sign up for our eNewsletters, please visit:
KensingtonBooks.com/TellUs.